LAST STAND

By Lindsay McKenna

D1596193

Blue Turtle Publishing

Dear Readers,

Welcome to my latest romantic military suspense series: SHADOW TEAM! SEAL Cal Sinclair met Lieutenant Sky Lambert, an Army Black Hawk helicopter officer, at a forward operating base in the last days of the USA being in Afghanistan. Cal has never given his heart to any woman, but there is something so deep and moving about her that it breaks every rule he ever set for himself when it came to the opposite sex. When Sky is wounded, and Cal saves her life, she is sent on a medical plane to Germany for surgery...and he never sees her again. It's as if Sky has disappeared not only from his life but there is no trace of her anywhere in the world. Undaunted, he leaves the Navy and goes on a mission to find her...or else.

Sky Lambert is a woman who carries many secrets and none of them are good. At the forward operating base, she meets and falls in love with Cal Sinclair. Fighting her desire to see him again, she knows she cannot drag anyone she loves into her nightmare existence. It's better to disappear and let Cal have a good life without her in it. Hiding in Peru, South America, Sky thinks no one will find her. Worse, another man, a Russian drug lord, is on her trail and wants her for his own. When Cal finds Sky, a war erupts when the Russian comes after them. Only one man will survive.

Dedication

To all the readers love my romantic military suspense!

CHAPTER 1

January 3

CAL SINCLAIR DIDN'T know whether to laugh in triumph or cry with relief. His boss, Jack Driscoll, a retired US Navy SEAL and owner of Shield Security, had finally located Sky Lambert after almost a year of searching to track down her whereabouts. Sliding his keycard into the outside slot, the door swung open into the global security agency based in Alexandria, Virginia. He took a deep, steadying breath. Would he FINALLY find Sky? It was 0630, the January sky dark, and it was snowing. Two years ago, his SEAL team had been stationed at Camp Nichols, near the Pakistan border with Afghanistan. They were there to stop weapons and drugs from coming across that border into Afghanistan via mountain ratlines. It was there that he met and fell in love with Medevac Army pilot, Lieutenant Sky Lambert.

The office hummed, even at this early hour and Cal said good morning to several of the men and women who working there. It was a 24/7/365 kind of place, where professionals in the Intelligence trade worked across three shifts a day, eight hours each, seven days a week. Jack met him in one of the smaller conference rooms in the massive three-story brick building that sat at the edge of Alexandria. At thirty-five, dressed in a dark red cowboy shirt, a set of Levi's and wearing a pair of old, well-worn cowboy boots, Driscoll entered the room. His black hair was military short and his pale gray eyes always reminded Cal of a raptor.

"I see you poured us coffee," Jack said in way of greeting. He nodded his thanks to Cal and sat down at the end of the table. At each seat was a computer terminal anchored into the polished mahogany. He opened the main computer to the latest intel he wanted to share with his employee.

"I just got done writing up my report on my last assignment" Cal replied. He took the chair to the right of Jack's elbow, firing up the computer in front of him.

"I saw it come through," he said, pleased. "What did you do? Get off the plane and go straight to your office to produce this report?"

Rubbing his chin, still bristly with a day's growth of beard because he hadn't slept, showered or shaved yet, Cal said, "Yes. When I received your message in transit from Ukraine, that you'd located Sky Lambert, I wanted to tie up loose ends on this assignment, so it freed me up for whatever you've found on her." He'd been on the front lines, fighting with Ukrainian soldiers against the Russian incursion.

Nodding, Jack, pointed to Cal's computer screen. "After nearly a year of searching under every rock, globally speaking, we finally have a solid lead on her. And how we found her is pretty amazing."

"It's been two years since I said good-bye to Sky at the military hospital at Bagram." He shrugged. "Now that I'm officially out of the Navy and no longer a SEAL, I can pursue her whereabouts." He pulled out a small notebook from the pocket of his long-sleeved blue flannel shirt and produced a pen. "So? Where is she located?"

"Cusco, Peru."

"What? That's South America. Why down there?"

Shrugging, Jack said, "Don't know. We found out her real name, too," and he tapped the information on the screen. A photo of her popped up. "Linda, our research specialist, had this intuition to check with the Witness Security Program or WITSEC people and she got a hit last week. Sky's real name is Ginny Rawlston. But for legality's sake, her WITSEC program name is the one you, the Army, and the rest of the world, have known her by. Sky's in Witness Protection and in their Security Program because of Vladimir Alexandrov. Both were foster children in the Zimmerman household, and he attacked her in her bedroom when she was seventeen. Her foster father and mother were at home and heard her screams and came running to help her." Jack's mouth flattened, his voice going deeper. "Alexandrov had a gun, shot Jack Zimmerman and then his wife, Marielle. Sky saw it all, but she was able to escape through a window and ran to get help. Later, they found out that Alexandrov was the son of the Russian Mafia leader, Yerik Alexandrov, out of New York. She provided evidence for the DOJ attorneys against Alexandrov. In doing so, they knew she'd become a target, so she was placed in the Witness Protection Program to protect her from being hunted down and murdered by the Russian mafia before they could go to trial. While Alexandrov was in jail after being charged, he broke out and disappeared, never to be found. Sky went into the WITSEC program, was moved to Seattle, Washington, and spent her eighteenth year in a foster home. She then went to college, graduated, and went into the Army and become a Black Hawk helicopter pilot, at which she excelled."

"And that's where I met her," Cal said. "I really fell for her. And I knew nothing of her former life. She never liked talking about herself. Now I know why."

Jack shared a quiet look with him. "I haven't figured out how or why people are drawn to one another yet, even with a degree in Psychology. It's an ongoing mystery to me."

Hitching a broad shoulder, Cal grunted. "Me either." Cal saw the sympathy burning in Jack's gray eyes. When he'd met Sky, she was a hell-bent-for-leather pilot flying a Medevac Black Hawk helo top secret ops missions to pick up wounded SEALs, Delta Force, Special Forces, or Rangers. Studying the updated photo from her Cusco employer, her hair was short, a golden wheat color, just like when he'd met her. She'd gained weight and looked good. *Happy.* Cal winced internally.

"What's Sky doing in Cusco?" he asked.

"She flies a Bell-212 helo, a twin-engine Huey, for an NGO, non-governmental organization, a charity called Helping Hands. They dig wells for remote Quechua Indian villages, as well as render medical assistance to the villagers. According to her service record, Sky received a medical discharge from the Army because she lost partial feeling in two of her fingers after being wounded. It disqualified her from flying any military aircraft. Once out of the Army, she headed to South America. Helping Hands hired her as a pilot to fly in pipe, workers, field managers, and medical supplies to a group of their traveling nurses that work in these back water areas of the Highlands. First, she was assigned up in northern Peru, the Iquitos jungle area, for the first six months until she contracted malaria. She was then transferred down to Cusco where the charity has ten Quechua Indian villages earmarked to have wells dug for them. All of them are in the Highlands at the edge of the jungle near the UNESCO World Heritage Site of Machu Picchu."

"I don't suppose you got an address where Sky is staying in Cusco?"

"We have the address for Helping Hands. We've actually provided services for them recently. Your SEAL team member, who you know well, Dylan McCoy, is down there providing security detail for one of their traveling nurses. We had no clue that Sky was there working for the same company. Dylan had sent me a mission report a few days ago, mentioned Sky Lambert, and informed us of some heavy drug lord activity moving into the regions that she and other charity workers are presently working in. Her owner and boss, Elizabeth Standsworth, upon hearing this from Dylan, is interested in procuring Sky a security guard as well. I'm officially assigning you to her. Who is better for the job than you? With any luck, you should be able to connect with Sky at the airport."

"We're all black ops trained. I'll find her one way or another."

"Which is why I've hired so many ex-SEALs," Jack said, smiling a little. "How do you think Sky will react when you show up in her life again after two years?"

Shrugging, Cal said, "I honestly don't know. After I saw Sky that last time at the hospital, the Navy sent her home aboard a C5 medical flight to the States the next day, and I never heard from her again."

"What if she's in a relationship right now, Cal? Or married? What will you do?"

He lifted his chin. "Walk away. I'm not interested in hurting her or disrupting her life. I like Sky one helluva lot. I know in my gut there's something good between us. We just never got a chance to find out what it was." He quickly perused her service record coupled with a quick scan of her Witness Security and Protection records. She'd been running since age seventeen. Now, Cal was hoping to stop her from running. Permanently. Only running TO him, not away from him. *Again.*

"I'm hoping she's not in a relationship or married," he admitted to Jack. "Based on her history, she avoided men like the plague at Camp Nichols until I came along."

Jack nodded. "She's probably afraid that Alexandrov will someday find her. And anyone she loves, which might include you, could become his target, also. That could explain why she disappeared from your life. She may have done it to protect you."

"Yeah," Cal growled, "flawed thinking. SEALs are masters of protection. That bastard would never get close to her or me if she'd have let me into her life like I wanted."

Jack gave Cal a worried look. "Remember our conversation about Sky a year ago?"

"I never forgot it. You didn't want me to pursue Sky if we found her, rather, let her come to me."

"Exactly," Jack said. "My gut tells me she's running scared, Cal. I don't doubt your drawn to one another, but most likely, she couldn't climb over that self-imposed barrier she's erected. Remember? She saw her foster parents murdered. She knows what Alexandrov is capable of. And if Sky was falling fast for you, it probably scared the living hell out of her. She'd seen two people she deeply loved, ripped away from her. And if she is attracted to you? Her fear that Alexandrov will find her again and threaten any relationship she got into, and that person would automatically become a target like she was. So, she has every reason to keep out of sight from him and you."

"Wished to hell she hadn't run and gone into hiding," Cal growled, unhappy. "You can't live your life like a monk."

Jack laughed. "What? Like you do?"

Cal gave him a dark look and muttered defensively, "I have relationships."

"Yeah," Jack teased, "one-night stands. Like those count?"

Jack had married Val Edwards, a physical therapist. He was not one to do one-night stands. "They count for one night," he said, lightening his tone.

Jack shrugged good naturedly. "She doesn't know how well SEALs protect their loved ones. She couldn't trust you as much as she probably wanted too. When you find her and if she's still single and unattached, your focus has to be on getting her to trust you, not bedding her down."

"I agree. I want her to trust me," he said, his gruff tone softening.

"Over time," Jack counseled. "Val and I went through some rough times, but what held us together was our trust with one another. It is everything."

"I got it," he promised, nodding.

Jack sighed. "I feel we know each other pretty well, Cal. There's five years between us. In some ways, Sky and you are similar. You both had really harsh, violent childhoods. And trust is a big issue for both of you."

"Sky saw her foster parents murdered in cold blood," Cal rasped. "And Alexandrov's assault, I'm sure, shattered her in another way. I know I'm not one to talk, my family is a dysfunctional mess, no question. That's why I left and joined the SEALs. I wanted nothing to do with my abusive, drunken father."

Scowling, Jack said, "Roark Sinclair was an outlier, Cal. He was an addicted, angry man, he beat the hell out of you all the time. He was a loner until the day he died of that unexpected heart attack. By that time, you were in the SEALs."

"Yeah, and I didn't go home for his funeral either," Cal growled. "Chad and Tracey, my younger brother and sister, stepped up and they ran our farm just fine without him around."

"At least you three are good friends. Your farm is in Oregon. Are you still in close contact with the rest of your family?"

"We're on good terms with one another, as well as all the other farmers in the Willamette valley," Cal said, "but I can't step foot on that farm without having bad memories, the beatings and fights, with Roark. He was a mean, miserable son-of-a-bitch. That's why I've built my own cabin outside of Alexandria, up in the woods. I needed some peace, Jack."

"I hear you, Cal. Alcohol and drugs can turn a man into monster," Jack agreed sadly. "Are you going to see Chad and Tracey before you leave to check out Sky and her situation?"

"No Instead, I'll Zoom with them and let them know I'm going on another assignment. They're used to not seeing me for six to nine months at a time and they know better than to ask questions about my whereabouts."

Jack's face grew serious as he caught Cal's gaze and continued "The situation down in Peru is more dangerous than we thought. Dylan informed me that there's a new player in the drug trade for that region. The Russian Mafia wants a piece of the cocaine trade, and they have been infiltrating the area and taking over coca groves hidden in the jungle by the villagers. I've worked my contacts and learned some troubling news. This is Top Secret intel Cal. Sky's foster brother, Vladimir Alexandrov, is leading up the Russian crew down there. It seems maybe she was right to worry about him finding her again.

"Does he know Sky is there?" Cal asked, a sinking feeling striking the pit of his stomach.

"We don't know. It seems unlikely at this point, because if he did know she was in the area, he would most likely have gone after her."

"You're right." Cal agreed. "I'd like to leave tomorrow morning, if you can swing it?"

Jack quirked a small grin. "Emily is putting together a travel package for you right now. This way? You'll have important connections already in place with the police and other federal organizations in Peru and in Cusco that you can call for assistance or information. If you need help, you'll be able to tap into it. Also, you know you'll have contact with us at any time you need it. Emily is setting it up so you'll reach Reagan International Airport at 0900, and from there, you're on a commercial airliner that will fly into Miami, Florida, change planes and head to Lima, Peru. There, you'll catch a next morning flight out to Cusco."

"Thank you, Jack."

"You'll have a bank account already in place by the time you land in Cusco. Any money you need, will be in there. It will all be set up via your smart phone, and Emily will give you that info later today. Why don't you get back to your apartment, get cleaned up, sleep, and then call in and speak with her on the details?"

"I need the shut-eye," he agreed. "And I'll call her after I get up."

Grinning, Jack gripped his hand. "SEALs always stick together. Maybe that's why we joined them in the first place?"

"I think you're right," Cal admitted, never thinking along that line. But then, Jack was not the usual operator, either. He was a genius, so the Navy said, and he'd made changes to SEAL operations that boosted him to Master Chief in less time than anyone had ever made that vaunted enlisted rank. Jack had left the Navy at age thirty and came to Alexandria to create an instant, overnight success with Shield Security.

Jack made it a point, whenever he could, to hire people coming out of the military. Black ops people were natural MacGyver's who could make something out of nothing, and that was an important skill to any operator out in the field. By the time Jack was thirty-five, Shield Security had become a global success, working in democratic countries whose Intelligence agencies relied on his skills, his top-drawer contacts, plus, the high caliber of people he hired to carry out very important and clandestine missions around the world. Jack was in a class by himself, and Cal was glad that they had teamed up with him once again, only this time around, as a civilian. He doubted any other employer would do what Jack was doing for him so he could go in search of the woman he loved. But then, Jack's own childhood read like his growing up years. Some things they shared in common, and they weren't pretty.

Cal wasn't about to admit how much his heart was involved in this mission. When he had sex, it was sex, with no emotions in the mix—just pleasure for the woman and a release for him. But after that one tender, sweet, searching kiss he'd shared with Sky, Cal would never forget it. Her kiss had brought up a ton of emotions within him. It had surprised the hell out of Cal. He had been caught completely off guard. Wanting Sky was more than about selfish sexual gratification. It was eating away in the center of his chest, driving him to find her. He HAD to find her. He HAD to know if what they felt for one another was justified or not. Cal knew it was. All he had to do was convince Sky of it. But he had no way of knowing just how Sky was going to react when she saw him. None.

January 5
SKY LAMBERT SAT in the right seat of her Bell 212 helicopter after just landing it. The international and domestic parts of the sprawling, massive Cusco airport were ramping down for the evening. No flights took off after dusk because of the violent, chaotic winds that blew down off the Andes Mountains that ringed this city nestled in a bowl-shaped valley. At night, hundred mile an hour winds would howl across the landmass. If a plane tried to fly in that kind of chaos, it would have its wings ripped off. They had enough airplane crashes to verify it.

The sun was setting as she pulled off her white helmet, dropping it in the left hand seat. She ran her fingers through her short blond hair and sat there feeling dizzy for a moment. Closing her eyes, she leaned back, allowing the tension to slough off her shoulders. They felt so tight. But when didn't they? Every day, Sky had to prove herself. She flew in twenty-foot lengths of pipe in a special sling harness beneath her helo, plus carrying cargo, well equipment, food and medical supplies to inaccessible places where Quechua villagers eked out a living in the Highlands of the Andes.

She'd contracted mild asthma by this high altitude flying without an oxygen mask, making it harder to breath at nearly twelve thousand feet above sea level, where Cusco sat. Sky opened her eyes and unconsciously rubbed her chest. Two years ago, she'd been shot in the left upper arm at Camp Nichols. The sensation in her left hand, the last two fingers, had never returned. She could still fly as a civilian, which was her only happiness. The asthma was new, but a lot of people who hadn't been born in Cusco acquired labored breathing issues. Some, like herself, developed irritating off and on asthma, which was a pain in the ass, but not a giant killer. When she was in Lima, which sat at sea level near the Pacific Ocean, she never had asthmatic symptoms. It was just the high altitude and her body's inability to adjust to it.

Alone again, as usual, Sky thought, carelessly opening the harness and releasing it from around her hips and chest. *Nothing new.* She'd been born alone. Abandoned by two drug parents who were meth and cocaine dealers. The only respite she'd seen in her life were the years spent with Jack and Marielle Zimmerman, who took her in, gave her real love, care, and nurturing. It was the first time in Sky's life she'd understood just how much she'd missed when it came to living in a healthy family environment.

Muttering under her breath, she leaned down and pulled her helmet bag from behind her seat and set it in her lap. *All water under the bridge.* Her life had always been a nightmare of one sort or another. There were no happy endings for her. *Ever.* Hiding out in the Andes in Peru seemed like a good place to Sky and she leaped at the chance to become a pilot for the Helping Hands Charity organization after separating from the Army when her wound had healed.

She looked around at the huge airport, the hangars and the planes that were parked in the shadows of the coming dusk, everything would come to a halt at all the different facilities shortly. Nothing would move until seven a.m. tomorrow morning when the winds reversed direction, and the air became tamer and flyable once again. Only a fool with a death wish flew out of this airport during the night hours. Sky stuffed her helmet, Nomex gloves and knee board into her flight bag.

Opening the door, she emerged from the cockpit. January was still the rainy season, but by mid-March, it would turn to the dry season and then the heat of the Equator would drive the temperature higher. She could dodge rain showers, which were common in the wet season, and still deliver life-giving pipe and supplies to the teams who worked at specific Quechua villages. It was a humid coldness that chilled her, as she pulled the green nylon Jacket more tightly around herself. The tan, one-piece flight suit she wore was too thin to take such temperature variations.

Sky saw the lights on in the hangar where they rented space to park the charity-owned helicopter when it needed maintenance and repair. In her helmet bag were papers she had to fill out and hand in to the manager of the charity. Elizabeth Standsworth, her boss, had a small office inside the same hangar. The woman was amazing to Sky. She was the daughter of Senator Curt Standsworth and had devoted her life to creating this charity. Elizabeth wanted to bring fresh, clean water to villages. So many died of dysentery because of fouled and polluted water. Wells, on the other hand, were clean and free of parasites, bacteria and fecal matter that killed so many babies and young children. Sky believed in Elizabeth's mission. No child should suffer.

Walking toward the opened hangar door, the lights turning the deepening dusk a little brighter, her breathing becoming more labored. On bad days, it made her dizzy at times to live in Cusco. If she took good, slow deep breaths, it compensated for the loss of oxygenation, and the dizziness passed. She always carried her emergency asthma inhaler with her. The wind blew hard and mussed the strands of her flattened hair. Hurrying toward the hangar, she didn't see the man approaching from her left.

"Sky?"

Sky jerked to a halt, hearing her name called. Turning on her booted heel, she saw a very tall man, shadowed by the dusk, coming toward her at a casual pace. Frowning, she her heart amped up. That voice…she knew it. From where? Her fine, thin brows drew down as she squinted, trying to see who it was in the deep shadows. She feared Vladimir Alexandrov finding her. Her Russian nemesis was six foot, five inches tall. And this man approaching her, whoever he was, was close to that height. A part of her wanted to flee mindlessly in fear. Sky felt the adrenaline tunneling through her bloodstream, making her hyper alert, getting ready to run. She always carried a .45 pistol on her, a sidearm she was never without. Her hand automatically moved toward the butt of it. She always left the safety off and a bullet in the chamber because if Vlad ever found her, Sky knew he'd kill her on the spot. Was this Vlad, or a man sent by Vlad? Was he here to kill her?

As he emerged from the shadows, Sky gasped. Her hand fell away from the .45 pistol, her eyes widening as she jerked to a halt. It was Cal Sinclair! Her lips parted and she felt a rush of so many conflicting emotions that it momentarily paralyzed her. He was free of his black beard she'd seen him with over in Afghanistan. But it was the same square face, those penetrating, narrowed gold-brown eyes of his, his broken nose and mouth, flat and hard looking. When she'd first met Cal, he'd scared the hell out of her because his body build that was almost identical to Vlad's build. But Cal was nothing like her tormentor.

Gulping unsteadily, curling her hand more tightly around the leather handle of the helmet bag as Cal slowed his approach toward her, she released her breath. The well-worn brown leather bomber Jacket outlined his massive, proud shoulders. There was nothing forgiving or weak looking about Cal

Sinclair. There never had been. He was a SEAL; one of the best trained black ops warriors in the world. And his walk, although casual and silent, belied the threat that always existed around him. He wore dark green cargo pants that were bloused into scarred, well-worn black leather combat boots. Even though these were civilian-like clothes, Sky knew they could not hide what Cal was: a warrior in every sense. Her heart raced, but it wasn't from fear. It was sudden happiness flooding her heart, soothing her fractured soul.

"Cal…," she whispered as he drew near and halted, his gaze only on her. Sky saw his thinned mouth relax. It was the only feature on this man's hard face that told her he was capable of humanity; that he wasn't a killer like Vlad Alexandrov. "W-what are you doing here?" Her voice sounded far away to her, stunned sounding, her words barely above a choked whisper.

Cal halted as he studied Sky. She looked good. He felt his chest tighten, his pulse ratchet up, and every cell in his body wanting to kiss her senseless right now. His gaze dropped to that luscious mouth of hers. Sky wore no make-up, but that didn't matter. He reined in his desire and said gruffly, "I've been looking the world over for you."

Sky faltered. "Me?" She had never forgotten their one kiss. It had melted her soul and touched her abandoned heart. Her whole world focused on him. He'd kissed her so tenderly and it had surprised her because he was a warrior, a man of deadly action. Remembering their first meeting in Afghanistan, Sky had been drawn and repelled by him. When Cal had kissed her, she suddenly realized that as rugged looking as he appeared, he was nothing like Vlad. His mouth sliding with invitation lightly across her lips had shattered and consumed her. And she'd never forgotten him. *Never.* He was the ONLY man who she'd ever dreamed about. Good, positive dreams. Vlad was always in her nightmares, but how Sky looked forward to dreams about Cal, cradling her, his mouth seeking, finding hers, filling her with his heat and his strength. Sky gulped, barely able to hold his intense gaze as he perused her in the thickening silence.

"I told you," Cal said, lessening the gruffness in his low voice, "that I'd find you, Sky. Today is that day." Searching her stunned looking blue gaze, those turquoise gems set with huge black pupils and a black ring around the outside of them, his mouth softened. "There's something good between us, Sky. And I wanted the chance to find out if there is…if you aren't already in a relationship."

Cal swallowed hard, afraid that Sky would bolt and run again. He saw that she was much thinner than in her employment photo, and that bothered him. Sky had an oval face and a stubborn chin and a wide, full mouth that made him ache to kiss her once again. Her blond hair, still sun streaked, was cut short in a pixie style around her perfectly shaped skull. She stood five foot seven inches tall. Her shoulders were small but proud, echoing her military training.

Sky looked down, unable to hold Cal's burning, searching gaze. She heard the hope in his low voice. An ache built in her chest, her heart contracting with so many emotions. She wanted this man like the air she breathed. Dazed with shock over his unexpected appearance, she lifted her head and stared up at him. Her voice was strained as she said, "I'm not in a relationship. How did you find me?"

"I'm black ops, you know that," and Cal gave her a careless smile meant to make her relax. Was Sky going to run away from him again? Tell him the same thing she did at the Bagram hospital? Tell him to walk away from her? Fear ate at Cal. Gazing at her, hungry for Sky in every way, he saw the strain of the two years after being wounded and nearly dying. She would have died if Cal hadn't help save her life. He just didn't want Sky to jettison him again.

"Are you on leave from the SEALs?"

"No. I left them two years ago. I'm a contractor with a security company in Alexandria, Virginia, now."

Frowning, Sky looked around. The night was closing in on them, the grayness outlining the Andes peaks to the west of them. Wiping her fingers across her brow, she felt trapped. And happy. And scared. "Why did you leave the SEALs?" and she tilted her head, drowning in his warm golden-brown, shadowy gaze.

"Because I couldn't get the time off that I wanted in order to find you, Sky."

Shock flared through her again. Cal was in top shape, not an inch of fat anywhere on his tall, powerful body. It was his hands resting relaxed on his narrow hips, that drew her. Hands that had gently framed her face as he leaned down to kiss her when she'd come out of surgery at Bagram, barely conscious. He'd kissed her so gently, and Sky swore she could feel the infusion of life, of joy, of hope, flooding her body, her senses, as his mouth softly took hers. How many times had she wondered what it would be like to have Cal's hands gliding across her naked body? They were scarred hands, calloused and rough feeling. But it had felt so good to Sky as she'd awakened in post op with his kiss. She thought of the fable of the prince awakening his beloved princess with one. She rubbed her scrunched brow, trying to think straight when all she felt were a kaleidoscope of emotions smothering her logical mind.

"Cal—"

He held up his hand. "Don't send me away, Sky."

She stared at him. Feeling like running. Feeling like running TOWARD Cal. To be held by him. Sky saw the ache and loneliness in his eyes for her. Cal wanted to hold her. To kiss her, to sweep her into his arms and never let her go. She had well developed intuition because of her past and she could feel all those yearning emotions around Cal and more.

"It won't work," she whispered wearily.

"I don't buy that."

She gave him a bare shake of her head, exhaustion tunneling through her. "I'm tired, Cal." *Tired of running. Tired of hiding. Tired to my soul.*

"Then lean on me."

Man of few words. That was the Cal she knew. He always went for the jugular. To the heart of the situation. One corner of her mouth lifted faintly, and she shook her head. "I can't."

"You won't. There's a difference, Sweetheart."

The endearment sent heat instead of ice or fear flowing through her. "You don't understand," she began with an effort.

"I understand you a lot more than you think I do, Sky."

She felt his stubbornness. Felt his fixedness regarding her. Cal wasn't leaving this time. Part of her felt safe for the first time in her life with him simply standing there. How badly Sky wanted happiness.

Her idealistic side dissolved though; it had all been smoke and mirrors. Sky remembered the hard, biting hands of Vlad upon her, tearing at her clothes, pushing her down on the bed. She shivered inwardly, never able to shake that assault by him. Or the bloody carnage left in the wake of her fighting him off and escaping. The loss of Jack and Marielle, whom she loved so deeply, who had given her the love she'd so hungrily needed as a child, murdered by Vlad when they'd raced to her room after she screamed for help.

And yet, Sky felt incapable of fighting Cal. He was so strong. Confident. Male. But also, she could feel that powerful, invisible embrace of protection that he automatically bestowed upon her once again. How good it felt! Comforting. If she could just relax for a little while, absorb what he wanted to give her. Why wouldn't she reach out and allow that to happen?

The silence thickened between them as the night began to cover them. "Okay," Sky whispered wearily, exhausted, "follow me…"

CHAPTER 2

January 5

THE WASHED-OUT LIGHT in the hangar revealed how tired and drawn Sky really was. She no longer strode with that cocky confidence she had possessed at the forward operating base in Afghanistan. Instead, she walked like a wary shadow; someone who did not want to be seen, rather, she wanted to remain invisible to the world around her. Her shoulders were drawn up, telling him she was very tense. Over his sudden appearance? As she walked into the busy hangar full of other aircraft, fixed wings and jets for maintenance, Sky peeled off to the left of the working mechanics and headed toward a row of small offices on the side of the cavernous building.

All the offices were dark. Quitting time, Cal knew, had come and gone. She headed toward the office with Helping Hands, *Manos Amigas*, in gold letters in Spanish and English across the window. He watched her fish out a key and open the door.

"Come in," Sky said, pointing to another chair at a second desk. "I have a flight report and some other stuff I have to deal with, first."

Nodding, Cal looked around. He saw a coffee pot in the corner. "Want some coffee?" He saw Sky turn, surprised.

"That would be wonderful…"

Just the sudden emotion in her husky voice riffled through him, a heated yearning blooming in his chest. "I'll make coffee, you go to to work."

Sky nodded. Cal's presence filled the small office like sunlight. She shouldn't relish his thoughtfulness, that powerful sense of safety that washed over her, but she did. Tired because of a lack of sufficient oxygen and because it had had been a bitch of a day flying-wise, Sky gratefully sat down at her desk. She pulled a pen from her flight suit upper arm sleeve and went to work.

Trying to remain immune to Cal's masculine presence was like having an elephant in the room and trying to ignore it. Her hand shook a little as she signed off the flight hours in her logbook. She turned on the desktop computer and waited for it to boot up. The pleasant sounds of coffee being made lulled Sky. Pushing her fingers through her hair, she caught herself. Why did she care what she looked like now? It was Cal. His overwhelming but welcomed presence soothed her guardedness. Sky never used cosmetics and her short hair was always flattened by the helmet she wore. His maleness was like a tsunami in the chilled office and impossible to ignore. Worse, Sky berated herself because she felt starved for Cal's sudden presence. *Two years.* He'd been out of her life for two years, but it seemed like yesterday to her. Shaking her head, Sky got to work typing up her daily report. The wafting scent of fresh coffee being made made her sigh.

"Smell good?"

Turning, she saw Cal with his hip hitched on the corner of the other desk, arms across his chest, casually watching her. Normally, a man staring at her for any length of time made Sky scared. Instead, languishing beneath Cal's golden gaze, she felt warm, snug, and blanketed by his care. "It does," she admitted, clearing her throat.

"You look tired, Sky."

Shrugging, she got back to typing up her report. "Comes with the duty." Sky heard him grunt. Smiling to herself, she thought, *this is pure Cal.* He never said much, but when he did, it was blunt and in your face. One did not guess what he was thinking; it was all there in front of you. She missed that honest quality; at least she knew where he stood. Most men did not broadcast that to a woman. Her fingers flew across the keyboard as she input the amounts of equipment and gear flown into the highlands today on each of her six flights.

Cal scowled, absorbing Sky's clean profile. She was fragile. Her skin was tight across her cheekbones. She was just this side of gaunt. He bet beneath that sexless flight suit of hers, he could see her ribs. She wasn't eating right. Why? Was it the job? The pressures on her? The danger of flying in these rugged mountains with their well-known hellacious wind shears was a challenge to all pilots. Cal sat quietly, absorbing her. He was glad Sky wasn't in a relationship. One of the first things he'd checked out was her left hand. There was no ring on it. In fact, she wore no jewelry whatsoever. Not uncommon for a pilot, though. In the military regulation, no jewelry was allowed to be worn during a flight. Sky was no longer in the Army, but Cal wondered if that regulation had followed her into civilian life. He tried to tamp down his hope that THEY could forge a relationship between them. It was a tall order, and he knew it.

The coffee was done, and he slid off the corner of the desk and walked over to the table. There were four mugs and he turned two of them over and filled them with coffee.

"You used to like your coffee black," he noted, lifting his head, meeting her gaze.

"Still do. Some things don't change."

Cal smiled to himself and set the mug down to one side of the keyboard.

Sky's heart thumped once in her chest. She saw the thoughtful expression in his face and realized he was being vulnerable to her. His SEAL game face was no longer in place. The cragginess of his face was there, and his eyes were alert and filled with gold dapples. She liked that his mouth had softened, no longer a hard, thin line as before. Sky reached for the mug, "Thank you…," her voice catching momentarily as an avalanche of unexpected emotions deluged her.

Sky was trying to concentrate. She was making a lot of typos because Cal was standing so close to her, that male heat of his surrounding her, his masculine scent like a perfume to her flaring nostrils. "Can you go sit down, please?" and she jabbed a finger toward the other desk.

"Why?"

"Because you're making me make a lot of typing mistakes."

Cal preened and grinned. "Okay," he murmured. He saw how ruffled Sky had become. Her cheeks stained a pretty pink hue, and he knew for sure it was her reaction to him. A damn good sign in his book. Cal had always been a reader of body language and facial expressions. Plus, he had a powerful intuition that never led him wrong. And it was telling him that Sky was happy to see him again, no matter what words were coming out of that soft mouth of hers?

He sat down, eased the squeaky, protesting chair back and sipped his coffee. Savoring her profile, her blond brows were drawn down in concentration. Her fingers flew over the keyboard.

"Do you do this every night after a day of work?"

"Yes."

"How much longer?"

"Keep chatting and it will be a lot longer."

Cal squelched his smile. That was the woman he knew in Afghanistan. He relished the taste of the potent brew. He always made strong coffee. He watched as Sky would stop, take an appreciative sip and then return to her typing duties. She was so damned easy to read. She didn't know how to hide how she felt.

He had always preferred a blond. Not a dyed one, but a real one. Sky's hair, although short, had streaks of gold combined with thin streaks of sienna and lighter hues of amber; indicative of her genetic heritage. Her skin was soft, and he saw no tan whatsoever. Flying a lot, not having down time to hike or be out in sunlight, was most likely the reason.

"How many hours a day do you fly?"

Sky lifted her chin, his low, deep voice like a roughened velvet blanket surrounding her. "Three to five hours a day, depending upon the amount of daylight. My helo is civilian and has no IFR gear in it. And there's a lot of ground time due to low lying fog or heavy rain on these flights. I'm usually out from dawn until dusk."

Cal grunted. "It's only Wednesday and you look like a skinny ghost."

One corner of her mouth quirked as she continued to type despite his interruptions. "Thanks."

"You need some sunlight. Some good, fresh air, a hike, maybe?"

"Sounds like a dream," Sky admitted, more touched by his care than she wanted to be.

"Dreams do come true."

At that, Sky gave a derisive snort.

"What?"

"Dreams are for optimists."

"And you're not?"

"Never."

"I'm not either. But I do believe in fresh air and sunlight."

Her lips thinned. "That's because your black ops boys operate outdoors most of the time."

"Got me there. Guilty as charged." Cal grinned, seeing a slight smile hook one corner of that full, soft mouth of hers. The woman made him ache for her. But Cal knew she was off limits. *For now.* At least Sky hadn't sent him away. *Yet.* And she WAS talking to him. Both positives in his world, and it felt like major progress to him.

"There," Sky muttered, finally closing the file and shutting down the computer. "Done." She turned in the chair and looked at Cal. He reminded her of a jaguar looking relaxed in that chair. It was deceptive. Sky could feel that tightly wound steel tension around Cal; as if in a second, he could explode into violent, focused action. Oddly, that gave her tranquility, not alarm. She'd felt that same wired, dangerousness around Vlad and had lived with it for two years in that foster home. He watched and stalked her. Cal was stalking her too, but Sky didn't feel threatened by it. Her heart was breaking because she knew she couldn't have any sort of connection with Cal as much as she wanted it.

"Good," Cal said, unwinding slowly from the chair. He walked over and took her emptied mug to the coffee table. Turning, he said, "Let me buy you dinner at the Palacio del Inka Hotel in Cusco where I'm staying?"

Sky hesitated, hands becoming damp on the fabric of her flight suit as she sat there staring up at him. "No—I—"

"I won't bite you, Sky. It's just dinner." Cal gestured to her. "You're underweight, Sweetheart. You need put some meat on your bones."

Sky flushed. She felt the heat come up off her chest, fly up her neck and settle with heated prickles into her cheeks. The look on Cal's face was earnest and sincere. She saw worry banked in those gold jaguar eyes of his. Biting on her lower lip for a moment, she relented. "Okay. Just ONE dinner, Cal. ONE. That's all."

Nodding, he rumbled, "One dinner coming up," and he slid his hand beneath her elbow and helped her stand. Instantly, Sky pulled away from his fingers, as if burned. She felt a moment of panic. Grabbing her helmet bag, she turned off the light and opened the office door.

Had his touched scared Sky? Cal wasn't sure. He saw panic rise in her blue eyes as he walked through the door and turned, waiting for her to close and lock up the office. Cal cautioned himself. He remembered Jack's warning words. Yeah, Sky was scared. Almost ready to run. *Again. Sonofabitch.*

Sky tried to quell her panic. She stared out into the parking lot outside the airport, scanning the surroundings. Cal had no wheels into Cusco from the airport that she could discern. He followed her to her beat up looking silver Toyota SUV that had lots of dents and some rust on its fenders. It had seen better days. Sky climbed in, her hands on the steering wheel. When Cal closed the door and looked over at her, the lights shining through the windshield, he saw angst in her shadowed eyes. Her mouth was pursed.

"What's wrong?"

She studied him in the quiet of the car. Sky could smell his scent, a combination of sweat, maleness and clean, unscented soap, and it was sending her body into hunger for him. "I need to go change first."

"Okay, not a problem." Cal was going to tell her she'd look good in nothing at all but clamped down on saying that.

"I guess I didn't want you to know where my apartment's located." She saw Cal sit back and relax his bulk. A jaguar resting, but always alert and ready. "I know you're black ops and, sooner or later you'd find my place, anyway." She watched his mouth twitch. Brows flattening, she gripped the wheel, fingers damp and cold.

Cal tried to keep his voice gentle, not gruff or threatening sounding. "I'm not your enemy, Sky. All I want to do is buy you one dinner. I'm not going to come over and beat on your door and beg to come in." Instantly, he saw the lines in her brow relax, that beautifully shaped mouth of hers soften. Groaning internally, Cal wanted to reach out, haul her slender form into his embrace, and kiss Sky senseless until they melted together, and they couldn't tell one from another. Damn, there was a Grand Canyon standing invisibly between them. How the hell was he going to breach it and get across it to her?

Nodding, giving him a rueful look of apology, Sky fished out the fob and the engine turned over. "Okay." Her voice sounded breathless. Relieved, maybe. "There can't be anything between us, Sinclair. You've GOT to get that," Sky warned him as she swung the Toyota out of the parking lot, heading down the highway toward Cusco.

Cal said nothing. He was relaxed against the seat, but his senses remained on high alert. It was dark, lit only by the flash of car lights leaving from the major airport that was shutting down for the night. Ahead, down in the bowl-like valley, lay the jeweled lighting of the city of Cusco, at nearly twelve thousand feet in altitude. He heard the wobble in Sky's husky voice, the emotion and fear behind her words. *Time. Patience.* Jack was right: he had to ease into Sky's life, not break down the door to try and reach her. Cal wouldn't put it past Sky to run again. It was what she'd done all her life, according to her WITSEC file, but he wasn't about to let on that he knew about it or her past.

Cal saw the major stone edifices along the cobblestoned streets that had been earlier fashioned by the industrious Inca civilization. Traffic was still light because it was only six p.m. He knew in South America, dinner didn't happen until at least nine p.m., or later. Sky's apartment was located in the center of the city near a major plaza, a Roman Catholic church at the other end of it. The building was a three-story yellow stucco with a lot of windows covered by green and white striped awnings. It was a clean place, well cared for, and between two other buildings with wide cobblestone alleys separating them. The Cusco air smelled cleaned as Cal climbed out of the SUV. Sky had parked near the sidewalk leading up to the rear of the building. Looking around, he saw the area was well lit. The city hummed with traffic, mostly taxis. Cusco was a dynamic place founded by the Incas. Later, Spanish conquistadors built their buildings over the sacred Incan stone temples that could be seen everywhere.

"Come on," Sky said, locking the vehicle door. She shouldered her helmet bag. Cal came up in a few strides and gently pried it off her shoulder and out of her fingers.

"Let me," he said. He saw what his touch did to Sky for a split second. Her eyes had gone warm and damned if he hadn't seen longing in them. Shocked by that unexpected discovery, just as quickly, Cal saw Sky button up her expression, so it was back to the wariness and distrust of him in her eyes. He smiled to himself. Sky really didn't understand how well SEALs read micro facial expressions; even fleeting ones that they thought no one would see. But he saw. And it gave him hope. Sky LIKED his touch, even if it scared her. Inwardly, Cal took a deep breath of relief.

Sky's apartment was at the end of a highly polished, mahogany paneled hall. The floor was composed of brick red tiles from one end to another. This was a beautiful place and Cal appreciated the wood, a carpenter in his spare time. He liked wood, liked carving it, and he had built his cedar log cabin by hand, over a seven-year period. Sky halted and opened the mahogany door that had an ancient looking brass doorknob.

"Come in," she urged, pushing the door open. "I need to grab a quick shower and wash off the sweat from the day…I'll be about half an hour."

"Take your time," he murmured. Cal quietly closed the door. As he turned, he absorbed the living room that was alive with tropical plants. The walls were a pale, cheery yellow, much the color of Sky's gold hair. The white leather couch and stuffed chairs sat on a handwoven tapestry-like rug with Incan symbols worked into it. The rug was a cream, brown, black, and gray design. There were pictures of tropical flowers in tasteful wooden frames here and there along the walls. He watched the sway of Sky's hips as she walked down the hall. She was slender, not curvy, but her hips were flared, and he could almost imagine his hands around them, holding her to him, giving her pleasure. Yeah, he could make Sky swoon, for damn sure. Reluctantly tucking away those torrid thoughts, Cal nosed around. He found himself in a small kitchen with a round wooden table and two wooden chairs. Everything was neat and clean, like Sky. There were no messes, everything sparkling, and the curtains at the window were a pale pink to add color against the white walls.

He heard music, classics, playing in the background. Sky must have turned on her iPod because that wasn't South American Latin music by a mile. He smiled a little, running his hand over the rose, black, and cream-colored granite counters. There was a small gas stove. It was a modern kitchen with modern appliances. He wondered how much she made to afford this place. Usually, his digs in a city as a SEAL weren't half as cushy or nice as her place.

Cal was curious about Sky. He knew a home reflected the person. He ambled down a highly polished hall and discovered her office. There was a desktop computer, a bright mahogany desk, and again, everything was clean and neat. Thinking about her messy past, her reaction was to have control and therefore, organization as a result. It made sense to Cal. His chest tightened as he remembered her dysfunctional past. Sky has been brought up by druggie parents who beat her regularly until she ran away at age ten, only to be caught by the police and brought home. According to her file, she had continued that cycle of running away into her teen years. Yeah, a neat, picked up house could reflect Sky's unconscious need for order when there had been nothing but chaos in her life for the first sixteen years of her life.

Cal found a stuffed gray kitty cat sitting on her rolling chair tucked beneath her desk. He grazed at the furry beast's head and stroked the fake fur with his fingers as he looked around. There were more prints of botanical plants and flowers up on one wall. She must love nature, he surmised, even if she didn't get out in it judging from her pale skin.

The door at the other end of the hall was closed and probably her bedroom. Cal found himself wondering what it looked like. Just then, the door open. Sky saw him and jerked to a halt. She wore a tasteful pair of tan wool slacks, a long sleeved dark pink silk blouse with delicate ruffles around the collar. He saw the small white pierced earrings set in gold, thinking it matched the gold flecks he saw in her blue eyes. Her hair was brushed and fuller. She wore a pink lipstick, but no other cosmetics, and she looked stunning to Cal.

"I was just admiring your office." It wasn't a lie. Sky gave him a wary look and pulled the dark pink vicuna shawl around her shoulders. He felt himself yearning powerfully for her as she walked toward him with that woman's grace of her. She had a long set of legs and Cal felt his hands getting itchy, wanting to slide his palms up them and feel how velvety and firm they were.

"Your black ops. Why wouldn't I expect you to be snooping around?"

Cal had the good grace to give her a bit of an apologetic smile. "Caught red handed. Actually," and he turned, pointing to one of the flower prints hanging on the wall, "I've decided you're a nature lover."

Sky laughed a little, feeling heat crawl into her face. "Oh, all my many plant pictures?"

Cal inhaled her scent as she moved past him. Sky's fragrance was part almond, maybe the shampoo she used on her hair, part wildflower soap that she caressed her skin, mingling with her own, unique feminine scent. It was a potent combination. Cal felt his entire lower body aching for her. He wanted her in the worst damn way.

He didn't make the mistake of cupping her elbow this time as they left her apartment. Instead, Cal contented himself with watching how Sky walked, her hips gently swaying down the hall as they sauntered toward the elevator. Her scent was driving him crazy. He ached to slide his fingers through that shining gold of her hair, kiss the short strands, to kiss her and never stop.

At the entrance to the street, Sky turned to him. "We can walk over to Plaza de Armas from here if you want. It's only a block away."

"Sure." Cal looked down at her shoes. They were sensible, low heeled brown leather shoes. "Let's go…"

"I don't wear heels," Sky drawled. She noticed the heat she saw in Cal's eyes. She could feel him inspecting her because wherever his gaze moved, her flesh tingled and then grew heated. He liked her. *A lot.* Cal didn't try and disguise how he appreciated her as a woman and for once, Sky felt herself grow lighter. Her lower body was contracting and feeling needy. She knew that signal. Was she wanting him? Absolutely. Had she done anything about it? Not for a long, long time. Now Sky was yearning for him, and she found herself weakening beneath his hungry gaze. No man had ever made her feel this feminine, this good about herself as a woman.

Cal didn't give her a look like Vlad had; a feral, vicious gaze telling her he owned her. No, Cal's gaze was so different that it shook Sky to the soles of her feet. It was raw male appreciation, she realized. Respectful, yet haunting and devouring to her in all kinds of good ways. Even her breasts tightened beneath his gaze, the nipples growing hard against the pink, silky bra she wore. What would it feel like to have Cal touch her breasts with those large, calloused hands of his? Despite his daunting physical presence, Sky somehow sensed he'd be a gentle lover with her. Not a predator like Vlad. With Cal, she wouldn't be his prey. She would be his equal, a woman walking into the arms of man who truly appreciated and respected her in every possible way. That made Sky feel good about herself.

"Good thing you don't wear heels," Cal rumbled, angling an index finger at her practical shoes. "They ruin a woman's feet forever." Cal pushed open the dark mahogany door that led to the street. "Come on, I'll buy you a good steak dinner and we'll put some meat on those bones of yours."

CHAPTER 3

January 5

THE RESTAURANT HAD just opened, and Cal had the maitre' d take them to a black leather booth at the rear of the massive room. From there, Cal could watch everyone coming and going from the restaurant. It was also near a second exit. He asked Sky to sit in the other seat, he saw her smile a little, a knowing glitter coming to her eyes.

"Don't say it," Cal muttered, sitting down and situating himself in the booth so he had a complete view of who was coming and going into the area. It was against the Peruvian law to wear a weapon, but he had one on him, hidden beneath his jacket.

"What? That you're in black ops mode?" Sky chuckled and shook her head and opened the menu. "You'll NEVER not be a SEAL, Cal."

He warmed to the soft smile hovering at the corners of her mouth. Picking up the menu, he said, "That's true," he agreed, amused.

Sky tilted her head, studying Cal in the dim light offered by a lamp on the wall above the booth. The planes of his face were angular and hard. He was not handsome in a model sense. Instead, he reminded her of a rough-hewn granite sculpture, his flesh sun darkened by years of being out in all kinds of rough weather and the even harsher elements. Her gaze followed to his lips, and instantly she felt her body contract. Her mouth going dry, she reached for the glass of ice water, barely getting a sip down her throat. Sex radiated off him like blinding sunlight. It had from the day she had met him at Camp Nichols. He reminded her of a raw, primal animal like the powerful jaguar that roamed the jungles of Peru. He simply could not be ignored. Sky saw him lift his lashes, his brown-gold gaze connecting with hers. A warmth flowed through her, sweet and good. Cal's gruff words, "There's something good between us," kept gently playing in her heart. Compressing her lips, Sky asked softly, "I thought you'd stay in the SEALs for twenty years."

Cal set the menu aside, folding his hands on the white linen cloth. "Things changed."

Her heart stopped and Sky said, "You didn't want to reenlist?"

"No."

Because of his commitment to find her? *Maybe.* The dogged stubbornness burning in his eyes struck Sky deeply. When Cal chose to solely focus on her, she swore he was like a magnifying glass with sunlight streaming hotly through it into her. Every cell in his body was attuned to hers. Sky could feel it, taste it, and sense it. Nostrils flaring, she caught Cal's male scent. "You have better things to do with your life," she whispered, giving him a confused, guilty look, "than tracking me down."

"No, I don't, Sky." Cal splayed open his hands. "There's nothing in this world that I want more than to explore what we might have, Sky. We never got time in Afghanistan. You were an officer, and I was enlisted. We couldn't have a relationship even if we'd wanted one." His voice grew grave. "And I wasn't about to put you in a position where you'd get court martialed for consorting with me on a personal level." Cal saw her eyes grow sad. But he also saw real warmth in Sky's gaze as he spoke about them. Embolden, he added, "Remember how we met? The afternoon I found you crying, it about ripped my heart out." He saw Sky's eyes widen. "Look, I'm not good with words, Sky. I'm a man who can show better than tell, but when I saw you alone, hiding behind that wooden hut, crying, it hurt me to my soul. You looked so damned beautiful, so fragile in that dirty damn place that only took lives. I wanted to lean over, scoop you into my arms and just hold you because I couldn't stand seeing you like that. It was only after you fessed up that an Army officer pawed at you over in the canteen that I understood why you were crying."

Cal watched Sky's expression carefully. For a second, he swore he saw tears moisten her eyes. But then, they were gone as fast as they'd come. When she swallowed, the slender column of her throat was more exposed, no longer hidden in the pink, fuzzy shawl she had worn.

"That was a terrible moment in my life as far as being part of a nearly all-male base," Sky agreed, shaking her head, picking up her menu and studying it.

"I worked at being a friend to you, not one of those guys who saw you as a piece of meat to be chased down and used," Cal offered quietly, apology in his voice as he opened his menu. His mouth flattened. "Now, looking back on it, I wished we'd had more personal time with one another, Sky. I guess I'm pretty black and white about life, about people. I reported the guy who harassed you. I wasn't going to let him get away with it, because I knew he'd stalk you and try it again. I was overlaying my rules of life on you." He gave her an abject look charged with emotions he couldn't name. "Now? I'm not sorry I reported him. But I know I took the control of the situation, out of your hands without asking you permission, and I shouldn't have. At the time I wanted to beat him into the ground."

The waiter came and took their order. Another waiter brought a glass of chardonnay for Sky and an icy cold beer for Cal. Sky felt her gut twisting with loss and sadness. The dark look in Cal's eyes told her he was being honest with her. "But you were right: I should have reported the guy and not try to run away from him and the situation," she told him, taking a sip of the tart chardonnay. Her fingers wound around the cool glass stem. "What happened with that guy was a similar event that happened when I was seventeen years old. I froze like a deer in headlights when the Army officer at the canteen started pawing me. You came along, stood up for me, reported the incident, and it shook me awake." Sky didn't want to get into details about her past, but she did want Cal to understand why she'd frozen up on the Army guy's assault upon her. After she'd finished crying and shaking over it, she told him she wasn't going to report him, too afraid that he'd come after her again in retribution. Just like Vlad had done to her.

That afternoon at the camp was indelibly etched in her memory. Cal had fervently pleaded with her to turn the guy in, or he'd do it again. She had said no, and she could see he didn't understand why she wouldn't do it. When Cal walked her to her hut, he turned around and reported the officer. And to her surprise, the guy was sent home, never to bother her again. It was a lesson she'd learned from Cal's actions. Instead of hiding and running away, which is what she always had done, he'd taught her how to stand her ground and fight back. She never forgot that lesson.

"Hindsight is always 20-20," Cal grumbled. "Camp Nichols took a lot away from you. You lost your dream of a military career Sky, when you almost died after being shot in that raid by the Taliban on us. I'll always be sorry about that for your sake."

Cal watched Sky tip the glass to her lips. He almost swallowed with her. Shaking himself, Cal had to stop being so damned distracted with Sky finally so close. His eyes narrowed. He needed to get on safer ground with Sky. Cal did not want to go into anything serious with her here in the restaurant. That would be saved for later.

"I didn't know you like nature so much," he said, changing the topic. Instantly, he saw her relax. "All the prints you have on the walls of your apartment have flowers in them."

Sky sat back in the booth, her hands folded in the soft pink shawl in her lap. "I grew up in a city, but in my heart, I have always pined for the country, wildflowers, fresh, clean air, quiet, lots of trees, a brook babbling, and solitude."

"Did you ever take any courses in botany or biology in college?"

"No." Sky found herself beginning to relax in Cal's presence. She could feel his sincerity in wanting to know more about her. "I love the many colors of the flowers." She set the wineglass down and opened her small white leather purse and drew out a small digital camera. "When I fly into a village and the supplies are being off loaded by the guys, I go hunting for the bromeliads and orchids around the area. I have a digital scrapbook on my desktop, hundreds of pages filled with flower shots I have taken up in the Highlands and down in the jungle." Giving him an embarrassed shrug, Sky admitted, "Its a past time, something that helps me relax. When I walk in the jungle or get a chance to stretch my legs, I always feel better afterwards." She saw unknown emotion in Cal's eyes. His face was not readable, but she could see changes in his large intelligent eyes.

"What are you dreams, Sky?"

Cal's low voice was deep, like the rasp of a cat's tongue against her flesh. Shrugging, Sky forced herself to look up at his shadowed face. "I guess…I never had any dreams, Cal. I know that sounds awful, but…" and she swallowed hard, unsure what else to say. Because if she said anything else it would open up a can of worms that she did not want to discuss with anyone. Especially not with Cal, because he was a protector by nature.

"Did you dream of flying?"

Nodding, relieved that he didn't dwell on her answer, Sky said, "My dad was a police helicopter pilot. Before that, he had been an Army Black Hawk pilot. When I was seventeen, he took me up on a flight and after that ride, I knew I wanted to fly."

The sudden passion in her voice sent waves of heat through Cal. Her eyes suddenly went from dull to shining. She sat up in the booth, engaged, lively and connected with him. The difference between the responses to the two questions was stunning to Cal. He knew Sky was being evasive with him, trying not to say much about her younger life, which he already knew about. She was talking about Todd Zimmerman, who had taken her in at sixteen as a foster child. Not blaming her for the deception, Cal knew that later, in her apartment, her hidden past was likely to come up. His gut knotted. He had no wish to cause Sky more pain, but once she found out more about him and why he'd showed up here, he knew that more than likely, all hell was going to break loose. He could feel a wall going up between them every time she mentioned her childhood. She didn't want to tell him about WITSEC or anything else. If only she would trust him.

"What does flying do for you?" Cal wondered, drowning in the joy burning in her wide blue eyes. This was the most animated he'd ever seen Sky and it tightened his chest and his heart churned with yearning that flowed sweet and hot through him.

"It sets me free, Cal." Sky lifted her hands and smiled shyly. "I can't explain it. When I'm flying, everything is all right."

"Only when you land do you get sucked back in by real life, right?" and he gave her a teasing grin.

"Well said," Sky murmured. She wasn't sure if it was the wine or Cal's company, but she was feeling highly relaxed. More so than normal. It felt good to be the center of Cal's universe. He rarely smiled, his face usually unreadable, but she sensed his emotional reaction toward her, nonetheless. Sky couldn't explain it, but it felt like she was wrapped in a warm blanket of his love and care. The concept was so foreign to her, it shocked her. For a moment, Sky frowned, feeling her way through that epiphany, through whatever was going on between them on the invisible realms.

"You, okay?" Cal saw Sky suddenly frown and then look away from him, as if something hit her hard and she was trying to wrestle with the emotions that had come with it. He saw her lick her lower lip and give a quick nod of her head. He was going to say something else, but the waiter appeared, bringing their considerable amount of food to the table.

Throughout dinner, Cal kept their conversation light, trying his best not to upset her. He cajoled Sky into eating half her medium-well cooked beef steak and a third of her mashed potatoes and the other steamed veggies.

"You're too thin," he told her, honestly concerned. "Why don't you eat more?"

"I can't eat when I'm upset."

He lifted his head. "What's got you upset then, Sky?"

Mouth grimacing, she muttered, "Oh, there's a lot of warring going on between two cocaine drug lords up in the Highlands where I fly well supplies into villages. Elizabeth, who owns the charity, is really worried that it will spill over onto our volunteer well drilling crews. Or on me." Sky pushed the plate aside, laying the knife and fork across it. "It's been steadily escalating, Cal."

"Has there been infil into the villages where you work?"

"No....not infiltration. But I'm afraid there will be at some point. It's a complicated situation. The Quechua people of these jungle and highland villages around Machu Picchu are very poor. They've been growing coca plants for thousands of years. The government of Peru wants them to stop, but they have no other way to make an income. The two drug lords are fighting each other for the territory. As a result, the Indians are going deeper into the jungle to grow the crops so they won't be found and destroyed by government soldiers. And then you have these two drug lords both promising each village more money to sell them the hidden crops instead of selling to their competitor. All so it can be turned into cocaine."

Frowning, Cal asked, "How about weapons?"

"Both drug lords have heavily armed mercenary soldiers. They're constant-ly battling one another. A few of the villagers have been killed by stray bullets. You know how it goes. You spent many years in Afghanistan on deploy-ments."

"Yeah, I understand," Cal growled. "Have they shot at your helicopter?"

"No. Not that I know of. All I do is haul pipe in a sling under the belly of my bird or I fly in other necessary drilling gear or medical items for the villagers. I'm not a threat to them. So far…"

Cal wasn't so sure but said nothing. "Dessert?" and he raised his brows, trying to coax her into eating more.

Sky puffed out her cheeks and placed her hand against her stomach. "No. I ate way too much already," and she laughed a little.

His heart thudded hard in his chest. His throat tightened. The sudden, husky laughter spilling out of Sky's slender throat, the lustrous beauty shining in her eyes, damn near did Cal in. In that one moment, when Sky was purely herself, not hiding behind the walls she always erected, on guard, wary and distrustful, Cal saw the woman he knew had been hiding in there all along. His heart expanded powerfully with emotions. He managed a cockeyed grin and said, "Okay." He looked at his watch. It was eight p.m. The restaurant was filling up with well-heeled patrons, the upper-class crust of Cusco was arriving. He gave the waiter his credit card and in no time, they were ready to leave. "May I walk you home?" and he stood, offering her his hand.

"Yes, thank you." She gathered up her shawl, pulling it around her shoul-ders. When Cal eased his fingers across the material, they momentarily brushed her shoulders. Groaning internally, feeling slightly dizzy, she knew it had to be from the wine.

"Ugh," she muttered, "wine and high altitude do NOT mix well in me…"

"Lean on me, Sky? I'll get you out of here and no one will suspect any-thing."

"That would be nice." Every muscle in Cal's body where Sky sank lightly against him sang with joy. He felt her freeze momentarily as his arm went around her shoulders, and then relax. She wasn't used to being held. He felt like a starving wolf absorbing her physically against him, the warmth of her against him.

By the time they got out of the restaurant and through the hotel lobby, Sky seemed to be enjoying being supported by him. For the moment, he gloried in her unexpected trust. But it was going to be temporary, and Cal felt grief. What would Sky do? Tell him to get out of her life? Cal wasn't sure of her coming reaction. As he guided her across the busy plaza street, he got her to the sidewalk where many couples strolled arm in arm. At night, Plazas de Armas came alive with lovers, Cal discovered.

They crossed to the other side of the plaza and walked down a block beneath a darkened, starlit sky to her apartment building. Once inside, Cal walked her up to her apartment door. There, he released her and stood back as she hunted for her key.

Turning, Sky gazed up Cal. He was so tall, so confident, his shoulders broad and thrown back with such natural pride. Her hand trembled as she slid the key in the lock. The door opened. Swallowing hard, Sky didn't want this night to end. Cal holding her beneath his arm across the plaza did something so melting to her as a woman, she could barely think straight. Her throat grew dry as she lifted her gaze to his.

"Thank you for a wonderful night, Cal. I—"

"It isn't over, Sky."

The warning in his voice made her freeze. "What do you mean?"

Cal looked in her apartment, and then down at her. There was regret in his expression. "May I come in and have some coffee with you? Talk at the table? There is some serious top-secret information, I need to share with you."

He stepped forward, his hand slipping around her elbow and gently guided her inside. He shut the door and released her.

"What is this all about?" she demanded.

"I need to talk to you, Sky. I didn't want to do it at the restaurant. I wanted the evening to be good for you, to make you happy, to see you smile...," because he'd never seen her smile before. Cal could see the sudden wariness come to her eyes, realizing that whatever trust he'd built with her during dinner had been destroyed. Could he have handled this differently? He didn't know, agitated because she was upset, her eyes flashing with anger. He had hurt her and the accusation he saw in her eyes spoke loudly: he'd tricked her.

Sky placed her purse and shawl down on the couch and walked resolutely into the kitchen, her back stiff and straight. Cal followed. Well, so much for Mr. Smooth. He'd blown this one. Sitting down at the table, his hands clasped, he watched her angrily make coffee. Sky turned, her eyes narrowed on him.

"If you think you're staying here—"

"It's not about that," Cal protested, holding up his hand. "This isn't some ploy on my part to get you into bed, Sky, so relax."

Her nostrils flared, and she glared at him. Her hands went on her hips, a typical aviator stance. Now she was in combat mode, Cal realized. Groaning, he rasped, "This is BUSINESS, Sky. I didn't want to discuss it at dinner. All right? That's all it is."

"You and I have no business!" she whispered, turning and walking to the cupboard.

"Yes," Cal said wearily, "we do. I just didn't want to mix it with dinner, was all." There was confusion and hurt in her eyes and for that, Cal felt like a bastard. He hadn't meant to hurt Sky, only make her feel good.

Her hands trembled as she poured them coffee and brought it to the table. He took the mug and thanked her. Sky sat down opposite him. She swallowed hard and tried to keep the quaver out of her tone. "So, what business do we have?"

"I was hired by Elizabeth Standsworth to be your security detail on your flights." Cal saw her eyes widen and she stared at him. He wasn't sure it was out of shock or joy. Most likely, shock.

Sputtering, Sky snapped her mouth shut, her back going ramrod straight. "Liz NEVER said a thing to me about this!"

"I asked her not to," Cal admitted quietly, holding her enraged stare. "I told her you and I had a personal connection and I'd like to break it to you myself. She said that was fine."

"No…," and Sky pushed away from the table, wanting to get as far away from Cal as she could get. "You're lying!"

Cal felt his heart shrink in grief. He'd screwed this up royally. Elizabeth should have told her, not him. Now, Cal realized, it looked like he had been manipulating her, positioning her to where he wanted her to tell her what had happened. "I'm not lying. Come on, Sky," he pleaded huskily, pointing to the chair, "come and sit back down. Please?"

"Like hell I will, Sinclair!" Sky's breath came hard, her heart pounding, fear tunneling rawly through her. How in the world was she going to fly with Cal in that helo with her? How? The man melted her. Distracted her completely. Made her feel soft and feminine. And none of that could happen in the cockpit of a helo she was flying.

Cal winced over her words. The desperation in Sky's face tore at him like nothing else. "Look, there's a REASON why I was hired," he told her quietly. Cal knew she wasn't going to sit down, so he went on in a reasonable tone of voice. "You talked about the two drug lords who are vying for the cocaine trade here in this area at dinner. Right?"

"Yes. So what?" and Sky balled her hands into fists at her side. Her emotions were in free fall, her heart wild and thrashing in her chest. Sky felt trapped; just as she'd felt trapped with Vlad living in the same house with her. Cal was pursuing her, there was no question. He'd just gotten himself hired as the shotgun rider in the helo.

What did Cal tell Liz? Did he lie to her to make her think she and the well drilling crews were in jeopardy? But no, the danger there was real. Hell, his friend, Dylan McCoy, an ex-SEAL who had been in Cal's team in Afghanistan, had been hired months earlier to ride with Julia, a traveling nurse who treated people at different villages in the area for the charity. Liz had hired him to guard Julia, afraid that the drug lords' soldiers might try and kidnap her. Sky hadn't faulted Liz for that decision. So why was she in an uproar that Liz hired someone as security for her? Why couldn't it have been anyone but Cal?

Cal took a sip of his coffee, deliberately taking his time, giving Sky a chance to absorb the info. She was in fight mode, her eyes blue fire, narrowed, her mouth thin, her entire body tense. He set the mug in front of him. "Okay, so here's some more dope that you don't know about and it's the reason why Elizabeth hired me. Dylan and I work for the same security company, Shield. I found out about it a few days ago after coming back from a European mission. You have more trouble in this area than you realize, Sky. Besides the two drug lords fighting each other under your nose, there's been an intrusion of a third force entering into this fray." His mouth thinned and Cal held her glare. "Russian mafia is down here, and a man named Vladimir Alexandrov, is their leader." Cal saw the instant reaction in Sky.

Gasping, Sky blinked. "What? What did you say?" All the old terror, the fear and pain came erupting up through her at the mention of Vlad's name. Cal sat there looking hard and impenetrable. He was relaxed in the chair, his one hand on the table, his other hand on his thick, hard thigh, studying her. "No, no, you're wrong about that…God…no…" and she choked, her fingers flying to her throat. She was 17 again, and Vlad had found her in her bedroom, grabbed her by the neck, and thrown her down on the bed, his fingers wrapping hard around her throat, closing off her breathing as she fought, kicked and screamed for help. Sky shut her eyes, taking a staggering step backward, feeling dizzy with terror.

Cal was on his feet instantly. He saw all the blood drain out of Sky's face. He reached out, and she shrank away from him. If he had any question about Vlad's assault on Sky and how it affected her, he was seeing it right now. Sky uttered, "No… this can't be true, Cal! It can't be…."

CHAPTER 4

January 5

S KY FELT HER world falling apart. *Again. Always again.* Cam's roughened thumbs gently removed the tears from her cheeks. The gesture was so touching that Sky felt her guarded heart open. She finally yielded to Cal's attempt to comfort her and allowed him to guide her onto the couch in the livingroom.

"Stay put," Cal growled, standing.

She gave a jerky nod. Vulnerable now, she missed his quiet, powerful presence. Wrapped in misery and shock, Sky's mind was bombarded with flashes of memories; of Vlad's short blond hair, his long, narrow face, and those dark green eyes of his alight with glee as he held her down on the bed. The images tore through Sky, eliciting a sob. The past was never far from her.

She felt Cal return even though her eyes were tightly shut. There was a sense of comfort as he sat down, their hips meeting one another once again.

"Here," Cal muttered, "maybe this will help…"

She felt the damp cloth move across her cheeks and then down the sides of her neck. The warmth felt good against her flesh. Her heart turned over as Sky felt Cal's tender, hesitant touch. Forcing open her eyes, she looked up into his hard face, his expression unreadable. It was his eyes that were alive with roiling emotions she couldn't possibly begin to interpret, except that he was shaken.

Sky lifted her hand, catching the cloth and taking it from him. "Thanks," she whispered. "I need to sit up more…"

Cal nodded and set the cloth aside. He stood, taking her hand and allowing her to reposition herself. He could see the abject misery in her face, her beautiful eyes marred with raw terror. He decided to give Sky some space and slid down to the opposite end of the couch. Gruffly, he said "I'm sorry. I didn't mean to upset you so much with this news, Sky."

She leaned forward, placing her elbows on her thighs. She forced herself to breathe deeply, knowing she needed to get more oxygen into her lungs. "I-I haven't cried since…well…Camp Nichols, after I got shot," Sky whispered, shaking her head.

Cal saw how drawn up her shoulders had become. Jack had warned him that he needed to learn some diplomacy, that his blunt honesty, while worthy, wasn't something people could accept all the time. Well, his blunt honesty had just triggered something very bad within her. Cal could literally see her quivering, such was the level of shock and fear he'd triggered in her. *Dammit!*

"I'm sorry, I should have said things better. I didn't mean to hurt you," and his brows knitted, remorse in his tone.

Sky stared at him, seeing he was scowling and unhappy.

"Tell me what you know about Vlad being in this area. How did you know it was him in the first place?"

Wincing internally, Cal leaned his elbows on his thighs, hands clasped between them, scowling. "Jack Driscoll, my boss and the owner of Shield, has contacts in the CIA and at SOCOM, for starters. He works with democratic countries around the world, and they share their highest levels of intel with our company. I was given a mission briefing before leaving for Peru on your situation." He held her marred, tear-filled gaze. When her lower lip trembled, Cal cursed himself. *Damn bull in a china shop.* Rubbing his hand across his face, he went on, "A mission briefing gives me, as your hired security detail, your entire past history before you came down here to work for Helping Hands. I needed to understand what was going on with you and in the region, you were working in, that's all."

"I-I see." Sky wiped her eyes with trembling fingers. "What kind of past history?"

Mouth slashing, Cal girded himself. He knew the truth was going to strike at Sky again, wounding her further. "In this briefing, I found out when you were at Camp Nichols, that you were also in Witness Protection and Security, Sky." He braced himself for her emotional reaction. As he searched her face, Cal saw her close her eyes, her lips compressed, her hands tightening until her knuckles whitened. He wished he could redo this night. Wished mightily that he had better diplomacy for her sake. Sky did NOT deserve this kind of pain he saw etched across her face.

"That far back?"

He nodded. "Dylan was already down here and was the one that raised the alarm to Jack about a new Russian gang entering the drug lord turf war. That's where Alexandrov's name popped up. And I was briefed on him….and then that led to you and he being in the same foster child household." He took a deep, serrated breath, holding her watery gaze.

"So you know all about Vlad, about my past with him…" Sky swallowed painfully and looked up at the ceiling.

"I knew nothing about your past when we were at Camp Nichols. I only found out about it in this briefing from Jack before coming down here a couple of days ago." He'd done enough damage tonight. He'd just hit her with the worst possible news that Vlad was in the area. That news alone had Sky terrified. And worse, he'd broken what little trust he'd built with her by the tactless way he had broken the news to her. Misery flowed through him.

"What else do you know about me, Cal?"

Grimacing, he muttered, "We have your military service record, WITSEC and Witness Protection files," he growled unhappily, "and your entire family history… all of it…"

Sky felt as if someone had struck her hard in the chest and she couldn't breathe properly. "Oh, God…" Her mind careened and spun. Cal was black ops. He had connections most people never had and somehow, he'd laid her entire life bare before her. If he could do that… Had Vlad done it too? Was that why the Russian was down here in Peru? Hunting her? Making good on his threat to find and kill her? Was he stalking her right now? Terror raced through her.

"Has Vlad been able to access my information, then?"

Cal shrugged. "I don't know, Sky. There's no way for me to tell." He saw the absolute devastation in her expression, as if her whole world had suddenly collapsed inward on her once again. Hadn't it? "Look, Jack's resources at the CIA tell us that Alexandrov has been in this general region for a full year. He's part of the Russian Mafia ring operated by his father, Yerik Alexandrov, out of New York City. The father sent him down here to try and carve out a piece of the cocaine region from those other two Latino drug lords for themselves. The Russian team is actively fighting them to take over their turf right now. And it's moving into the area where you're presently flying in and out of. That's why Liz acted, and that's how I got assigned."

"Then," Sky whispered, her voice hoarse, "Vlad's been in this area for a year?"

"That's what Jack's contact says. Why?"

"Because the only soldiers Liz and the other charity workers who are in this region have seen are those who work for the two drug lords."

"Have any of you seen men carrying weapons on them?"

Shaking her head, Sky nervously twisted her fingers. "No… not that I know of." She shot Cal a look. "Are you SURE about this? That Vlad is here?"

"I am." Cal made a face and added, "Look, Army Special Forces has two three-man black ops hunter-killer teams down here in this area and their orders are to find his gang. Their job, once they find him, is to take them out, permanently. This is Top Secret info, Sky. The CIA has picked up cell phone chatter between Alexandrov and his father in New York City, several times. Jack's contact, a South American CIA analyst, feels like he's scouting the area, getting to know the tactics and strategy of the two drug lords, who are the players and his enemies. Intercepted communications indicate that the father wants his son to take over this region, work directly with the Quechua Indians in these villages in the Highlands and the jungle region near Machu Picchu, and grab the entire cocaine production for the future."

"That's awful," Sky rasped unevenly. She searched Cal's face, saw the grim set of his mouth, the hardness in his eyes. He wouldn't lie to her and she knew it. "Liz hired Dylan three months earlier for Julie, one of our traveling nurses. She rides a horse and has a pack mule with medical supplies. Her route encompasses a circuit of ten villages in the jungle and the Highlands. There's been more activity between the drug soldiers and Liz was worried for Julie. We all knew Liz hired Dylan to ride with her and protect her. I didn't think beyond that and it seemed like a reasonable call on her part to keep Julie safe."

Nodding, Cal said, "It was a good call on her part to protect her employees."

Sky chewed on her lower lip. "And that's why Liz hired you? Or did you go to her with all this intel?"

Cal drew in a deep breath and released it. "There's more to this story. Like I said earlier, Dylan had called Jack and tipped him off that Russians were in the area, but he didn't know who. He'd met up with one of those Special Forces teams, and they'd filled him in and warned him to be careful. That's when Jack went to his resources at the highest levels of U.S. Intelligence to verify the info. I originally was coming down here on my own time, to find you. When I found out through my briefing before coming down here about Alexandrov and your past with him. Because of the danger this poses, Jack contacted Liz by phone. She knows him through her father, the Senator. That's when Liz asked to have one of Jack's security contractors sent down here to guard you when you were out in the field. I've got a degree in electrical engineering, and Liz thought I'd be the perfect candidate to be with you. I could use my mechanical knowledge, volunteer my help on these well digs if they needed someone who knows about electrical interfaces. Liz asked me for my resume, Jack sent her the email of my records. She called Jack the next day and offered me a job as a security contractor to protect you."

Rubbing her face, Sky muttered, "Liz never told me…"

"That's my fault," Cal said. "I convinced her because of our military past, that I'd break the news to you." He gave her an apologetic look. "I didn't do it very well, and I'm sorry."

Sky nodded, her emotions twisted and roiling within her. "I don't know how you could sugar coat that kind of intel."

Cal admired her maturity, but it still didn't relieve him of the guilt he felt. "Well," he muttered, "you've been through enough. I didn't need to add to your misery and scare the hell out of you on top of everything else."

For a moment, Sky saw his Cal's mask disappear. She heard heavy regret in his voice and saw the apology in his eyes. "I know you didn't mean to hurt me. Okay? I guess I'd rather know about Vlad than not know. I can't believe I've been here a year and never seen him." Shaking her head, Sky muttered, "Unbelievable."

"He's not actively tailing you. I don't think he knows you're here." At least, Cal prayed he wasn't aware of Sky's presence. But there was no clear proof one way or another, which made him damn glad he was on scene. This way, Sky would be kept safe from that sick, murdering bastard.

Lifting her chin, she asked, "Does Liz know Vlad is in the area?"

"No. This is all top-secret intel, Sky. Dylan was read in on it since he's Julie's security detail. This intel was on a need-to-know basis only."

"But…Julie should know…."

He looked at his watch. It was nearly midnight, and he knew both of them were exhausted. Sky looked fragile and it scared the hell out of him. "No disagreement there but I need to connect with Jack and Dylan to update him on the latest intel." He saw relief come to Sky's face. Cal could almost see what she was thinking: that Vlad could kill Julie and Dylan.

"We need to get some sleep, Sky. Can I hitch a ride with you tomorrow morning out to the airport?"

"Yes. Be here at 0700. Where are you staying?"

"The Palacio del Inka, the same place we had dinner. I'll see myself out. Good night, Sky. If you need me, here's my cell phone number," and he handed her a business card.

Sky felt Cam's larger than life presence withdraw as he quietly left and closed the door behind him. She was still in shock. Vlad was out there. Where? Did he know she was in the vicinity? Was he actively stalking her? Or was his focus just on the cocaine? Sky tried to quell her raw emotions. Thinking it through, if Vlad had been around for a year and she hadn't seen him, that boded well for her. Because Sky knew, if he discovered her here, he'd come after her in a heartbeat. He'd always told her that he loved her, that he wanted to marry her. Sky had never loved him. She was deathly afraid of Vlad from the day she'd met him. He talked of marriage. Of the beautiful children they would have. All lies, as far as she was concerned, to lure her into his bed. And when that didn't work, he'd tried to take her by force. She shut her eyes, trying to push all those bloody memories away.

Sliding her fingers through her hair, Sky frowned. Should she contact WITSEC and let them know she was leaving the charity? Run again? She was so tired of running. Sky thought she was safe down here. No one comes to this part of a third world country. How short sighted of her to not realize cocaine was made here, which in turn would attract the attention of criminal organizations like the Russian Mafia. So many questions and no answers.

Sky pushed to her feet, exhausted. Wanting Cal here, she knew it was impossible. She couldn't trust herself with him. Alone, she slowly walked down the hall toward the bedroom. Tomorrow morning would come early enough.

January 6

VLADIMIR ALEXANDROV LOUNGED in his chair at an outdoor cafe on the main street of Aguas Calientes. The small Peruvian tourist town sat at the base of the well-known World Heritage archeological site of Machu Picchu. He savored the thick, strong, hot espresso coffee and waited for his second-in-command, Lev Zuyev, to show up at the appointed time. A scruffy black dog, starved-looking, wandered into the portico area and sat down near his combat boots that were still wet and muddy. The dog looked how he felt. Vlad wished he could take the train to his Cusco apartment and get a hot shower to wipe off three weeks of grime, mud, and sweat. He tossed the dog several scraps from his plate, which the dog scarfed down quickly, a grateful expression coming to its face.

Lev, who had been a sergeant in Spetsnaz fighting at his side for the past seven years before coming to Peru, rounded the corner. He was dressed like a tourist, something they did to blend into the tourista trade in order not to draw unwanted attention to themselves. At thirty years old, the hard-faced blond with small blue eyes nodded in his direction. He wore jeans, a dark green t-shirt and a blue baseball cap. Compared to other touristas, he fit in. Vlad smiled a little as he sat down opposite him at the small black wrought iron table. Lev wore his combat boots just as he did, despite the rest of their costume.

A waitress hurried out. Lev gave his order in thick Spanish, a huge breakfast along with four cups of espresso. The waitress, a young woman with black hair and light brown eyes, looked shocked over his massive order. Lev, who was six foot two inches and two hundred pounds of pure, rock-hard muscle, grinned and repeated the order. He teased her, saying he was a hungry, growing boy. They were out in the jungle for three weeks at a time, climbing over rocks and rugged terrain or fighting the fucking jungle with machetes. It made everyone toughen up, almost as tough as when they were in black ops in other Russian controlled countries. Their mission was to find and the Islamic rebels who refused to obey the peace accord between themselves and Mother Russia.

"He's a growing boy," Vlad confirmed to the girl in Spanish, who was probably in her late teens. He could feel himself growing hard, his eyes level with her full, young breasts hidden beneath a white pheasant blouse. "Give him whatever he wants. I'm paying."

"Si, si, Señor," she said breathlessly. "And you? Do you want *desanyo*?"

A local word for breakfast, Vlad knew. "Give me the same order."

"And four espressos, Señor?" she asked, almost gasping.

Vlad gave her a curt nod. "Si. Vamoose!" and he waived her off with a sharp movement of his long hand. The girl was stupid, but she had a nice, young body. The kind he preferred. And she wasn't bad looking, although all Vlad really cared about was burying himself in her tight, virginal warmth between her thighs.

"You look like a wolf on a prowl," Lev said, giving him a wicked, knowing grin. He rubbed his bearded face with his large, scarred hand.

"I am. Three weeks in that fucking green jungle and I need to have a woman."

"Makes two of us. She is what I'd like."

"Hands off," Vlad warned. They had to use Aguas Calientes as their second home when not in the jungle or Highlands. As much as Vlad wanted to screw some of these local women, he didn't. They had to use this town as a base of operation, and like the Russian wolves he and his men were, they didn't shit in their own back yard. They had to come and go as quietly as possible and remain under the radar. Vlad didn't want to raise the interest of the corrupt local law enforcement, who were too busy getting pay-backs from tourist companies to look the other way. They were into corruption up to their asses and back. If he and his men took a woman by force, just one time, their cover would be permanently blown, and they would lose this valuable base of operation. Vlad had given strict orders for his men to go only to the local whore house and leave the other women who lived here alone.

"When are we going to Cusco?"

"Soon," Vlad promised, finishing off his espresso and pushing the small cup. He leaned down and fed the dog the last of the scraps. The dog looked up adoringly at him.

Lev needed a shave, his blond, thin beard itching like hell. And he stunk. "The rest of the men are coming in later this afternoon."

Nodding, Vlad saw the girl reappear with a large tray. On it were all the cups of espresso. She looked harried and quickly set them in front of the two men. Vlad could smell her, and he liked her female scent. Nostrils flaring, he picked up the fragrance of a sweet perfume she wore as well. Lucky for her, he wouldn't pursue her. She had a young, voluptuous body, the kind a man could knead his hands around her breasts, full hips, and her fine ass. She was the daughter of the owner though, so he forced himself not to be interested. He thanked her and she turned away, hurrying back into the restaurant.

Lev took the first espresso, gulping it down. He made a satisfied sound as he put the tiny cup on the tabletop. "I miss coffee out there."

"I miss fucking a woman."

"That's second on my list," and Lev grinned, downing the second cup.

"We'll have our fill back in Cusco." Vlad frowned. "I need to get with my Spetsnaz contact about intel on these two drug lords. We'll take a week and rest up in Cusco and then get back out in the Highlands and jungle and keep finding the new trails. I need to see the satellite flyovers of this area to spot where the Indians have been growing new cocaine fields."

Snorting, Lev muttered, "Those satellite images save us a helluva lot of time in finding them when there is almost always ground fog around."

"We need to find those new cultivation areas," Vlad said. "Every field we find, we kill the drug soldiers guarding it and it's one more field I own."

Lev sprawled out his long legs, giving a satisfied grunt, the third cup in his large, meaty hand. "We're making progress, Vlad."

"Not fast enough for me."

Shrugging his thick, heavily muscled shoulders, Lev tipped the espresso into his mouth. "Rome wasn't built in a day, Comrade."

Scowling, Vlad growled, "I want that damned well drilling charity out of the area. How can we scare them out of this region?"

"It's not a bad idea to force them out of our area," Lev agreed. "If we get into firefights and bullets fly between us and the drug soldiers, as they inevitably will, one of those American volunteers could accidentally get wounded or killed. Then the US government will send Marines down here to investigate. Then, we're fucked. It will delay your schedule. Right now, we are still under everyone's radar. It's the best place to be for a take-over."

"Tell me about it," Vlad muttered. His blond brows knitted as he considered plans. "There's a red-haired American woman who is a traveling nurse that rides between those ten Quechua villages. I've been thinking about kidnapping her... Make an example of her. That ought to get the charity's attention. They can't afford to have their women volunteers raped," and he smiled a little, thinking about the American nurse named Julie. He liked women with red or blond hair. He always had. And she was beautiful. His loins tightened as he thought about taking her, watching her face, listening to her scream and try to fight him off her. It was a turn-on for Vlad. It made sex even better for him. Terror in the victim always heightened his experience and pleasure.

Lev scowled. "That nurse has an American security contractor with her," he warned. "He's armed and he knows what he's doing. We got glass on him the other day. He's not some novice, that is for sure."

Shrugging, Vlad murmured, "Then, we'll just have to use our sniper abilities, won't we? We'll observe, be patient, get down their rhythm, what trails they take, and their habits. Then, when the American contractor is away or distracted, we'll grab the nurse. End of story."

Lev didn't look convinced as he finished off the last espresso. "He's black ops by the way he operates," he warned Vlad. "Not your run-of-the-mill security contractor. He's an operator just like us. It's going to take a lot of time and patience to pull this off right."

Vlad smiled a little. "It's on my list. He may be an operator, but we'll think of something. A diversion of some sort that lures him momentarily from guarding her." And if that didn't work, Vlad would order his sniper to put a bullet into his head and capture the nurse afterward.

Scowling, Lev shook his head. "You will have to be careful. You know the US ambassador down in Lima will send up a Marine investigation team. We cannot have our fingerprints on her flesh. We have got to do this right so if she's found dead, the Marine investigators won't know who did it."

"I'm wanting them to blame either of the two other drug lords," Vlad murmured. "And they will. No one knows we're operating in this area. At least, not yet."

Smug, Lev nodded. "We're good at what we do, no question."

"Well, once we get the team rested up in Cusco for a week, I'll turn my attention to the nurse," Vlad said. "That charity is a pain in my ass and I want them permanently out of our area."

"Collateral damage," Lev agreed, sitting up as the young woman brought out a large tray with their breakfast on it. "Come on, let's eat. I'm starving…"

CHAPTER 5

January 6

"JULIE? ARE YOU ready for me to close this pannier?" Dylan McCoy called from outside the hut. He leaned over the large, rectangular box that would carry the medical supplies for her next circuit through the ten villages. The morning was cool in La Paloma, the Quechua village where they stayed. Nearly a hundred Indians, remnants of the mighty Incan empire, lived a hardscrabble life here. Dylan saw her come to the open door, the sunlight highlighting her red hair pulled up in a ponytail.

"No…," she said, stepping outside the hut for a moment, "I just got off the satellite phone with Sky. There's been a medical package just come in at the Cusco airport and she's flying it up here this morning. Keep it open, Dylan."

"Will do." He slowly unwound from his kneeling position. His M4 rifle was leaning against the mud and straw hut; close enough for him to grab if necessary. Julie hurried his way, in her usual jeans, a dark blue t-shirt, and her hiking boots. To the outside world, she looked like a beautiful, freckle-faced, college-aged young woman. Few would guess she was a registered nurse whose whole existence was focused on helping the poor in Peru. She'd been with Helping Hands Charity since she graduated from Ohio State University with honors. The blue of her t-shirt emphasized her light blue eyes and large black pupils as she approached where he had crouched. He saw her frown and knew she was mentally going through the detailed last minute check list of medical items that were needed for this trip. He'd already filled one pannier, but the second was only half full.

Kneeling at the pannier, she began rapidly pulling items out of the box she had carried over, setting it down on the tarp. "Did you put the malaria pills in there?"

Dylan grinned and knelt behind Julie. He slid his hands around her waist, gently drawing her against him. "I did," he rasped, kissing her temple, inhaling her sweet scent, "ramp down, okay? You always get hyper like this the day we're supposed to leave."

Julie made a half laugh and sank trustingly into Dylan's arms, leaning against his hard, fit body. Blowing a huff of air between her lips, she uttered, "You're right. I know what you're going to say," and Julie angled a look up at him, her lips pulling away from her teeth, "to take a few, slow, deep breaths. Come back to Earth," and she chuckled.

Dylan settled back on his heels, more than strong enough to hold the woman he loved in his arms. He hadn't meant to fall in love with her. As a security contractor, he was taught to keep his distance. But working closely with her over the first month, he had fallen helplessly in love with this incredible, heart-centered woman. She fit against him like a long-lost puzzle piece. Her hair tickled his three-day growth of beard along his jaw. "I have a better way to reduce your hyperactivity," Dylan hinted darkly, pressing a kiss to her cheek, feeling her velvet flesh so warm and firm beneath his lips.

Julie laughed. The helicopter's coming…"

"Too bad… You're missing one helluva love session with me," he whispered against her mouth.

Sighing, Julie reluctantly eased away from him. She pulled out the black baseball cap that Dylan had given her and plopped it on her head. "Maybe later? If we get a chance?"

"Just say the word," he said, releasing her so she could stand.

January 6

CAL WAS GLAD to see his SEAL team friend once more. Dylan stood beside a young, red-haired woman as Sky lightly brought the helo down for a landing. A grin slid across his mouth. He had known Dylan was somewhere in the area but was not sure where. *Damn*. Happiness thrummed through Cal. He felt even better knowing a former teammate was here with the Alexandrov problem hanging over their heads.

As Sky was shutting everything down, the blades moved slower and slower. Cal pulled off his set of earphones. "You see that guy out there with the woman?"

Sky looked up from her duties. "Oh, the security contractor?"

"Yeah." Satisfaction rang in Cam's voice. "That's my SEAL buddy, Dylan McCoy. We were on the same team for six years."

Sky heard the undisguised surprise and happiness in Cam's voice. "Good friends?"

He slid her a glance. "Damn good. Dylan's nickname in the SEALs was Viper. He was our sniper."

"Viper?" she asked, sitting up and releasing her harness. "As in poisonous snake?"

Grinning, Cal said, "Yes. Dylan was the best damn sniper on our team. I didn't realize he'd be at this village."

Sky lifted her hand and waved back at Julie, who was enthusiastically waving at them. "Dylan knows about Vlad, but Julie doesn't. Right?"

Cal nodded. "Right. Jack called me before I came to your apartment this morning. He wanted Dylan brought up to speed. The two of us are going to have a little sit down in one of those huts over there," and he pointed in the general direction of the village that sat about a quarter of a mile to the left of the makeshift helipad.

As Cal dismounted from the helo, he saw Dylan's broad smile. His SEAL friend trotted out, grabbed him by the shoulders, and slapped the hell out of his back in welcome.

"I can't believe it!" Dylan said, releasing him, grinning up at Cal. "How did you end up here? I knew you were coming down, but we've been out in the mountains without any contact."

Cal grinned, looking around, always on guard. "Might ask the same of you. You dropped off the friggin' radar the moment you left for Peru. Jack was always grousing that you weren't checking in when you should."

Dylan matched his smile. "It's the mountains, Cal. Bad comms. You know how it goes?" He became serious, lowering his voice so only he could hear him. "Hey, the village chief told us when we arrived that a group of Russian men came through here two days ago. Vladimir Alexandrov is their leader's name. He was talking to the chief about going with them on cocaine production and dropping the drug lord who currently pays them for the product. He promised the chief more money if he would go with them, instead."

Scowling, Cal muttered, "The chief was sure it was Alexandrov?"

"Yes. The chief didn't like him and told the Russians he'd think about his offer, and then they left. Because of the mountains, I couldn't get out to call you or Jack about this new development. When you fly back to Cusco this afternoon, will you send this intel on to Jack and his people?"

"You bet I will." He looked around at the quiet, placid village. Children were barefoot, playing games with one another. It was so peaceful. But it wouldn't be for long with the Russian intrusion. He clapped Dylan's shoulder and saw Sky and the red-haired woman chatting, laughing, and enjoying their time with one another at the panniers. "Hey, is that Julie the traveling nurse?"

"Yeah, she is a fine-looking woman," Dylan said. "And she's mine." He looked up at Cal. "We just got engaged. We're going to marry in six months after her contract is up out here. Then, we'll go stateside."

Shaking his head, Cal gripped the SEAL's shoulder. "I thought you'd NEVER settle down. Does Jack know about this?"

He laughed good-naturedly. "No, not yet. We are going to finish this circuit and once we're back in Cusco, I can tell him the good news, plus, give him my report." He grinned a little. "She turned my world upside down and inside out."

Cal understood that very well. The same thing had happened between him and Sky. He would be glad to get her flights to the villages finished so they could get back to Cusco by dusk.

January 6

"YOU'RE WORRIED ABOUT something," Cal observed as he sat at one end of the sofa after having dinner with Sky. He was surprised she'd invited him in for dinner after landing back at the Cusco airport. He tried to hide his reaction, more than happy to spend some more quality time with her. Maybe seeing her best friend Julie and spending time with her today at the village had changed something between them. He'd talked at length to Dylan about an update on Alexandrov when they were alone, out of Julie's earshot.

"I am worried," she murmured.

"About?"

"Alexandrov." Sky sat at the other end of the sofa; one leg pulled beneath her. Giving Cal a strained look, she quietly admitted, "Honestly? I want to run again. That's what has kept me ahead of him finding me." She saw Cal nod, his dark brows drawing downward.

"I thought you might be considering that option." The tension was back in Sky's face. He could see her wrestling with her fear, the terror, and the memories that crowded into and stained the present. "What do you think you'll do? Tell Liz you're quitting? Go find another flight gig somewhere else in the world?"

Sky sighed. "I... I don't know, Cal. I'm torn."

"What's to keep you here?" He'd just found her. The last thing Cal wanted was for Sky to suddenly disappear on him again.

Turning, Sky wrapped her arms around herself, resting against the sofa. Frowning, she studied the polished white tile floor in front of her for a moment. Desperate to change the topic, she said, "You know all about my family history. Tell me about yours. What was your childhood like?"

Cal felt his gut tighten. This was a crossroads. Normally, he never talked about his family. Not ever. With Sky, however, Cal wanted her to know him, warts and all. But it was tough because Cal's knee-jerk reaction was to push back and shut down. That's how he'd survived and made it this far in his life. The coaxing warmth in Sky's searching gaze unhinged all his defenses, however.

His mouth tightened and he said, "My father was an angry, abusive alcoholic. I have a younger brother, Chad, and a sister, Tracey, who are two and three years younger than me. When our father would drink, he turned into a rageaholic. I would lead him away from them, and I'd make myself his target. It was my responsibility to protect Chad and Tracey. When I was seven, he went after Tracey, and I attacked him." Cal pointed to his nose. "He turned and let me have it."

Sky uttered a sound, her heart breaking for Cal. "Oh, no...."

"It was all right," he assured her. "From then on, my dad picked on me and left Chad and Tracey alone, which is what I wanted."

Her heart felt torn up as she stared mutely at Cal. No wonder he was as hard and tough as he was. Sky grimaced. "When my father was high on drugs, I hid. If I didn't say anything, kept my mouth shut, I was safe."

"That worked for you and I'm glad," Cal rasped. Although she was tough on the outside, Cal sensed and knew how delicate she was beneath that exterior. And he knew he could feed her his strength and help her get strong over time, if only she'd let him. That was a big if.

"Did he beat on you until you were eighteen?"

"Not even." Cal sprawled his long legs out before him. "When I was in the third grade, my teacher accidentally saw some welts and bruises on my back. She was horrified, called the police and the rest was history. Me, Chad, and Tracey were taken away from our father and we were put into three different foster homes." His brows fell. "The only bad thing about it was I never saw them again until I was eighteen. I didn't want to lose them, and I haven't. We're tight as three peas in a pod, today. They now run my father's fruit farm in Oregon, after he suddenly died from a heart attack."

"When I got put in Marielle and Jack's care," Sky admitted quietly, "I was so scared. I didn't know what to expect. But Marielle just hugged me, kissed me on the cheek, and told me everything was going to be all right. That I was safe and loved. I stood there in shock, I guess. I had run away from age ten, onward, to get away from my druggie parents. I was sixteen when the state finally took me out of there. I didn't know what it was like to be fussed over instead of being hit or kicked at."

"I'm glad you had the Zimmerman's, Sky, because I think it helped you in many ways."

"Did you have a good foster family, too?" she asked, giving Cal a hopeful look.

"No. I got bounced around through three families by the time I turned eighteen." He saw the stricken look Cal to Sky's face and hastily added, "I was an angry, rebellious kid, believe me. I couldn't handle my rage. I was always fighting authority."

"Because your dad beat the hell out of you all the time," Sky muttered, shaking her head. "It's enough to make anyone angry and want to lash out."

"It did," Cal said, "but then I joined the Navy, and went into the SEALs, and they straightened me out. They helped me understand what integrity, teamwork, and pride were all about. They became my family. I never had another problem with authority after joining the teams."

"You were probably glad to leave that childhood behind you?"

"No joke," he growled.

"As much as I loved being with Marielle and Jack, it was a nightmare in another way."

"Because Alexandrov was a foster kid under their care?" Cal watched her tense a little, worry entering her expression.

"Yes. The moment we were introduced, I was afraid of him. I felt…violence…around him, Cal."

"Did your foster parents feel the same way about him?"

"No. I don't believe they ever saw the monster in him. He'd been with them since he was nine years old and he was sixteen at the time they brought me into their home." Her mouth thinned. "I felt danger around him." She shivered. "I could always sense someone who was capable of hurting others. I feared for my foster parents as much as I did, for myself."

"You knew what he was because you came out of a home of violence."

She stared at him, pulverized by his startling insight. Finally, her throat tightening, Sky managed, a "Yes…"

Frowning, Cal asked, "Did he stalk you?"

"At first, no. But I think…," and Sky looked up at the ceiling for a moment, trying to find the right words. "I think, Cal, that he was jealous of me coming into the household. Marielle fussed over me a lot. I think Vlad was jealous by my presence, so he began to constantly stalk me."

"His type is competitive and controlling," Cal said. "By you coming into the home, you upset what he had with them. The focus was no longer solely on him."

"He was always sniping at me, making horrid comments when they weren't around. The first year I was there, I was verbally tortured by him." She shivered. "He used to pull wings off flies and butterflies. It sickened me."

"He did it in front of you?"

Sky's eyes rounded. "How did you know?"

"Because he's a sick sonofabitch and a sociopath. He has no feelings, no sense of right or wrong. All he knows is power and disempowering others, manipulation, and revenge. I've seen his type of way too often over in Afghanistan."

Shaking her head, Sky muttered, "I hid from him, stayed away from him, tried too never be alone with him."

"Why didn't you go to your foster parents and tell them what was going on?"

"I was afraid they'd see me as the reason for the problems, and make me go away," she whispered. "Cal, I was getting love for the first time in my life. You'll never know how scared I was of losing my foster parents... I'd just found them and..." her voice thinned, and she closed her eyes, fighting back tears of grief.

To hell with it. Cal stood up and moved next to her. He opened his arms toward her. "Come here," he coaxed. He could see she wanted to come but was hesitant. "We all need comforting, sometimes, Sky. That's all I want to do, nothing else." Cal was risking everything. Everything. Sky could push him away. The tenuous trust between them could be broken. It was such a risk, but he had to try.

It was so easy to lean against Cal. As his arms gathered her up, bringing her against him, she released a broken sigh and rested her cheek against his chest, feeling the taut, muscular strength of him beneath the fabric. Sky felt small within his embrace as she surrendered over to him, her brow resting against his jaw. A serrating breath slid between her parted lips, and she kept her eyes closed, absorbing Cal's maleness, the way he held her tenderly in his arms. This wasn't a sexual advance on his part. It was one human trying to comfort another. As she moved her hand against his chest, beneath her palm she could feel the solid, slow beat of his magnificent heart.

"Just relax, Sweetheart," Cal rasped against her hair. "You're safe now..."

Tears jammed into her tightly shut eyes. Sky fought her reaction to his low, husky voice. Of late, all she could do was cry like a baby. Unsure of why, she felt the tears squeeze out from beneath her lashes and begin to trail down her cheeks. Sky tried to stop them. Ever since Cal had shown up again in her life, she felt like so many pieces of her were slowly fragmenting and tearing apart. Was that why she was letting her guard down, allowing him in when she hadn't before? Or was it Vlad slamming back unexpectedly into her life, shattering her sense of security once more? Sky didn't know, but when Cal eased his fingers through her hair, a sob tore out of her.

"Shhh, it's all right, Sky. You can let go. I'm here... It's all right..."

Cal's voice was like a rumble of faraway thunder through her. Fingers digging into his t-shirt, feeling his flesh tighten instantly in reaction, Sky pressed her cheek more deeply against him, her tears running freely. They soaked into his t-shirt as she sobbed, her entire body shaking like a tree leaf caught in a violent storm. It was a storm that had been long held at bay within her.

She'd cried intermittently after leaving the Bagram hospital, understanding she was no longer whole. Somehow, she'd found the grit to stop the tears, like she always had. As Cal gently eased his fingers through her hair, she started to let go. Really let go. No one except Marielle had ever held her like this. No man had given her this kind of tenderness. Only Cal had. Only this hardened warrior who had such a hellish childhood, she couldn't even begin to comprehend, had the capacity to reach out and care for her so profoundly. She began to cry. She cried for Cal and for herself.

Sky lost track of time. She breathed his masculine scent deeply into her lungs as his hand moved gently up and down her spine, continuing to soothe her. He cared. He genuinely cared for her, Sky realized as she slowly opened her eyes, the room blurring for a moment. His t-shirt was soaked and darkened with her emotional release, and she slowly moved her hand, feeling the dampness of the fabric beneath her palm.

"I got you all wet," she said in a hoarse voice. Sky felt Cal laugh. It was a rumble in his chest. She honestly didn't want to move, didn't want to leave the circle of his powerful arms. His reassuring touch had dissolved her terror. And when she felt his lips press against her hair, she quivered, but not out of fear. It was from something so deep, so good, welling up through her, that it caught Sky off guard.

"It's okay," Cal rasped, enjoying sliding his fingers through her silky hair. Each time, he could feel Sky absorbing it. She wasn't making any sounds, but he sensed her emotions because he was so damned attuned to her on that intuitive level. He was sure Sky didn't realize his heightened perceptions. Before, his nearly psychic abilities had saved lives on his SEAL team. Now, it was helping him monitor and know what supported Sky and what disturbed her. He referred to his abilities as a kind of emotional radar of sorts, glad to have it because there were so many craters, he could fall into with her on this path. Cal couldn't read a person's mind, but he could sure as hell read their body language. And he heard gratefulness in her tear-stained voice. And that's all he wanted to do, to give Sky a modicum of sanctuary. He would always stand between Sky and any threat to her.

Sky closed her eyes, wanting to be held but sitting up. "At Camp Nichols," she said in a strained voice, "I was drawn to you, but it scared the hell out of me, too."

Cal leaned back. He could feel her rapid heartbeat, hungrily absorbing her softness against him. "Because of your past, right?"

Miserably, Sky choked out, "I didn't want to fall for you, Cal, because of my history." Rubbing her face, Sky placed her hand against her eyes, unable to hold Cal's understanding look. "People die who are around me, Cal. I... I can't live with any more dying. I honestly can't…" and her voice broke.

Cal whispered her name, gently easing Sky's hand from her face, watching the tears gather in her wounded gaze. Without a word, he drew her back against him. This time, she came without hesitation, flowing against him like sunlight moving silently across the land of his body. Sliding his arms around her shoulders, Cal kissed her temple. "Listen to me," he growled, "no one has died because of you, Sky. Your head is messed up with what. Vlad killed your foster parents. You didn't."

"B-but, if I hadn't screamed when he was trying to pin me down on the bed, Jack and Marielle would never have come to save me!" Sky choked out, "Don't you see that?"

Cal sat up and framed her wet, pale face. "No, you did NOT cause what happened, Sky. You were a VICTIM in it just like your foster parents were. Vlad was the aggressor, the murderer." His nostrils flared as he forced her to hold his stare. "You were abused by your first family, Sweetheart. Abuse victims often take on the fault for what has happened to them and others. Listen to me," and his fingers tightened slightly around her face, his voice suddenly emotional, "you are INNOCENT in all of this, Sky. You always have been. You always will be. This is not your burden to carry or to feel guilty about any longer. If anyone should feel guilty, it's Alexandrov, but he's a sociopath and he feels NOTHING. You're carrying HIS load and yours. Do you see that?" and Cal drilled a look into her widening eyes.

Sky swallowed painfully and pulled out of his hands. She saw the anguish in Cal's eyes, heard it in his hoarse, low voice rampant with feelings. She'd never seen him like this. The suffering she saw in his face was for HER. *Her.* His words careened through her mind and heart. She grappled to embrace them, but it was so hard to do. Her fingers slid down her throat and her voice ached with feeling. "I… I never looked at it that way, Cal."

He shook his head, grazing her cheek. "You couldn't, Sweetheart. You were caught up in the middle of an ugly mess that had played out. It's easy for anyone who's standing outside of it to see it. There's no fault here, Sky, but I really need you to get that you were a victim of Vlad just as much as your foster parents were."

Rubbing her eyes, Sky nodded. "Okay… I'll think about this…" Her heart expanded with the quiet love she'd always held for him. How long had she ached to kiss Cal once again? The thought sent a frisson of joy skidding through her. Sliding her hands around his face, understanding the courage it took for her to take that step, she barely caressed his lips with his own. It felt as if she were on the edge of the world, but she pushed through that un-sureness as she felt Cal briefly tense. His mouth softened, and she heard him groan, his hands coming to rest on her shoulders, easing her closer to him. A groan caught deep in Cal's chest as she deepened their kiss, becoming bolder, asking him to become a partner to her. As Sky opened to him, a sweet, fine quiver raced through her. He was a past master of a woman's subtle signals as he rocked her lips open beneath his, and she began to melt.

There was something pulverizing beautiful in lingering against his searching mouth, as she invited his further exploration. She trusted him, feeling the moment as a sacred trust being built silently between them. He treated her like fine, delicate glass.

Sky's breathing quickened. Her fingers flexed against Cal's thick shoulders. A sheet of white-hot heat dove downward, reminding her of how long it had been since... She was lost in the heat, senses wide open, feeling him wanting her all the way and yet, reigning himself in, waiting for her to give the word— or not. Her mind was blown by his mouth cajoling, teasing hers and how badly she wanted him to curve his hand down between her thighs and feel her, touch her heat, know that she wanted him just as voraciously as he wanted her.

"If we don't stop now," Cal rasped against her wet mouth, "Tell me what you want?"

A tremble went through her as she drowsily opened her eyes, drowning in the golden brown of his. She felt the calloused strength of his fingers trailing teasingly against her skin. There was taut tension in his face, almost agony. There was no question she wanted him. All of him. In every way. Her lower body was throbbing with a fire of its own. She felt the wetness pooling between her thighs.

"Y-yes," she whispered. "Please... I want you... all of you..."

Those were the most beautiful words Cal had ever heard. He gave her a very tender look. "Okay, we'll take it slow and easy, Sweetheart."

"But I'm not protected," Sky protested, giving him a worried look.

Cal took a deep breath and rasped, "And I don't have any condoms on me." He hadn't really believed Sky would EVER consent to go to bed with him. He saw the consternation in her look, the sadness and disappointment. *Of all things...* The worst of timing. He gave her a look of abject apology. At this time of night, pharmacies were closed in Cusco, too. There was no recourse and he sure as hell didn't want to get Sky pregnant. He saw she shared his disappointment. "I'm sorry, Sweetheart. Bad timing."

"It's all right," Sky whispered, feeling suddenly embarrassed.

Cal couldn't disagree. "Let me hold you?"

She came willingly into his arms, her head resting against his chest, her palm over his thudding heart. There was no way Sky couldn't feel his erection against her hip. If she did, she didn't pull away. And there was no need to apologize.

"Well," Cal told her wryly, kissing her temple and cheek, "this is one for the history books."

"Why?" Sky asked, absorbing his tender touch, his kisses. Her body felt like a bright, burning flame, her lower body flexed, crying out for him.

"If Dylan ever finds out, which he won't, that I didn't have a condom on me, I'll never live it down. I always carry them."

Sky laughed softly and shook her head. "You are the kind of guy that had a lot of women in his life, that's why."

Shrugging, Cal smiled down at her, chasing a few blond strands away from her temple with his fingers. "All I care about is what you think of me, Sky." His brows drew down as he drowned in her lustrous blue eyes a man could lose his soul in. "With you, it's different." It had always been different, but Cal didn't want to explain further right now. When he saw confusion in her eyes, he realized she didn't understand the enormity of his admission. "You're beautiful to me, Sky. You're all heart. You're a kind, giving person. Today, out there with the kids in that village, I saw you relax for the first time. I saw you free of stress. I saw you smile. I saw your eyes light up. And I heard your laughter. You have a beautiful laugh. There are a thousand ways you make me feel good." He purposely avoided the word 'love,' because he was afraid, she might run from him at that admission.

She sat up, her hand on his knee. "We need sleep. I have a lot to think about, Cal."

Easing to his feet, he barely caressed her hair. "You're right. I'll see myself out and I'll come back at 0800 tomorrow morning?"

Nodding, she whispered, "Yes…I'll see you then, Cal. Good night."

CHAPTER 6

January 6

"HEY," LEV GROWLED, on his stomach lying on a small jungle hill above a main trail, "look what's coming." He handed the binoculars, over to Vlad, who lay at his side. The trail below, half a mile away, was used by everyone in the vicinity. The jungle in this part of Peru was a twisted puzzle of woody vines that made it impossible to traverse or cut through. Even if a man had the sharpest machete, it would pare him down in a matter of minutes. The hard, twisted vines were so thick and cumbersome, no human could get through them. As a result, these paths had been cut out by the Incan's hundreds of years earlier. The local animals, wild pigs, jaguars, as well as the villagers, used them to this day. And as of late, so did the drug runners.

Vlad scowled as he saw a woman riding a sturdy Peruvian pony in the lead, a pack mule heavily loaded down behind her, and a man on another horse bringing up the rear. "Well, well," Vlad murmured, interested in the woman's red hair caught back in a ponytail. "What have we here?"

Lev snorted. "This is the first time we've scouted this particular trail. I thought only drug runners and locals used it." He pulled out a small notebook and pen from his camouflaged shirt pocket. It was his job to note GPS, any activity on it, and who they saw. As soon as he got done, he'd use his digital camera and take photos of them.

"Americans?" Vlad murmured out loud. For a moment, his focus was on the woman in the lead. She wore a black baseball cap like the man bringing up the rear. His brows scrunched. "That guy in the rear is a fuckin' operator," he muttered in warning.

Lev's brows went up and he lifted his head, squinting at the couple on the trail. They were far enough away not to hear their low voices. "A real one? Not someone playing black ops?"

"Yes," Vlad said. "He's got an M4 in a sling across his chest. He's a damned former SEAL if I don't miss my guess." His own black ops background and familiarity with US operational groups had long ago been ingrained into Vlad.

"But she's not."

"No." He angled the binoculars, trying to read the white letters in Spanish on the side of the mule's tarp. Chuckling a little, he said, "It's an NGO. Says Helping Hands Charity on the fabric."

Lev scowled and tucked his notebook back into his pocket. He took photos. "What do you think? Are they on a mission of mercy? It could be the same two I've seen before. The woman has red hair. We talked about her at the café in Aguas Calientes."

"I think you're right," Vlad said, scoping out the operator in the rear who was alert and looking around. He was definitely black ops. No question. "I'd say it's the woman with that charity, that traveling nurse you told me about. Nice looking…" and Vlad felt himself becoming hard. The only problem was the operator with her. He wouldn't go quietly to his death.

They dropped into silence as the couple drew near. Vlad knew an animal would pick up minute sounds like low voices a long way off. Lev held the camera and took a quick photo before they were within earshot. They lay unmoving among the tall ferns, well hidden. Wearing camouflage gear and floppy hats, their faces painted with green, black, and gray paint, they were invisible in this jungle backdrop. Vlad watched the operator closely. The American was doing his job, his gaze raking the area, always looking, watching, and sensing. Were they on this trail for the first time? Or was it the other way around? This was a new path for Vlad and his men, and they had only been keeping twenty-four-hour surveillance on it for a week to see who and what was using it.

It was a pleasant surprise to find this American woman available, instead of sickly Quechua Indians trundling with huge packs on their backs, carrying loads of coca leaves used to produce the cocaine that was prized so much. Vlad remained immobile. Any fast movement would alert the animals and, more than likely, the operator. His breath was slow and deep.

Finally, after they disappeared down the slope and around a curve, he moved. He gave Lev a grin. "Same one? She's a fine-looking bitch."

"Yes, it is the same woman. I was thinking the same thing about her, too." Lev slowly got to his feet. He too had an erection. "I'm so damned horny I'm ready to fuck a tree with a hole in it."

Snickering, Vlad rose and brushed off his pants. "Find a llama. Let's follow them. Call up two other men and have them take over our position here. They can continue to watch this trail." He craned his neck, looking at the empty curve of the trail below them. "I want to find out who they are."

"That operator really means business," Lev warned.

"Yes. Unfortunate. But a sniper's bullet can take him out of the equation, no problem. I feel like having a red head." He watched Lev's grin increase. In the past, Vlad would kidnap a young woman from a Quechua village and carry her off after gagging her so she couldn't scream for help. Then, his men would have their way with her after he was done. Then they dumped her body over a convenient, nearby cliff, never to be found except by the jaguars or condors.

January 7

"STAY IN THE chopper," Cal order Sky after they landed at the La Paloma village. At every stop, he was training her up on security procedures and she had to change her habits. He saw her give him an irritated look. She was used to climbing out and getting the job done. Instead, he would survey the area, then climb out of the helo and clear the area first of possible intruders or unidentified men.

M4 in his hands, Cal knew this stop in the Highlands was the safest of all the villages that Sky served. It sat on the slope of a rocky mountain, and one could see for miles in all directions. It would be tough for Alexandrov to sneak up on her at this spot. Earlier, down at two other villages located near Machu Picchu, it was an entirely different story. Cal wore his protective vest. It was lightweight and cost an arm and a leg, but it fully protected his upper body from any type of bullet, fragmentation grenade, or shrapnel. And instead of weighing thirty-five pounds, it only weighed three pounds. He wore it over his olive-green t-shirt.

Sky fumed. Cal had become a mother hen about protecting her. She had become his PSD, he told her, personal security detail, her bodyguard. Was he ever! She drummed her green Nomex gloved fingers incessantly on the cockpit console, watching him walk around the front of the helicopter, alert, missing nothing. Glancing at her watch, they were nearly an hour behind schedule! At every stop, he got out, circled the craft, and then came back to give the all-clear. She always kept a bullet in the chamber of the .45 she wore strapped across her chest, the safety off. Sky wasn't very gung-ho about this walk-around business. She could do the same from her cockpit Plexiglass windows. Did he think he'd turn her into a SEAL?

Cal gave the all-clear with a hand signal. Another training for her was learning silent hand signal language so they didn't have to speak to one another if the enemy was around and give up their position. Cal was over-reacting as far as she was concerned, Sky thought, as she climbed out with the day's manifest in her gloved hand. This was their last stop, the sun low on the western horizon. More medical supplies had come in and needed to be stowed in Julie's medical hut. As Sky leaped off the lip of the helo, she saw Pilar, the headman's wife, hurrying toward her, a concerned look on her forty-five-year-old wrinkled face.

"Señorita Sky!" she called in Spanish, lifting her arm to get Sky's attention.

Frowning, Sky rounded the nose of the craft where Cal was waiting, rifle in hand, barrel pointed upward, ready for action. Pilar wore a brown bowler hat with a dark brown grosgrain ribbon around the felt. Her gleaming black hair was in two long braids that nearly reached her waist.

"Hola, Pilar," Sky called, walking up to meet the woman. Pilar was very short and overweight. She was huffing as she came to a stop, her dark brown eyes squinting up at Sky.

"Señorita, I need to speak to you."

Sky knew Spanish well and moved into that language. Her Quechua was not as good, and thankfully, Pilar spoke Spanish well. "What's wrong, Pilar?"

"Señorita Julie and Señor McCoy," she breathed, plastering her hand to her ample chest beneath the white blouse she wore. "They were VERY angry with one another before they left on the medical circuit." She pointed toward the corral where the mule was kept. "Is there something wrong between them?"

Frowning, Sky felt Cal's approach. She twisted a look in his direction, wondering if he understood Spanish. The look in his eyes told her he did, but he came to a halt at her shoulder and said nothing. Sky introduced him and then said, "Pilar, were they upset about something in specific?"

"Eh? They were shouting and yelling at one another!" She shook her head. "I have NEVER heard them raise their voice to one another, señorita. The señor wanted her to go home to the U.S.A., that it was too dangerous for her to remain here. I was wondering is there something going on around here?"

Cal put his arm on Sky's shoulder for a moment. "I know what this is about," he said quietly to her in English. "Let me handle this?"

Nodding, Sky heard Cal speak very fluent Spanish to Pilar.

"Señora Pilar, it was a lover's spat. You know how it is? They just became engaged to one another. It was about a certain dress that cost *mucho soles* and Señor McCoy didn't feel he could afford the *soles*." Cal gave an elegant shrug and opened his hands. "You know how it is with young people in love? *Sí?*"

Pilar's face fell and she patted her chest, relief in her expression. "Si, si, I do, Señor Cal. That is good to know. I felt badly for them. They are such good, kind people. And they love one another."

Cal gave her a slow smile. "True, but this is marriage jitters, Señora. That is all. By the time they return from their stops, they'll be all smiles and kissing one another again. Okay?"

"*Si, si, okay. Buenos*, good. Thank you," and she turned a waddled back toward the village, her black skirt flapping in the gusty breeze.

Sky gave him a dirty look. "What a liar you are. I'll bet the fight was about

Vlad being in the area and Dylan becoming more protective of Julie?" Like Cal was with her.

Cal gave her a patient look. "It's a white lie." He hitched his jaw in the direction of the path that led out of the village. "I had a second chat with Dylan after you and I buttonholed him about Alexandrov. Dylan loves her and he's scared to death for Julie. He said he was going to ask her to break her contact and leave now, not three months from now. I know he made a call to Liz to get her out of the contract and get a male nurse to replace her on this circuit."

A gasp escaped Sky. Her eyes rounded as she stared up at Cal. "What?"

Cal gave her a frustrated look. "Julie IS a target, Sky. Just like you are. You stand out in a population of brown-skinned people. Dylan understands the threat that Alexandrov brings even if Julie doesn't."

Rubbing her brow, Sky muttered, "Wow. Then the fight was him wanting her to leave for the U.S., and Julie digging in her heels to stay here?"

Shrugging, Cal growled, "Well, the mule's gone and so are they. That pretty much tells me Julie won this round of their argument." His mouth turned down. "Dylan's right, though. She needs to get out of here sooner, not later. Break the damn contract and she'll remain alive, albeit pissed. It's the better of the two options on the table."

Her head was beginning to ache. The pressure of Vlad's threat made her feel raw and vulnerable. "Don't get any ideas you're going to railroad me out of here like that. I'm staying."

Cal gave her a dark look. "You're military trained. Julie's a civilian. If Alexandrov and his men hit Dylan and Julie on the trail, he's alone to defend both of them. One man against God knows how many Spetsnaz-trained Russian soldiers." Giving her a grim look, Cal growled, "Julie is putting both of them at high risk whether she realizes it or not."

Sky could understand Julie's position. She loved the Quechua people and had spent many years among them. To her, they were like extended family, and she couldn't see herself anywhere else but here. Cal looked upset. "Okay, look, I need those medical supplies moved. Want to help me take them to the hut?" Sky asked.

"Yeah," and he clipped his M4 to his chest harness, so it was within easy reach in case he needed it. Seeing the turmoil in Sky's eyes, Cal knew he wasn't going to be able to cajole her into leaving either, as much as he wanted to.

After dropping off the last load, Cal climbed back into the bird and slid the side door shut. Sky was already up in the right-hand seat, her hands flying knowingly across the console, getting ready to start the first engine. He harnessed up in the left seat, his rifle nearby between the seats. Putting on the headphones and drawing the mic to his lips he said, "What's the schedule for tomorrow?"

"A day off," she said, looking to the right and left before starting the first engine. "Why?"

"Good. I'm going to go talk with Liz," he told her.

Sky snapped her head to the left and stared at him. "About what?"

"To give her a better understanding of why Julie and Dylan are in real-time danger." He scowled. "I'm hoping she has more sense about this situation than either of you two do."

Anger sparked in Sky. "Don't you DARE include me, telling her I should leave!"

"You can come with me if you want."

Nostrils flaring, Sky watched the gauges jump and come to life as the first engine came online. The helo started a subtle vibration, as if awakening. "I will let her know how I feel, because you are NOT going to tell her I should go home, too. I won't do it, Cal."

Cal noticed how pale Sky had become as she flew them back to Cusco. The sun was setting when she got out of the bird that housed the charity's busy hangar. He walked with her to Liz's office. She was already gone for the day and one of her assistants took the paperwork from Sky and wished her goodnight.

On the way back to her apartment in her car, he asked, "Are you feeling okay? You look a little pale."

"Just a headache," Sky muttered, rubbing her temple that pounded. "I get them sometime due to the high altitude. No big deal."

"Because of the stress of today?" He drove the car into an underground garage.

"Mostly," Sky admitted.

Cal parked the car and got out, moving to the other side and opening her door. Even her eyes looked dull with pain. "What can I do to help?" he asked, gripping her hand and helping her out.

Grateful for his care, she murmured, "Nothing. If I take a hot shower and go to bed, I can usually sleep it off. I've got an oxygen tank and I'll get some O2 into me and that will help a lot." Sky gave her a worried look. "Will you be okay eating at your hotel tonight?"

He smiled and picked up her helmet bag, carrying it in one hand. Shutting the door, Cal slipped his other hand beneath her elbow. "No worries. Look," he urged, opening the door that led to the elevator, "we'll call it a night? I need to hunt for an apartment around here. Instead of coming over tomorrow morning for coffee and breakfast, you sleep in and just take the day off and rest while I find a place to call my own?"

It sounded good, although Sky knew she'd miss Cal's presence. "Honestly, that's a good plan. Let me call you tomorrow sometime? When I feel better? Maybe have dinner over at my apartment?"

Cal wanted to do just that, but his sense cautioned him that Sky needed time and space alone. Privately he felt the headache was a result of the shocking news about Alexandrov. He'd seen it eating at Sky ever since he'd told her about it. And the argument between Julie and Dylan inflamed the situation for her. It was hitting home with Sky and it was stirring up her well-justified fears. "I think you need some downtime, Sweetheart. How about tomorrow is all yours? I have plenty to do in getting an apartment."

"Okay," Sky said, walking into the elevator. "Sounds good." She would miss Cal acutely. It was for the best though, Sky told herself. She needed space after so much had happened so fast. Maybe Cal was right: she simply needed a full day off with plenty of rest.

January 9

WHEN CAL KNOCKED on Sky's door two days later, she was slow in answering it. It was 0700, a time they normally met for coffee and breakfast. When the door opened, Cal gave her a hello smile. Sky looked like her old self, her eyes sparkling with life once more, a bit of flush to her cheeks. She was dressed in her flight suit. "Good morning," he murmured, stepping in. He held out a sack to her. "For you."

Sky smiled, absorbing Cal's powerful, quiet presence. Her spirits automatically lifted. "What's this?" she asked, opening the bag.

"I was out hoofing around for an apartment and came across a bakery in another plaza yesterday," he said, enjoying the curiosity in her expression. Sky could be like a little girl at times, he was discovering. It sent sweet, hot fire through him. "You'd mentioned awhile back you liked cinnamon rolls."

"Ohhh," Sky whispered, excited as she dug into the sack, drawing one out. "This is great! Where did you find them? I never could find a bakery that knew what they were, and I've searched Cusco from one end to the other."

Shrugging Cal watched her bite into it, savoring it. He liked making Sky happy. "Up on the plaza where the Catholic church sits at one end of it. I can't remember the name, I walked so many plaza's yesterday."

"Mmmmm, this is good, Cal." Sky spontaneously opened her arms, the sack in one hand and a roll in the other. She leaned up, giving him a swift hug of thanks.

Cal didn't even have time to capitalize on her unexpected embrace. His body tingled wherever she had pressed momentarily against him. The fragrance of almonds encircled his nostrils, the flowery-scented shampoo she'd recently used on her hair. "Hey, if I can get a hug for bringing you cinnamon rolls, I'll bring one to you every morning," Cal teased, grinning down at her. He saw Sky's cheeks deepen in color before she turned away and walked into the kitchen, munching happily on the pastry.

There was an unspoken rhythm to them working in the kitchen to make themselves breakfast. Cal whisked up some hollandaise sauce for their eggs Benedict. Sky was happy to pour them coffee and set the table. She placed a cinnamon roll on his plate and ate a second one. He'd bought her three. Over his shoulder he said dryly, "You can have another one, Sky."

She laughed a little, putting the sack in the trash. "You go ahead and eat it. You deserve something for your trouble.

Cal as he sat opposite Sky. "How's your headache? Did it go away?"

"Yes, I drained half a tank of O2 and then I slept the rest of it off."

Another reason not to push his need of her too much, Cal thought. "Good," he murmured, spooning out the sauce and drizzling it across her egg, ham, and English muffin. "You look well rested this morning. Better than I've ever seen you." Except at Camp Nichols. There, she had been a good weight and was feisty, a hell-bent-for-leather combat pilot who flew dangerous missions to rescue operators out in the Badlands. Cal could clearly see the toll the last two years had taken on her.

"How'd the apartment hunt go? I know it's tough getting apartments in the downtown area."

"Are you ready for this? I got an apartment one floor up from where you're at in this same building." Cal preened and grinned, pleased with himself, and watched her mouth drop open and then quickly shut.

"No way!"

"Way."

"Well, that's good in one sense because you can meet me down in the garage and we can drive over to the airport together." Sky's heart skittered with other off-the-table possibilities. She saw the very satisfied look come to Cal's face. "You got lucky."

"I did," he agreed amiably. "I didn't even know about it day before yesterday. I got up this morning to keep hunting. I spent all day looking with no luck. I was coming back from walking half the city late yesterday afternoon and I saw the woman in the office put a FOR RENT sign up in the window as I passed by it."

"Is it furnished?"

"Yes."

"Are you staying there instead of the hotel tonight?"

Nodding, Cal said, "Absolutely. I'm moving in today, lock, stock, and barrel."

"Good. We'll have to have a housewarming for you." Sky hooked a thumb behind her at the pantry. "I made chocolate chip cookies last night. I started feeling better late in the day and I wanted something sweet to eat. You can take half a dozen with you for lunch if you want," and she met his smile. Cal made no secret of liking dessert.

"Thanks. Want tuna sandwiches for lunch today?"

"Mmm, absolutely. You making them?"

"Yep."

"Maybe you missed your calling, Sinclair. You should be a chef. Everything you make is delicious."

"Just because I was a SEAL doesn't mean I don't have other talents," he reminded her archly.

"Isn't that the truth," Sky chuckled. Cal was hardly single-faceted. Every day, she was learning something new about him. At La Paloma, she learned he spoke fluent Spanish. The man was a Chinese puzzle. But an interesting one.

"I bought some nice-looking beef steaks from a downtown meat market. How about I make us a nice meal tonight when we get home?"

"I'd like that," she said.

CHAPTER 7

January 23

S KY AWOKE FEELING happy. It was a foreign emotion to her as she turned slowly over in the bed. Blinking drowsily, she looked at the clock. It was 0600. Time to get up. She'd dreamed last night that Cal had made love to her. Flopping down on the pillow, Sky closed her eyes, remembering how good it felt. Her heart expanded with deep feelings for him. She lay there remembering everything. Cal had been incredibly gentle with her, as well as tender.

Gray light peeked around the drawn dark blue drapes at the window and Sky wanted to languish, to remember that dream in every detail. She'd never had any man who was anywhere near his skill level. Ever. A pleasant, throbbing warmth had filled her lower body. Cal had been right all along: there was something good between them. He had been showing her that since coming to Cusco. And in her dream last night, he'd treated her like a beautiful instrument, fine-tuning her, and putting her in complete touch with herself as a woman. Being an equal partner, especially in the realm of sexual matters, was important to her.

How long had it been that she felt like that? Sky pulled her arm from across her eyes and stared up at the ceiling. *NEVER. Not like this.* Sighing, she turned on her stomach, burying her head in the pillow, just wanting to absorb the afterglow that continue to linger, wishing he was here, beside her, right now. Could it really be that exquisitely good? If it could be with anyone, she was sure that it would be with Cal.

"Crap," she muttered, throwing off the quilt and sitting up. She wanted the real thing. She wanted Cal. ALL of him. Did he have condoms? Rubbing her face, she needed a shower to wake up. Shrugging into her pink chenille robe, she moved drowsily down the hall to the bathroom.

After a long, hot shower, washing her hair, and climbing into her tan flight suit, Sky headed for a cup of coffee, the kitchen filled with the dark roasted aroma. Instead of taking down one mug, Sky took down two. Cal would be here in less than fifteen minutes. A new warmth thrummed through her. She'd fought so long and hard to run from him, to cut him out of her life. And here he was. Larger-than-life, once again. A thoughtful man with keen intelligence. What was she doing pushing him away all the time?

Groaning, Sky sat down at the table and rubbed her face. Her heart warred with her fear. Cal gave her a sense that she was going to be all right, that things would work out. He effortlessly infused her with hope. The hope of a future. A happy one. But would it be so? Sky was so lost in her chaotic thoughts that she almost didn't hear the soft knock at her apartment door. Frowning, she got up and hurried to answer it.

Cal stood there in his olive drab cargo pants, combat boots, and a black t-shirt that showed off his powerful chest and shoulders in delicious detail. In his hand, he held a bouquet of red roses. Gulping, Sky stared at them.

"What?" Cal said, giving her a teasing look, "you don't like getting flowers? You have pictures of them all over the walls of your apartment."

Stunned, Sky managed, "Well… ummm… I… no, they're beautiful." She reached for them and stepped aside to allow him into her apartment. Closing the door, she whispered, "Thank you. I didn't expect these…"

Cal turned and saw how rosy Sky's cheeks had become as she buried her nose in the fragrant blooms. How easily touched she was. He felt the exhaustion of barely sleeping last night, just one floor away from her. There was a deep, powerful drive within him to make Sky happy. Cal wanted her to focus on the good things that life could give her. That HE could give her.

"I smell coffee," Cal said, smiling down at her and heading toward the kitchen.

Sky followed, shutting, and locking the door. Something magical had shifted between them. Was it the dream last night? Cal fulfilling her? Giving her that edgy, exquisite pleasure of orgasms? Sky looked at his large, scarred hands differently this morning as he poured himself a cup of coffee. He was so tall, but in her dream last night, he'd been nothing but a tender lover with her. And how she'd lapped up every touch, every kiss Cal had given her. He was her rain and she, the parched desert. Until now. How she thirsted for him!

Walking into the kitchen, Sky placed her cup next to his and he filled it for her. She noticed he had not shaved, that dark growth giving him an even more dangerous look if that were possible. On their weekday flight routine, he didn't always shave. Moving around him, she pulled a vase from beneath the kitchen sink and filled it with water. The roses were fresh and heavily scented, already beginning to fill the kitchen with their fragrance. It felt as if they were living together, Sky mused. Cal sat down at the table, mug in hand. Sky had a tough time not staring at him because he was like eye candy to her. One glance at that strong mouth of his and her whole body went into a meltdown of anticipation. The man could kiss, no question. The dream teased her wickedly. Her lower body felt cranky and needy. For HIM. What to do? To say?

Sky looked distracted this morning. What was bothering her? Cal sipped his coffee, watching as she placed each rose into the crystal vase.

"Did you get much sleep last night?"

Turning, Sky shrugged. She brought the vase with the roses and sat it on the side of the table so they could admire them. "I had a dream," she muttered, going over and retrieving her coffee. She sat down opposite Cal. Because if she was too close, Sky would want to reach out and touch his dark-haired lower arm. She could see the corded muscles, the thick bicep stretching the black material of his t-shirt. Veins stood out prominently on the lower half of his arm and the backs of his hands. Those hands that had sent her into a fiery heaven of unadulterated pleasure. Giving an inward shake of her head, she wished to hell he wasn't such a sexual, primal animal.

"At least it wasn't a nightmare. What kind of dream?"

Finally, she gave him a dark look. "I was dreaming of you."

"And why do you think that is?" He held her confused blue gaze. This morning, Sky was open to him, despite her defensiveness. So, she dreamed of him. That made him feel hopeful. Cal didn't feel the walls she always kept in place with him as before. For that, he was more than grateful.

"Ever since you found me at Camp Nichols crying, I've felt safe around you, Cal. I just didn't want to admit it, was all..." Sky held his dark, intense gaze. He sat relaxed, his thick, broad shoulders telling her how well he carried heavy loads. Even hers.

"A question of trust?" Cal wondered.

"Yes," and she licked her lower lip, feeling a little embarrassed. "Nightmares scare the hell out of me. I was glad that it wasn't one."

"As a kid did you have nightmares?"

"If I cried out when I was sleeping, it drew attention to myself and that was never good. My father hated me breaking up his sleep. I jammed my feelings down deep inside myself. Or I hid in the closet and pressed fabric against my mouth, so he couldn't hear me and find and beat me."

"I'm sorry that happened to you, Sky." He shook his head and gave her a sad look. "Crying," I found out, "is good for men and women," Cal said gently, holding her unsure gaze. He could see Sky wrestling with her being emotional around him. Cal didn't mind it. He wanted it. Would she allow herself to trust him once again? Knowing her past, she wasn't used to crying in someone's arms. "Tears are never bad, you know?" He raised his brows, meeting and holding her gaze.

"Sure," Sky snorted. "Like you SEALs cry when things get tough?"

"SEALs cry, believe me. When one of our team is wounded or dies, we're all crying. We might not do it in front of one another, but trust me, we do."

Sky gave him a look of relief. "That's good to know. You guys are supermen. Or at least, you make all of us believe you are indestructible, that you can handle anything and tough your way through it unlike the rest of us mere, fallible humans."

Moving his fingers around the warmth of the cup, Cal said, "We are tough. And we're good at what we do. Emotions have no place in combat, Sky. It's one of the worst distractions a man can have because it will throw off his rhythm, his reflexes, and he won't be as alert as he needs to be."

"All of that is true," she acknowledged. "In the cockpit of my helo, I'm all business. I put my emotions aside, too."

Silence lulled between them. That dream called to her, enveloped her, and she sighed inwardly. What would Cal think if he knew she wanted to go straight down the hall to her bedroom and have him join her right now? Sky was feeling needy, much to her surprise and consternation. That had never happened before! All Cal had to do was look at her in a certain, smoldering way, and Sky was responding to him. She saw his eyes grow tender, his expression thoughtful. His hands moved around the cup, and she remembered his skill with those fingers. That dream had set her up! All she could do was see everything through a sexual filter this morning!

"Where are you?" Cal wondered.

Licking her lower lip, suddenly nervous, she whispered, "Remembering my dream from last night and thank goodness, it wasn't a flash back."

"At least it wasn't one of the bad ones," he said, partly in jest. And relief. A warmth spun through him as he saw the sudden expression of shyness being reflected in her face. There was so much Cal wanted to say to her, but he clamped down on all of it. Even a dream was hopeful news to him.

"You're right. It was a good one," she admitted.

He shared a warm look with her as he sipped his coffee. "Sounds like the dream has broken something loose in you, Sky?" Women weren't sex machines like a male was, and he knew that. They were built entirely differently from a hormonal standpoint. While there was no doubt there was magic between them, Cal knew the long-term relationship he wanted with Sky meant it wasn't something they should rush into. First, she had to get used to him being around. Second, and more importantly, she had to learn to trust him.

"Yes, the dream seemed to open doors I'd never knew existed…" Nervously, she stood and walked to the counter. "Breakfast?"

"Yeah. Do we have time?"

Looking at the watch on her wrist, she said, "Plenty. I've got some pipe coming in from Lima this morning. It won't arrive until 0900. We're in good shape, timewise."

Cal unwound from the chair. He placed his cup on the counter. "Tell you what," he said, "I'll make YOU breakfast. I'm pretty good in a kitchen."

Sky closed her eyes, her hands resting lightly on the counter, feeling Cal's bulk nearby, his powerful body two feet away from her own. Literally, she could feel the heat rolling off the man. He hadn't touched her. He hadn't gotten too close to her, but that didn't seem to matter to her body. It had a mind of its own, thanks to that torrid dream. "That...," she managed, "sounds wonderful... thank you...," and she forced herself to step away.

Over a breakfast of scrambled eggs with shredded cheese, chopped onion, red peppers, and zesty spices, Sky found herself physically hungry. Cal had fixed some French toast to go with the eggs. He'd added some peanut butter and Kahlua liqueur into the batter and she found herself gobbling up three slices in quick order. It was completely unlike her to eat so much! Cal had used a dozen eggs and two-thirds of them were on his plate along with four-stack of the French toast. The man tucked it away, no question. Sky found herself happier than she'd ever been. The kitchen smelled wonderful, and Cal was there with her, sharing the meal.

"This is nice," Sky admitted, reaching for the syrup.

"What is?"

"Us. You. I mean, being here with me. It's—different."

"Different can be good," he teased, meeting her gaze. Cal saw gold dancing in the depths of her blue eyes, feeling Sky's happiness despite her distractedness. It made him feel damn good about the future. About them, as a couple.

"This just feels so normal to me," she said, looking around the kitchen. "Like we've been doing this for years."

He'd like exactly that, but kept his mouth shut. If Sky knew his end game with her, Cal knew she'd freak out and run. Instead, he said, "We have something good building between us, Sky. I've said that from the gitgo."

"At Camp Nichols, I didn't believe you."

"Oh," Cal murmured, giving her a rueful look, "I think you did. You just didn't want to admit it, was all, for a lot of good reasons."

"You're probably right. We didn't have much time together because I was an officer, and you were enlisted."

"That was our impasse," he agreed.

"Two years apart and it's as if we just picked up where we left off."

Cal could see Sky trying to understand or perhaps rationalize what they shared. "What we have, Sweetheart, isn't a head trip. It's a heart trip. And it's kinda nice you can dream about us."

Sky sat there feeling her way through his gritty words and observation. She sliced the last piece of French toast with her knife and fork. "I never thought of dreams in those terms," she admitted.

Cal looked up. "Have you ever been in love, Sky?"

Giving him a groan, she said, "Love? Never."

"Why do you think you dreamed of us last night?"

Cal's unsettling observations once more reminded Sky he was a SEAL. They didn't miss details. Ever. Their lives depended upon it. And she knew that skill set was used just as much now as then. It didn't matter if Cal was now a civilian.

"I think," Sky began quietly, feeling her way through the words she wanted to choose carefully, "that because of my past, I never really trusted anyone with myself. I couldn't trust my real parents. And my time with Jack and Marielle was only two years in length."

"You trusted them, didn't you?"

"With my life," Sky said, suddenly emotional. "It took me a year to believe they honestly loved me, Cal. And then, when I realized it was genuine, that they really did, I surrendered over to them and poured all my love I had been holding onto into them."

"It was a good time in your life," Cal agreed gently. He saw the sadness in her eyes, the fact they were no longer alive. "But you knew letting anyone close to you meant they could also hurt you."

Frowning, Sky ate more slowly, considering his observation. "You're right. I learned that early on as a young child."

"And the men you let walk into your life? Did you ever trust them?"

She held his blunt stare. Compressing her lips, she said, "Not much…" Sky pushed her plate away, finished with the meal and wiped her mouth with the yellow linen napkin. "When Vlad attacked me, it scared the hell out of me, Cal. I went through four years of college fighting off boys who wanted me in their bed. And I knew that's all it was. I got stalked by Vlad. And I felt that same stalking from the guys who chased me later in college. It was so unsettling to me. I wanted no part of it. I got tripped up twice by them."

"Yeah, as a breed, men aren't too subtle, are we?" and Cal gave her a sad look filled with irony.

"No, you guys are pretty black and white," Sky agreed, feeling less nervous admitting her lack of partners to Cal. "I had a very brief affair in my junior year. I was really suckered in by his lies. The guy got me drunk and I don't do alcohol too well. I couldn't believe he thought I was beautiful and attractive, so I drank with him. I thought that was what I was supposed to do. I'd never touched a drink until that one time and I didn't realize I could get drunk, which is what he was waiting to happen…"

Cal said nothing. Helluva way to lose one's virginity. But then, a lot of young women fell for that kind of trap. "What about the other guy?"

"Well," she said, raising a brow, "I wasn't drunk on my ass the second time around. At least I learned from my previous mistake." She saw him smile a little and nod. Somehow, telling Cal wasn't making her feel guilty or apologetic. Sky suspected he was trying to understand her experience… or rather lack of experience, in the realm of relationships.

"The last time happened when I was in helicopter training. The officer was one of my instructors, and I fell hard for him. He lied to me. He told me he was single." Her voice dropped. "Two months into our affair, I found out he was married and had three kids. I about died of shame. I would NEVER have dated a man who was married. What does that make me?"

"You're not the kind of woman who'd knowingly do that. And it doesn't make you a bad person for falling for his lies. You were the victim here, Sky. He knew what he was doing."

It meant a lot that Cal believed her. Sky pushed some hair off her brow in frustration. "Men lie to women. That's what is burned into me from my college experiences. They lie to get you into bed, to have sex with you. To them, a woman isn't a human being. We're just a body to be screwed. We're not seen as worthy of respect, as an equal in their reality."

Cal felt her justified anger and frustration. "Well," he said blandly, getting up and gathering up the plates and utensils, "there will NEVER be any lies between us. EVER," and he gave her a dark look of promise that spoke volumes. "I never stalked or chased you at Camp Nichols, either. I wanted a serious, long-term relationship with you, Sky. I knew it wasn't possible at that time and I was hoping that once we got transferred back to the States, we could pick up where we left off." He put the plates in the sink and added, "I'm after a serious relationship with you. And I want to gain your trust."

"You were trustworthy at Camp Nichols," Sky offered quietly, "with your blunt nature, honesty has always been your only policy, now as it was then. I really appreciated your honesty back then. You didn't stalk me, although other men tried."

Cal rinsed off the plates in the sink. "What you see is what you get. If anything? I'd like to hear someday from you that you do trust me. That's a gift I have to earn and I'm okay with it. With trust comes honest talk between two people."

Nodding, understanding he was serious, she offered, "I've never been in a long-term relationship, Cal. This is all new to me. I appreciate that you're not pressuring me."

"Because I'm in with the long haul with you, that's why. Cal turned and wiped his hands off on a towel. "How do you see me, I wonder?"

"You are easy on the eyes," Sky admitted.

He preened a little. "Thanks... that's a nice compliment."

Cal was SUCH a hunk! She could imagine women swooning over this man. He oozed sex appeal. It wasn't anything Cal did in particular. Sky could count on one hand of all the men she'd met in her life who had that kind of blatant and charismatic sexuality. With Cal, it was in her face, completely raw and there for a woman to feel and react too. And he didn't even seem to be aware of it! Cal just had a seemingly easy going, casual kind of way of moving through his life. But maybe, Sky figured, because she'd had less experience with men in her life, she was gun-shy? If she allowed Cal into her life, what did that mean? Where was their burgeoning relationship going? Was a long-term relationship really what she wanted? What were her priorities? Above all, Sky felt the drenching cold of fear overwhelming her once more. Vlad Alexandrov was out there, somewhere. Stalking her. And if he ever found her, Sky knew he'd kill Cal and then he would rape and imprison her and force her to be the mother of his children. She never forgot those chilling words he rasped at her as he sprawled her out on the bed, and she was trapped beneath him. He wanted her to be the mother of his children! That had shocked her into action, and she started to scream for help.

She looked up at Cal's strong back and wide set of shoulders as he dried off the plates and flatware. He was the man standing between her and terror stalking her. And it was enough to slow Sky down. Just as Cal had said earlier: distraction could get a person killed. And it was true. Was Vlad in Cusco? If so? Where did he stay? Did he know she was living in Cusco? Was he actively stalking her? Sky rubbed her neck, in thought. Somehow, she knew she would pick up on Vlad if he was in her vicinity. And she'd not gotten that feeling—yet. But if she threw herself into a relationship with Cal, it could mean trouble of the worst kind. If they were locked in with one another, they would both be distracted. And that is when Vlad could strike, when they were not alert to his proximity.

CHAPTER 8

January 25

C AL NOTICED JULIE seemed aggravated as she worked in the jungle village of Kurmi, two days later. It was a Quechua name meaning 'rainbow,' because they would often see them during thunderstorms that rolled across the area. He'd helped the well drilling workers offload the necessary pipe for their project. Dylan had been tense, and he was on edge more than normal. Knowing they were at sixty-five hundred feet, the village carved out of the jungle, he had a good idea as to why. This area was ideal for growing coca plants, meaning it could have fallen into Alexandrov's territory. He sauntered over to where Dylan was standing on guard, M4 in hand. The morning was coolish, long white wisps of clouds silently stealing just above the triple layer canopy of the jungle.

"Hey," he said, coming up, "everything okay?"

Dylan snorted. "Walk with me?"

Cal saw Sky walking with Julie and helping her set up an outdoor area where she could give vaccinations to the children who needed them. Already, there was a line of mothers and children forming. "I haven't got long. We're on a tight turn-around schedule today," he told his friend.

Dylan walked slowly along the edge of where the jungle stopped and the cleared, hard-packed red earth of the village began. "I tried to talk Julie into breaking her contract and leaving because of Alexandrov's presence a couple of days ago." His mouth flattened. "It didn't go well."

"Both of them are independent and focused," Cal agreed. Lifting his head, he felt a prickle along his nape. It was a warning sign. They'd flown in forty-five minutes ago. The helo sat out in a field. "You told her everything?"

"Yeah, I told her that Sky had been assaulted by the bastard, that he'd murdered her parents." Dylan cut him a swift glance. "I didn't say anything about her being in Witness Protection and Security."

"Thanks," Cal murmured, his gaze moving slowly up to a jungle-clothed hill above the village. "Julie looks pissed off as hell."

"Yeah. She told me I had no right to tell her what to do."

"She's a civilian, bro. She doesn't understand the threat assessment."

"And dammit, I can't make her," Dylan growled, kicking a small rock with the toe of his boot. "She thinks she's abandoning these villagers to the wolves if she leaves. Never mind Liz would hire in a male traveling nurse to take her place and the villages won't suffer at all."

"Julie was going to leave in six months, anyway," Cal pointed out. He halted, his eyes narrowing on the hill. Someone was up there. He could sense it. And whoever it was, they weren't friendly. "You see any activity on that hill in front of us?" Cal turned and lowered his head. The enemy, if stared at, would see it, so a swift look was all that could be had at this point.

"No… nothing. Why?"

Rubbing the back of his neck, Cal said, "Got a hit on that hill. You might watch it."

Nostrils flaring, Dylan said, "Probably Alexandrov and his goons reconning the area."

"Maybe… I don't know." Cal wished he did. "I talked to Sky this morning on the way out here about Alexandrov's habits. She lived with him before he jumped her."

"Oh?" Dylan took off his sunglasses and wiped his perspiring face. The high humidity in the jungle made everyone sweat profusely. Sliding them back on, he said, "Anything we can use?"

Shrugging, Cal continued to walk slowly, his gaze active. Jungle shadows could be a man waiting and hiding, well camouflaged, unseen. And every time he saw something, he'd check it out. "The bastard continually harassed her. And being so young, she didn't realize he was stalking her at first. Sometimes, she'd leave her bedroom and he would be standing next to her door for no reason. It would startle her, but Sky was innocent and thought nothing of it. When it happened several times in a row, she did ask him and he said he was walking to his room, which was across the hall from hers."

"He made it look perfectly normal," Dylan said, frowning.

"Yeah, and Sky never caught on. I think he was listening at her door. He couldn't see into it, but he was there, waiting and watching."

"Gets his rocks off on stalking his victim and they never know it," Dylan muttered.

"He's calculating, and he enjoys the hunt."

"Is there anything else you can get on him through your resources?" Dylan demanded.

"I'm working on it. Maybe by tomorrow. I have a CIA contact who's digging deep into Spetsnaz intel and looking for his name. My hunch is this bastard was involved in going after the Chechynian rebels." Cal's mouth thinned. "And you know they weren't kind to any of them if they were caught."

Snorting, Dylan said, "Spetsnaz has never taken the Geneva Conventions, the treatment of prisoners, seriously. Nothing new there."

"Damn straight." Cal halted at the edge of the village, casually looking around. He could see the colorful clothes of the women in the center of the thatched-roof village. Dogs and kids were running around and playing. He envied the children's sense of freedom, having no awareness that danger was all around them in the form of drug runners and drug lords. He saw Sky helping Julie, handing her syringes of vaccine. Their two heads stood out like sunlight in the darker jungle surrounding them, one blond and one red.

"This is your last stop before you head back to La Paloma?" Cal asked.

"Yeah. Can't hardly wait to get the hell out of here. I've had a sense we're being followed." Dylan gave Cal a frustrated look. "It's hell not being able to order a drone or satellite fly-by with thermal imaging to find out who's around here."

Grinning a little, Cal said, "Yeah, it sucks being a civilian contractor, doesn't it?" All their normal military tools to find the enemy were no longer at their disposal. It came down to basics: being alert, following one's intuition which could alert them to possible danger, and that was it. "You'll be in La Paloma in what? Two days?"

Nodding, Dylan began his walk around the other side of the large village. "Yes. We take another trail, more straightforward, to get home."

"Good. You've got an apartment in Cusco, right?"

"Yeah. You ever get one or are you still the hotel?"

"I managed to get an apartment in the same building Sky's living in," and he smiled a little.

"Was that planned?" Dylan demanded, grinning.

"No, but I'm not bitching about my luck. I want to be close to her." Even closer than that, but Cal didn't go there.

"My apartment is a block off Plaza de Armas," Dylan said, walking though the muddy red earth, his boots caked with the damp clay. It was always raining sporadically and the clay never dried up. It was a red glue that stuck to everything, and one could never get it off their boots or clothing.

"My kitchen is up to speed. How about when you two get back to Cusco, you come over for dinner? I make a mean rare steak."

Lightening in mood, Dylan nodded. "Sounds good."

"Might give you two a breather with one another," Cal murmured. "Something different. Besides Sky is Julia's best friend. It could be a good evening and maybe a chance for all of us to relax."

"We can't talk about this," Dylan grumbled. "Julie's really hot over this. I've never seen her on war footing before."

"She probably sees it as you taking away her reason for living," Cal said drily. "Put it into our terms. What if someone came up and told us we had to quit the SEALs because it was dangerous?" and he grinned a little.

"Yeah, I know," Dylan said. "I should have been more PC. I just didn't expect this kind of blowback from Julie."

"You love her," Cal said, slipping a little in the slick mud. "And you've picked a woman who's not only a pioneer, but stubborn."

"Just like me," Dylan laughed a little, feeling some of his worry recede.

Cal clapped him on the shoulder. "Give her time. She's got to know you love her and you worry for her. It's natural."

Sweeping the jungle, Dylan said, "She knows that. Julie is mature. She's not going to stay angry at me forever."

"Maybe a few days off in Cusco and a good dinner with us will help put things right."

Vlad damn near came unhinged when he saw Sky Lambert emerge from the Bell helicopter earlier. His heart started a slow pound of excitement as he watched her walk with a very tall, lethal-looking man carrying an M4 rifle. There was no question he was an operator, someone hired to protect her.

Vlad couldn't stop smiling. At last, after all these years, he'd found her again! He loved Sky. He wanted to marry her, but she spurned his advances every time. Part of him wanted to kill her for it. His heart, however, wanted her as his wife. She would bear him strong, fine sons.

"That's her?" Lev growled, laying at his side. They lay beneath a camouflage netting so that they blended into the surrounding plants and brush. "The girl you always talk about?"

"It is," Vlad said. "Did I tell you I found out through my father, who had a contact in Witness Protection, that she now calls herself Sky Lambert?" Too bad the contact had been killed. His father had been pushing the man to find out where Sky was hiding for him, and he was grateful to his father for his efforts. The last he'd found was she had been deployed to Afghanistan at a black ops forward operating base. And as hard as their best computer hacker tried, they couldn't break into the Witness Protection program to find out more. He wondered why Sky was here and not still in the Army.

"A blond and a red head," Lev said, pleased as he watched the women through the sniper scope.

Putting down the binos for a moment, Vlad wiped the sweat off his camouflaged face. He slapped at an ant crawling along his neck, finding and squeezing it until it tore in two. Throwing it away, he muttered, "One for each of us. You can have the nurse. I want HER," and the word ground out of his mouth. He would break Sky, make her realize he owned her, that she had no options but to do as he demanded. And he'd get her pregnant. There would be no turning back once he got his hands on her this time.

"It's going to take a lot of planning," Lev warned. "Those two operators are former SEALs. They won't be easy to get around in order to grab the women."

Vlad settled the binos to his eyes, scanning the women and children in the central square of the village. He felt an erection stir as he watched Sky. If anything, she'd matured as a woman and was even more beautiful than before. Vlad wanted her. Badly. But his experience in Spetsnaz took over. "You see the name on the side of that helo? Helping Hands Charity?"

"Yes. So?"

"I'm going to check it out. Sky's got to be flying in and out of Cusco. I think I'm going to take a week or so off and do a little recon. Find out more about this NGO, where it's based, and then find out where she's living."

"The Russian wolf is on the prowl," Lev chuckled.

Vlad had all sorts of scenarios racing through his mind. Sky had to live somewhere in the city of Cusco. If not Cusco, she was operating out of Lima, but that logic didn't hold water. Lima was on the coast of Peru, built at sea level and near the Pacific Ocean. It would stand to reason Sky worked for this NGO and she was based in Cusco because of the deadly shift in wind currents from the Andes range of mountains that happened at every dusk until dawn. No one flew anything in the night hours, or the wings of the craft would be torn off.

"We're going to stand down on this nurse for now," he warned Lev. "I'm leaving you in charge of the unit until I return from Cusco. Tail the nurse, watch her movements, but do NOT engage." He slid him a warning look. "Sky is my priority now. Not her."

Lev growled a curse. "I need a woman."

"Well," Vlad snarled, "it's not going to be that nurse. Not yet. You're going to have to wait. Go find a llama or alpaca."

Sky felt out of sorts. She struggled to understand what was causing it as she met Cal near the helo. It was time to leave if they wanted to stay on schedule today. She wiped the perspiration off her brow and settled the baseball cap back on her head, opening the right door of the Bell. Glancing around, Sky felt a threat. Was it her imagination? Could it be Vlad? It FELT like him. This area of the jungle was where the drug running took place. Shaking her head, she pushed her aviator sunglasses on and climbed into her bird.

Cal slid the rear door shut and locked it after he entered through the cargo area. Moving forward, he saw Sky frowning.

"Everything okay?"

"Yeah," she muttered, buckling up. "I'm jumpy. My imagination is going crazy. I keep thinking Vlad is out there, watching us. Watching me." Her lips compressed as she took off her cap and dropped it behind her seat on top of her go bag and donned her helmet. "It's probably just me."

Cal harnessed up, gazed out the windshield, and saw Dylan walking toward where Julie was giving vaccinations to the children who were lined up. "I felt something too, so it's probably not your imagination."

Her hands froze and she snapped a look at him. "What? Are you serious?"

Cal nodded. "My neck prickles when there's a threat around," he said, safing his weapon and taking the bullet out of the chamber. Laying it across his lap, he added, "Dylan felt it too." He saw the blood drain from Sky's face, sudden terror rising in her eyes. Reaching out, he gripped her gloved hand resting on her thigh. "You're safe. I'm not going to let anything happen to you, Sky."

His hand was large and warm over hers. Sky swallowed hard, her gaze moving toward Julie and Dylan. "But… what about them? Julie?" and she couldn't stop the memories from flooding back through her mind as much as she tried to ignore them.

"Dylan's on top of it." Cal heard the sudden, emotional wobble in Sky's voice even though she began the pre-flight sequence. Her eyes were narrowed, and she was focused in on her flight duties. He tried to ease her concern. "Look, Dylan has a sat phone. He has my number as well as Liz's number at the office at the Cusco airport. If anything happens, we can be here in a short amount of time." Cal put on a pair of earphones that were plugged into the ICS, inter-cabin system, within the helo. Through it, they could continue to speak to one another as the craft roared to life.

Sky felt her gut churning as she started the first engine and then the second one, engaging the blades. She adjusted the mic near her lips. The helo began to sway and shudder. It was familiar and soothing to Sky's screaming nerves. "Why wouldn't you stay with Dylan? Isn't two men better than one if Vlad really is nearby?"

Cal nodded. "I suggested it to Dylan, but he said no. I also suggested they both fly back with us today, but he declined my offer."

Letting out an exasperated breath, she nailed Cal with a look. "What IS it with you SEALs? You think you're Superman? Dylan is one man against how many Russians? You've told me before that Vlad has a force of mercenary soldiers with him."

Feeling her frustration, her terror, Cal grazed her pale cheek. Any excuse to touch Sky was a good one. He knew his touch always calmed her; centered her. He watched her mouth relax a little after he grazed her cheek. "Sweetheart, it's not about ego or us being SEALs. From what you've told me about Alexandrov, he's a patient man who plots and schemes long before he ever makes a move. Besides, Julie would refuse to leave here, and then they'd get into another argument. Dylan said it wasn't worth trying to convince her to fly back with us because she would simply refuse to go."

Sky pushed all her fear aside and she concentrated on lifting off the Bell. The blades whirled at full speed, and she slowly brought it straight up, the air punctured and shaking and invisibly rippling around them. Only after they'd gained altitude and were heading for the next village, Tuyur, at the edge of the jungle, did she speak through the mic. "This scares me, Cal. What if Vlad is out there? What if he saw me? Maybe he didn't know I was here until right now?"

"It's wiser to assume he knows you're here, until we can prove it one way or another from a security standpoint, Sky."

Well, that made sense too, she admitted sourly to herself. The sky was filled with high humidity, the color leaching out as they left the jungle below them. Sky always flew two to three thousand feet above the canopy in case there was engine failure. If the helo had a thousand feet of altitude, she then had a chance to do a hard landing below. If it was less than a thousand, then they'd auger in with no hope of surviving the crash. She forced herself to keep her mind on the gauges and dials as well as the computers. Cal's presence was comforting.

"I guess," Sky admitted after a while, the flying soothing her raw nerves, "I'm overreacting."

Cal gave her a sideward glance. "No, you're not. You have a right to how you feel, Sky. Don't deny it and don't apologize for it. Okay?" He desperately wanted to take her into his arms, to give her that sense of safety he knew he could always bestow upon her. Sky licked her lower lip, something she did when she was really worried about something. Mentally, Cal cursed Alexandrov. His shadow was long and still ran her life in so many ways. He wanted to find the bastard and kill him.

Cal drove Sky home after they'd landed at the Cusco airport and walked her to her apartment. It had been a long day for both. He was finding that some days Sky didn't have much flight time and on others, it was like a rock skipping over water. They landed at eight out of the ten villages today, delivering medicine, gear, food, and drilling necessities. Cal had come to know when Sky was tired, and this was one of those evenings. What she needed was to be held. What he wanted to do was love her. The tan flight suit she wore had dark blotches down the center of her back from the humidity and temperature, plus spots beneath her armpits. He smelled of sweat, too.

As Sky came to a halt at her door, Cal stood aside, her helmet and go bag in his one hand.

She pushed the door open and dropped the key into her pocket. The day had been especially nerve-wracking for her. She turned, looking up into Cal's shadowed eyes. She saw him worrying about her. Sky had waffled about Cal in her life. She'd torn apart the why's and what for's all day long. No answers were ever forthcoming except that Cal made her feel lighter, happier. But she'd been afraid to reach out to him. If she made love with Cal, would he want a continued relationship with her? Where would it go? Despite a lack of clear answers, something today had shaken her out of her indecision.

Throughout her misgivings, desires, and fears about Cal, Sky realized today that her reactions were based upon her past experiences. As she met and held his warm gaze, heat flowed sweetly through her, erasing so much of her fear and trepidation. She remembered Cal telling her that he would never pressure her or push to get her in bed. And he hadn't. He'd backed off completely, giving her latitude to be in charge and in control of the situation.

Without warning, Sky stepped forward, pushed up on the toes of her boots, slid her hand around the nape of his neck, and drew Cal's head down to her lips. Closing her eyes, Sky wanted to drown in Cal's mouth, wanted to feel his arms slide around her. She felt him tense for a second before he relaxed, his one arm coming around her waist, hauling her against him, his mouth curving gently against her own. There was a sense of possession in his kiss, but not brutal animal lust, although Sky felt him tremble as she pressed her breasts against his chest. She gloried in the strength of Cal's lips sliding against hers, felt him monitor how much pressure he met and returned her kiss with.

Sky eased from his mouth, her breath accelerating, a hot glow and ache settling deep within her. Cal's eyes were stormy looking, narrowed upon her and she felt her heart fly open beneath that intense, burning look. "You said I had to come to you," Sky whispered unsteadily. "I'm here. I want to love you, Cal…" She saw him give her a faint smile, his hand moving to her cheek, his thumb stroking her flesh.

"Sounds good to me, Sweetheart." Cal lifted his head and peered into her apartment, which always reminded him of life with all the plants in it. "Want to grab a shower first? I know I do." The thought of taking Sky into the shower was provocative, but not wise. Not right now, at least.

Nodding, Sky stepped out of the circle of his arms, relief sloughing through her. The decision felt right. "That's a good idea," she admitted. "I feel like I've been in a locker room. Do you want to go up to your apartment and meet me down here afterward?" She felt her body humming with heated anticipation. That dream had never left her. She saw Cal give her a very confident smile.

"Yeah. And I'll bring some condoms along," he added.

"Okay, that sounds good. See you in a little while?" and she drowned in that intense, heated look he gave her.

"I'll be back," Cal promised, leaning down, sliding his mouth hotly against hers. He felt Sky hungrily return his kiss. Cal gave her the helmet and go bag, watching her walk into the apartment and close the door. He turned, frowning. What had suddenly made Sky decide to take the next step? Heading for the elevator at the end of the hall, Cal moved through the possibilities. This wasn't survivor sex, which was a bad reason to screw around in the first place. Had the idea that Vlad might have been watching her in that jungle village scared her? Was she wanting the sense of safety he afforded her? Confusing sex with safety? Rubbing his jaw, Cal turned the corner and punched the button for the elevator. The doors slid open, and he walked in, deep in thought, with no forthcoming answers.

As Cal showered and shaved, he wondered about Sky's reasons. Afterward, he padded into his bedroom. He dressed in a pair of gym shorts and a black t-shirt. His hair was short and damp, and he ran his fingers through it, taming it back into place. Normally, he didn't shave at night, but for Sky, he would. By the time he was heading down the elevator to the second floor, Cal had cleared the decks of his mind. Sky wanted him. Why the hell should he question her as to why?

CHAPTER 9

January 25

CAL EASED QUIETLY back into Sky's apartment. He entered the bedroom. She lay naked in the center of the bed, waiting for him. The light from the hallway moved weakly into the room. It was a little after midnight, and although it had been a long day, he was wide awake in every sense. Meeting her eyes, they appeared luminous, and he sensed in her a hunger that matched his own. Cal moved to the bed and eased in next to her. She slid into his arms, pressing her body against his. Her skin was moist from her earlier shower.

Sky nuzzled beneath his jaw, content to feel Cal's arms grow tighter and hold her solidly against his hard male body. All he had to do was give her that smoldering look of his, and she was lost. This was even better than her torrid dream, feeling how their flesh met and seemed to melt into one another.

Cal eased Sky on her back, watching the moonlight sift silently through the east windows, highlighting her exquisite body. His gaze moved appreciatively from her brow to those incredible blue eyes that were wide and aroused. Her nose was fine and clean, her cheekbones high, and her mouth soft with promise. Groaning inwardly, Cal would never forget the shape of her full lips, the way the corners turned upward. "Well," he growled, "I've lost the battle AND the war when it comes to you," and Cal trailed his lips down her temple, the short strands of silky blond hair tickling his nose and cheek.

Closing her eyes, Sky inhaled his male scent combined with the soap he'd used earlier, a faint pine fragrance clinging to his skin.

"I like feeling the way you move, like the sensual cat you are, against me." He saw her eyes grow dreamy as he pressed his erection more deeply into her soft, yielding belly. The fire of arousal burned brightly in her eyes, and he grinned, nipping her lower lip playfully, feeling her respond, her hips meshing hotly against his.

"Mmm, for sure," Sky sighed, feeling his hand move and linger around her breast. She arched into his palm, wanting more, wanting the pleasure she knew he could give her.

He slid his hand up across her left hip, his fingers splaying out across her belly.

Sky opened her eyes, drowning in his gaze.

He moved his mouth against her lips, feeling their softness opening like a flower beneath his exploration. Cal felt heat bolt down through his body as she pressed upward against his chest, her breasts tight, nipples hard and dragging suggestively through the hair on his chest. "I like the idea of finally making you mine…"

A low sound of pleasure vibrated in her throat as his hand ranged down from her belly, easing her thighs open, his fingers slowly teasing her wet folds. His gritty words only made her contract more, the fluids stimulated as his finger eased just inside her entrance. Her breath left her lips in a soft cry and Cal swallowed it, his mouth sealing against hers, his tongue finding hers, emulating the rhythm of his finger stroking that sweet knot of nerves just inside her.

Sky became lost in the white-hot pleasure he was building within her, felt his mouth leave her lips to settle on one of her hardened nipples pleading for his touch. A moan rose out of her as he suckled her strongly. Her whole lower body flexed. He knew how to milk her, to tease her mercilessly, bringing her to a state of orgasm so quickly, it tore through her like a scalding, rippling tsunami. Her ragged cry was drowned in his mouth as he took her lips, moving his fingers within her, moving deeper against her thrashing hips, giving her unbearable pleasures that mounted one on top of the other.

She had arched upward as he felt the walls within her contract, the honey-like fluid flowing hot and thick around his fingers. She went wild, caught up in the fire that he'd ignited within her. She was writhing, her fingers digging frantically into his shoulder, telling him how much she was enjoying the feelings now coursing through her. She was lush, so responsive, so damned hot, that he ached to thrust himself into her right now. But Sky's pleasure always came first. *Always.* Cal knew a woman was slower to get turned on than a man. But once a woman was warmed up, prepped, and allowed to soar on a series of orgasms, she could outperform a male by miles. And now, as he eased his fingers from her, she would be more than ready to receive him.

Sky was fearless, Cal had discovered with delight. She liked sex as much as he did. And she wasn't afraid to experiment. Sky trusted him, completely. And that made Cal feel grateful in ways words could never express. He would show her through his care, his protection, and by loving her. Her little cries slowly faded as he felt her collapse back onto the bed, her breath ragged, her eyes dazed looking, telling him she was still on that magic carpet ride of feeling as the multiple orgasms flowed sweetly through her. He cupped her breast, feeling the tautness of it as it rested in his calloused palm. She needed a break. To rest just a little, to catch her breath. Right now, Cal was sure she was feeling super sensitive. In a few minutes, the sensation would ebb, and then he could stimulate her again and give her another orgasm.

Her eyes shuttered closed, and Cal smiled to himself, watching as her wet, slightly swollen lips parted as she relaxed completely in his arms. That sweet expression on her face told him how much he'd pleased her. He lived to gratify Sky. To somehow give her the happiness she'd never had. His erection throbbed. He was hungry for her. But patience was a virtue, and no one knew that better than he did. He'd had tight control over his body as a SEAL and he ruthlessly applied that brute dominance over himself now. The moonlight peeked around the curtains, and the milky radiance flowed across the hills and valleys of her long, slender body. He moved his hand across her pearlescent belly, wondering if her hips were really wide enough to birth a baby. He was a big man. She'd be carrying a big baby in this slender body of hers. The need to impregnate Sky was nearly overwhelming, and it came out of nowhere, stunning him. The desire was so damned strong, it caught him off guard.

"You," Sky whispered, opening her eyes, holding his hooded ones, "are incredible… you make me feel so alive…"

Her wispy words only made him ache even more. "I always want to please you," he growled, kissing her lips lightly, assessing her, seeing if she was ready once more. Just the corners of her mouth curving softly upward, made him ache. If he couldn't get into Sky soon…

"And now? It's your turn…" Her throaty purr damn near had him coming. As she moved against his erection, Cal growled and gripped her hips, bringing her solidly to him, a promise of things to come for both of them. "I'm going gentle with you tonight," Cal warned her, leaning over, lightly nipping her shoulder. He felt Sky shiver, a little sound of pleasure escaping her lips.

"That would be best… it has been a long time…"

"All you need to do is tell me to stop and I will." He saw her nod and saw the gratefulness in her expression. That was all the permission Cal needed. He moved to the exposed nape of her neck, kiss her smooth flesh, feeling her purr. Lifting her hips, she rubbed suggestively against his erection, teasing him mercilessly, trying to steal his massive control away from him. Easing his hands around her, cupping her tight breasts, he felt her sigh and simply collapse against him. Easing her thighs apart as he moved above her, he felt her wetness flooding against his erection pressed at her sweet gate to mind-blowing pleasure.

"I'm taking you," Cal growled near her ear. He felt and heard her breathy laugh.

"I'm more than ready for you…"

Moving against her entrance, Cal felt her hot slickness surround him. Sky pressed boldly against him, trying to lure him into her depths. Gritting his teeth, he settled his hand around her hips, gently positioning her. He slid into Sky, waiting momentarily as her body adapted to accept him. Easing his hips forward, feeling the fist-like tightness of her smaller body grip around him, he again halted and waited. It was worth the hesitation, because as she began moving her hips, challenging him to move even deeper within her, the feeling was incredible. His fingers dug into the soft flesh of her hips, and he drowned in the instant heat that fully surrounded him. A groan tore out of Cal as she began to rock him and he felt himself thrust deep within her, losing all context of reality, his erection was scalded by her body's sweet fluids, held prisoner so tightly within her. Her hips moved with a heightening rhythm. His mind melted and the primal, animal instincts to mate tunneled through Cal. He thrust into her, hearing her cries of pleasure, feeling her walls contract around him, the fluids boiling around him, making him even hungrier to release.

Her rhythm was swift and intense. Cal could feel her body becoming explosive and he knew Sky was as close to orgasm as he was. More than anything, he wanted her to come with him. Simultaneous orgasms were the peak experience for a couple and something that didn't happen often. But it was going to happen tonight, he knew, feeling her body give, accept and accommodate him. Cal felt more animal than human as she took him relentlessly, her hips sweaty, his hands tightening to hold on to her, to keep her angled in a way that gave them both unbelievable, white-hot pleasure.

It felt as if they had melted into one another, and he was unable to tell where one began and the other ended. Sky suddenly cried out and she gripped his shoulders, her lips parting, and Cal heard that raw, wonderful sound lodging in her throat, her body telling him she had orgasmed.

It was then that Cal allowed himself to flow into her. The bolt of burning heat slammed down his spine, rupturing his tightened body against hers. Frozen, Cal couldn't move, only growl, his teeth clenched, his back arching like a bow that had been pulled too taut. And through it all, she moved her hips, drew him in deeper, then pulled away, and pushed back into him. The pleasure spun him into another universe, lights exploding behind his tightly shut lids, his breath jagged, groans tearing out of him as his climax seemed to go on and on forever.

Cal eventually collapsed against Sky. He eased out of her. Gathering her into his arms, holding her, breathing unevenly, sweat sliding between their trembling bodies, he fiercely absorbed her against him. Little sounds of satisfaction trickled up her slender throat as he weakly lifted his head, kissing her lips. This went beyond good. Never had he felt as virile, as powerful as tonight, sharing himself with her. Cal had no idea why he felt like this, but this ranked up there with the best sex he'd ever had in his life. And that was saying something. He felt Sky collapsing within his embrace, sinking into her orgasm, swimming in her own mindless pleasure.

She sighed languidly and sought Cal's embrace, kissing the column of his sweaty neck, seeking and finding his mouth. As she curved her lush lips against his mouth, their breathing ragged, she pressed her hips wantonly against his. Automatically, Cal kissed her with all the passion, all the love, that he held in his heart for her. Sky made him feel as if he'd entered the mythical Nirvana. Her body and heart were a luxuriant garden, overflowing, ripe and willing. Sliding his hand over her hips, Cal cupped her hips and he felt his erection already starting to harden once more. She moved sinuously, like a cat against him, her nipples hard, trailing through the damp silky hair across his chest, her mouth wreaking havoc on his spinning senses.

"Mmmm," she whispered against his mouth, "you are soooo good, Sinclair. You make my body sing…"

Her husky words made his erection strong long before it should have, pressing insistently against her gate once more. "You're insatiable," he growled, drowning in her opening eyes. Cal felt her smile against his mouth, inhaling her warm, moist breath into himself. Sky was life. She was HIS life. The milky light caressed her, shadowing and highlighting the clean, sculptured lines of her features. She was like a beautiful Greek goddess, flawless to him. The love he saw burning in her eyes for him totaled Cal in an unspoken, powerful way. He loved her and he knew she loved him just as much. It didn't get any better than this.

January 27

CAL GOT A call from his CIA analyst friend, Tom Jorgensen. He had just arrived at his apartment after a long day of flying with Sky.

"Hey, Tom," he said, standing in the kitchen with a sat phone, "what have you got on Vladimir Alexandrov?"

"Hello to you too, Cal," he said. "Sorry I wasn't as quick in turning this one around, but we all got grabbed for a crisis over in Ukraine."

"No problemo, compadre," Cal said, sitting down at the table and pulling over a piece of paper and a pen. "Shoot."

"Okay, this guy is a nasty piece of work. He arrived in Russia at age eighteen."

"Yeah," Cal growled, "he was on the run after murdering Sky's foster parents, Jack and Marielle Zimmerman, back in the U.S."

"Right. Well, his father, Yerik Alexandrov, has connections to Spetsnaz.

He was a former Spetsnaz interrogation officer himself, back in his younger years. Vladimir followed in his footsteps and joined the military, moving into Spetsnaz while he was in Russia, avoiding US law enforcement. The last time we talked, I told you the son was in this black ops group."

"Right, and that he went and fought in Chechnya."

"Correct, but the shit I got on him now makes him out to be a sick bastard. He raped Islamic women in front of their husbands, whom he was torturing to get intel out of them."

Cal's nostrils flared. "Twisted."

"Alexandrov is a sadist and a sociopath. He's a sexual predator. He rapes the woman in every way you can imagine. The reports I have on this sicko is that if the woman doesn't die during it, he slits her throat afterward."

Rubbing his face, Cal uttered, "Damn…"

"Yeah, you're playing with fire down there. Alexandrov was in Spetsnaz as a field officer for ten years, earned a lot of medals, killed a lot of Chechens and he murdered hundreds of innocent villagers. To Russia, he's a bonafide hero. To the Chechens, he's a monster with a huge price on his head. After leaving Spetsnaz, Vladimir started to work with his father, Yerik, who by that time held the reins of the Russian Mafia in New York City. He's the kingpin. Yerik is just as sadistic, although he doesn't have his son's sexual mean streak. Since Vladimir was a wanted man in the U.S., Yerik sent his son to South America, where he isn't wanted for anything. Yet."

"How long ago did he leave New York and come down here?"

"A year ago. Yerik is funneling millions of dollars into his son's account in a Lima bank. And what's worse is that Vladimir has twenty men from his former Spetsnaz unit there with him. Now they're drug-running mercenaries working for Yerik. There's an exception on his team. He hired two Ukrainian combat medics: Alexei or Alex Kazak and Nikita or Nik Morozov. They were born in Ukraine, on family wheat farms, and are the best of friends. As young men, they both joined Spetsnaz and were combat medics. Vladimir heard about them and talked them into signing up with his team here in Peru. They refuse to take part in the raping of women or the murder of villagers. Cal, this is a rogue enemy unit even if they aren't in the military anymore. Alexandrov makes the laws, and his men abide by them. The second-in-command, Lev Zuyev, is a sexual predator, like his boss. I got a thick file on him, also. He's no better than Alexandrov and in some ways is worse. He doesn't leave any survivors who might turn him over to law enforcement and identify him."

Cal's lips lifted away from his teeth and hissed a curse.

"I told you, this is ugly. His men are armed with the latest Russian weapons, thanks to his father's money and connections. And the bullets they use are of an armor-piercing variety."

"What's Alexandrov's end game?"

"The bad news is that Alexandrov is making inroads into destroying the two local drug lords who hold the territory where your presently at. Three weeks ago, a CIA field agent posing as a travel writer in Aguas Calientes talked to a scared Quechua drug runner who told him Alexandrov was mapping out each of the trails in the jungle. It doesn't say Alexandrov was a sniper, but he's behaving exactly like one. He's carefully recording each pathway. He puts men at different parts of the trails and watches who uses it. They keep tally of everyone, including taking photos."

"So, he's laying the groundwork to take over the entire region," Cal muttered. He pushed his fingers through his hair in an aggravated motion.

"Exactly."

"What about those two Army Special Forces units? Are they on the ground yet?"

"Yeah, they just HAHO'ed in a week ago."

Cal was familiar with the high altitude, high opening parachute jump from a plane at thirty thousand feet and then opening their parachute right away in order not to be detected when coming into an enemy held area. "WHERE are they?"

"I'll give you their GPS positions. I've got a line into them since I'm on the Alexandrov case. Got a pen?"

"Yeah," he growled, "go ahead. And give me their satellite phone passwords." Cal quickly wrote down the coordinates.

"They have to find Alexandrov first," Tom warned him. "The CIA field agent couldn't get any more out of that Indian. He was scared. He said Alexandrov would kill him and his family if he knew he'd given them even that much intel."

"Is Alexandrov in Aguas Calientes? Do you still have a field agent in place there?" Cal demanded.

"Yeah, our agent has been in place for six months. But this is the FIRST time he's gotten any leads. The Indians down there are scared to death of Alexandrov. No one's talking. Even with money, good money, the Indians can't be bribed into giving us intel."

"Does this agent know where Alexandrov is at? Does he stay in Aguas Calientes? Cusco?"

"No one knows. The case officer thinks Alexandrov and his team come into town disguised as tourists. Our field agent got a photo of this guy, lucky for us."

"Send it to me," Cal growled, "to my laptop. It's got an encoded scrambler and I can receive it no problem."

"Roger, that. Our case officer feels he's working the jungle area right now. That's not good news for you because Sky is flying to those villages who are getting wells. She's not staying overnight at any of these villages, is she?"

"No. She flies in and out of the Cusco airport daily. But Julie, the nurse who works for Helping Hands Charity… well, that is a different problem." Cal got a sick feeling in the pit of his stomach.

"The agent feels Alexandrov is mapping the trails in and around Machu Picchu because that is the territory he wants to eventually claim and take away from those two other drug lords."

"Can you get a satellite fly by to map these trails from above?"

"Hell, we've been trying. The problem is constant cloud cover over the area. Actually, it's mostly ground cover fog. It's hiding a lot of these trails from us. The map guys are slowly piecing it together, but not fast enough for any of us. We're lucky to get an hour or two of clarity a day to see the trails. They're going to switch to infrared satellite. That should help us see those trails."

"How long before that happens?"

"I don't know. I wish I did, Cal."

"Damn…"

"Yeah, my sentiments exactly."

"Okay, send that photo of Alexandrov and anyone else you know who is in his gang. Can you do that? I need eyes on them. I need to put a name to a face."

"Yeah, I got fourteen out of the twenty with photos and military intel."

"Why not send the entire file on Alexandrov to me?"

"I can't do that. I wish I could, but I'm risking my job as it is by working with you as a civilian security agency."

Grimacing, Cal said, "I appreciate whatever you can do for me. Right now, Dylan McCoy and I are badly outmanned and outgunned down here."

"Two ex-SEALs against twenty ex-Spetsnaz isn't exactly good odds. Can you leave the area? Will Sky and this gal, Julie, leave?"

Cal's mouth turned downward. "No, both are refusing."

"What a FUBAR situation."

"Yeah."

"Contact those two Army hunter-killer teams who are setting up shop to operate in our area and introduce them to us? Maybe, if we get in trouble, they might be able to swing some firepower, men or intel our way."

"I'll make it happen. They're on the ground, undercover. Each team has a sat phone and you have the GPS and code for both of them. There's no available helos, high altitude drones or anything else to help them or you out of the hot zone."

"Yeah, I hear you. It sucks not being in the military right now." If they were, they'd have the availability of such logistics to help them in an emergency.

"One good thing," Tom said, brightening. "The Special Forces teams have got Raven drones on them."

"Really?" Cal felt his heart thump hard once to underscore that piece of good news. SEAL teams used the small raven-sized drone all the time on missions.

"I'm going to contact the sergeant in charge of each three-man unit and give them your their sat phone number and photo ID, in case you folks can hook up down there."

"I appreciate that," Cal said, meaning it.

"Okay, I gotta go. I'll be in touch as I get more intel. In the meantime, stay safe down there?"

Grimly, Cal rasped, "You can count on it."

January 27

DYLAN MCCOY SAT at Cal's apartment table, moving through the photo array of Alexandrov's gang, their names, and backgrounds. His face was hard, his hazel eyes narrowed as he looked over at Cal who sat opposite him. "This is a clusterfuck just waiting to happen. You know that."

"No question about it. If those Special Forces teams on the ground run into Alexandrov and his gang, it's going to be like a buzz saw cutting through those Army teams. They have to remain undetected." Cal shook his head, draining his cup of coffee. It was early in the evening, and Julie and Dylan had just flown back to Cusco with him and Sky. Liz was sending Julie away for a week to the U.S. to get her yearly medical check-up. Dylan, in the meantime, had nothing to do, so Cal wanted his thoughts and experience since they'd worked together for years as a team over in Afghanistan. He trusted Dylan with his life and vice versa.

"I've been in contact with both sergeants running those spec op teams," Cal told him. He pulled out pictures from another envelope and handed them over to him. "Here's all six men, their ranks and names."

Hungrily, Dylan went through the photos and the intel, committing it all to memory. "Do these dudes realize Alexandrov has twenty Spetsnaz-trained men with him?"

"They do," Cal said grimly. "Not a job I'd volunteer for if I was those Army grunts."

McCoy agreed. "I know these Army guys are good, but they're in the same boat we are: up against a superior force with better firepower than we've got.

And we have NO backup if things go south."

"And to make this even worse," Cal growled, "there's no logistics available if we get in trouble. I'd sure like a Predator drone available to us, loaded with Hellfire missiles. And the Army operators don't have any, either."

Dylan shook his head, compressing his lips, exhausted emotionally because Julie couldn't be convinced to leave Peru.

Cal stood, getting up and pouring himself another cup of coffee. "I don't know how much to tell Sky. She already knows Alexandrov's M.O., modus operandi. The spooks, the CIA, are just now getting a gander at him and his team's lethality. I want Sky to get the hell out of here now, not later."

Dylan leaned back in his chair, hands resting on the jean fabric across his thighs. "How much of this can I tell Julie?"

Grimacing, Cal slowly paced the kitchen, thinking. "Everything we've been given is top secret."

"At this point," Dylan said wearily, "I'd be able to warn Julie about them in highly general, vague terms, and nothing else."

Cal frowned. "Do you think it will scare Julie enough into leaving?"

"Hell," Dylan muttered, "I don't know. I knew she was committed to this work. But I never knew she had this kind of stubborn streak in her."

"She's not military," Cal told his friend, putting a hand on his shoulder. "If she was, it might make a difference."

"It hasn't with Sky, so far," Dylan said, giving him a narrowed look.

Cal shook his head. "It's different with her. She's staying because she's tired of running from him. I'm not convinced Alexandrov knows she's here. I think if he knew, he'd have been after her immediately. He's been here a year and Sky hasn't been attacked or seen him."

"So? She's staying to face him down? *Mano a mano*?"

Cal smiled faintly. "In a way. Sky wants her life back. I'm willing to stick around and help her make it happen. I'm going to try and find Alexandrov before he finds her. Tom, my spook contact, is feeding me intel on the side, as it comes in. The big problem is the present satellite array can't penetrate that jungle canopy fog. If I could get photos showing him and his men on a certain trail, I could begin tracking him down, but we don't even have that. At least, not yet."

Dylan wearily got up and walked over to pour himself another cup of coffee. He looked around the small, pale-yellow kitchen. Cal had closed the curtains across the only window in the room; a typical black ops reaction. His friend didn't want anyone looking into his apartment. "I feel tied up in knots," he admitted.

"It's a bad situation," Cal agreed, seeing the pain and worry in Dylan's eyes.

"For sure, it's not easy, Cal. I didn't mean to fall in love with her. It just happened." He gave Cal a twisted grin. "Not like when we were in the SEALs, when we had our pick of woman at Coronado. We had a lot of sex, a lot of fun, and no strings attached."

"Yeah, well those days are long gone for you and me," Cal muttered, sitting down.

Dylan gave him a curious look. "You love Sky?"

Grimacing, Cal said, "I try not to call it anything."

Laughing, Dylan shook his head. "Oh, I see, bro. If you don't call it love, it isn't? If you don't say the word, it doesn't count? You're living in la la land. Or ignorance is bliss and all that shit?" and Dylan laughed even harder.

Giving him a sardonic grin, Cal shrugged. "Sky hasn't admitted it, either. I'm not going to force the issue."

Wiping his eyes, Dylan said, "You two are something else. At least I have the balls to admit I love Julie. And vice versa," he added.

"It doesn't make any difference," Cal growled.

"I would NEVER have thought any woman would ever rope you and tie you down."

Cal shot him an irritated look. "I didn't think it would ever happen, either."

Dylan sat down, leaning his elbows on the table, still grinning. "If the guys in our old SEAL team knew this, they'd die of shock on the spot. You're a legend, Cal. Dude, this is rich karma..." and he laughed heartily once more.

Cal gave him a dark look but ignored him and sipped his coffee.

Dylan studied him thoughtfully for a moment. "So? You going to marry her?"

"It hasn't gone that far, yet."

"But if she tells you she loves you, what then?"

Needled, Cal growled testily, "I'm still getting used to the fact she's the one."

Brows shooting up, Dylan marveled, "How do you know it?"

"I knew from them moment I laid eyes on her at our forward operating base. When she flew her Black Hawk in and landed it, I was in Ops delivering some intel from our mission. When she walked in..."

"Remember? I was with you the day she arrived at Ops. You didn't show ANY indication she'd grabbed your attention."

"I've always known which woman was right for me," Cal muttered defensively. "And I'm sure as hell not gonna broadcast it to the world."

"Yeah, but she was no one-night-stand, bro." Shaking his head, Dylan stared at him. "You've always had damned good, honed intuition. You saved our asses out in the Sandbox so many times I lost count because of what you sensed."

"I'm never wrong," Cal muttered, eyeing him.

"No, you weren't. But...," and Dylan looked up, considering for a moment, "to know the woman you're going to love, going to marry, just like that? Pretty heavy duty, brother."

Shrugging, he growled defensively, "Sky is special."

"I know that one. I feel the same way about Julie," Dylan whispered.

"Something's bothering me," Cal said, scowling. "Remember when we were in that Indian village with you and Julie last week?"

"Yeah."

"There's a trail just outside of that village. It's one of the main ones on an east-west axis. Do you remember feeling anything? My neck was taking off. I felt like we were being watched."

"Phew," Dylan said, rolling his eyes, thinking back. "I was distracted, Cal. I don't remember feeling particularly threatened. But you did?"

"Yeah, and I wasn't distracted like you." He suddenly got up, pacing the kitchen, thinking. "What if Alexandrov or some of his men were scoping out that trail? There was a hill about half a mile away from us. What if they saw Sky when we flew in? If they're taking photos, then Alexandrov would see those photos. He'd have them of Julie and Sky."

"I know," McCoy uttered, sitting up, tense. "And if they got the name of the charity off the helicopter, then Alexandrov would easily find out it's based here in Cusco."

Rubbing his jaw, mind racing, Cal growled, "Sonofabitch."

"He's after Sky."

"Yes. And if she's been ID'd in a photo...," and Cal's voice trailed off as he thought about possibilities.

"They'd have photos of us, as well."

Cal snorted. "He won't have the capacity to ID us at all, Dylan. I'm not worried about that." He put the mug on the counter, throwing his hands on his hips. "What I am worried about is if Alexandrov see's Sky's photo, puts two and two together, and he comes to Cusco to find her."

"Is Sky registered under her real name? Or a fake one?"

"I don't know. Probably her real one."

"Would Alexandrov go to Liz's office over at the airport?" There was fear in McCoy's voice as he stared up at Cal.

"It's likely. Thank God Liz is in the U.S. with Julie right now."

"Who's running the office, then?" Dylan demanded.

"Her two office assistants. They're both Peruvian women."

"How easy is it to break into Liz's office?"

Snorting, Cal said, "Too damned easy."

"Does she have a file where she keeps all the employees' names and info?"

"We need to get out there NOW and find out. If for nothing else than to remove the four files on us if we can find them."

Instantly, McCoy was on his feet.

Cal disappeared down the hallway and pulled the SIG Sauer pistol from the dresser drawer in his bedroom. He tucked it in his belt behind his back. Returning to the kitchen, he started formulating his action plan. "Listen, I need to go down and get Sky. I'm going to move her up to my apartment, just in case. The first place Alexandrov will go is to her apartment."

"But won't your address be on file?"

"Might be too soon. I don't know," Cal said.

"I'll be right back," Dylan explained. "Gotta pick up my go bag from my apartment. It's stashed in my closet."

Cal nodded. Every SEAL had a go bag. It held the weapons they might need. "I'll meet you at your place after I get Sky situated up here. I'll need a few minutes to talk with her and fill her in on what's happening. I'll borrow her SUV, pick you up at your place, and we'll go to the airport together."

Twenty minutes later, Cal pulled up outside Dylan's apartment building and took the elevator to the fourth floor. Dylan saw Cal had armed himself well also. He had put on his protective vest and transferred the SIG Sauer into a drop holster low on his right thigh. He sported an H-gear tactical harness that fit around his chest and shoulders, holding eight clips of ammo for the M4 rifle and his pistol. McCoy took two flash bangs and smoke cannisters out of his go bag just in case they were needed.

"Let's rock it out," Cal growled, hefting the bag off the table, hauling it with him. They took the fire exit stairs quickly, walking swiftly to the SUV in the parking lot and driving out into the dark of night.

"How's Sky taking this info?" Dylan asked as Cal drove through the wet cobblestone streets.

"Not good, but she's going to remain in my apartment until I get back."

"She got a weapon on her?"

"Yeah, she's armed, and she knows how to use it."

"Good," McCoy breathed, watching the traffic begin to thin out as they got out of the city and started for the airport. At eight p.m., the airport was shut down, most people gone for the night. "What's the plan?"

"There's a second entrance/exit to the airport. It's closer to the charity hangar. I'll douse the light's once we get in through security. You got your passport?"

"It's on me."

"Good," Cal said, his hands tightening on the wheel. "It's possible Alexandrov has already broken in."

"Or not at all."

Grimly, Cal said, "We'll find out shortly. If our files are a mess in the drawer or missing, then we know he's beat us to it."

CHAPTER 10

January 27

SKY'S HEART JUMPED and adrenaline flowed through her when she heard the three knocks on Cal's apartment door. She'd been pacing like a caged animal, prowling around, her hearing keyed up for any sounds out of the ordinary. Two hours had passed since Cal and Dylan had driven to Liz's office at the Cusco airport.

Heart banging, she wished the door had a peephole so she could make sure it was Cal standing outside of it. He'd set up the three knocks as a way to let her know it was him and not Vlad. Opening the door, her throat tight with tension, she saw him and Dylan, with grim looking expressions, standing there. They quickly made their way inside and she closed and locked the door behind them. They went straight to the kitchen. Following them, she sat down between them.

"What did you find out?" There was an underlying quaver to her voice.

Cal pulled four files out of his go bag and set them on the table. "Alexandrov hasn't been there yet. There was no evidence of the lock being tampered with or jimmied, and the files were all still in alphabetical order."

A slow trickle of relief spread through Sky. "But that just means he's not gotten into the office yet?"

Cal reached out, seeing how pale Sky was. Her eyes were dark with worry, and he sensed her terror although she was fighting to keep it hidden. "Right." He knew Sky was thinking that Alexandrov could hack into the charity's servers and get the information another way. Just because they had the files in hand didn't mean much at all, not in today's computerized world.

Dylan gave her a sympathetic look. "Understand, Sky, we're working off assumptions here. We're assuming that what Cal felt out at that jungle village, that we were all being watched, was accurate. And we're assuming if we were being watched, it was by Vlad. Cal felt a threat, and that is all we have to go on."

She rubbed her face. "It's better to assume it was him. I also felt something out there."

Cal's mouth thinned. "On the way back, I made a sat phone call to Liz and filled her in. I painted the unvarnished picture for her. She's going to encrypt everything on their servers so if Alexandrov hacks in, he can't read the files and find out who's working there. She's setting that up tomorrow morning with her IT team back in D.C."

Dylan added, "And Cal asked Liz to stay in the U.S. and keep Julie there as well."

Sky heard the relief in Dylan's voice and saw it in his eyes. She understood.

Another concern struck Sky, "But there are two laptops and a desktop in Liz's office."

"Not anymore," Cal said. "We took them with us. There's info on all of us on them. I told Liz I was going to erase everything having to do with the four of us and she was okay with it. I'm going to ask Tom, my spook contact, to have one of their intel specialists encrypt everything else on all three computers so the info can't be lifted. That will happen tomorrow, too."

Sky became grim. "Getting all the info encrypted is a good start. It will slow him down if he hacks it."

Cal got up and poured himself coffee. He lifted an empty cup toward them. "You two want coffee?"

"Yeah," Dylan grunted, scowling, "we need a cup," and he saw Sky nod her head.

"I gotta tell you, a pisco sour sounds damned good right now. I want a drink, but I don't dare," Sky muttered. High altitude and alcohol did not mix well. She saw a grin leak into Cal's tightened mouth.

Cal sat down after giving them each a cup of fresh coffee. He exchanged a long look with Sky. "What name did you lease this apartment under?"

"My own, Sky Lambert." And then she gulped. "Oh, God… would Vlad know I've changed my name?"

Cal shrugged. "No way of knowing. But if he was on that hill and saw the writing on the side of the helo's fuselage, he knows you're associated with the charity. And if he can't get evidence to trail you from the office, I'm worried he'll grab one or both of Liz's assistants and torture them to get the information." Cal didn't go on with what else Alexandrov would do to his victims. Sky was shaken enough.

"Did you tell Liz this?"

"Yes," Cal said, sipping his coffee. He looked at her over the rim of his cup. "Liz has already called her two assistants and told them to stay home and NOT go back to the office until she tells them to return. They can work at home for now. They know the office laptop computers have been removed." Cal moved his chin in the direction of his black nylon go bag at his feet.

"They're in my bag. I told Liz I'd keep them until this has blown over."

"Good," Sky whispered, giving them each a tense look. "How is Liz going to run things down here then?"

"She can run it from stateside," Cal said. "She's flying to her headquarters in Alexandria, Virginia. She's already told her father, Senator Standsworth, what's happening."

"Yeah," Dylan said, "and we're hoping the senator can cut loose some more help for us down here. He's the chairman of the Armed Services Committee."

"That would be wonderful if he could," Sky said, giving Cal an optimistic look. She saw him nod.

Cal then set the cup down and laid out his conversation with Tom to her. He avoided the sadism of Alexandrov and his second-in-command, Lev Zuyev. He watched the skin growing tighter across her cheekbones, the darkness in her eyes deepening. She was scared, and he didn't blame her.

"He's got a superior force," Sky said after hearing their intel. "Two of you can't go up against him and hope to win."

"SEALs are good," Dylan said, "but there's a reality check, too. Cal and I wouldn't be able to overcome Alexandrov's force without extra support and information."

Sky got up, unable to remain still. She slowly paced the kitchen, deep in thought. "Cal, what am I going to do about my apartment?"

"It means you're going to leave your apartment," he murmured, giving her an apologetic look. And then he added, "You'll move into my apartment, and I'll go down to the office and give the secretary our assumed married name. That will throw Alexandrov off if he gets to Cusco and tries to find you."

"Okay," she said. "Your idea is sound."

"I'll help you move tomorrow morning," Dylan said. "I'm here under an assumed name, so I can't be traced like you can, Sky."

She stood, arms against her chest. "And I thought I'd be safe down here."

Cal felt for Sky. She wasn't black ops. He was going into that mode right now and was going to make damn sure she was kept safe. "What we need to do right now," he said, "is get to bed and get some sleep." He looked over at Dylan.

"Yeah, me, too," he grunted, getting to his feet. "When do you want to meet tomorrow?"

Cal looked at his watch on his wrist. "It's 2300 now. Let's make it 0700? Come over and I'll make everyone breakfast here at my apartment."

Sky said goodnight to Dylan, thanked him, and then closed and locked the door to Cal's apartment. She felt him come up behind her and she automatically turned. He embraced her.

"It's going to be all right," Cal murmured, holding her, kissing her hair. "You've got to be fried by all of this?"

Her voice was muffled against his chest. "Yes. I keep having moments of sheer terror." She trembled, shutting her eyes tightly. "It's like it was yesterday, Cal. I'm so sick and tired of all of this. Tired of running. I'm so damned angry right now. I want that bastard dead. I'd give anything to kill him myself."

Cal smoothed his hand down her back, feeling the tension in Sky. "My little tiger woman," he teased. Easing her away from him, he said, "I want you to go get ready for bed. You're staying with me from now on. I'm not letting you out of my sight until we can find Alexandrov."

Her eyes widened. "Find him? Are you going AFTER him, Cal?" Her heart arced in fear. She knew how deadly the Russian was and feared for Cal's life. She searched his hard face and realized he was in operator mode right now. The look in his eyes was one of pure intensity and focus.

"That's the plan," Cal murmured, kissing her brow." He turned her around and patted her rear. "Go on, get a bath? I'll stay out here and guard. When you're done, I'll get a shower and you stand guard. Okay?"

Shaken, Sky nodded. She'd brought her robe and toiletries with her when Cal had taken her up to his apartment. "Okay," she whispered.

Sky couldn't go to sleep even though she lay in Cal's arms, her head resting on his shoulder. His bedroom was dark, with only hints of moonlight sifting from around the window drapes. Earlier, she'd seen him place a bullet into the chamber of his SIG and set it on the nightstand where he could easily turn over and grab it. SIG's didn't have a safety and all Cal had to do was lift it and fire.

She felt Cal's fingers trail down her arm. They were naked and Sky absorbed his quiet strength, his calm. His arm was around her shoulders, holding her close.

"You need to try and sleep."

Sky nodded, pressing a kiss to the column of Cal's neck. She inhaled his male scent, and it helped her calm down. "My mind is moving a million miles an hour. Isn't yours?"

"No," he answered. Cal squeezed her a little to reassure her. "We have a plan and the odds of Alexandrov finding this apartment are small. We're safe here, Sweetheart."

The endearment only made her heart ache more. "I'm so damned scared, Cal."

"You've got a right to be," he rasped. "Look," he said quietly, "I know you don't want to hear this, Sky, but I think the best thing you could do is get out of Peru for now. Leave this to me and Dylan."

Sky tensed and slowly sat up, the covers falling around her hips. The moonlight gave her just enough illumination to see his hard face, his glittering eyes. There was nothing soft, tender or loving about Cal right now. She was seeing the SEAL on guard. "I've thought about it," she admitted softly. Moving her hand across his chest, the silky, soft hair across it tangling in her fingers, she sighed. "But… why do you have to stay behind? There's a CIA agent on the ground in Aguas Calientes and two Army Special Forces hunter-killer teams looking for Vlad. Couldn't you leave with me? You and Dylan? This isn't your fight."

Cal felt relief that Sky wasn't going to fight him on leaving Cusco and flying stateside to remain safe. He sat up, resting against his back against the headboard. He picked up her hand, squeezing it. "Because things have changed, Sky." He held her shaken gaze, saw the strain in her face, heard the subtle tremble in her husky voice as she spoke. Cal could see she was trying to be strong, to keep herself together under the circumstances.

"What do you mean?" she demanded. "Nothing's changed! He's still after me, Cal. That's old news."

He gave her a faint smile, rubbing his thumb across the back of her hand. "Everything's changed, Sky. Between you and me." Cal saw her face crumple, tears glisten in her eyes. He held her hand a little tighter. "I've waited my entire life for you, Sky, and I'm not losing you now. If Alexandrov isn't found, you'll always be running. You don't deserve to be hunted down like a dog." His mouth flattened. "I'm putting a stop to it once and for all. That's why Dylan and I will stay behind. We want that bastard dead."

She sniffed, her heart widening with such love for him. "But," she quavered, "he could kill you instead, Cal!"

He gave her a careless smile filled with confidence. "No way, Sweetheart."

"I suppose you and Dylan have already decided this. That you're going after him?"

"Yeah, we're going to work with the two Army Special Forces teams. We've been in touch with them and we're going to coordinate with them and their resources. We're on the northern flank of Alexandrov's area. They're on the southern end of it right now. We're waiting for the CIA to give us infrared satellite photos of those trails through the jungle between us and them. Right now, they are still utilizing the old satellite system that can't see through the fog."

Shaken, she stared at Cal, feeling the warm, dry strength of his hand around hers. "No one's asking you to do this. I haven't. I don't want you out there trying to find that monster."

Cal whispered her name as he coaxed Sky into his arms. She reluctantly came, her eyes filled with anxiety. Only it wasn't for herself, it was for him. He settled her against him, guiding her head to his shoulder and then holding her close. "Listen to me," he rasped against her temple, "we're trained up for this, Sky. You know this better than most. You're ex-military, and you were at Camp Nichols with us."

She slid her hand across his broad, capable shoulder, her heart pounding with dread. "But he's got a bigger force and more fire power than you do, Cal. If you ever got into a firefight with him, you're heavily outgunned."

"Well," Cal murmured, kissing her temple to try and calm her mounting fears, "that may change soon. With Liz going to the Senator, we may well get some more logistical support down here from the U.S.. If we can get a high altitude Pred drone over us, it will be a huge help. That and getting some Apache helicopter protection in case we need to call them in for their firepower."

"But Peru doesn't allow US combat weapons or military assault helos in their country," she protested.

Cal took a deep breath and said, "There is a history of it. There was an Apache squadron down here, very close to Machu Picchu. They had a huge cave complex where the helos were protected from everyone's sight. They flew day and night missions out of there to stop the drug runners. The woman who created the plan, Army Major Maya Stevenson, had an all-woman pilot Apache squadron. Now," Cal said, his voice turning amused, "it was all top secret and the Peruvian government HAD given their permission for them to operate in this area. So, I lobbied Liz to get her father to try and bring down at least two Apaches and utilize that cave complex again. It's a perfect spot for them and it's in the operational area where Alexandrov is at presently."

A breath escaped Sky and she lifted her head, meeting Cal's dark, gleaming eyes. "That would be a huge help."

"Yeah, but it's not reality yet. I'm going to contact Senator Standsworth directly sometime tomorrow. Liz gave me his sat phone number. She's a lynchpin in all of this, Sky. I hope she can persuade her father to bring military assets and logistics to bear to find that bastard. And because it's his little girl who is down here in Cusco, who is a target by proxy, the senator has a personal, vested interest in finding Alexandrov and his gang sooner, not later. Liz is spitting nails that she can't come back down here until this situation is cleared up. She's like Julie: a pit bull when it comes to being of service to those in need."

Sky sighed and laid her head on his shoulder, closing her eyes. "They're passionate about their commitment to helping others."

"Yeah," he drawled, "but not at any cost. Giving their lives for it isn't part of the deal they signed up for."

Her nostrils flared and she dragged in his scent, a mix of male with his recently used soap that reminded her of the piney fragrance of the Rocky Mountains. Right now, Sky wished they could both be out of here. "No," she murmured, "no one should be murdered for helping others."

"But it happens with these NGO's," Cal growled. "One example is that there were too many innocent lives lost over in Afghanistan when the NGO's were there. They finally got smart and pulled out."

"Yes, I remember that all too well." Sky's heart was in turmoil. She didn't want to lose Cal. Lose what they had just claimed with one another. She fought her anger and felt tears stinging her eyes. Her voice was with low with emotion. "Cal... I'm so afraid. I'm more afraid for you than myself." She sat up, his arm moving around her waist as he studied her. "We've just found one another," and her voice broke. She saw Cal's face melt, his mouth flex, his eyes growing warm with sympathy.

"Hey," he rasped, sliding his hands around her face, holding her tearful gaze, "We'll be fine down here." He felt her quiver. The fear in Sky's eyes tugged at his heart. "I know you're worried," Cal said thickly, kissing her mouth lightly, "but I've survived just fine in the SEALs and come through all kinds of situations unscathed, Sky. Besides, our boss, Jack Driscoll, is working with Tom, my CIA contact. Jack has influence in places he doesn't, and I know he's working with a special mission team back at his HQ in Virginia to come up with more support for Dylan and me, plus those Army Special Forces teams who are already in the area."

He eased back just enough to hold her glistening eyes. Sky held his heart whether she knew it or not. But Cal didn't want to add that stress to her right now. Later, when they got past this challenge, he'd sit her down and confess his love for her. Cal had dreams of telling her about his two-story cedar cabin in the Virginia countryside, a home he dreamed would be hers as well. But right now, above all, he was committed to finding and killing Alexandrov. She could never relax, never let her guard down, until the bastard was taken permanently out of her life. Cal knew he could give Sky her freedom. Only then he could watch the terror leave her eyes, the tension that always hovered around her dissolve, and finally see Sky truly at peace.

CHAPTER 11

"I F I'M NOT flying the helicopter anymore," Sky told Cal the next morning at the kitchen table, "I'm going to have to speak with the mechanics and get it properly mothballed at the hanger. I need to call them and schedule that maintenance today."

Dylan McCoy sat with them at the breakfast table, sipping coffee. "Can't you just call it in?"

Shaking her head, Sky said, "No. I have to sign off on certain procedures within the cockpit or the FAA will hit me with violations. There are things I have to do or oversee that a mechanic isn't allowed to do. And all the paperwork is sent to the FAA. I can't risk losing my license, Dylan. I've got to be there."

"I'll take you up there," Cal grunted. He cleared away the plates and silverware, setting them on the kitchen counter.

"Everything's happening so fast," Sky muttered more to herself than them. Cal had already had a conversation with Senator Standsworth. He'd called at 0600, waking them from their too-brief slumber. Cal snapped awake when his sat phone buzzed, and Sky listened to the long, involved conversation. The good news was that the Peruvian government had approved an Army Black Hawk flown by two Night Stalker pilots along with their mechanics and software crews to be flown in. They nixed the Apache gunships and the Predator drone. It would take a day for the Black Hawk team to arrive at Cusco. A high-altitude drone was being rerouted to start a racetrack high in the sky over the Peruvian Highlands and jungle area. It was armed with infrared cameras to detect body heat even through the cloud cover. By the end of today, it would start its flight duties in their region. The non-weaponized drone was coming in from an Ecuadorian CIA station and would arrive shortly over that area. That made Cal very happy. Where there was body heat, there were human beings or animals. An analyst looking at the video could easily tell the difference and then alert them via sat phone potential targets. One of those infrared blips could turn out to be Alexandrov and his men. Sooner or later, they would be found.

As Sky had climbed out of bed to take a quick shower, Cal got on the sat phone with the two Special Forces teams on the ground. They were relieved to have a high-altitude drone coming in as well. It would make their job of hunting down Alexandrov, a lot easier. Just as she emerged from the bathroom, dressed in a bright red tee, jeans, and her flight boots, Cal received a call from Tom, his CIA contact. He wanted to know how Cal had gotten those assets cut loose so quickly to help them down in Peru. Cal explained that the Chairman of the Senate Armed Forces Committee had done it, to aid the situation for his daughter who operated her NGO in the area. Everyone was thrilled with the changes that would help them now and in the future.

Sky noticed that Dylan didn't look very well. Pale, maybe. Sad? She reached over, briefly touching his shoulder. "Are you okay, Dylan? Do you feel sick?"

Dylan roused himself. "No... no, I'm okay."

Cal shot his SEAL brother a dark stare. "You look like shit warmed over. What's going on?"

Sky squelched a smile and sat back, letting Cal pry open his friend. McCoy hadn't eaten half as much as Cal did at breakfast.

Running his hands through his brown hair, Dylan muttered, "Julie called me late last night."

Frowning, Cal sat down, his gaze never leaving his friend's face. "And?"

"She's flying back down here today. She'll arrive at Cusco at ten a.m."

"What?" Sky gasped. "Oh... no... she can't, Dylan! It's too dangerous!" and she nearly came out of her chair if not for Cal holding his hand over her forearm.

Cal growled, "That makes no sense..."

Dragging in a broken sigh, Dylan shook his head. "She's like a horse with blinders on. She's upset that Liz wanted her to remain stateside. And then, when she found out that Sky was leaving today and there would be no pilot to make the rounds to the villages, she thew a tantrum. She's worried that no one with medical experience is here, and a lot of children who are sick right now and a few will die without continued medical intervention. Liz has already hired a male R.N. to take over Julie's circuit, but he won't be down here for a week."

"She can't come back down here, Dylan," and Sky gave Cal a terrified look.

"Can you meet her at the Cusco terminal?" Cal demanded. "As soon as she gets off the plane, confront her? Hell, I'd be buying her a ticket right now and turning her right back around that turnstile and get her out of here as soon as possible. Get any flight to Lima for her, Dylan. She'd be safe down there, but not here in Cusco."

"Look," Dylan muttered, weary, "Julie broke off our engagement last night…"

Gasping, Sky teared up as she saw the raw grief surface on Dylan's face. He didn't try to hide it. She gripped his hand. "I'm so sorry, Dylan. Maybe… this is just a misunderstanding? If you could just talk to Julie after she lands? She loves you! I know she does. Don't give up on her. Okay?" and she choked, her emotions swamping her.

"Damn," Cal muttered blackly, pushing his chair back from the table. He rose in one fluid motion, moving to the sink where he placed his hands on the counter, glaring at the curtains across the window.

Miserably, Dylan uttered, "Sky, I tried EVERYTHING with Julie last night. I apologized. I told her I loved her. I begged her to stay stateside for her safety."

"Didn't she realize you love her enough to want to protect her?" Sky asked, shaking her head, disbelieving her friend would do that to him.

"Look," Dylan rasped, "I don't understand what's going on with her. Liz tried to convince her too. She told Julie it was too dangerous to come down here right now and continue her medical circuit. And then, when Julie found out you were leaving today, that did it. Something snapped in her. I can't explain it… She's not thinking rationally."

Sky shot Cal a desperate look as he turned toward them, hands on his hips, his eyes angry. "Maybe I should stay, Cal?"

"Hell no," he growled. "You're leaving today Sky. I don't know what's with Julie. This is NOT good. She's completely untrained and unprepared for this evolving situation." His mouth turned down and he glared over at McCoy. "I don't care what you have to do, but when you meet her at that plane today, you kidnap her and make damn sure she can't take off for the Highlands."

"She's already lined up another helo ride down to the villages," Dylan said quietly. "Julie knows the players here at the airport and she's hired another pilot to fly her in to pick up the medical supplies and take her to those villages."

"Guys," Sky whispered, getting up and standing between them, "maybe there's another way? How about if I meet Julie at the gate? Take her to the cafe that's up on the second floor of the main terminal and try and talk some sense into her?"

Both men glanced at one another and then looked at Sky.

"Okay," Cal growled, his voice vibrating with anger. "That's a better plan."

"Yeah," Dylan said, "maybe it takes another woman to get through to her, but Liz couldn't." McCoy rubbed his temple, a headache coming on. "Julie worships Liz. And if she refused to hear Liz's reasons for staying stateside and blew them off, I don't know what ELSE you can say to persuade Julie to turn around and get a flight out to Lima, Sky."

"At least let me try?" and Sky gave Cal a pleading look. She knew he was going to stick to her side like glue, his M4 in his hands until she got on the last flight out just before dusk. He wasn't going to let her go anywhere without him. In the terminal, there was no way he could show up carrying an M4 rifle. Any automatic weapon was not allowed in Peru. Luckily, he and Dylan, as well as herself, had permission to carry concealed pistols in the country's government. But to show them off in public would be a disaster. Cal would have to settle for his SIG tucked in his waistband beneath his jacket if he accompanied her to the airport.

Cursing, Cal said, "We don't need this! Not right now. We don't know if Alexandrov is around or not. If he is, and we expose ourselves out in public, we're all targets, Sky."

Dylan looked hopeful as he held Sky's gaze. "I know it's a risk," he said, his voice thick with emotion, "but I'd do ANYTHING to get Julie to leave as soon as she could."

"Okay, then," Sky said firmly, "I'll do it." Cal said nothing else. Love made people make bad decisions, Sky realized. And Julie had been one of her closest, dearest friends. For her to break off the engagement though, came as a shock to Sky. And it was a traumatic life-changer for Dylan, whose bleak-looking expression made her heart wring with sadness for him.

"She doesn't even realize she's putting ALL of us in jeopardy by being so damned pig-headed," Cal growled, stalking to the living room, shaking his head.

Sky gave Dylan a sympathetic look, silently asking him to remain where he was. She knew Cal well enough that when he got upset, he needed to be alone to work it out. And Dylan probably already knew that, because he gave her a slight nod and sat back in the chair, his face a pool of devastation.

"It's all set," Sky told Cal, getting off the sat phone. The apartment was quiet in comparison to an hour ago. Dylan was already on his way to the airport, and she was going to have to follow soon. Cal was sitting at the kitchen table, cleaning his weapons, a hardness to his expression. He looked up when she placed the sat phone on the table.

"When can the mechanics start to work on that bird?" Cal demanded, wiping down the pieces of his SIG in front of him.

Sky grimaced. "This afternoon. I asked the head mechanic to hang around instead of going home after lunch. Told him I'd pay him extra and bring him a sack lunch." She smiled a little, trying to relieve the tension she felt in the apartment. Cal was on war footing. He was intense and focused. His gaze was alert and flinty looking. Sky understood the need for him to be like that.

"How long is that going to take?"

"About an hour, more or less." She tried to sound upbeat. "I'll have plenty of time before we have to drive over to the domestic terminal to meet Julie."

Grunting, Cal swiftly put his pistol back together with years of experience. Everything was muscle memory at this point. He glanced up and saw her expression. "I'm sorry you're getting dragged into this, Sky. This isn't your fight." And dammit, he wished like hell he hadn't agreed to let her talk to Julie. His intuition was shrieking at him that Alexandrov was hot on their trail, that it was just a matter of time until he found Sky. He knew a Spetsnaz-trained soldier was just as stealthy and competent as any SEAL. Worse, some of them were amoral killers. There was no ROE, Rules of Engagement, with those men. No Geneva Convention rules, either They were the law unto themselves, and they were more than willing to kill any civilian who stood in their way.

Sky moved behind him, encircling him with her arms and resting her head against his shoulder. "I'm sorry too. I know how upset you are."

"Aren't you?" Cal growled, wiping his hands off with a clean cloth.

She pressed a kiss into his back, inhaling his maleness, her senses stirring. "I'm sad for Dylan. He's a wonderful person, Cal. And I'm puzzled by Julie's behavior. I don't understand why she broke off the engagement to Dylan."

He turned around and captured her hands. "Maybe she realized she doesn't really love him."

"Always to the point," she murmured. Sighing, Sky admitted, "I thought of that, too. I just didn't have the heart to suggest that to Dylan."

"He already knows," Cal said bluntly. "He's been around. Dylan loves her, but Julie may have realized she really doesn't love him. Maybe it took this crisis for her to realize it?"

"Perhaps. I don't think anyone saw this coming," Sky whispered, closing her eyes, feeling very old and very tired right now. All she wanted was to have this over with. The thought of getting on a plane and leaving Peru lifted her spirits, but her heart was heavy with dread for Cal. He and Dylan were on the hunt for Vlad. Someone would die and she didn't want it to be Cal, Dylan, or those Special Forces guys. But she knew Vlad's deadly intensity. She'd seen the look on his face when he'd lifted that Glock and shot her foster parents. He'd been smiling. An iciness worked through her.

"Hey," Cal murmured, releasing her hands tucking her against him, "you doing okay? This is hard on you, too."

Sky sat down on his lap after he'd led them to the kitchen chair. She slid her arm around his shoulders, trying to give him a smile, but failing. "I'm jumpy, Cal. Freaked out if you want to know the truth. I feel Vlad's nearby. It's nothing I can prove, but honest to God, I can feel him coming for me."

Nodding, Cal embraced her. Sky nuzzled him. He felt her relax, a soft, ragged sigh escaping from her lips. "You're tired from running from that bastard," he ground out, moving his hand against her nape, beginning to massage the area. Cal heard her moan and become putty in his hands. Inhaling her scent, the almond fragrance of her shampoo, he smiled a little. "You know what?"

"What?" Sky sighed, feeling her tight muscles unknot beneath his coaxing fingers.

"You're a very, very brave person, Sky. I hope like hell Julie realizes how much of a friend you are to her. You're risking your own life to warn her."

"She's a good person, Cal."

"So are you, but you have far more sense than she does."

"Julie is committed."

"She's a damned fanatic."

"Julie sees herself as a champion of those who have so little. She's done so much to ease people's suffering here in Peru, Cal, helping save children's lives. What price do you put on that? Julie can't stand to see people suffer."

"Julie needs her head examined."

Laughing softly, Sky shook her head. "Don't hold back. Just tell me how you feel."

Cal moved his fingers across Sky's tight shoulders, feeling them relax beneath his coaxing. "I may be blunt, but I'm honest, Sweetheart." Sky moaned, a sound of utter pleasure riffling through him. More than anything, she trusted him. Fully. Cal was so damned grateful, feeling like a man who was overwhelmed with gifts. Sky had become the sun in his life. She lifted him from that dark place he always lived in. Made him laugh. Her kindness had softened him. There was nothing weak or cowardly about Sky. *Nothing.* She deserved someone like him. She deserved to be loved breathless, to be held and cherished for every minute of the rest of her life. Cal was committed to her. Only death would remove him from her life now.

Sky wanted to lay against Cal and absorb him on every possible level. She was flying out at dusk, and she had no idea when she would see him again. It made her sad. And it worried her.

"I have a gift for you," Cal rumbled, sliding his hand down her back and patting her rear.

"You do?" and Sky lifted her head, meeting his hooded eyes. Her neck and back felt like warm butter, soft, and relaxed after his massage.

"It's something you'll need when you get stateside," he said, digging into his cargo pant pocket. Pulling it out, he said, "Open your hand."

Sky held out her palm. Cal placed a security pad for his home into it. She frowned and gave him an inquiring look. "What's this?" Cal had insisted she make a one-way ticket from Cusco, Peru, to Washington, D.C. He hadn't said why, what the plans were when she arrived.

He wrote down a set of numbers on a note pad, tore off the paper, and handed it to her. "This security pad is to my cabin I built by hand outside of Alexandria." Cal slid his hand around her waist, drawing her against him, watching her brows dip down as she studied the electronic pad.

"I'm looking forward to seeing your cabin."

He grunted. "When you get to Reagan International Airport, Jack Driscoll will pick you up at the airport and take you to your new home." Cal drew a photo of Jack from his pocket and placed it in her palm. "This is what he looks like. He'll get your luggage and then he's going to drive you up to our cabin." He saw her brows rise in surprise. "It took me seven years to build the place, one log at a time. It's where I go when I'd get off SEAL deployment and have sixty days of leave on my hands. It was my therapy if you will. After I left the SEALs and I went to work for Jack, I was able to finally finish it. I've always liked being in the mountains of Virginia, absorbing the quiet and the woods around me." Cal saw her eyes glisten, her face soften with emotion. Tears always tore him up, but he was never going to tell Sky not to cry. She had a lifetime of tears to get rid of and Cal understood that she'd never really had a home of her own. She did now.

"Well," he prodded, "will you be there waiting for me when I get home?" and he held her gaze, seeing how much she was impacted by his gift.

A lump formed in her throat. Sky's chest tightened. "Oh, Cal...," and she gave him a distressed look.

"I want you there, Sky, when I come home. It's a beautiful place. A healing place. It's calm, like me," and he grinned a little. "There's a nice little creek in the meadow below my home. You can sit beside it come Spring and watch the fish swim by."

Shock rolled through her. "I guess," she whispered off key, "I could find a job as a helo pilot while I wait for you?"

"No way," he said. "Until we can catch Alexandrov, I want you somewhere safe. Jack has his facility nearby and you'll have them as your guard dog. My cabin is wired with the latest surveillance, and there's a perimeter security alarm system a half a mile around it. You'd know in a heartbeat if someone was coming and so would Jack's people, who monitor it at Shield HQ. All the alarms are connected directly with his security company's monitoring system. He has women and men manning those computers twenty-four hours a day. They'd SEE who was coming, what kind of car, the license plate and anything else. And if it didn't conform with the known car type and plate they have on file, they're on it. You'd be alerted within a minute or two of them discovering the intruder. And," Cal added, frowning, "if it became necessary, Jack would place a former SEAL operator at the cabin itself, to keep you safe until I returned."

Nowhere in the world was safe for her, Sky realized, once more. She saw the seriousness in Cal's shadowed eyes, heard it in his deep voice. "Okay, I can do this. You're right, I should go to ground until Vlad is caught."

"Killed," Cal said, the word gritted out with finality.

The corners of her mouth tucked inward. Her fingers closed around the security pad, and she gave him a soft look. "You've thought of everything, haven't you?"

"Sky, you're my life. I'll protect you or die trying." And then he added, "I'm not intending on dying so don't give me that stricken look, okay? I'm coming home to you."

She chewed on her lower lip, nodding, feeling the weight of the pad in her hand. This was her future with Cal. He'd never said he loved her. It was too soon. And there were so many challenges facing them right now. The words wanted to tear out of her mouth and Sky forcibly stopped them. She didn't want him to worry, didn't want it to become a distraction. Holding his intense gaze, seeing the love in his eyes, Sky felt torn and joyous all at the same time. Love wasn't easy. It was a mine field. There was such pain. But the happiness was equal to it, too. "I won't worry," she lied, making her voice sound steady and light. "You can take care of yourself. You have Dylan at your side. You've worked as a team before, and you'll find Vlad. I know you will." Would he believe her? His eyes changed, became a lighter brown, telling her he did. They only got dark when he was upset or worried.

"Okay," he murmured, adding a business card. "Here's Jack's private cell phone number. I'm sure he'll be there to pick you up at the airport, but just in case, you can always connect with him."

"Will I have contact with you, Cal?"

He nodded. "Yeah. Jack's going to loan you a company sat phone when you arrive. He'll have my number and his number locked into it, as well. Don't call me, though. Let me call you?"

Nodding, Sky understood why. She could distract him at the wrong time. "You know how much I'll look forward your calls?" She saw him give her a male grin.

"If I could reach through that phone and love you, I would."

She caressed his cheek, feeling the stubble beneath her fingertips. Tipping her chin, she searched and found Cal's mouth, feeling him tense, his arms coming around her, rough and strong, claiming her. Sky unraveled as he cupped her breast beneath her tee. She never wore a bra, just a camisole, because her breasts were small, and she hated bras anyway. Cal's fingers slid provocatively around the curve, teasing the nipple, sending heat sheeting down through her. She moaned, the sound drowning in his mouth as he breathed it into him. His hand roamed lower, sliding between her jean-clad thighs. He began slowly rubbing the area and she gasped, breaking the kiss, feeling the surge of wetness beneath his knowing, coaxing fingers. Gripping his shoulders, she felt the gnawing yearning for him begin. "Cal…," Sky managed, closing her eyes, sinking against him, opening her thighs wider to him, "this isn't fair…."

He chuckled darkly. "I told you, Sweetheart, a woman's entire body is an erogenous zone." Cal gave her an intent look and then stood up, bringing her into his arms. "Come on," he growled, "we have time for one more round of loving before we have to leave…"

Laughing softly, Sky shook her head and placed her arms around his shoulders as he carried her easily through the living room. "I think we're sex addicts."

"Ask me if I care…"

Her laughter floated down the hall as he nudged open the door to his bedroom. There wasn't a day that went by when he didn't want to be inside Sky, feeling her sweet grip, those scalding fluid surrounding him, driving him off the edge of the universe. Sky had no idea just how sexy she was, but Cal was going to let her know just how much she turned him on and inside out. This time, though, their last time together in Peru, was for her. Only for Sky. As Cal sat her down on the bed, drowning in the heat of her smile, that fearless look she gave him, he began to undress, dropping the clothes to the floor, not caring where they landed. Her fingers were trembling as she pulled off her tee, exposing those small, perfect breasts of hers, the nipples already pushing against the silk of her white camisole, telling Cal she wanted him too. It felt good to be wanted like this. Cal had never spent more than a few hours with any woman. With Sky, he wanted to spend a lifetime…

CHAPTER 12

January 28

THERE WAS A haunted look on Julie's face when Sky met her at the exit from the security area of the Cusco airport. Dark shadows were beneath her pale blue eyes, her hair seemed uncombed, and she didn't look to have taken good care of herself. Sky forced a smile as she approached. Julie always wore jeans, a dark green tee, hiking boots and an old Levi jacket that had a colorful horse embroidered on the back of it. She loved horses and horseback riding, having grown up on her parents' large Virginia farm.

"Hey, how was the flight?" Sky asked, coming forward and giving her a gentle hug.

"Okay. I didn't expect anyone to meet me here," and she warily looked around.

"Dylan told me you were coming in and I wanted to see you, Julie." Sky frowned. "You look very tired. Are you all right?"

She grimaced and shrugged, pulling the red canvas bag with a white cross on the side of it over her left shoulder as they walked. "Yeah, just a long flight." Julie chewed on a fingernail, looking around again. "Where's Dylan?"

Sky heard the pain in her hushed tone. Julie didn't have a loud voice. It was wispy and reminded Sky of the way a sweet flower fairy might sound. There was something ethereal about Julie. There always had been. She was even thinner than she was before, despite her curviness. "He's with Cal," she said quietly. That wasn't a lie. They were here in the airport, just unseen for now. Once they got to the lobby, she pulled Julie to a stop. "Can we stop and get some coffee at the cafe upstairs? I'll buy?" Tension thrummed through Sky. Vlad could be nearby. She felt him.

"Yeah, sure. I've got the time." Julie pushed her fingers through her red hair that lay about her shoulders. "I'm starving to death. I hate airline food."

Smiling, Sky slid her arm through Julie's. "No argument there. Come on...," and she walked with her toward the stairs that would take them to Cafe Lindo in the domestic terminal. It was a relatively quiet, upscale restaurant with decent food. She noticed Julie walked without much energy. She seemed beaten down. Depressed because she broke off the engagement to Dylan? Most likely. As they traversed the busy airport, major flights arriving one after another, taking advantage of the favorable winds, Sky saw Cal and Dylan out of the corner of her eye. Julie seemed unaware of just about everything. The two ex-SEALs looked like travelers, each carrying a shoulder bag. Dressed in their American tourista fare, they blended into the crowds who were coming and going.

At the restaurant, Sky selected a black leather booth at the rear of the restaurant, near an exit door. Cal had insisted she find one nearby in case they needed to escape in a hurry. As Julie scooted into her side of the booth, Sky kept her back to the wall and saw the two men go to the bar, keeping an open line of sight on them and the entrance from the domestic terminal.

The waiter came over. Julie ordered coffee, fresh fruit, and toast. Sky had already eaten but ordered coffee.

"So," Sky said, folding her hands on the table and holding Julie's exhausted gaze, "what's going on between you and Dylan?" For a moment, Julie teared up and she wiped her eyes with her shaking fingers. Sky felt badly about asking, but she had to know.

"Look," Julie said quietly, putting her elbows on the table, her hands on her chin, "there's something I have to tell you, Sky." Julie sniffed. "You've known me for years now, right?"

"Yes." Sky watched her dig into her canvas bag and pull out a tissue. Julie blew her nose and blotted her eyes. "But I've never seen you like this, Julie. Something's wrong. I can sense it." Sky gave her a pleading look. "I'm your friend. You can talk to me."

Julie crumpled wearily against the back seat of the booth. She stared at her. Wiping her eyes, she stammered, "I have incurable brain cancer. I found out last week when I flew home with Liz. I was getting headaches. I couldn't figure out what was wrong." Julie swallowed hard. "I went in for an MRI and the doctor found a cancerous growth in a part of my brain that cannot be touched by radiation or chemotherapy. And if they tried to operate on me, it would kill me. It's inoperable." She cleared her throat and added hoarsely, "They say I have six months to live. I-I wanted to spend three of them down here, doing what I love doing, Sky."

Staggered, Sky sat back, shock rolling through her. Julie was twenty-nine years old. She should have had a whole lifetime ahead of her. Blinking, she asked, "Then… does it affect you emotionally?" She was thinking of the exaggerated reaction Julie had when Dylan begged her to leave Peru.

Nodding, Julie said, "Yes, it's starting to interfere with my normally very placid, happy personality," and she forced a smile that broke.

"Getting suddenly angry at Dylan?"

Julie hid her face behind her hands, struggling to capture her emotions. Taking several deep, calming breaths, Julie let her hands fall to her lap. "That's what got me to tell the doctor in the states about my unexpected mood swings. It wasn't like me to ever be angry with Dylan. I had a horrible headache that day and I never told him about it. Between the pain and what he asked of me, which shocked me to my soul, I just lost it." She gave Sky a sad look. "He didn't deserve what I've done to him, Sky. He's there to protect me. I know that. But the tumor, as it presses on the frontal lobe of my brain, I get overly emotional. I'm not able to fully reason out my reactions and decisions."

"Then," Sky whispered painfully, "when Dylan talked to you the other day? Why did you break off the engagement, Julie? He loves you. You KNOW that."

Tears welled up in Julie's eyes and she compressed her lips and hung her head. "I don't deserve him, Sky. He's been the most kind, the gentlest man I've ever known. We were so happy…"

"Then why break off your engagement?" Sky asked, her voice dropping with agony.

Julie pulled on her reserve strength and stared at Sky. "Because I'm going to die. Because I don't want to be an invalid, a vegetable that he thinks he has to take care of, watching me rot away one brain cell at a time day in and day out."

Stunned, Sky had no words as she saw the anguish in Julie's eyes. Swallowing hard, she opened her mouth, but nothing came out. She watched Julie putting up her walls, trying to protect herself from whatever she might say.

"It's better this way, Sky."

Mouth quirking, Sky whispered, "Maybe you should let Dylan be the decider of that? You've not told him about your condition yet?"

Shaking her head, she muttered, "No. And I'm not going to. And you aren't telling him, either Sky." She tapped her index finger on the table. "This is between you and me only."

"But, Dylan is suffering so much, Julie. He's so confused—"

"I'm not going to tell him! I'm not going to force him to stay with me, feed me baby food and watch me rot like a banana from the inside out."

"Do your parents know?"

"Yes. When the time comes, I'll go home. They'll take care of me," she whispered.

"Oh," Sky said, her voice cracking, tears coming to her eyes. "I'm so very sorry, Julie." She reached out, sliding her hand into hers, squeezing it gently. "What can I do? You know I'll support you any way I can."

"Liz said you're leaving later today to go stateside?"

Sky nodded.

"Do me ONE favor, Sky. Could you fly to the U.S. on another day? Get your ticket changed so you can fly me into Kurmi? I've got a helo and pilot rented to fly me, but that's three days from now. You could get me there in time. There are three babies there that are in desperate need of IVs or they're going to die of dysentery because of the bad water. I've brought new medical supplies with me. We can load them into your helicopter, and you can fly me there much sooner than the other pilot can. I'll just cancel my trip with him."

Blinking, Sky's mind spun. "But... that's in the area where Vlad is at."

"He's not after me, remember? He's after YOU."

Stung, Sky held on to her anger. It wasn't like Julie to be snarly and aggressive like this. She calmed herself. It had to be the brain tumor's influence. "You're right, he is."

She shrugged and made a face. "What's he going to do? Kill me?"

Feeling as if she'd been slapped, Sky sat for a moment, watching the anger leap to Julie's eyes. This simply was not her like her to be like this. "It's what he does before he kills you that is horrifying," she managed, her voice cracking. "He rapes, he tortures women..." Julie looked at her as if she didn't care. She was dying. Had she lost all fear of death?

"I'll be okay. Liz told me she is finding a permanent replacement male pilot who flies helos. She hopes to have another pilot to take over your duties within the next week. I can stay at that village until the hired guy can pick me up and fly me to the other villages."

"But—"

Julie made a cutting gesture with her hand. "Dylan said no one knew where Alexandrov was. Has that changed, Sky? Do you know where this ghost is at?"

Miserably, Sky shook her head. "No... we don't know. Only... a sense that he's out there somewhere. Cal is sure he's in the area near the villages you and I service."

"Then given my death sentence," Julie said strongly, "and that no one has seen this dude, I'm going. I've been here for years and he's apparently been in the area for at least one year, and we've never run into one another." Her mouth twisted. "Logic tells me luck is on my side, Sky. I'll take my chances. I want to spend three months being a nurse, giving life, not losing it. I want to die knowing I served, knowing I made a difference in struggling people's lives. Please fly me out there today or tomorrow at the latest? Do this one, last thing for me? Because we're friends?"

Squirming inwardly, Sky kept her emotions off her face. Julie was changing without warning. "Do you think you can be a competent nurse out there under the circumstances, Julie?"

"I talked to my cancer team," she muttered. "They said if I saw abrupt, severe personality changes, to come home. Until then, I can still add, subtract, run a computer, talk, and chew gum at the same time, and make sense. None of those functions are impaired, yet. If they are? I'll leave Peru. I won't endanger my patients. Liz agreed with me on this approach."

Pushing her fingers through her hair, Sky said, "Look, I need to talk to Cal about this. And Dylan. You know they're staying behind to find Vlad?"

"No, but I figured they would. I know Cal wants you out of here and I think it's a smart idea, Sky. But can you fly me into that village later this afternoon or tomorrow at the latest?"

"Yes, I can do that…" She would have to call the mechanic and tell him to stop the mothballing process that would take place at noon. And, instead have him prepare the helo for flight, instead. "Cal would come along, too. He won't leave my side. Not now."

Julie frowned. "All right then, maybe Dylan can stay behind to guard me. I'll have to find out." Her voice wobbled. "Sky, I love him so much! It hurt me to break off the engagement, but it's best."

"Listen to me," Sky said, gripping her hand, giving it a small shake, "Dylan loves you. I can't speak for him, but I'm pretty damned sure he'd want to be at your side all the way through these three months here in Peru, Julie. He's a SEAL. He's seen everything. If anyone could handle this situation, it's Dylan."

"B-but I'm so afraid to face him! I'm living in terror of seeing how much I've hurt him," and Julie pressed her hands to her face. "He's suffered enough, Sky."

Sky shook her head. "If you love someone, you want to be with them no matter what kind of shit happens to them. Dylan has handled a lot in his life and survived it. You're going to need someone like him. He'll be the strongest support you'll ever have." Cal had shown her this in the short time they had shared their lives together. He fed her strength, confidence, and hope. Sky knew Dylan did something similar for Julie.

Sniffing and wiping her tears away, Julie saw the waiter approach with their food order, interrupting them.

"Look," Sky said after the waiter left, "I need to make a phone call to Cal and Dylan. I can't just fly off without him and I won't. I'll be back in a few minutes?"

"Yeah, sure," Julie managed, staring at the food, not hungry at all.

Sky took a deep breath as she hurried out of the restaurant and walked far enough into the domestic terminal so that Julie could not see her. She turned to look around. Cal and Dylan were walking up to meet her. Moving to the wall, she waited until they were near enough for her to speak. Her voice was low with emotion. She knew she had to tell them everything given Julie's unbalanced mental state, as difficult as it would be. Reaching out, her fingers wrapping around Dylan's hand, trying to somehow protect him from Julie's news, she forced herself to tell him.

Cal watched his friend blanch. Dylan's face went white as Sky quickly covered Julie's deadly illness. He reached out, putting a steadying hand on Dylan's other shoulder, feeling him rocked to his soul by the information.

"Look, I'm sorry, but I need to get back to Julie," Sky said, looking toward the door of the restaurant. "She's scared and she's one-pointed. She wants to go to Kurmi this afternoon. She wants me to fly her in." She sent Cal a pleading look. "After we eat, I'll take her over to the hangar area. I'm not sure if I can fly her in today, more than likely, tomorrow morning. Maybe there in the office, she and Dylan can talk because I know you will both be flying with me if you let me drop her into that village."

Dylan pushed his shoulders back, as if internally shoring himself up. He glanced at Cal. "I can't leave her now. I'll continue to be her bodyguard. You understand."

Grimly, Cal nodded. His mouth hardened. "I do, brother." He looked around. "Take a taxi over to the hangar with her, Sky. We'll be waiting for you over there."

"Okay," Sky said.

CHAPTER 13

January 30

CAL TRIED TO not feel anything, one way or another, after they arrived and drove into the hangar. Julie was standing with Sky when he and Dylan climbed out of the SUV. The look on Julie's face slashed at him, no matter what he tried to do to remain impervious. She immediately broke into tears upon seeing Dylan. He walked swiftly up to her, gathering her into his arms, not allowing her to pull away.

Cal saw the tears in Sky's eyes, and he knew she was thinking the same thing he was: what if this was them? He had a key to Liz's office and opened it, clearing it first before gesturing for Dylan to take Julie inside and have a private talk with one another. Dylan nodded his thanks, Julie huddled in his arms, her sobs wracking, helpless to stop them.

Closing the door, Cal turned grimly to Sky who was standing near the SUV looking pale and upset. Walking over to her, he forced himself to remain alert and on guard. Emotions were deadly and a complete distraction to keeping her safe.

"You, okay?" Cal asked her gruffly, squeezing her upper arm.

"Y-yes," Sky whispered, giving him a brave smile, seeing the angst in his eyes, the tears in them. Cal was no less affected than she, but he was trying damned hard not to show it.

"Okay," he said, clearing his throat, "here's the plan. Your helo is in here and so is the mechanic. Let's get the normal maintenance done this afternoon. Tomorrow around eleven hundred, we will take Julie and Dylan out to Kurmi." He glanced toward the office, the Venetian blinds drawn over the windows so no one could look in on them. "They need time to sort this out. I don't think Julie will throw a shoe over flying down tomorrow morning instead of this afternoon, do you?"

"I don't think so… but it's hard to say, Cal. She is very volatile right now." Sky looked at her Bell sitting in the center of the hangar, "I've told my mechanic to cancel the mothballing process. So, you want me to get the bird fueled up and prepare it for flight at 1100 tomorrow?"

"Yes, go ahead." Cal scowled. "I'll cancel your flight to the U.S. for this afternoon. We'll get another ticket for you leaving in a day or two. That should give us plenty of time to drop them off at the village and get back here."

"Good plan." Sky drew in a ragged breath. "Cal, I'm devastated by Julie's cancer. None of us knew."

"Look," he growled giving her a hard look, "we'll talk more tonight. Right now, I feel Alexandrov snooping around. One of us needs to remain alert. I'm going to hide over there," and he pointed toward the edge of the hangar opening. "I want you to go about your normal, everyday duties you'd do with the Bell and your mechanic, regardless. Don't look toward me, don't come over and talk to me. We'll leave here in the SUV when Julie and Dylan are done talking in the office. Okay?"

Compressing her lips, Sky nodded. "Understood," she said quietly. She felt her throat tighten with so many emotions. Forcing them back, moving into her old military mode, Sky turned and walked toward the head Peruvian mechanic who was servicing another, smaller helicopter on the other side of her aircraft. She had work to do for the next hour.

After nearly two hours later, Cal stirred from his hidden position. The hangar sat a long way away from the busy main international and domestic terminal. It allowed him a good view of the airfield, where he could see the many trucks and cars coming and going from a long way off. With his senses screaming that Alexandrov was near, he remained on high alert. Occasionally, he'd hear Sky's voice over the mechanic's voice as they spoke to one another in Spanish. Once, she laughed, and his gut immediately loosened, and Cal felt the tension sliding off his shoulders. He loved Sky so damn much that he couldn't even begin to give it words. Tonight, he'd show her. Cal was better at showing than telling, anyway. And after this jagged day of emotional highs and lows, Cal needed her as much as she clearly needed him. The only good thing that had come out of this, Cal thought, was that he got one more night with Sky in his arms, where she belonged. He had no idea how long it would take to find Alexandrov. It could turn into months. At least now, the two Army Special Forces tag teams would be coordinating the hunt with him.

His mind churned and he struggled not to get caught up in thoughts of his friend Dylan. Cal knew he'd give Julie her dying wish and stay here. Maybe, when it was all said and done, he could talk some sense into Julie, and she'd agree to go back stateside with him sooner than three months. Cal did not expect Dylan to take part in finding Alexandrov under these stressful circumstances. Dylan loved Julie and he needed to be at her side. Cal's mouth flattened as he tried to not think any further than that. SEALs knew life was short, and that it could be snuffed out in a blink of an eye, ripped away, suddenly, without any warning. If Julie had six months to live, Cal hoped Dylan and Julie would have that time together, to make the most of it. Maybe that could be a silver lining in this whole miserable event.

Sometime later, he heard the door to the office open. Twisting his head, Cal glanced to see Julie and Dylan emerge. They both looked sad, pale, and grief-stricken. Who the hell wouldn't be, Cal wondered. He saw Dylan walk Julie to the SUV and helped her into the back seat. He turned and walked toward Cal.

"What's up?" Cal asked quietly as Dylan moved to his side, remaining hidden behind the door.

"I'm going to marry Julie," he said, his voice hoarse.

Cal's brows rose and he twisted a look at Dylan. "Now?"

"Yeah, right now. Can you drive us over to that Catholic church on the other plaza in Cusco? Julie's Catholic and she knows the padre over there. She wants to marry me today."

Surprised, Cal said, "Yeah, no problem." Who was he to judge what they should do under the circumstances? "Then... you've patched things up between you?"

Dylan rubbed his jaw and nodded. "As best as we can. Julie was running scared. I managed to get her to change her mind, let me be with her until..." and he choked, suddenly looking down at his boots for a moment. Lifting his head, his voice tight with tears, he managed, "Until she dies. I'll be with her every second of the way. She's not dying alone."

Cal reached out, patting his friend's slumped shoulder. "The way it should be. SEALs don't leave anyone behind," and he met Dylan's dark, grief-stricken eyes. His gut tightened. What if he lost Sky like this? How would he feel? He couldn't bear the thought. "What else can we do to support you?"

Dylan turned and looked toward the SUV. "Drive us to the church and the padre will marry us. If we can push the flight to Kurmi out until tomorrow morning, Julie wants to get to a few more supplies gathered since we don't know how long we will be out there. She's worried sick about three babies there who have dysentery. If she can get them on IVs by early afternoon tomorrow, she can get them over the worst of the symptoms, and they won't die.

Nodding, Cal scanned the front of the hangar before returning his attention to Dylan. "I had figured we would need to push travel off until tomorrow, so that works. Sky is getting the helo fueled up and ready for flight tomorrow morning. I told her not to tell the mechanics when she'd fly it because I don't want our schedule known by anyone. I figure if we leave here at 1100, we can be at Kurmi by noon. Would Julie be okay with that kind of schedule?"

"Yeah, that works for us," Dylan muttered. He wearily pushed his fingers through his hair. "Thanks, for everything, brother. You're making this easy for us."

Giving him a slight grin, Cal growled, "I'd move heaven and earth for you. You know that."

Dylan gave him a wry look. "Yeah, and I'd do the same for you." He shoved his hands into his pockets. "How's Sky holding up?"

"She's rocked by Julie's diagnosis. They're best friends. She's grief-stricken by it."

"This is hard on her, too," Dylan said, nodding.

"Look at it this way: you'll get married and then take your bride to your apartment afterward and you have a whole night together. That's something to celebrate."

Dylan brightened a bit. "She was saying the same thing."

"She's probably glad you talked some sense into her."

Dylan shook his head. "It's the tumor, Cal. It's making her rash, causing her to make emotional decisions she normally wouldn't even begin to consider. Sitting her down and talking quietly with her, I was able to get through to her."

"You could always tame the wildest of fillies," Cal said, grinning, wanting to lift his friend's shattered spirit.

A sad smile cut into Dylan's thinned mouth. "I've always been good at soothing fractious animals. I guess it's my mother's wolf energy or something she passed on to me?"

"You've always had a way with women, too," Cal agreed. "You weren't exactly a monk in the SEALs," and he chuckled. That got a wan smile out of Dylan. Some of the darkness in his eyes lifted. It made Cal feel good that he could reach inside his friend and support him in small but important ways.

"Let's get going? You drive? I want to be with Julie in the rear seat."

Cal nodded and saw Sky give him a sign that she was ready to go. She looked worried. She hadn't talked to Julie yet, who was sitting alone in the SUV. "Yeah, let's do this, brother…"

"They've got to be emotionally wrung out," Sky whispered against Cal's neck as she lay naked beside him that night in his apartment.

Cal heard the stress in Sky's low, emotional voice. The couple had been married by Padre Francis and Cal had driven them over to Dylan's apartment. He'd been looking for a tail, another car shadowing them, but he hadn't spotted anyone. He could feel Alexandrov looking for them though, in his bones. Just because he had those nearly telepathic intuitions, it didn't tell him where Alexandrov was at. Cal wished to hell it did, it would solve so many problems they were running into right now. Moving his hands lightly up and down Sky's upper arm, he said, "I'm sure they are. But at least they're happy. And that's all that counts."

Sky closed her eyes, desperately needing Cal's quiet strength and grounding he always gave her. "I just feel so torn up for them... to only have six months with the person you love."

Cal heard the tears in her voice and eased Sky onto her back. He rose on one elbow and leaned over her, kissing her wet, salty lips. She was so easily shaken by tragedy, but why wouldn't she be? She'd lived a tragic life up until their meeting one another again here in Peru. Cal moved his mouth reassuringly against her warm, softly giving lips. And tragedy was still striking from all directions. He knew Sky was tired to her soul. She'd been devastated once more with Alexandrov being in the area. And now learning her best friend was dying.

Easing from her lips, Cal cupped her cheek and looked deeply into Sky's glistening eyes. The moonlight silently peeking from around the window drapes were just enough to show the strength in her face as well as her beauty to Cal. "Listen to me. This isn't going to happen to us. You need to put what's happened into perspective, Sweetheart. I feel badly for Julie and Dylan, but they have a different path to walk with one another than we do." Cal moved several short blond strands from her wrinkled brow. Soothing the lines on her brow away with his thumb, he growled, "I want you home, Sky. At my cedar cabin. You have the security pad. Jack will be there to pick you up at the airport. You're going to be safe, and you're going to wait until I come home to you. And I AM coming home to you." He dug deeply into her shaken gaze knowing this incident with Julie had destroyed her confidence she'd been building while they were together. Life was rough. No one knew that better than Cal. Two tears drifted from the corners of her eyes. He kissed each of them away. "Talk to me," he rasped, his heart wrenching in his chest. He could stand everything except her tears.

Sniffing, Sky reached out, sliding her fingers along his roughened jaw. Cal hadn't shaved today. "I... I just worry for them, Cal. They aren't safe out there in those villages anymore. You know that."

Scowling, he nodded. "That's true." There was such anguish in her eyes that he added, "Look, the Special Forces teams are now in the vicinity of Kurmi. I called Sergeant Mace Killmer, one of the team leaders, with info on our coming flight schedule. He's going to try and meet us there, but it's going to be close. If they arrive in time, they can be a back-up squad, if you will. They've got Raven drone footage on a group of men about ten clicks ahead of them on one of several trails leading near that village where we're landing. The sergeant thinks it's Alexandrov. He can't be sure, but they've got streaming video from the Raven on a group of white men, all Russians, all armed, on that trail. So, he and I are convinced they are Alexandrov's men until we can prove differently."

Sky closed her eyes, homing in on Cal's calloused fingers gently moving from her brow to wiping her cheeks free of dampness. Tonight, as never before, she wanted him, her heart opening fiercely with love for him. "You make me feel safe in a world that I know is anything but safe," she whispered thickly, nuzzling her nose against his neck, inhaling his masculine scent. She felt Cal groan, whisper her name, his strong, warm arms coming around her, bringing her against him, their hips meeting. Tonight, Sky wanted to love him as never before. Julie's tragedy brought home the raw terror of each losing the other. Before, it had been mental. Now, it was raw and emotional.

"I-I've just found you, Cal," Sky whispered brokenly against him, tightening her arm around him. "I don't want to lose you…" She heard a laugh rumble through his chest.

"Sweetheart, I'm going NOWHERE. Heaven doesn't want me, and hell sure doesn't, either." Cal pulled her away just enough to connect with her gaze. "I know you'll worry while I'm down here hunting Alexandrov, but I'll do my level damnedest to call you by sat phone as often as I can. I know you're a born worry wort," he teased her gently, kissing the tip of her nose, watching her eyes lighten with hope. Tonight, Cal wanted to feed Sky on every level. Give back what was torn away from her. He realized too late that asking her to meet with Julie hadn't been good for Sky at all. It had been for Julie, but not for the woman he loved.

"Vlad is a lethal schemer, Cal. I know… and that's why I'm so worried."

"Hush," he whispered against her lips, seeing fear come to her eyes. He moved his hand downward until he cupped her small breast, feeling her gasp against mouth. "Now," he added in a thick voice, "let's concentrate on us, huh? We've got one last night with one another. Let's make the most of it?" and he moved his thumb across her hardened nipple. Instantly, Sky reacted, pushing hungrily against his erection, and he smiled to himself. Loving Sky was as easy as breathing. She was his breath, his life. Cal leaned down, capturing that peak, hearing and feeling Sky react, wanting to engage her heart, mind, and soul to focus them on only one thing: him loving her. He wanted to steal this moment, turn Sky's emotions from grief and worry into aching, hungry need for him. He loved her so much. So much…

January 29

SKY COULDN'T HELP but feel happy as Julie and Dylan entered the SUV the next morning at Cal's apartment. Both looked so much in love with one another. No longer was there sadness in Julie's eyes, or shadows beneath them. Dylan, if she could guess, was relieved. He was a SEAL. He knew what they were getting into by going out on the medical circuit again. He knew Alexandrov was out there somewhere. And she could see the worry banked deep in his hazel eyes, but he'd kept it all to himself. Julie was fragile but determined, and Dylan wasn't about to destroy her resolve, wanting to give her these months that meant the world to her. He loved her enough to risk his life, if necessary, to protect her while she fulfilled her dying dream. Sky forced her tears deep inside herself. This morning, she'd had chills off and on and tried to ignore them. What now? She felt slightly feverish, as if a nasty flu was coming on. She didn't share it with anyone, needing to support her friend and Dylan on this last flight to the village. As Cal drove them to the hangar at the airport, she put on her own game face and slid into the stoic comfort of her military mindset. She had to be that way to fly alert and safely.

The mechanics looked surprised when she asked them to get the Bell ready for flight. It would have to be brought out with a push-pull tractor and then she would do a walk-around to ensure the tires were in good shape and look for leaks or metal stress issues on the external parts of the helo before taking off. After the bird was moved outside the hangar to its designated take-off area, a pallet of medical supplies would be loaded on and then strapped down with thick nylon straps to the deck of the helicopter. As the mechanics prepped the helo, Sky called in for the weather in the area she would fly and filed her flight plan from Liz's office. Finally, she was ready to go. She had dressed in her light tan single pieced flight uniform, her well-worn leather flight boots and a white silk scarf tucked inside the neck of her uniform. It protected her sensitive skin from rash created by the harsh fabric of her flight suit as she swiveled her head. Sky donned one additional garment today as well. Cal had specially ordered her a special light, bulletproof vest like his own, and had it rushed by courier to Cusco. It had arrived just in time for her to wear that life-saving vest on this last flight she had to make. Dylan wore his as well. Julie however had refused, as she did not believe in wearing one.

Sky saw Cal and Dylan both on guard, not obvious to anyone else, but alert and intense. They made several circuits outside of the hangar as well, taking nothing for granted. She felt tense inwardly, sensing Vlad nearness. Several times, Sky swore she felt his eyes upon her, but then shook it off. It had to be her wild, overactive imagination.

When the helo was ready, Sky climbed in. Cal sat in the right-hand seat. Julie and Dylan would sit on two seats in the rear of the helo, the anchored pallet in front of them. As Cal adjusted his ICS earphones and microphone close to his lips, he said, "That spec forces team is trying to make Kurmi by the time we arrive. It's going to be close, though. They've been up all night, hiking down that trail to make the link up."

Sky nodded, slipping on her aviator glasses, and starting the pre-flight check list. "I feel better with them in the area," she muttered, relieved.

Cal said nothing, his wraparound sunglasses on, his gaze never still. He had the sat phone in his harness and easily accessible. If Sergeant Killmer and his men arrived there before they did, he'd feel a helluva lot better. If they didn't, he was going to feel damned exposed in a military sense. This village sat on the edge of a huge oval meadow that had been hacked and cleared from the twisted, wooden vine jungle of a thousand years before.

There was ample room for the helo to sit down, but it put them within twenty feet of the jungle wall and the surrounding hills. That wasn't a good landing area from a strategic standpoint. Inwardly, Cal was prepared for an attack. He hopes it didn't happen, that Alexandrov was elsewhere, and not in their vicinity. Killmer had picked up movement two days earlier on a parallel trail, however. And since then, the ground fog had covered the area, leaving the spec force team once again blind. Their infrared drone had experienced thermal imaging issues and was now in Lima awaiting parts from the U.S. to be repaired. The downtime was going to be three days. Killmer had the AeroVironment RQ-11 Raven drone up and did not have infrared capability. Unless this fog began to break up and let sunlight through, it couldn't give them eyes on the enemy, either. Cal wiped his mouth, his brows flattening. If Killmer and his team saw anything, Cal would get a call. And they'd waive off the landing at the village.

Cal knew Dylan could be counted on if things went south after they landed. Julie was in a world of her own though and Dylan refused to tell her what could happen. Sky, on the other hand, was military trained and and had the emotional fortitude to handle it. Rubbing his unshaven jaw, Cal hated this mission. Damn, this last flight was a clusterfuck just waiting to blow up in their faces. He hoped like hell he was wrong.

Cal asked Sky take two slow turns over the jungle area where the village was located. Luckily, the fog was thinning, and there were breaks in it here and there, more by the minute as the heat of the sun burned it off. He and Dylan had binoculars and they were looking like raptors for prey hidden in the foliage along the edge of the walled jungle. The noon time sun didn't help their attempts, the rays slanted such that shadows became muddied and nothing stood out to get their closer or more clear inspection. The back of Cal's neck tingled in warning. Damn it, he knew Alexandrov or some of his men were waiting nearby. As Sky completed the second swing, a thousand feet above the canopy, Cal made one last call to Killmer. He was one mile away and coming hard, pushing his team to their limits to get there. It wouldn't be soon enough. He was about to turn and tell Julie that he wanted to wait, but he heard her cry out. It was a cry of joy.

To his chagrin, he saw most of the village of about fifty Quechua Indian families spilling out of their huts and waving their hands skyward, faces uplifted and smiling as the bird flew around them. The Indians knew what it meant to have the Bell in their area. It was food, medicine, and badly needed health care. Julie was sobbing, her hands against her mouth as she looked out the window where she could see the villagers gathering. The look in her eyes, the need to care for these people, couldn't be ignored. Not even by him. Cal didn't have the heart to tell her the spec forces team would arrive too late. Cursing to himself, he ordered Sky to land.

Cal gave Dylan the intel on Killmer's team who was hot footing it in their direction, but they were going to be behind by fifteen minutes. He saw Dylan frown, nod, and say nothing, his gaze intent on his wife, who couldn't quit crying because she was coming home to where her heart and soul had been for so many years. He saw Dylan reach out and gently rub Julie's shaking shoulders, trying to sooth and comfort her. The look Julie gave her husband melted Cal's heart. Damn, but he wished things were different for his brother. The love these two people held for one another was like the love he held for Sky. Sometimes, life sucked, and this was one of those moments.

Sky brought the shaking, trembling helo slowly down on a smooth, grassy area about twenty feet on either side of the jungle at one end of the meadow. She glanced and saw the villagers waiting patiently in the distance. Wiping her sweaty brow with the back of her glove, she knew the villagers understood about not to get too close to the swinging blades. One gloved hand was on the cyclic, the other on the collective, boots on the rudders, bringing the bird in for a soft landing in the long armed, waving, swirling grass. The blades were pushing the grass outward in circular pattern so that it looked like long strands of thick hair being blown and rippling rhythmically in the powerful wind kicked up by the blades.

Cal gripped Sky's shoulder. "Keep this bird at take-off speed."

Sky gave him a startled look, her lips parting, but she understood why he asked. He wanted the helo at just below take-off speed, eighty miles an hour. Because if shit happened, they could all dive back into the bird for protection, but it would be several seconds before she would be able to lift off. That was time enough for all of them to be killed. The helo landed.

"Rock it out," Cal growled into the mic to all of them. He gave Sky one swift, last look, gripped her shoulder, and squeezed it after unharnessing. Dylan opened the sliding door on the craft facing the village, extending his hand upward, asking her to wait until he cleared the area. Cal was out of the Bell after working his way around the pallet of medical goods. Wet clods of grass, torn up by the helo's blades, slapped him hard, like a boxer's punch, across his body. The force of the blades turning at such a high rate of speed stopped Cal from hearing anything. The blasts from the blades buffeted him and Dylan as they moved in a semi-crouched position, M4 rifles up, each taking a different route around the helo as soon as they were outside the blade radius.

Cal kept his feet well apart, fighting the sinking wet soil, the grass that tangled and whipped around his calves and knees, slowing his progress. He saw the villagers about two hundred yards away from them, anticipation on their collective faces. His gaze probed the darkened jungle, the thick, twisted woody vines that were like a ten-foot-high fortress wall with the canopy of leaves of much taller trees above them. How anyone could get in there to set a trap was beyond him. SEALs would never use such a place because there was no ability to move to exfil and escape quickly, if needed.

Cal met Dylan on the other side of the copter. Dylan gave him a wordless thumb's up and made a hand signal to meet at the door on the other side. The wind was powerful and almost knocked them over, so they crouched to reduce the chances of it happening. Clumps of grass continued to tear free, smacking them hard against their bodies. The soil was soggy, and a high wind could easily hurl the mud into the air like heavy, wet billiard ball sized clumps at them.

Dylan reached the opened door first and held out his hand to Julie, who took it. Cal moved in front of them and kept Dylan's back covered as he helped his wife egress. She would have been knocked over by the helo chop if he hadn't put his arm around her waist, making her duck low and then run in a crouch until clearing the turning blades. Cal turned. The double whine of the two engines mounted on top of the helo pummeled his ears and he couldn't hear a damned thing. His neck crawled with warning and his stomach knotted. Where the hell were these tangos? Turning, he pointed his M4 in the direction of the jungle opposite of where the group of huddled Quechua Indians stood anxiously waiting.

Something wasn't right.

Cal turned on his heel, yelling out a warning through his lip mic to Dylan.

There were several winks of light from the jungle. Cal saw Dylan suddenly fall, blood on his left thigh, the M4 slipping out his hands. Instantly, Cal laid fire into the jungle where the lights had originated from. He saw Julie scream and run to where Dylan had fallen. Cal wanted to tell her to go prone behind him to protect herself but had no way to reach her over the thundering of the helo blades. As she knelt next to her husband, more fire erupted from the wall of jungle. Villagers screamed and scattered, running back toward their homes.

Julie took three hits. Cal cursed, running, and firing toward the jungle. He wasn't about to leave them. He gave Sky an order to lift off. She could at least save herself. Boots sinking into the mud and grass, Cal dropped to one knee, firing short bursts. The tangos were now firing at him, instead. Grimly, his eyes slits, Cal kept his focus. Julie lay unmoving several feet away from Dylan's unmoving body. His friend was either unconscious or dead. Cal wasn't sure which. To his frustration, Sky did not take off! Damn her! Cal wanted her safe, not on the ground! They'd kill her too if she didn't get the hell out of here!

Panting heavily, Cal slid to a halt. He dropped to his knees, throwing himself forward on his belly, firing into the jungle, following the wink of the rifles. There were at least four or five firing at them. He was outnumbered and outgunned. Where was the Army spec ops team? Cal gripped the sat phone, making the call to Killmer as mud erupted all around him as firing focused heavily upon him. He heard the snap of several bullets near his head; the slugs so close they broke the sound barrier, making a sharp cracking sound.

He got Killmer! They were four minutes away! Cal gave the Army team their GPS and a layout of what was happening. His voice was cool and calm as he spoke, as if nothing were happening around him. Releasing a spent magazine, Cal rolled onto his side, yanking another mag from his harness, and slapping it into his M4. He rolled back over on his belly, taking careful aim. His shots were counting. He saw one man tumble out of a tree and he was white. A Russian. Grimly, Cal kept choosing his targets. SEALs were taught to slow fire and make every bullet count. He couldn't help Dylan or Julie if he didn't end the fighting first. If he could just hold out for another four minutes, he had three well trained operators coming to help. Then, the tide would turn.

CHAPTER 14

"DON'T MOVE, PET."

Sky froze. Vladimir Alexandrov's low, snarling voice filled her headset. Somehow, he'd gotten on board and grabbed a pair of ICS earphones hanging near the door. That was his nickname for her when she lived in the Zimmerman household. She felt the cold metal of a pistol pressed into her neck, making a deep, painful indentation. Her heart flew into a terrified gallop. Outside the cockpit window, she saw Cal fighting for his life. She heard Vlad laugh indulgently. He adjusted the ICS mic he wore closer to his mouths.

"Stay exactly where you are. In a minute, the last operator will be dead. My men are coming on board. And then, you're flying us out of here to Siquta," and he handed her a piece of paper. "Set up these coordinates on your Bell's computer. Now."

Shaking, Sky couldn't stop herself from wanting to cry. *Cal! Oh, God, no!* Vlad had set up this ambush! How did he know they'd be coming here? How? Her gloved finger shook as she punched in the coordinates. The whole time, her gaze moved between the computer on the console and the cockpit Plexi-glass window. Cal was firing slowly, another man falling out of the trees across the meadow. The mud was flying up like geysers all around him. Julie was down, lying motionless near Dylan. Neither was moving.

Oh, God!

Vlad chuckled. "Americans are stupid, Pet. Your nurse runs her life on her heart. How deadly that proved to be for her…pity…"

Suddenly, she saw Cal slump to the ground, his rifle falling listlessly out of his hands. She gave a cry, the harness biting into her shoulders.

"Cal!" she screamed, frantic.

"SIT!" Alexandrov snarled, his hand clamping like a vise on her shoulder, shoving her hard back down into the seat.

Sobbing, Sky wrenched her head toward Vlad. It was the first time she'd seen him since she was seventeen years old. Horror and ice coursed through her. His glittering forest-green eyes were filled with triumph. His full, sensual mouth was drawn into a pleased, twisted smirk. She felt his fingers soften slightly. "Please, please, let me go to them! You can't leave them to die!"

Shaking his head, Vlad muttered, "You haven't changed at all, Ginny. Or is it Sky now?" He kept his hand on her shoulder and spoke into the mic at his lips in Russian. He turned and ordered the last of his men into the helo.

Tears blurred Sky's vision. She sobbed, her glove against her mouth, staring out the cockpit Plexiglass. Cal didn't move. From this distance, all she could see was blood alongside his head. Shot in the head... *Oh, no, please... please don't let him be dead!* A sob tore from her. Sky saw four men clad in cammo gear, weapons in hand, hard looks on their camouflaged faces, as they sprinted across the short distance from the jungle wall next to where the craft was located. They carried a fifth, a dead man, between them.

"Get out of that harness," Vlad snapped, stepping back, holding the pistol on her. "Now! Hurry!"

Hands shaking, Sky removed her headset and released the harness. As she rose to stand between the seats, Vlad grabbed her by the shoulder. He was an inch shorter than Cal and he was bent over in the cabin, leering at her. The helo rocked as the other men, all heavily armed, leaped on board. Within moments, they released the medical pallet's nylon straps holding it snugly to the deck. They easily pushed it out the other door and it tumbled to the ground, the medical items scattering in all directions beneath the whipping blades of the chopper.

Vlad yanked Sky past him.

"Pilots, get up here!" he snapped. He hurled Sky into the rear of the helicopter.

Sky landed hard on her left shoulder and hip. She rolled and fell against another soldier crouched in the corner. The roar of the helo erased whatever it was he snarled at her as he kicked out at her. His boot landed squarely in her ribs. Her breath was knocked out of her. Sky cried out, rolling onto her other side, curling up, arms around her torso. She heard Vlad's roar of orders above the engines, but it was in Russian, and she had no idea what he screamed at his men.

Her face was pressed against the cold aluminum of the deck. The doors slid shut. Two men stepped around her, heading for the cockpit. She felt someone jerk her onto her back, grabbing her wrists with his large hands. His lips grew into snarl, hatred in his eyes for her. Within moments, thick plastic zip ties were painfully tightened around her wrists. Another soldier turned her around, gripped her arm, helping her to sit up. He placed her up against the bulkhead, next to him. The helo powered up. Through her tears, Sky saw two Russians now at the controls of the Bell. Alexandrov knelt in a crouch behind the two seats, every now and then, keeping a watchful eye on her. There was pride in his expression, like a primitive animal who had successfully captured his prey. He made a gesture and snapped an order to another soldier crouched next to her over the mic close to his mouth. As they lifted off, a pair of ICS earphones and a mic were placed on her head and near her lips.

Sky could barely breathe. She was in shock, her heart, her soul, back in that meadow. Cal was dead! Everyone was dead! And all because of Vlad! He had been waiting for them. How had he known?

"So, Pet, we are together again at long last, eh?" Alexandrov said over the comms. "I've always loved you, you know? I will marry you. You will carry my children. Finally, here you are. My dream has come true after all these years. I am a lucky man, eh?"

Sky lifted her lashes, the tears refusing to staunch, and Vlad's face blurred. "Go to hell," she spat, her breath coming in gasps, her bruised side aching. His laugh made her skin crawl. It was a rich laugh with serrated edges to it, one that had always made Sky feel nothing but terror for what he'd do to her later.

"Ah, as you've matured, you've become the hell cat that I always suspected was hidden within you." Vlad gave her a confident grin. "I like angry women. They've taught me a lot. And I've always had the ability to choose warrior women who knew how to fight back." He flexed his gloved right hand, moving it slowly into a fist and then relaxing it. "And I'm really looking forward to seeing you fight, Ginny. Oh, that's right…," and he placed his finger to his chin. "Witness Protection gave you a new name, didn't they?" He licked his full lower lip, grinning. "I actually kind of like your new name better, so I will call you Sky."

Sky's stomach lurched and rolled. She saw hatred etched in the hard faces of the Russian soldiers who were crowded into the cabin with her. The stench of sour sweat filled her nostrils. The bird could carry ten fully armed soldiers in its cabin. These men were carrying heavy rucks, state of the art automatic weapons, and each had a pistol at his side, along with a knife in a sheath strapped to one leg or the other. Their eyes were like Vlad's: dead looking. No life. Just… hatred. All except for the one soldier who crouched next to her. Looking distressed, he gave her an apologetic look. Sky trembled inwardly, the flex cuffs so tight that the circulation to her hands was cut off and she could no longer feel her fingers. Vlad must have noticed as she tried to move her hands around in her lap, to find some relief from the pain. He gave an order in Russian. Instantly, the man beside her leaned forward. His hands were gentle upon hers and he took his knife, cutting the zip ties. It allowed circulation back into them, pain drifting up into her wrists and forearms.

"See?" Vlad crowed, "now you cannot say I'm without a heart, my beautiful Sky. I want your beautiful hands roaming my body, pleasuring me."

The gravity pushed her against the deck as they gained altitude. They were flying the chopper hard and fast. The village of Siquta was twenty-five miles away as the crow flew, on the edge of the rocky, cold, windy Highlands. Her mind and heart wrenched back to Cal. Her heart was breaking. Grief washed over her and Sky's fear for herself dissolved in tears as she closed her eyes, sobbing for the man she loved and who had died right in front of her eyes.

Cal groaned and rolled over. He heard the helo taking off, felt the blast of downward pummeling air slamming him like fists as it roared overhead. He watched it struggling and taking the full length of the meadow to gain enough altitude to clear the jungle canopy of hundred-foot-tall trees at the other end of the meadow. Unable to go after it, he followed the sound of the helo and the direction it was flying. Blood was running down into his right eye. He rolled over, his head throbbing, ears ringing, his orientation screwed. A pounding headache was making his brain hurt. In the distance, screams of Quechua Indians filled the air. Then, he heard the hard pounding of boots coming in his direction. Looking up, his vision starting to clear, Cal recognized the Special Forces team. Sergeant Killmer, a man as tall as he was, his rifle up and watching the jungle tree line intently, was rapidly advancing in his direction. His other two men had spread out in a fan-like pattern, on guard and alert. Damn, his head ached like a sonofabitch.

Sergeant Mace Killmer saw the movement of one man lifting his hand weakly, waving him forward. How many of them were still alive? They'd heard the gunfire while running up the hard, flat clay path. It was so damned slippery because of constant thunderstorms, and he and his Special Forces team members skidded and slid their way toward the sound of the helicopter. They arrived too late! He saw two other bodies along with the operator who lifted his hand, a few feet away from them.

"Nate, Tony, get to those two who aren't moving. Stay alert," he ordered them into his comms mic.

"Roger that," Tony said. "Looks like an ambush got 'em."

Mace gave a sharp nod. He dropped to his knees, placing his weapon nearby. "I'm Sergeant Killmer," he said. "Which one are you? McCoy or Sinclair?"

Cal blinked and focused on the Special Forces sergeant looking down at him, pulling out his blowout kit from his lower right cargo pant leg. "Sinclair," he managed. "Ambush..."

"Yeah," Killmer rasped, breathing harshly, "got that. You were hit by a grazing bullet on the side of your head. Hold still," and he quickly wiped away the blood away with a piece of gauze.

Cal grunted and sat up. "The other two," he managed hoarsely, turning their direction.

"My men are on it. Stay where you are."

Cal's head swam with pain. The Army operator was fast and efficient. In no time, he had the bleeding from his scalp staunched and had special tape across the slice to hold the flesh together. Cal tried to turn.

"My teammate," he said to the sergeant, struggling to get up.

Mace relented and helped the operator get to his knees. "Your friend has a thigh wound. A bad one. Nate's an eighteen Delta corpsman, a field combat surgeon. No one better to have around here right now, so rest easy. If he can be saved, Nate will do it."

Cal blinked, his vision clearing. He saw a black-haired sergeant with green eyes working quickly to put a tourniquet around Dylan's upper left leg. Wincing, Cal saw the other sergeant had gently laid Julie out on her back in the tall, swaying grass. She was dead. She'd taken three shots to her center mass. Blood had bloomed out across her white blouse, dyeing it pink and red. The color of death. Choking back on bile, Cal turned away. He had to think! Pushing the heels of his hands into his grit filled eyes, he rasped, "A woman with blond hair? She's the American pilot. Have you found her?"

Mace looked up from his duties as he placed a dressing across his head wound and then quickly wrapped it three times around the operator's head with an elastic bandage. "No. I just see three of you. Where was she at?"

"In the helo," Cal muttered, pressing his fingers against his brow. Or was she over in amongst the medical items near the wall of the jungle where the Bell had landed? Dread filled him.

Mace quickly repacked his medical kit and then put it away in his cargo pocket. "All we saw was the helo taking off to the north. We haven't seen another woman." His mouth thinned. "You and your teammate are lucky," he said, hauling his Toughbook laptop out of his pack and flipping it open.

"She's either here in this meadow, or they took off with her in the helo," Cal growled, his vision clearing. His gaze was fixed on Dylan. The 18 Delta corpsmen were the best in the world at combat medicine, trained field surgeons utilizing their incredible skills in battle torn areas, saving lives that would surely have been lost without their expertise and help. He watched the man called Nate work swiftly and confidently, strapping on a thick nylon tourniquet above the wound on Dylan's mutilated thigh. McCoy was unconscious from blood loss and shock. He watched the medic pour Celox, a blood coagulant, into the open wound to stop the last of the bleeding, having already staunched the major arterial bleed.

"I just got a call an hour ago that the Army Black Hawk landed at Cusco."

Killmer said, and looked up at Cal. "That's good news for all of us."

Cal nodded, studying the jungle. He saw four dead men. Four Russians. He felt vicious satisfaction in taking them down. It was payback for killing Julie and wounding Dylan. He'd killed a fifth man but didn't see his body.

Typing in a password code to the scrambler, Killmer said "I'm callin' it up here. If we don't get your friend out of here pronto and to the Cusco hospital in time, he's not going to make it." Mace looked up, squinting at Sinclair. "And you need to be looked over, too. Plus, we have an American aid worker, dead. There's a whole lotta paperwork to fill out on her," he growled, frowning.

"Take McCoy and his wife Julie out of here," Cal rasped," but not me." He slowly forced himself to his feet. Wobbly, he planted his boots wide apart until the dizziness passed. Cal picked up his weapon, slinging it across his chest. "I'm going over to that pallet and search for Sky Lambert, the pilot." Looking up, he saw his own ruck was shot to hell, and he shrugged out of it. "I gotta hope they pushed the other ruck out of the bird, too." He headed for the massive carnage heaped upon the ground, praying to find Sky there.

His hopes were quickly dashed, as he found no sign of her amidst the stacks of broken, scattered, and open supplies. Cal cursed, understanding that Alexandrov had pulled this op off brilliantly. He'd managed to recapture Sky, and Cal wanted to vomit. The Army spec ops sergeant came over to him as he located Dylan's ruck among all the strewn medical boxes. It remained undamaged, and the four gallons of water contained in it held were in good shape. "I'm going after Alexandrov. This was his ambush and he's got Sky with him." Cal's mouth turned down. "He's going to torture, rape, and then kill her."

"Hold on," Killmer growled, "let me get this typed in and sent to my contact. We'll go with you. That helo has flown due north. There's only one village, Siquta, about twenty-five miles from here. They may be going to land around there. It's one of the places we had pegged as a layover spot for the Russians."

Cal stood there looking at McCoy. His friend's face was leached out, looking like wallpaper paste. A few feet away, Julie had been covered with the space blanket, only her red hair visible and splayed out across the green grass surrounding her. His heart felt heavy with grief for his friend, Dylan. If he lived, once he became conscious only to find out Julie was gone... What would Dylan do? Shaking his head, Cal turned away, bile again rising again in his throat. Leaning over he vomited violently and then spat, gulping for air. Grabbing his CamelBak line attached over his shoulder epaulette, he sucked water into his mouth several times, spitting it out and clearing it. The frightened Indians were peeking out of their huts, warily watching them.

"Better take the four bodies of those Russian ex-Spetsnaz soldiers with you, too," Cal muttered, gesturing toward the jungle tree line where they had fallen. "See if they can be ID'd. Our Spooks will like any intel you can find on them, photos, and documents, too."

"Yeah, I'll make sure they're brought on board in body bags," Killmer promised, scowling as he typed with two fingers on his Toughbook laptop.

Cal tried to think. Where was Alexandrov taking Sky? The helo had headed north to the only village in that area. "Did you have a Raven in the air coming up here?"

"Yeah," Killmer muttered, finishing off the order and transmitting it to the satellite. It would then be sent to the Night Stalker Army Black Hawk in Cusco. He switched to the viewing program on his laptop. "Come here," he said, gesturing for Cal to look.

Cal walked carefully, still getting his shaky legs back under him. He bent over the broad shoulder of the operator and looked at the video feed from the Raven. It clearly showed Alexandrov jumping into Sky's helo. Cal couldn't see inside the craft, but he was sure Alexandrov had removed her from the cockpit and made her his prisoner. Shortly after, he saw other Russians make a break from the jungle and leap into the bird, carrying one dead operator with them. He'd shot five of them in total. Alexandrov's men quickly pushed the pallet of medical supplies and other unwanted items out of the door of the bird. The door was then slid shut. Squinting, Cal saw two men in the cockpit through the Plexiglas. Where was Sky? His heart started beating harder. His mind went wild with terror. Was she being stripped and raped in the cargo hold of the helo right now? Swallowing hard, Cal knew he had to stop this line of thinking. He couldn't function, he couldn't be of help to her if he let his emotions run rampant. Swallowing hard, he croaked out, "She's our pilot and she's not in the cockpit."

Killmer grimaced. "Could be in the back of the bird under guard?" He twisted a look up at Sinclair, who had a dark, worried scowl on his face. "I don't think Alexandrov would let her fly if he had replacement pilots, would you? She'd auger them into the ground if she got a chance. She's a former Army Medevac pilot."

Cal wouldn't disagree with his analysis. And it was much better scenario than what his mind was concocting. But then, Killmer wasn't aware that Alexandrov had a penchant for Sky, either. "After the Black Hawk arrives, your team is going with me?"

"Yeah. Ms. Lambert is an American citizen in trouble. We'll come along."

Nodding, Cal felt his throat tighten. "Thanks," he said gruffly.

"Where are you going?" Killmer called.

"I'm taking the only path that goes on the other side of that village," Cal told him. "I'm going after them."

"To where?"

"Your raven showed the Bell was heading north. The only village in that direction is Siquta. It's the only village north of here and in that specific direction. The fastest way to it is by that path there," and Cal pointed toward a trail in the distance on the other side of the meadow.

"That's a helluva hike," Killmer reminded him.

"Yeah, I know." Cal headed toward the medical supplies strewn about the meadow by the buffeting of the helicopter's blades. He wiped the sweat off his face, lengthening his stride, picking up a few items, stuffing them into his thigh pockets. Thirty-minute miles carrying sixty-five pounds was doable for a SEAL like him.

Killmer closed his laptop and shoved it back into his massive ruck sitting next to him in the grass. "Can you give us a bit of time?"

"No," Cal said. He pulled Dylan's ruck across his shoulders. Cal strode toward Killmer, who was standing and hauling on his heavy ruck across his broad, thick shoulders. The sergeant looked his way.

"Thirty-minute miles?"

"Is there any other?" Cal drawled, slowing to a stop.

"My men and I have been running hard all night to get here. We're lucky to make fifty-minute miles carrying the weight we do." Killmer gestured to his team working on McCoy. "We're beaten to shit, Sinclair. We need to refuel, hydrate, and get an hour's rest or we can't push. You haven't been running all night."

"That's why it's important I take off now. Listen, can you send your corpsman into the village? They've got three babies that need IVs because of dysentery. That's why we flew up here to this village, to save them."

Killmer's full mouth flexed and his black brows drew downward. "It will happen. As soon as Nate is done stabilizing your brother, I'll send him into the village to find those children. Don't worry about it. He takes care of babies and women just fine." He scowled at Cal. "You're one going up against how many? They're ex-Spetsnaz that Alexandrov employs. Isn't that a little much even for an ex-SEAL?"

Cal gave him a twisted grin. "No, we consider that good odds."

Snorting, Killmer said, "We'll make sure we take good care of your brother, here and get him loaded on the Hawk after it arrives. I think he'll make it."

Cal extended his muddied hand. "Thanks, Killmer. Thanks for helping those sick kids, too. Julie, the nurse who died, was supposed to take the IVs to them after we landed. But your corpsman can do it and we appreciate it. Catch up with me when you can. We'll stay in sat phone contact. Get that Raven drone pointed toward Siquta. Check and see if Sky's helo is on the ground once they land. See if it can pick up and identify her or if we can get photos of the sitrep on the ground?"

"I'm on it," Killmer promised, griping his hand a strong shake. And then he added, "I wished like hell we'd gotten here in time."

Cal became somber and released his hand. "You did the best you could. Each of you is carrying a hundred and twenty pounds of gear. The time it took to get here must have set a new black ops time record. You guys made Olympic time under the circumstances." He didn't want Killmer's team to feel like they failed. Only another operator could understand the brutal physical demands on a man's body, the elevation, the humidity, and the steepness of the path as it led to this village at fifty-five hundred feet in elevation. He saw relief come to Killmer's gray eyes.

"Hey, Frogman, we'll be hot on your heels. We just need an hour to revive."

"Good enough for me." Cal smiled a little. "Too bad the military doesn't buy light weight vests for you boys. Three-pound bullet proof vest versus forty-five pounds of level 4 Kevlar weight that each of you are wearing, slows you down, too," and he patted his vest hidden beneath his black t-shirt. "I'll be a helluva a lot further ahead of you because I'm carrying half the weight you are. Get there when you can. I'll be giving you reports as I draw near the village once it's confirmed that its where they're holding Sky prisoner."

Killmer grunted, "Do you SEALs ever get tired of always playing hero?"

Cal gave him a confident look and grinned sourly. "When you're the best, you don't need to even brag about it." He threw the sergeant a salute. "I'll see you in a bit…" and he turned and walked over to where Nate was still working over McCoy.

"How is he?" Cal demanded, looking at the medic dressing the wound.

"Bleedings stopped and I'm giving him an IV of saline with pain meds to stabilize him," Nate told him, glancing up. "He'll make it because we're in that golden hour with the Blackhawk coming our way."

"If you weren't 18 Delta, I'd have my doubts," Cal said. He saw the Army medic give him a big grin.

"We bring 'em off the battlefield alive. Even you SEAL types know that. No one does what we do."

Cal nodded. He leaned over and patted the medic's shoulder. "Thanks for saving him, Doc. I know McCoy will forgive you that you're an Army doggie who is saving his SEAL hide."

That brought a howl of laughter from the Army team as they looked at each other, grinning broadly. Inter-service black humor and rivalry was alive and well.

Cal leaned down on one knee. He knew Dylan was unconscious, but he also knew people could hear a person talking to them even in that state. He gripped Dylan's shoulder gently and leaned close, his lips near his ear. "Hey Brother, you're in good hands. You're going to make it. I'll see you after I find and rescue Sky." His voice changed and tightened. "I'm sorry about Julie, buddy. I'm so sorry... just get better and I'll see you in a little while," and Cal broke contact with Dylan and stood up. His head ached fiercely but he wanted to go say good-bye to Julie. Cal knew it would be the last time he would ever see her.

Kneeling near her shoulder, Cal gently drew back the space blanket just enough to reveal Julie's calm, waxen face. The Special Forces team member Tony had put tape over her eye lids to keep them closed in death. Cal hoped her parents would someday know the care with which they treated their daughter out here in the jungle where she was murdered. Running his fingers through the limp strands of her red hair, Cal tried to smooth them into some semblance of order around her bloodless face. Sadness overwhelmed him. He couldn't be angry that Julie wanted to be here. She had a strong heart for those who had so little and needed so much. She was the daughter of a very rich Virginia farmer, and yet, she'd devoted her life, literally, to these economically deprived people. To him, she was an angel without wings for all of them.

He looked up at the villagers who were frightened and hiding in their thatched huts. Their lives would be changed too, Julie was no longer their fierce nurse protector, ministering to their medical needs and keeping pain, suffering and death at bay. Luckily for them, however, a male nurse would replace her shortly. Tears burned in his eyes and Cal gently stroked the cool flesh of her cheek. "Sleep the sleep of Angels, Julie, because you are one... Safe sailing, Sister..." He pulled the blanket gently across her, a gutting sigh escaping his tightened lips.

Rising to his feet, Cal blinked back his tears. He'd covered Julie, her red hair no longer spread tangled and twisted about in the long grass around her head. It would be the last memory he'd have of her. Swallowing hard, he saw Killmer was watching him through narrowed, saddened eyes. Giving the hardened black ops sergeant a final curtesy nod, Cal turned and began a ground eating stride of a trot, heading directly for the village and then to the trail beyond it that would take him north to hopefully find Sky.

The humid, hot equatorial temperature rose, and Cal could feel the sweat popping out on him, being absorbed by his special SEAL Crye Precision jungle colored cammo pants and his black t-shirt. The vest would absorb its share of his sweat, too. In no time, Cal knew he'd be soaked. He would take constant swallows of water from his CamelBak water supply on his back. When it emptied, he'd dig into Dylan's ruck and fill it again. Those four gallons of water would get him to Siquta.

As he drew close to the Quechua village, Cal saw the terror, the shock and tragedy written in the faces of the people. The women were openly crying. The children were frightened, sobbing, clinging to their mother's skirt, peeking out behind the material gripped in their little hands. The men looked grim, and grief stricken.

It was a shitty day for everyone.

Cal increased his speed outside the village, easily locating the three-foot wide red clay path. On either side of him rose the dense vine jungle that was a carved, wooden wall ranging from ten to twenty feet high. Growing through it were one-hundred-foot trees creating an umbrella-like canopy. Cal breathed a sigh of relief, glad to be in the shade once again instead of the hot, druzy sunlight filling the meadow.

Sky. He loved her so much; he thought his heart was going to burst with anguish and he'd end up having a heart attack. Cal knew he couldn't begin to imagine what was happening to her. How was Alexandrov treating her? Had she been wounded? Yet, Killmer's quiet, logical explanation seemed on target. Alexandrov wouldn't want her flying because she sure as hell would auger her bird into the ground, taking her life to snuff out the Russians on board. Sky would have done it. She was made of that kind of steel courage.

As he trotted, the jungle getting darker quickly, his footfalls soft along the wet and muddy trail, Cal settled into a ground eating stride. He tried to mentally reach Sky. He knew there was an invisible energy connection between team members on a patrol. They never spoke to one another. And most of the time, they never needed silent hand signals either; they were that much in sync with one another. He felt that same closeness with Sky. His eyes burned. His heart lurched with so many withheld feelings that poured through him as he tried to send her a message to hold on, that he was coming. To do whatever she had to do to survive because he loved her. Cal would love her no matter what happened. *Just stay alive…*

CHAPTER 15

January 30

C*AL IS DEAD.* Sky tried to think, tried to figure out a way to escape as the helo flew to the village. She kept her eyes down, refusing to meet Vlad's open, triumphant stare. She could feel the collective hatred of the soldiers toward her. The smell of unwashed males, muddied, sweaty and bleeding, assailed her nostrils. Inwardly, her stomach quivered with old terror and knowing what was coming. Vlad would torture her. Rape her. And he'd enjoy every moment of it.

She heard Vlad speak to his men in English through the intercom system.

"We're landing at Siquta, Lev. Everyone disembarks except for the two pilots. Return the helo to Aguas Calientes. That way, when the CIA starts looking for the stupid Americans, they'll find a cold trail. Wipe all surfaces down. Remove your fingerprints."

Sky shut her eyes, hot tears jamming into them. She flashed back to seeing Julie being shot three times. She'd stepped into the line of fire after Dylan was wounded. She didn't know if Dylan was alive or dead. If he was alive, it was because of Julie's unhesitating courage to protect him.

"And then what?" Lev demanded over the intercom.

"We stay at the village for a day or two, waiting for the two pilots to return and hook back up with us."

Sky snapped up her head, glaring across the filled cargo space at Vlad. He was smiling at her. But it never reached his eyes. She saw one of the soldier's glaring at Vlad and he spoke up.

"We don't have THAT kind of time, Comrade Commander."

Licking his lips, Vlad didn't even look at Lev. "Yes," he gritted out, "we do."

Sky saw the other soldiers looking at one another, sneers, and disagreement on their unshaven faces. These were hard, ruthless men.

"Take her right now," the soldier snarled, jamming a finger in her direction, "because you're putting us all in danger if we stay two days anywhere! We live because we keep moving and stay nowhere very long."

Snarling a Russian curse, Vlad turned, his fist balled, smashing it into Lev's big, hawk like nose.

Sky winced, hearing bone crunch against flesh. The man named Lev grunted. He was huge, well over two hundred and twenty pounds, stood six-foot 2, and was lethal looking. Blood went flying around the cabin. He toppled like a felled ox, his eyes rolling back in his head as his skull brushed against her feet where he fell. Sky stared, gasping. Blood was pouring from the man's broken nose like an open faucet.

"Now," Vlad said in a conversational tone, looking at his other men, "anyone else have anything else to say about my orders?"

Sky gulped, her heart in her throat, making it ache. She tried to move away but was boxed in by Russian soldiers on either side of her. There was nowhere to hide. The big Russian called Lev, suddenly jerked awake. His pale blue eyes were almost colorless, dazed, as he sat up, spitting blood and cursing. She watched Vlad. His dark green eyes glittered like a viper as the man clasped his broken nose. Blood was gushing down across the man's lips and chin, dripping onto his dark green cammos. The metallic odor was cloying, and Sky felt nauseous in the enclosed cabin. The sweat, along with the raw male testosterone odor mingled with the scent of blood and made her gag. Sky turned her head to one side, vomiting. The soldier beside her gripped her shoulder, supporting her, trying to help her.

Saliva dripped from her mouth afterward, her eyes watering and her nose running. The humiliation, the terror, all of it combined as she retched. Spitting several times, Sky felt the soldier who had held her steady move away. The next thing she knew, she felt the man pulling her up and wiping her mouth and nose with a damp cloth. The gesture was one of care. His hand was firm without being painful on her shoulder, keeping her upright so she wouldn't fall back down into her pool of vomit and the blood. A canteen appeared in front of her. It was pressed to her lips, and she drank some and then spat it out on the deck. She was given more water. Sky cleaned out her mouth. The third time the water was offered, she drank the tepid fluid eagerly, dying of thirst, feeling feverish.

"Well, well, Alexei," Vlad purred, "how HUMANE you've suddenly become. I didn't know you had it in you."

Sky dragged her chin up, her gaze falling on the black-haired, hazel-eyed Russian soldier Vlad called Alexei. The man was as tall as Cal, with a square face. The look in his eyes was one of concern toward her. Sky was trembling physically and just his kindness was helping her to stabilize. He wasn't good-looking, reminding her of a farm boy with a broad face, high cheekbones, a fine, thin nose, and a strong chin. His hazel eyes reminded her of Dylan

McCoy, and she felt grateful he was helping her. He turned, giving Vlad a hard look, but he said nothing, continuing to support Sky in an upright position.

"Clean it up," Vlad ordered the combat medic. "I don't want to smell her vomit for the rest of this flight."

Alexei turned, gave her an apologetic look, and then settled Sky gently against the rear bulkhead of the helo. He took a damp cloth from his medical pack and quickly cleaned up the blood and vomit and threw it in a plastic bag that he'd pulled from his nearby ruck, which bore a red symbol with a white cross in the middle of it. He tied it shut with his large, calloused hands and tossed it near the locked door.

"You always did vomit when you were scared," Vlad growled at Sky. "I see that hasn't changed."

Sky dropped her gaze, never wanting to spar with Vlad. There was safety with the soldier whose hand remained comfortingly on her shoulder. Alexei was tall and large boned, reminding her of a farm hand's kind of body. He settled her between his long, opened legs. It almost felt as if he were trying to protect her from Vlad, but Sky didn't fool herself into believing that. Shutting her eyes, she frantically searched for some kind of internal compass, some strength, to help her find a way to escape. Vaguely, she realized her fever was climbing incredibly fast and she felt woozy and out of control. What was happening to her? Why was she feeling like that? Instinctively, Sky realized she must have a very high fever because she couldn't think coherently at all. Sweat covered her face and her cheeks felt red hot. Had she picked up a jungle virus? Her mind canted and there was no answer forthcoming, feeling with every passing minute physically weaker. If it weren't for the medic, his supportive hand on her back, she knew she'd topple over and fall flat on her face to the deck of the helo.

As the helo landed outside the village, red dust kicked up by the blades, Sky was dragged out the door by one of the other soldiers. Fresh air washed over her, a relief even if it was gritty and dust filled. The other Russians quickly egressed from the bird. She took some comfort as Alexei trotted up and pointed towards the village, telling the soldier to take her over there to the hut area. She felt herself being dragged across the field; the brutish soldier's vice-like grip on her arm leaving bruises. At the beginning of the packed dirt road of the village, she was handed over to Alexei. He steadied her, his grip was far gentler and guiding.

Sky's feet weren't working, and she felt oddly feverish. Why? And then, she groaned to herself. She'd contracted malaria in Iquitos, a jungle area of Peru while working with the charity in that area six months earlier. Since then, she had to take anti-malarial pills daily or the malaria would return with a vengeance. The first symptom that always roared upon her was nausea and vomiting, followed by a high, raging fever lasting four to six hours. That was followed by an hour of lucidity, then the terrible bone-breaking chills would begin. Sky would become so cold that there was nothing she could do to get warm. Her teeth would chatter, her skin goose bumped, and she'd roll into a fetal ball, the iciness making her want to die.

Another period of lucidity was then followed by returning nausea. That cycle could go on for two or three days. Terrorized that she was coming down with malaria again, Sky stumbled over the rocks and clumps of dirt, starting to fall but the medic caught and steadied her. Dizzied, she realized that she hadn't been faithfully taking her daily anti-malaria medication since Cal had arrived. With all the stress and drama that had been occurring, she had managed to miss several doses. That made her vulnerable to a relapsing malarial attack.

As she fell forward, once more, she was caught by Alexei. He embraced her, ordering the other soldier to let him take care of her. The Russian gladly complied and returned to the helo. Sky felt her legs going rubbery beneath her. Alexei hauled his arm around her waist, easily bringing her up against him, and guided her towards the village square.

Vlad scowled. As his combat medic dragged Sky through the field, he saw how pale she'd become. She had practically collapsed into the arms of Alexei Kazak. What the hell! He wanted her in good shape to rape her, not sick as a flea-bitten mongrel! Perhaps it was a reaction to being captured, that was all. He'd lost half his men in that firefight. That one operator had killed five of them. Luckily the other ten men of his team were on another exploration path far north of the skirmish area, and they would return to this village in an hour, meeting back up with everyone. He would need them for guard and perimeter duty for as long as he wanted to stay here.

Sky felt her temperature climbing even more. She knew within an hour; it could reach a hundred-four or a hundred and five degrees. She'd begin hallucinating. Worse, if it climbed higher, convulsions would occur. Maybe death. Right now, death didn't look so bad to her. She'd lost Cal. What was left? They arrived in the main square of the village, and Sky was brought to a halt, leaning heavily against the tall Russian soldier who held her. She saw the terror in the eyes of the Quechua women and children. She saw anger in the men's eyes, but they were too afraid to react. They had no way to defend themselves against military weapons. There was something about Vlad's power and stature that automatically instilled fear in people. They took him at his word. Sky understood that better than anyone as she sagged weakly against the medic called Alexei.

Vlad ordered Sky was hustled into one of the larger huts. The medic opened the door. There were Peruvian woven rugs across the hard packed floor and a small fire in the corner with a smoke hole above it. It was warm inside, but not stuffy. A bunch of guinea pigs ran around them. These were a main meat source for the Indians. Every family had ten or twenty of the creatures at any given time living with them. They bred often, had big litters, and gave the Indians a good source of meat. He saw that the occupants had fled from it.

Sky sagged in relief as the soldier crouched and guided her through the shorter door. Indians weren't very tall, and Vlad's men were all six foot or taller.

"Here," Alexei murmured to her in stilted English, "sit down." He guided her to the floor, setting her on a woven carpet. Sky nodded, her feet crumpling beneath her. She felt dizzy from the fever starting to climb in earnest. He turned and shut the door.

"Please," she whispered in English, "I-I've got malaria. I forgot to take my pills for several days. I'm starting with a high fever. I need help. Please…" and she looked up at him, pleading with him as he stood over her. She saw him frown. Without a word, he opened his palm and placed it against her sweaty brow.

"You are not well," he agreed thickly in English.

"Listen," she wobbled, "I'm going to go unconscious. I get a high temp, a hundred and five or six. I'll need water. I'll dehydrate if I don't. It could kill me…" She saw his gaze turn sympathetic.

"No need to tell me about this disease, I have it myself." He scowled. "You have not been taking malaria pills daily?"

Shaking her head, miserable, Sky said, "N-no, not daily… well… hell…"

Jamming a finger down at the floor, he said, "THIS is hell."

Sky was beginning to feel woozy. "I-I need your help…"

"I am a combat medic. My name is Alexei. My friends call me Alex. I will help you the best I can with my medical supplies. I have some malaria pills in my pack to give to you. I must buy some more the next time we go to Cusco." He set his pack on the hard packed dirt and opened it up, producing a bottle of malaria pills. In no time, he gave her a tablet followed with drinking water from a canteen. "Taking the pills now… it will not stop the cycles, but it will shorten the length of them. You may have these symptoms for two or three days instead of a week. You won't die, but you will want to die."

"T-thank you for your help. W-what will your commander do to me?" Sky asked faintly, tipping her head back against the rocky wall, dizziness assailing her. Would Vlad put a gun to her head? Shoot her on the spot once he found out she had malaria? Right now, the way Sky felt, it would be a relief.

Alex mumbled something in another language. He leaned down, releasing the flex cuffs they'd put around her wrists before they left the helo. "Stay here." He drilled a hard look into her glazed looking eyes. "If you DARE try to escape, I promise you, he will make you regret every breath you take. Listen to ME? Stay here. I will try to help you."

Licking her dry lips, Sky whispered, "I'm not going anywhere. I need water… please…"

Alex prowled around the three rooms of the hut and found a large clay jug of fresh water. He brought them to Sky's side and carefully filled the pottery cup he'd found nearby.

Sky gave him a grateful look. "Thank you…" and she tried to lift the cup. It fell from her trembling hand, spilling across her and onto the rug.

Alex knelt, patiently refilling it and then holding it to her lips. "After a while, you aren't even going to be able to drink. You'll burn up with fever, sweat until you are nothing but a dripping rag. Drink all you can now, and we will hope it will see you through the hours of fever to come…"

Sky felt herself growing weaker, unable to do anything but lay down on the rug near the stone wall, closing her eyes, sinking deeper into the fever. She felt Alex's hand come to rest on her upper arm.

"Remember," he warned her darkly, "stay in this hut. I will return. No one will dare come in here. I and my medic partner, Nik, are the only ones who will be here to help you through this. Nik will be here shortly with another part of our team coming in to rest for the night."

Alex watched the woman nod, her face red, sweat standing out on it. As a combat corpsman, he was more than knowledgeable about jungle diseases. He'd had malaria and hated every time it came around to fell him for three to four days if he forgot to take his daily pill. As he slowly got off his knee and stood, he frowned. Why did this American woman have to look so much like his sister, Kira? When he studied Sky, it scared the hell out of him. Kira was the same height, slender in build, with blond hair and dark blue eyes. They were the same age, or nearly the same age, he thought. His younger sister had been an Army nurse at a Russian forward operating base when Chechen terrorists overwhelmed it. They had killed the wounded men they cared for, the doctors, and raped the nurses, Kira among them. He saw his happy, beautiful sister who had always made him laugh become a shrunken shadow of her former self.

Alex stood there, torn. He heard the American moan as the fever probably hit a hundred and five. She was sweating profusely, lying on her side, her arms wrapped around herself, knees drawn up toward her chest. He knew his commander was going to rape her. It was only a question of when. His gut churned. Alex never took part in such things precisely because he saw what rape had done to his beloved sister. Now, she remained at home, a recluse, happy to garden and cook, but afraid of all men. At times, Kira was even afraid of him if he came into his family's home unannounced. She'd scream, an unearthly terror filling her eyes. Alex couldn't bear her tears and sobs after he'd accidentally frightened her.

Unsure of what to do with the woman pilot, Alex decided the best course of action was to go to his commander and let him know that she was very ill. A small part of him hesitated. Alex knew few women lived through a night after being raped by this band of men. And these same Russian soldiers always mocked him and Nik Morozov, who was like a brother to him, for refusing to participate. They were teased and derided as homosexuals. Alex and Nik were not, but they didn't try to defend themselves against these ruthless soldiers, either. The only reason they tolerated them was simple: If they got shot or went down with a killing fever like malaria, they knew they could save their lives, so they didn't goad them too much on this point. In truth, he and Nik were as red-blooded as any man. He preferred the woman he desired to come to him, not be dragged fighting and screaming against her will. Alex cursed, taking one last look at the American who wouldn't be in her mind for another three or four hours. She would need constant medical supervision and care, an IV of saline to given hourly to her. She would need continuous fluids, but he wasn't sure what his commander would do or say about it. Would he allow him to use the life-saving IV fluids to save her life or not?

Vlad looked up when Alex was told to enter the hut. He was eating a roasted guinea pig that he'd found on a skewer over a fire. "Well? Is she ready?" he snapped.

Alex remained standing in front of his leader. "Sir, she has malaria. I just took her temperature and it's a hundred and five and still climbing." Alex saw Alexandrov's brows slice downward. He threw the half-eaten guinea pig to the ground in disgust.

"That's impossible!" he exploded. "She's lying!" and he heaved to his feet, angered.

Alex stared coolly at him. He was nearly the same height as Alexandrov. "Sir, I am one of your medics. I especially know malaria from treating it so often among your own men, as well treating myself. She has malaria. She is not faking it."

"Shit! Is she conscious?"

"I doubt it."

Vlad glared over at the corpsman. "Come with me!"

Alex walked with his commander two huts down. There wasn't even a guard at the entrance and Vlad cursed.

"No sentry? Where's your head, Kazak?"

Alex wasn't one to get rattled. He always kept his voice low and quiet. Maybe because he was a combat medic. Or maybe he'd learned not to be loud because Kira would cringe and become frightened if he talked in a normal tone of voice. "Because there was no need for one, Commander. Go see for yourself."

Cursing richly, Vlad dipped into the hut. He allowed his eyes to adjust and spotted Sky laying in a fetal position against the wall. He strode over to her. Kneeling on one knee, he jerked her upright by her collar. She gave a cry, throwing her arms up to protect her face.

"Enough of this!" Vlad hissed. He saw her eyes were glazed over. He roughly touched her cheek and brow that were hot and damp. "Talk to me, Sky!"

Sky didn't know if she was in a nightmare or if it was reality. Vlad's angry face danced before her. She saw hatred in his narrowed green eyes, studying her with intensity. "Y-yes, I see you," she whispered, feeling so thirsty. "Please… water…," and she swallowed hard, her mouth and throat dry. She was burning up, so hot she wanted to tear her clothes off, but she was too weak and uncoordinated to do so.

Vlad thinned his lips, placing his hands on either side of her flight suit, jerking it open. He felt her upper chest, just above the damp white camisole she wore. She was perspiring heavily. The camisole was sticking to her small breasts. He felt himself stir, harden, as he stared at her covered breasts, their roundedness beneath the damp, clingy material. Breasts he'd felt once before when he'd tried to make her his at seventeen, but she'd fought back, tearing his hands away from them. Now, Sky hung in his hand like a rag doll, as if filled with sawdust. She slumped, semi-conscious, leaning heavily into his hand where it wrapped tightly into the shoulder material of her flight suit.

With a growl, he started jerking the one-piece suit off her shoulders. He would rape her anyway.

Alex blanched. He heard the American woman give a weak cry, unable to defend herself.

No! He couldn't stand that Alexandrov was going to rape her, here and now. Alex knew if he interfered, his commander would more than likely turn and pull his pistol, shooting him in the head. But he couldn't bear the mewling sounds tearing out of her mouth as Alexandrov thrust his hand down inside her flight suit to grab at one of her breasts. The specter of Kira being assaulted overwhelmed Alex. He moved forward, his large hand snaking out.

Gripping Alexandrov's shoulder, he yanked the man away from the crying woman. He was just as tall, just as strong as his commander, and he hurled him across the floor. Alexandrov landed with a grunt against the stone wall of the hut. His eyes widened with surprise.

Kazak leaned over him, breathing harshly, gripping his collar, snarling, "She is sick! You will NOT rape her! She is under MY CARE. Get out of here!"

For a moment, Vlad saw death staring him in the face. He had no idea that Kazak possessed this kind of hatred, but he saw it now. The medic's lips were peeled away from his clenched teeth, the rage clear in his squinting eyes as he glared down at him. He'd drawn his pistol, holding it steady against his chest. Vlad had no question that Kazak would kill him if he tried to rape Sky right now.

Hissing a curse, Vlad pushed away and broke out of his hold. "You stupid bastard!" he spat, struggling to get to his feet. "She's just a woman!"

Kazak was breathing hard, his pistol held on his commander. "You said you loved her. You've talked many times of marrying this woman from your past. How," he grated, "can you rape her when she is so sick?"

Glaring, Vlad roughly swept off the dirt from his dark green t-shirt and moved toward the doorway. Breathing hard, he growled, "Take care of her, then! Dammit, I want her alive when this over! And well. Do you hear me, Kazak?" He punched the soldier in his broad chest. "If you let her die, you die. Understand?" he breathed in his face.

"I will take good care of her, commander," he responded evenly, unblinking, holding Alexandrov's insane glare. "You will allow me to use IV's to keep her hydrated?"

"I don't give a shit what you do! Just keep her alive! I want her, but I want her fighting me." He jabbed his index finger at Alex. "You ever draw a pistol on me again? I'll shoot you where you stand." He gave Sky one last glare, spun around, and stormed out of the hut.

Alex smiled a little after his commander left. He turned and saw Sky laying exactly where he'd dropped her into the ground. Holstering his pistol, knowing he dodged death for now, Alex swallowed hard. His heart was pounding in his chest. He couldn't stand to see another woman raped. Because he and Nik were medics, they would plead with Alexandrov not to rape any child or young girl, but he and his band of men jeered and laughed at them. They would leave, not wanting to see it happen, not wanting to hear the screams. How much more of this could he take? Alex tried to tell himself he was with the group for a good reason. That he desperately needed the good money that came with the job. He had to take care of Kira, himself, and his family farm in Ukraine. He had to give her back her life and this was the only way to do it.

Kneeling, Alex said soothingly to the woman, "Come on," and he gently positioned her and made her more comfortable. Her eyes were rolling, and he saw the terror in them, but she was utterly helpless in every way. He placed his jacket beneath her head as a pillow. "It is time to get some fluids into you. You are safe for now. He will not come back in here. Rest... just rest..."

Cal was breathing hard after five miles at this fast a pace. He stopped, now deep in the jungle, feeling the sweat coursing down across his body. Purposely, he avoided thinking about Sky. All it would do was open a can of worms for him. His sat phone vibrated and he took it out of his harness pocket, answering it.

"Sinclair, this is Killmer. Where are you?"

Breathing hard, Cal rasped, "Five miles in. What do you have?" He prayed it would be intel from the Raven drone.

"Raven's on station over Siquta. We spotted Alexandrov going from one hut to another, pissed off as hell from the looks of it. We count four other Russians, but are watching for more. It appeared that part of his team was on another mission, and they arrived an hour later. I figure ten men are in the other half of Alexandrov's group and they hadn't gone to Kumri for the ambush. Originally, he had twenty men. Now he has fifteen. We've not seen them or Sky Lambert. I'm hypothesizing she's in one of those huts. Oh... wait a minute..."

Cal wiped his brow, wanting to see whatever Killmer was seeing. Sky had to be there!

"There's a Russian carrying what looks like a corpsman's ruck. It's got a red cross on it. He's going into a hut two down from where Alexandrov's hut is located. I don't know what that's all about. But he's not from the Kumri group."

"Could be I wounded some of the Russians that got away and he's taking care of them?" Cal suggested, looking ahead at the dark tunnel between the twisted vine walls. It was 1700, five p.m., and the sun was going down, the place getting darker.

"Most likely," Killmer replied.

"What about Sky's helo?"

"We saw it land there but couldn't make out much except it was the Bell. We saw some of the Russians disembark, but too many other huts and trees were in the way for us to see everything. Now, it's gone. No sign of it. Looks like Alexandrov had his pilots drop him and his team if soldiers off at this village. It was heading down the slope toward Cusco and my guess back to that airport."

"Why?"

Killmer snorted. "I can't even hazardous a guess. We've seen his team stay there overnight sometimes, a sort of base of operation up there. Right now, I see three guards taking up posts outside the village, making their sentry rounds."

Grunting, Cal asked, "Did your Black Hawk arrive?"

"Yes, just lifted off with everyone on board. Your friend McCoy is stabilized. Nate says he's going to make it. Nate also gave IVs to those three young children. They're stable and he left the families medication to give them. They should make it, too."

"At least there's some good news," Cal growled.

"Look we're saddling up here. We want to make up time if we can. I won't be on the laptop looking at live video feed from the Raven. Once we take a rest, maybe after pushing a couple of hours, I'll look at it and give you another update?"

"Yeah, fine. Thanks, Killmer. For a Special Forces guy, you're doing outstanding." He heard the sergeant laugh.

"Go Army," Killmer replied, amusement in his low voice, signing off.

Cal grinned briefly at the friendly military interservice rivalry and felt his spirits lift, if but momentarily. He was a SEAL. He was used to operating as a team. He'd had many missions with other military branches black ops sister groups and there was always this camaraderie. It felt damn odd to be out here alone on a mission. He missed his team acutely, wishing they were back together once again. Everyone could rely on each other to do their jobs, to have one another's backs. He drank huge swallows of water, hydrating. His clothes stuck to his body, wringing wet. Physical suffering was something he lived with a SEAL. It would not change his pace or affect his mission. As the old SEAL saying went, pain was guaranteed, suffering was optional. He wasn't going to waste one second on suffering.

Shifting the weight of his ruck, Cal made sure his rifle was tight in the sling across his chest and then took off at a striding trot. He would clock himself, checking to make sure he was trotting thirty-minute miles. He wasn't a man to pray or even think about God, but as he beat out a rapid pace, he did both. He prayed to God that Sky would be protected and somehow, be spared from Alexandrov.

And just as quickly as he said the prayer, he shut off his emotions because Cal just could not go there. Emotions tore a man apart. They slowed him down, took over his operational mind and the mission turned into a clusterfuck. Choking down all his feelings into his internal kill box, Cal breathed through is mouth, sucking in draughts of stifling, humid air as he raced up the trail. He was running toward Sky. Running toward saving her at all costs.

His mind ranged over the cabin he'd built. The security pad to his cabin was in one of her flight suit's pockets. He'd seen her slide it in there before takeoff. How could so much go so wrong, so quickly? This morning, his body shimmered with sexual gratification and his heart was light with joy after he'd satisfied Sky. The soft sighs, her moans caught in her throat as he pleasured her, gave Cal the greatest gift of all. He absorbed her voice, seeing the druzy quality in her azure eyes, shining with such love reflected in them for him alone. She was the only woman in the world for him. He was twenty-nine. When Sky walked into his life, across the tarmac and into the Ops building at Camp Nichols, Cal now realized she had stolen his heart from that moment onward.

Stinging sweat ran into his eyes. Cal blinked hard several times. His vision blurred. With a frustrated sound, he wiped his eyes to clear them. But they blurred again. He couldn't be crying! He just couldn't be! *Not now. Especially not now!* Why the HELL hadn't he told Sky he loved her this morning? Damn! Of all things! He should have whispered it in her ear, or whispered it against her soft lips, and then watched her melt with happiness over his admittance. Why hadn't he told her?

CHAPTER 16

January 31

C AL WAS ONE mile from the village at 0630 the next morning. The Special
Forces team was moving as fast as they could to reach his position. But he
wasn't going to wait. He sat inside a group of tall rocks, about four to five feet
high, out in the middle of a plowed field. From this hidden vantage point, he
could watch the three Russian soldiers on duty who constantly patrolled the
village, watching for intruders, their rifles at the ready. He impatiently awaited a
call from Killmer, who was setting up in the jungle with his laptop hooked up
to an overhead satellite, watching the Raven drone feed.

It was barely dawn at this hour, the horizon a reddish ribbon. As Cal sat,
he devoured a protein bar and then drank the last of his water. He'd spent four
gallons of water making this run. His legs were cramping, and he popped some
salt tablets, hoping like hell they would relieve the knots in his calves. His back
ached, his knees felt like they were working bone against bone, the cartilage
gone. Every muscle in his body was tight and he tried to do some deep
breathing and relax. It was damned hard under the circumstances.

In another sat phone call during the night, Killmer had been patched
through to the CIA at Langley, Virginia, and provided updates on the mission.
The Peruvian government was refusing to allow the Army helo to come in and
give Cal a lift if he needed it after he located Sky, for fear of fallout if any
casualties were to occur. Diplomats were still wrangling with one another about
the permission over phones, but it didn't do Sky any good. He was on his own
out here. The one piece of good news, Dylan McCoy had pulled through
surgery at a Lima hospital and was going to make it. Cal was sure his brother
was going through a special hell after he'd been told about Julie's death. It had
to be hard on him. And he wished he could be there to support him. But this
job wasn't finished yet.

Cal squinted, looking through the Night Force Scope he had placed on the
barrel of his M4. It had infrared and he could see well through the darkness
and the lurid, sluggish dawn that wouldn't break for another hour. Though the
weapon wasn't a sniper rifle, the scope gave Cal an eagle's eye view on the

activity in the village. He'd timed the Russian guards, and he knew when there was an opening with no eyes on this part of the landscape for about two minutes between guard shifts. The plowed field was large. Not a sprinter, Cal estimated he'd have to rely on sniper-like movements to reach the village; run when no one was looking, hit the ground, fall into a furrow, and not move a muscle when the patrol returned, then get up and sprint again, until he could get to the hut where Killmer thought Sky might be held.

As he watched the guards make their rounds once again, his sat phone vibrated and he pulled it out of his harness pocket.

"Sinclair. What do you have?"

"Killmer. The drone shows all but three Russians are asleep in those huts. Plus, there's two medics. One stays in the hut most of the time by himself. The other carries medical items into him, mostly IVs from what I can make out, and then he leaves. The second medic shuttles between his hut and Alexandrov's hut."

"Why do you think that is?" Cal asked, shoving another protein bar into his mouth. He was starving.

"Reporting to Alexandrov?"

"No sign of Sky?" Cal was hoping against hope they might see her, confirm she was with the group.

"Negative."

Nostrils flaring, Cal stared off into the cloudy morning sky. He knew in his soul that she was in that hut. His instincts had never been wrong. The wind was cold and nasty, turning from flowing off the high Andes peaks surrounding the area and moving in the opposite direction by sunrise. "How many men have been to that hut where this medic's located?"

"Just the other medic. Both wear red armbands with a white cross on it. They're taking care of someone or several people in that hut."

A little relief trickle through Cal. If the Russians were raping Sky, the men would be standing in line, hovering around the hut, waiting their turn. Cal didn't want to think about the alternative: that Sky had been gravely wounded and these two Russian medics were trying to save her life. She could be dying. Pushing his fingers through his wet, dirty hair, Cal muttered, "Okay, that narrows it, then. IF Sky's in there, she's injured. They could be taking care of her. Or maybe other men with her who were injured in that firefight with Dylan and I earlier."

"Likely," Killmer confirmed without emotion.

"I'm going in. I've got a mile to that hut. I'm leaving my ruck in this rock fortress out in the middle of this field on the eastern side of the village. I'm taking my M4, flash bangs, putting my slide for a grenade launcher beneath it, and carrying what I can in my cargo pants. I can't wears my harness and carry as much ammo as I want. I have two minutes between guards making rounds on this end of the village. I'll sprint, drop, hide, and wait. I figure if all goes according to plan, I'll call you once I'm near that hut."

Killmer's voice came back amused. "Nothing ever goes according to plan."

Cal grinned wearily. "Roger that. But you should know my game plan just in case."

"That's a copy. Sounds solid."

"I plan to recon that one hut we think Sky is in. If she's there, I'll try to find a way in. From what you've seen from drone feed, no one else is coming or going from that hut. Right?"

"Confirmed. Just the two medics."

Glancing up at the turbulent looking, dark sky, Cal muttered, "And if I get damn lucky, it might start raining at dawn."

"Good cover for you. Kills sound. Water camouflage for you to escape in."

"Yeah," Cal said, "guards don't like being out in a cold rain, either. They get sloppy. They want to be inside where it's warm and dry. It's a damn good distraction."

"These are ex-Spetsnaz. I don't think they'll drop their guard."

"Roger that. IF I can get Sky out of there, I'm going to make a run for that same trail I just came out of. About half a mile below, there's a large meadow, and maybe I'll eventually meet you. This village is surrounded by wide open spaces and rocks. Nothing to hide behind. I hope like hell she's ambulatory or there's gonna be a shoot-out in that village."

"You SEALs get your rocks off in that kind of drama."

Grinning a little, Cal heard the worry in Killmer's voice. He was a damned good operator and he respected him mightily. Under these circumstances, the Army was saving Sky, not him. Without their eyes in the sky, their willingness to support his mission, Cal would have been screwed. He doubted he'd have been able to find out where they'd taken Sky at all. "Yeah, we're kinda flamboyant operators, aren't we?"

Killmer chuckled darkly. "I'll have you put that in writing when I see you."

"I'll see you, but it'll be a cold day in hell I'll sign anything away that the doggie Army wants me to agree too," and Cal chuckled softly.

"Hold on...," Killmer said, getting serious, "I just got an alert from the CIA case agent assigned to this mission. She's saying that Army Black Hawk CAN fly into your area for a rescue. The Peruvian government has just reversed their decision and granted you permission. Our U.S. diplomat must have convinced them. Do you copy this?"

Cal's eyes glittered. "Oh, hell yeah, I copy it loud and clear." Hope rose powerfully within him.

"Give me a call when you have the package in hand? Assess your GPS position and any other info and tell me if I can unleash that bird in your direction to pick you two up? Code word: Bingo."

"Roger that, bingo. Music to my ears," Cal grunted, twisting around, looking at his watch and seeing a Russian round the edge of the village.

"Good luck, Sinclair. You're going to need it."

"SEALs don't rely on luck, you know that Killmer," and Cal grinned. "Out." Wrapping the sat phone in a gallon-sized zip lock bag, he shoved it in one of the large thigh cargo pants pockets. If it got wet, he'd lose his one line of communication for support. He felt the first large, slashing raindrops begin to fall. Cal had a lot to do before he started his final sprint and stalk. He placed the rail system beneath the M-4 and loaded it with five grenades, the most it could carry. It would be more important to have ammo for his rifle. The protein bars gave him the badly needed sugar energy he'd have to rely on for the stalk.

There was a pounding, reverberating roll of thunder above him. Cal got ready to sprint, watching the guard disappear around the corner. With a grunt, he took off, boots digging into the hard, slippery, rocky earth, fading into the darkness.

Alex watched the American woman slowly become conscious after three hours of chills. He'd gathered as many blankets as he could find around the village to keep her warm. Nik had come in to assist him whenever he could. His friend also gave Alexandrov the updates he demanded regarding Sky's condition. Alex was glad he hadn't come back to try abuse her again. Sky Lambert was thin and underweight, and he knew when a person was in a weakened condition, that malaria could kill them. Fixing another IV of saline he added pain medication providing her an edge of comfort. He'd kept her well hydrated, although during the fever and chill phases, he'd worried about her pulling the IV out of her arm. To stop that, he tightly wrapped a blanket around her and held her.

His heart twisted as he sat cross-legged next to her after easing her to the rug in front of him. She slowly opened her eyes, and he saw the glaze over them. Alex had wanted to remove her wet flight suit but had second thoughts about it. If Alexandrov came back and realized she was naked beneath those blankets, he might decide to rape her after all. And Alex wouldn't allow that to happen. He'd pull the pistol on his commander if he tried. Alex also knew that Alexandrov could come in at any moment, shoot him in the head, and rape her, anyway. Alex had seen him kill other soldiers under his command for far less infractions than the one he'd committed earlier. No solider had ever disobeyed the commander's orders and lived to talk about it. Alex knew that Alexandrov would punish him sooner or later, he just wasn't sure how. A bullet in the head, most likely. Probably the only reason he was still alive was because he was tending to Sky, and he wanted the woman to survive the malaria attack. But after that… Alex knew his hours and days were numbered, and so was hers. He might have only hours to live. Everything was tentative. Alexandrov looked gut shot when Alex had hauled him off the pilot. He couldn't believe Alex had dared interfere. Mouth tightening, Alex felt his life was forfeit, leaking away, minute by minute. It was only a matter of time when it would end.

Right now, Sky was quiet, resting on a blanket he'd formed as a make-shift mattress for her lay upon. The six blankets were tucked tightly around her after he'd repositioned her onto the floor.

Having had malaria, Alex hated the chills the most. It felt like every bone was fragile and would break painfully in his tortured body. Every joint was weak, as if it would crumble into fine dust if stressed. There was no way to control the chattering of one's teeth or the horrible spasms that wracked a person's body during that phase. Sky had just come out of it, physically exhausted, barely able to raise a finger. Alex understood. Nik had found one old Quechua woman who was making chicken soup in a pot. He'd paid her handsomely for some and brought a mug of the warm broth back to Alex to give to Sky when she regained consciousness. Alex had put a pinch of salt into it because her body lost so many electrolytes. Salt during the fever and chill phases helped stop the muscle cramping.

"Sky?" he called gently, leaning over, his head almost parallel to hers so she could see him. "Sky? It is Alex. Can you open your eyes? I have some chicken broth for you. I need you to drink it."

Sky heard the man's low voice and faintly recognized it. Her mind was disjointed, thoughts colliding, nonsensical. She felt his hand lay gently on her blanketed shoulder. Yes, she remembered this man's voice. Remembered he'd held her as she raved and screamed during her fever stage. Remembered him holding her, so many blankets around her as her body jerked and convulsed with spasms because she was freezing cold. And he was still here. A sense of safety came to her as he spoke in a low, quiet tone to her. Something about chicken soup.

"I am going to lift you up, Sky. Get you into a sitting position across my knees. The soup is here. I want you to try and drink it, eh?"

It was an effort to lift her lashes as Sky felt Alex lift her into his arms and then cradle her against his huge body. Her head lolled against his barrel chest and shoulder, too weak to lift it. She felt a cup carefully pressed against her lower lip.

"Drink, Little One, for you are very, very in need of this nourishment. It will help revive you. I promise." And then his voice turned amused. "Do not be like my beautiful sister, Kira. As a little girl, when it was my duty to care for her when she caught the flu, she would refuse me. If Mama did not serve her chicken soup, she would not drink from the cup I brought. You look like her, but I know you are wiser about such things… Come now, drink just a little for me…"

The salty, warm fluid tasted so good that Sky sucked greedily for more. It took all her energy to swallow, but it tasted so good! She felt like a sack of flour in this man's comforting embrace. She heard a smile in his voice as she finished drinking the entire cup.

"Very good! Indeed, you are far smarter than my Kira."

She couldn't even lift open her eyes, simply too weary. Sky felt the IV in her arm. She couldn't remember where she was. But the man wasn't Cal. She missed Cal. What had happened to him? Why wasn't he here? And who was this man caring for her? She heard what she thought was thunder growling nearby, and then rain beating down around her. Somewhere. She just didn't know where.

Alex had tucked one long leg beneath himself and held Sky easily in his arm as he reached for the large clay mug bearing the soup. He poured more into the smaller cup. The thunder was caroming across the slope of the Andean mountains, shaking the hut like a dog shaking off fleas. He glanced toward the rattling door, feeling and hearing the sudden, powerful gusts of wind pounding against it.

Alex leaned back against the wall, feeling Sky relax and trust him, her hair tickling his jaw. He ached for his sister. At one time, he would hold her like this when they were children growing up. When Kira was frightened, she would crawl into his gangly, growing arms. After the rape, she would not run to him for safety anymore. She would go to her room, close the door and sob until he could no longer stand the sounds. Feeling so helpless, Alex had wanted to kill those bastards who had done this to her, who had broken and shattered her. Kira was a shell of her former self, no longer a living person, but someone who walked in the darkness, afraid of all men. Even him, her brother who loved her with a fierceness that would never die, was to be distrusted.

Sky moaned as Alex gently moved her into a more comfortable position in his arms and pulled her across his lap. "Shhh, little one, you are safe. That is just a big storm outside. We are safe and dry in here. Come," he urged, pressing the cup to her chapped lower lip once again, "drink a little more for me?"

He watched with sudden happiness as Sky began to drink it thirstily. It was a good sign she was regaining her strength between the phases. If she could do that, Sky had a chance to make it. And then, icy cold swept through him. What was he doing? Getting her well so that she could be raped by Alexandrov later? And the other men if she even survived his commander's brutal assault?

Bile entered his mouth and he he took the emptied cup away from her lips, blotting them with a piece of clean gauze. When Sky barely opened her flawless blue eyes and Alex saw they were no longer glazed looking, but that she was really here, he smiled down at her.

"Welcome back, little one. You have had a rough time. Do you know who I am?" He'd told her each time she'd move into a lucid phase, which would last about an hour.

Her fine, thin blond brows drew down as she studied him. "Cal?" she whispered, her voice hoarse. "Where's Cal?"

"Who is he?" Alex asked, wanting to draw her out, get her mind focused instead of free floating as it did when malaria hit.

Sky slowly opened her mouth and tried to talk, her voice barely above a whisper. "I-I love him…"

Alex's heart twisted. She was so beautiful. Harmless. Innocent. And in love. He felt guilty. Just the way she said it, he felt so many emotions rise up in him. Kira would never say this about any man. She would never marry. Never know love. Not now. Not ever. Alex managed a weak smile as she studied him, perplexed. "And I'm sure he loves you," he said.

Thunder struck and the entire hut shuddered and shook. Alex sensed rather than saw someone at the front door. Before he could react, a lethal looking American in military gear, his M4 pointed at him, slipped in, and slammed the door behind him.

Cal was breathing hard, his eyes stony and glittering as he saw Sky in the Russian's arms. His finger was on the trigger, and he was ready to put a bullet through his head. With a silencer on his rifle, no one else would hear it. His heart leaped with joy seeing Sky. At the same time, he was terrified, seeing an IV in her arm.

"Speak English?" he growled at the soldier, seeing his medic bag nearby.

"Yes. Do not shoot. You might harm her. I am Alex Kazak, a combat medic…"

Cal gave the tall, deeply muscled looking soldier a stripping look, checking for hidden weapons on him. His gaze swept across the floor, and he saw the emptied nearby cups. "What are you doing to her?"

"Helping her. She has malaria. I was feeding her chicken soup because she is in her lucid phase." Whoever this was, Alex thought, he was going to kill him. The look in his eyes was hard. But every time he looked at Sky, Alex detected an emotion not there before. "She is gravely ill," he warned the American soldier.

"Who else is here in this hut?"

"No one. Just Sky and myself. Nik, the other medic will not be here for another hour."

"Did Alexandrov touch her?" he ground out, looking quickly right, and left.

Alex rasped, "Not yet. He wants her well and healthy." He saw the man's face change and grow taut. "I have cared for her, that is all. I swear, I would not touch a woman in that way."

"Lying sonofabitch. I know your kind. Now gently lay her down and kneel in that corner to the right. You make one move; I'll blow your head off your shoulders. Got it?"

Alex nodded. "Yes."

Cal saw a lot of emotions in the Russian's hazel eyes. He was Spetsnaz, no question, but he wasn't like most of them he'd seen. But he was a medic, clearly, because he'd helped Sky. Cal wanted to rush to her. Hold her. But he couldn't. He was in a village surrounded with enemy operators.

Alex gently placed Sky on the floor. She'd closed her eyes, limp, and he knew she'd gone into an exhausted sleep. He looked up. "Are you Cal?"

Cal flinched. What the hell? He drilled a black look into Kazak's face. "How do you know my name?"

"Her," he said, pointing at the woman. "When she enters the fever stage, she cries out for you." He shrugged. "If I did not hold her, she would tear out her IV which is standing between her life and death right now. I hold her to protect her from herself. That is what you saw. That is all."

Confused, Cal watched the Russian slowly move, keeping his large hands splayed and out in front of him. He slowly knelt on the floor, his hand going behind his neck in a position of a prisoner. The rain was becoming harder. The thunder louder, sounding like kettle drums being struck hard. Cal looked about. He saw Sky and gulped, his throat tightening. She looked like she was dying, her eyes shut, lips parted, unconscious.

Relieved Alexandrov hadn't raped her, he wasn't sure if it was a good idea to take her out in this cold, biting mountain storm in her condition. What the hell should he do? The medic was watching him, a concerned look on his broad face. And then he recalled getting CIA data on Alexandrov's men in Cusco earlier. Amongst the faces and names, there were two medics with the unit: Kazak and Morozov. This was Alex Kazak. And Cal didn't see hatred in the man's eyes, only genuine concern for Sky. He swallowed hard, remembering these two men were from Ukraine. Maybe they weren't the same as the rest of Vlad's goons?

"I need to get her out of here," Cal told him harshly. "I'm not letting Alexandrov touch her. Can I move her during this storm? What will it do to her? I don't want her to die." Cal's throat tightened. It was unlike him to invite the enemy's ideas on an escape plan. Yet, Cal sensed this man had some integrity. Why or how, he didn't know. Sky looked untouched. He'd obviously cared well for her with the thick alpaca blankets wrapped snugly around her, feeding her chicken soup and giving her constant IVs to keep her from dehydrating. There were at least six other used IV pouches stacked in the corner. The Ukrainian was good for his word and Cal felt grateful to the man.

Alex said, "You must take her now. Because as soon as the rain lets up, my commander will be over here to check on her." He gave Cal an apologetic look. "He will rough her up, shake her, and try to get her conscious. She doesn't need that." His voice grew more urgent. "If she's wrapped in these blankets, I can hook an IV bag to your shoulder loop. It will be high enough to allow gravity to flow the saline into her artery. She needs to be continuously hydrated. She is very weak."

Cal's mouth flexed. "Yeah, on that you and I agree. What else?"

Alex figured out the man standing crouched before him was a Navy SEAL. He had the posture of one, that M4 barrel never wavering an inch from his head. He didn't let emotions get in his way. The drop holster on his thigh with the SIG Sauer in it gave his military branch away. Of all the black ops, Spetsnaz feared the SEALs the most. They were the finest trained men in the U.S. military arsenal, and they knew how to kill without even thinking about it.

Alex swallowed. "I am not your enemy. I am Ukrainian," he said, holding the SEAL's black gaze. "My sister, Kira, was raped by Chechen terrorists years ago. She no longer is herself." He glanced toward Sky. "She looks so much like my little sister. I do not want to see her harmed by my commander. But we must act swiftly. I can get her ready for transport wherever you must take her." Alex saw the man's eyes widen momentarily. "And when you are ready to leave, I will need you to strike me hard enough with the butt of your rifle, so it knocks me out. I must be found unconscious by the others, or they will kill me. I have already stopped my commander from trying to rape her once. I do not think he will allow me to live if you take Sky from this hut."

Cal straightened. He tried not to show his surprise. "I can do that," he growled. "Now get her ready for transport, pronto." He wouldn't have a problem taking the butt of his rifle and knocking this soldier unconscious. The way Cal looked at it, the man was saving Sky's life, so instead of shooting him dead, he'd let the man live. He was Spetsnaz. He'd understand the tradeoff. And besides, if Kazak was telling the truth that he'd stopped Sky from being raped, then Cal owed him. A lot.

Alex moved slowly from his knees, allowing his hands to come to his side. He knew any swift movement would earn him a one-way ticket to hell. The SEAL would shoot first, ask questions later.

Cal moved aside, keeping watch on the medic as he took out dark green duct tape from his medical bag and set to work. Alex quickly duct taped the blankets around Sky's body. It would stop the blankets from falling off and exposing her to the inclement weather or possibly leaving a trail for Alexandrov and his men could follow if one fell off. Next, he quickly retrieved a syringe from his bag.

"Whoa," Cal growled. What the hell is that syringe filled with?"

Kazak held the bottle out toward him. "Lorazepam. It is an anti-anxiety medication. It will keep her asleep. You do not need her waking up and screaming. Sky does not know where she is. She remembers nothing because of the fever." He glanced at his watch. "She is almost past her lucid phase, and she will enter the nausea and vomiting phase in about an hour. After that, she will fall into fever for three to four hours."

Cal handed the vial back to him. "Okay, give her the shot. Be quick about it. No funny stuff."

Nodding, Alex gave her the shot into the IV injection port after pulling the blanket aside. Pulling the blanket back into place, he hurriedly dropped the syringe and bottle back into his pack and retrieved a full IV of saline. "I do not know how far you are going." He quickly packed the IV in between the blankets and duct taped it closed so it couldn't change position or fall out.

Cal nodded. He wasn't about to say anything. He pulled out the sat phone and made the call to Killmer. When he answered, Cal said, "Bingo," and then hit the off button. Bingo was the agreed-upon word for the Black Hawk to be called from Cusco to the GPS position at the head of the trail. That was a two-mile run across open area. By the time he hit the head of the trail, it would be hidden from the village and Russian soldiers. There was a nearby meadow, just big enough to land a Blackhawk in. If he could make it there, they would make a safe, clean getaway. How long was this storm going to last? Cal couldn't hit the dirt when the guard came around the corner of village with Sky in his arms. *Damn.*

Torn, Cal's mind worked feverishly outside the box, thinking of ways to make that two-mile run and not get caught. He stared hard at the Ukrainian. How trustworthy was Alex? Was he telling the truth about his sister being raped? Kazak was in with a bunch of Spetsnaz animals. Cal found it tough to swallow. But he didn't have any other options. Killmer's Special Forces team was far too late to get here in time to lay down a wall of interlocking fire if he needed it. He was alone and it was a FUBAR situation.

"Were you telling the truth about letting Sky escape?" Cal demanded.

Alex finished preparing Sky for transport. "Yes. Why?"

"I have a two-mile run I've gotta make with her across open plowed fields. There's no place to hide. The three sentries who walk around this village will spot me sooner or later. I need a distraction."

"What kind of distraction?"

"Can you toss one of my grenades toward the west end of the village? Not in a hut, but near one? It would draw everyone's attention to the opposite direction of where I'm going to be heading." Cal watched the man's expression. He could tell the Ukrainian was thinking about it.

"I can do it, but then, you must shoot me." Alex pointed to his calf. "Here. In the meat. A through and through. I could throw the grenade and you shoot me, then you run away with her."

Cal grimaced. "Why the hell would you do that for us?"

Alex said, "May I pull a photo from my right pocket?" and he pointed slowly in that direction. Any fast move would earn him a bullet. "I believe it will explain everything to you?"

Nodding, Cal lifted the barrel of the M4, following his every movement. The medic pulled out a photo. He held it our toward Cal.

"This is my sister, Kira, when she was twenty-four. She was an R.N., a nurse in an Army medical forward unit. A band of rebel Chechen terrorists attacked. They killed every wounded man, every doctor in there, and then, they raped every nurse who was there, many times over."

Cal stared at the photo, giving Kazak a startled look. "She almost looks like Sky's twin."

Alex nodded. "Your Sky reminds me of my beloved sister, Kira. There was nothing I could do for her when she was raped, but," and Alex turned and looked down at Sky, his voice growing stronger, "I can do something for her. Help her avoid what Kira had no control over."

Cal handed the picture to Kazak. "I'm sorry about your sister. Let's get this show on the road."

CHAPTER 17

February 1

THE FIRST THING Sky saw when she dragged her eyes open was a strange man standing at her side. Her mind was empty. She felt his comforting strong hand around hers. Her voice was hoarse. "Who are you? Where…"

"Hospital in Cusco," he told her quietly, holding her wandering gaze. "You're coming out of a cycle of malaria. You're safe and you're going to be okay, Sky. And I'm Cal. Just rest." He watched her trying to remember him. The doctors had told him not to expect that she would know who he was at first, but that as the malaria released its grip on her, she would remember him fully. He tried not to be bothered by it.

Her brow furrowed and she studied him a long minute. Voice hoarse, she managed, "Cal?"

He'd seen a shift in her eyes, that glaze that was always present, was almost gone, at least for an instant. He smiled and wrapped his hand around hers that rested on her midsection above the blankets. "Yes, that's me. Do you remember me?"

She closed her eyes, moving her mouth and then opening them again, staring at him. "I-I think I do…"

He held up her left hand so she could see the blue diamond engagement ring still on her finger. "Do you remember this?"

For a moment, she stared at it, her gaze drifting upward to him, studying him. And then, "…Oh…," and she whispered, "Cal?"

This time, he saw that she knew who he was, and his throat closed with tears of gratitude. "Yes, it's me, Sky." He gently laid her hand on the blankets. "It's your engagement ring we bought here in Cusco," he managed in a low, emotional tone. "I love you…" and he watched her fade away, the glaze returned to her eyes once more. Taking hope, he dragged in a deep breath, simply holding her hand, loving her more than anything ever, in his life.

February 2

IT WAS 0800, and Cal had just gotten a shower and change of clothes from his apartment and then hoofed it over to the hospital to be with Sky once again. Earlier, 0600, he'd come over to see her. And to his relief, she recognized him, if briefly. There were IVs in both her arms. The Night Stalker Black Hawk had picked them up at the edge of the jungle trail at the designated GPS position in the meadow. And Alex Kazak had been good for his word. He'd distracted Alexandrov and sent him and his men in the opposite direction, allowing Cal to carry Sky that brutal two miles in the rain, the fierce winds, slogging through the slippery clay furrows of the fields to reach the rally point in that meadow. The downpour was so bad, their escape had been completely hidden by a thick, gray veil of rain. The Russians never spotted them. He considered that a miracle.

All that was behind them, now. Cal was sore as hell, having sprained an ankle slipping and nearly falling with unconscious Sky in his arms halfway to his objective. Right now, he had duct tape wrapped around it. It was the SEAL way of dealing with a sprain when out on an op. The Black Hawk crew had picked them up, a paramedic on board to take care of Sky, and in less than an hour had transported them to the Cusco hospital.

He'd gone into her hospital room and saw that she was sleeping deeply. Touching her meant everything to him, but he didn't want to awaken her. The doctor said to let her sleep, that it was the most healing thing he could do to help her get better, so he simply sat by her bedside, wanting to be with her in case she woke up.

The door quietly opened, and Cal looked toward it. The man standing in the doorway was dressed in Army cammos, muddy as hell, with camouflage paint on his sweat-streaked face.

"Sinclair?" he demanded in a quiet, gruff tone, hand on the doorknob.

"Yeah." Cal recognized his voice and stood up, heading for the door. "Killmer?" He kept his voice low so as not to disturb Sky's sleep. The man nodded. He walked out into the hall and quietly shut the door to Sky's room, turning to him.

The Special Forces operator grinned tiredly. "How is Ms. Lambert doing?"

"She's going to live."

"That's good to hear. We just got airlifted to Cusco by that Night Stalker Blackhawk earlier this morning. Got a second you can spare me?"

"For you, I do," Cal said, smiling a little. Killmer had short black hair and penetrating gray eyes that missed nothing. The man was built like a well-muscled boxer with broad shoulders and a deep chest. He didn't have any weapons on him because Peru's law did not allow them, but Mace Killmer was still lethal, nonetheless. There was mud on his combat boots, splattered halfway up his legs. He was still wearing a Kevlar vest beneath his harness. To

Cal, it appeared he'd just come off an op.

"You finally get out of that green hell of a jungle for a while?" Cal asked. The stench of jungle smells, musky, rotting odors, surrounded him.

Killmer removed his floppy camouflage hat and raked his long, spare fingers through his damp hair. "Could say that Sinclair. We were monitoring your comms with the Black Hawk as you were carrying her to the rally point." Killmer moved his strong chin in the direction of Sky's room. "I told my team, once they released us for some R and R, that first, I wanted to come to the hospital to see how she was doing and see if you were still gimping along with that sprain."

He held out his hand to the Army Special Forces sergeant. "I'm still mobile and Sky is doing much better. We owe you, our lives. If you and your team hadn't been in place, hadn't made the decision to support us, we wouldn't be standing here discussing it."

Mace gripped the SEAL's hand, a lopsided grin pulling at his exhausted features. "Just remember, it was the Army that saved your ass, Navy."

Cal met the man's grin with one of his own, Killmer's grip firm and strong. "Yeah, this is one for the history books. Usually, it's the other way around." He watched the man who appeared to be in his early thirties, smile sourly and released his hand.

"Thank God for inter-branch military rivalry," Killmer murmured, settling his hands on his hips. "Look, I'm here for a two-fold reason. I got permission from my people back at Langley to come here and see you in person." Mace looked around, making sure the hall was devoid of people, his voice low. He became somber. "After you lifted off, we finally arrived at the village sometime later. We surveyed Alexandrov and his men systematically looking for you and Ms. Lambert. We got orders to take them out is they didn't want to surrender." Mace's eyes glittered with satisfaction. "And we did because nine of them did, but the rest wouldn't surrender. Gave no quarter. We killed three of them, but two others escaped. One is Lev Zuyev, second-in-command, and the other, Nikita Morozov, a Ukrainian medic. The Peruvian police rounded up those that surrendered, and they are in custody within the country and will be prosecuted. The bodies of the other three who wanted to shoot it out with us came here to the morgue in body bags. That still left one man unaccounted for."

Gulping, Cal stared at the operator. "You killed Alexandrov?" His heart took off at an unsteady beat.

"Yeah," Mace said, satisfaction in his deep voice. "He was mine."

Relief tunneled through Cal, and he drew in a ragged breath. "That was more than I had hoped for. I was going to go back out there and personally hunt him down as soon as Sky was in recovery." Now, he wouldn't have to. Cal could take her home. Home to his cabin, home to where she belonged: in his arms. She'd never have to look over her shoulder again and worry if Vlad was there to jump out of the shadows.

"Here's where it gets interesting," Mace added thoughtfully. "Going hut to hut after the firefight, to try and find the last Russian, we found, instead, the second Ukrainian medic by the name of Alexei Kazak. He'd been shot in the leg in a hut, slowly bleeding to death. He said he helped you and the woman escape. Is that true?"

"Yeah, every word of its true. How is Alex? Did he make it?"

Mace nodded, his mouth softening. "He's here in this hospital, but I figured no one would tell you that. As soon as that Blackhawk dropped you and Ms. Lambert off, they flew back to help us. Alex is a stand-up dude. He's on the third floor, room 308. There's an American Marine detachment from Lima guarding his door for the duration, to make sure he doesn't go anywhere or that the Russian mafia doesn't send in a hitman in here to finish him off. He's beaten to shit, but he's going to make it." Mace settled the hat back on his head. "Alexandrov nearly beat him to death earlier, before we arrived, because he accused the medic of allowing Sky to escape. The Indians in the village were afraid of Kazak, being part of Alexandrov's crew. After we came into their area, and we were hunting for the last drug runner, they led us to him. They wanted him out of there, fearing retribution by the other drug lords who are fighting the Russians' intrusion. They didn't want to get caught in the middle of it."

Cal rubbed his jaw, eyeing the sergeant. "Alex Kazak is a combat medic, and he's the one who took care of Sky. If he isn't granted asylum or help from our country, then something's really screwed up. The man deserves our help, not a prison cell. And I won't sit still and say nothing in his defense." Cal saw the glitter in the sergeant's eyes, a careless half smile tugging at his mouth.

"Stand down, SEAL. You don't have to do anything. Between what you'd told me over the sat phone and what he told me after we found him, I put it all together. Nate stopped the bleeding on the bullet wound you nailed him with. Kazak filled us in on everything. He seemed relieved to know his commander was dead. Anyway, my CIA handler back at Langley is clearing the way for him to be transported to Balboa Naval Hospital in San Diego for recovery as soon as the docs approves it here. He's asked for political asylum in the U.S. The right people from the State Department will fly out to San Diego and interview him. Then a decision will be made."

"What do you think? Will he be granted it?" Cal was adamant that he'd become an advocate for the Ukrainian medic.

Grimacing, Mace shook his head. "The jury is out on that one, partner. On the plus side, he sacrificed himself to save you and Ms. Lambert. What's against him is that he worked for the Russian Mafia, as a drug runner. I don't know how the State Department is going to view him or what will happen. Another thing in his favor is that he and the other medic, Nik Morozov are not Russian. Nor are they members of the Communist Party. The people of Ukraine are a democracy. The U.S. supports Ukraine and its citizens. But," he shrugged, "all of this is above our pay grade as to what their final decision might be."

"Well," Cal growled, "I'm throwing my weight in on the side of granting him asylum."

"Yeah, but it's a thornier issue than that. Alex's family lives in Ukraine. The Russian Mafia will take their revenge, if he's granted asylum in the U.S., and they will kill his family. What the State Department needs to do is offer asylum to the rest of his family to come over here, too. Otherwise, they're all dead men walking."

Grunting, Cal nodded. "This is messy," he agreed. "But give me your CIA handler's name and number. I'm pushing my nose into this fray and making it my business."

Killmer grin tiredly.

"Already knew you'd go there, Navy." He pulled out a dirty piece of badly folded notebook paper with a name and phone number scrawled across it from his pocket. "Here. Everything you need to be a partner in this dance with us. My handler knows you're weighing in on this and that you're a serious player. They haven't disagreed with my request, so go push your considerable SEAL weight around and get involved. See what mountains you can move…" He slid the paper into Sinclair's outstretched hand.

"Where are you going now?" Cal asked.

Mace smiled a little. "My team and I are being given three weeks R and R in Lima. Los Flores area. We're staying overnight in Cusco, gonna get cleaned up, get a hot shower, change into our civilian clothes, find some damn fine Latin food, down a half a dozen pisco sours, and catch up on sleep. Then we'll head out for Lima and party. After that, we come up to this area we were assigned, and re-establish our presence like before a certain SEAL broke into our mission and blew it all to hell." His eyes glinted with amusement as he watched Cal's silly-assed grin spread across his face.

"Shit, you boys would die and go to heaven to have an op like this drop into your lap. You were fucking bored just mapping trails in the region. You're all about direct action missions, just like we are." Cal's grin widened. "Having to hump twenty-five miles carrying a hundred and twenty-five pounds on you is what you're really bitching about," and he chuckled.

"About right, partner," Killmer drawled, giving him a look of respect. "You did some serious humping yourself with half that weight. We really didn't think you were going to make thirty-minute miles, but you did."

Smugly, Cal said, "I'm a SEAL. What else did you expect?"

Chuckling indulgently, Killmer allowed his hands to fall from his hips. "Listen, your name is on a short list of people who are permitted to see Kazak. You need to present your ID to the Marine guards, and they'll let you go in and see the dude. He's in rough shape; broken nose, broken jaw, three cracked ribs, bruised kidneys, and two black eyes. Alexandrov worked him over pretty good."

"Spetsnaz methods," Cal growled.

"Yeah, that's what Kazak said. Alexandrov bought Kazak's story hook, line, and sinker. But he still beat the tar out of the poor bastard even with a wounded leg. Kazak couldn't defend himself at all."

"Now you realize why Alexandrov had to be taken down."

"Yeah, he was one sick fuck." Mace lifted his chin, giving Cal a slanted look. "I took him out with a head shot."

"One of us was going to do it."

"The two that go away? We're going to try and round 'em up when we get back on duty in that nightmare of a puzzle piece jungle. Alex said that Nik Morozov, the other medic, was forced to escape with Lev, the second-in-command, or he'd have put a bullet in his head, too. Alex is hoping at some point that Nik can peel off, hide, and make it back to Cusco and contact the State Department through the U.S. ambassador down in Lima."

"Nik helped Alex save Sky. He's not a bad guy, either."

Nodding, Killmer said, "Yeah, Kazak already told us that, but your word carries equal weight. If we find the dude, we'll try and bring him in and offer him asylum like Kazak."

Cal felt relief. "Good to know. He aided Sky, brought in the IVs that saved her life."

"I'll be putting all of this in my report. A copy will go to the State Department. Maybe we'll be able to track him down when we get back on duty. It's a big jungle out there though, and I don't hold out much hope of that happening."

"Can I buy you and your team a round of drinks when we get down in Lima, Killmer?"

Mace grinned. "Yeah, for sure. You flyin' out of Lima sometime later this week?"

"Yeah, if my woman is medically fit enough to do so. Let's keep in touch? We have sat phones and I can call you once we're in Lima. The least I can do is buy you and your team as many rounds of pisco sours as you want."

Mace grinned, his teeth white against the green, black and gray camouflage paint over his face. "This is one for the history books. Gotta get a cell phone picture of a Navy SEAL paying for Army boys' pisco sours," and he chuckled, shook Cal's hand, and strolled down the hall, heading for the elevators. "And then I'm gonna splatter it all over the Internet. You SEALs will NEVER live this one down," he called over his shoulder, laughing deeply, the sound echoing up and down the hall.

Alex Kazak was surprised when he saw the Navy SEAL enter his room that afternoon. The pain meds were keeping him comfortable, even to the point of being able to manage a lopsided smile of welcome for the operator even though his face was severely swollen and bruised.

Cal took the medic's extended large hand. "I'm Cal Sinclair. I just found out you were here. How are you doing, Kazak?"

Alex's jaw was wired shut, but he could still speak to an extent. "Better now, thanks."

Looking the Ukrainian over, he was dressed in a blue gown that didn't fully fit his large frame, sitting up in Fowler's position in his bed, an IV in his left arm. "I just got done talking to the spec ops sergeant who found you in that village. I didn't think this would happen to you," and he pointed to his injured face.

Managing a grimace, Alex said, "I expected it. Our plan worked perfectly. When I threw the grenade and you shot me in the leg, everyone came bailing out of their huts in the middle of that downpour. My commander bought my story. And then he asked about Sky." With a grimace, Alex said, "I lied and told him I saw you pass by the window, and I went out after you, leaving Sky unguarded." Alex's eyes, barely visible through the beating he'd taken, sparkled. "He went ballistic, ran down to the hut and did not find her. Ran back to me, screaming and demanding which way you went with her. I pointed opposite of where you were heading." Alex smiled as much as he could. "My commander believed me. He and the rest of his team searched for two ghosts they never found."

Cal heard the pride in the man's voice. His face looked like ground meat. "And then Alexandrov came back and beat you?"

Alex managed a grimace. "Yes. He tried to kill me. I lost consciousness from the beating, and I think he thought I was dead. When I woke up, I had been left without any medical help. The wound you gave me bled more than I had hoped, but I had no way to care for myself. With broken ribs, I could not move. I could not reach my medical ruck."

"And then, the Special Forces team found you with the help of the Indians?"

Closing his eyes, utterly exhausted, Alex nodded. "Yes. Otherwise, I would be dead by now."

Grimly, Cal gripped the medic's shoulder. "Tell me about the ambush at that village. Do you know who killed that red-haired woman?"

Alex opened his eyes. He made a face, but it wasn't much of one. "Lev Zuyev, second-in-command, did it. The commander had told us to focus on you two, not the woman. He wanted her alive because she was a nurse. He had plans to kidnap her, rape her, but Lev killed her."

"And Lev Zuyev is the one who escaped," Cal muttered, scowling.

"Yes, he and my medic brother, Nik Morozov, ran. Zuyev is heartless. No morals or values. Our time in Chechnya made him into a monster. Nik is like a brother to me. He is from Ukraine, as I am. He was born on a communal wheat farm next to where my family lives. He would never rape a woman. He was as sickened by it, as I was. We both got beat up several times when we tried to stop the rapes. Alexandrov told us if either of us tried to interfere again, he'd put a bullet in our heads. I'm sure Lev put a gun to Nik's head and forced him to run with him away from the village. These men know how badly they need a medic when in the jungle. I do not think Nik would leave me behind of his own volition. Nik would have come back to find me. He the brother I never had. He would not have abandoned me under those circumstances. I am sure he was forced to leave with Zuyev or he'd have killed him right then and there."

Cal nodded and eyed Kazak. "I'll be sure and put this in my report so that Nik isn't seen as our enemy, rather an ally who helped save Sky's life. Why weren't you two like the rest of your team?"

Opening his bruised, swollen hand, Alex whispered, "...I am a farm boy from Ukraine, just like Nik. We grew up together, the best of friends. My family has lived for generations on the land. I grew up seeing life and death. My parents, bless them, taught me the value of life toward all beings, that they should all be respected and preserved. War can take your soul if you allow it. I would not let it take mine," and Alex tried to give a shrug, but the movement caused him immediate pain. "Nor would Nik. He believes as I do."

"Well, you and Nik sure as hell got me and Sky out of a bad situation and I owe you," Cal said, meaning it. He held the medic's weary gaze.

"Yes, Sky loves you. It made me feel good to protect Sky from my commander. She will never live a half-life like my sister Kira, who is imprisoned within that one event for the rest of her time here on Earth..."

Cal settled his hand gently on Alex's shoulder. "I'm sorry that happened. Look, I'm going to push hard to get you asylum in our country for you and your family. Just know that. I've got some powerful contacts, and I'm going to call in my markers to see if we can make it happen." He saw Alex's eyes water. Tears fell out of the swollen corners of his eyes.

"My only family left in Ukraine is Kira. She is all I have left alive. I know what the KGB or Russian mafia will do to her if they ever find out what I did to help you escape. The commander's father, Yerik Alexandrov, is a very powerful Russian mafia lord in New York City right now… I worry for her, and I cannot reach her to tell her what has transpired. But Yerik can."

"Look," Cal said, "stop worrying. Give me contact information on Kira. You need to concentrate on getting well. I'm making some calls as soon as I leave your room. I'm down on the second floor where Sky is recovering. If you need me, it's room 210. I'll leave word with the Marines guarding you outside this door that I'm allowing such contact between the three of us to take place."

Barely nodding, Alex whispered unsteadily, "You are now turning around and saving the life of my sister and I… and for that, I will be forever in your debt and grateful…"

"One step at a time," Cal cautioned him. "Let me make those calls. Get some things in motion for you. I'll drop by later this evening and check in with you. Right now, I need to be with Sky. Her fever is starting to go down, finally…"

"Of course," Alex agreed, his voice thick. "Stay with her. Love will see her through this, as it will with you."

Gently squeezing Kazak's shoulder, Cal said, "Get some rest, buddy. I'll see you later and bring you up to speed on what I've found out."

Sky was fully awake this time when Cal quietly entered her room. His heart took off as he saw how distressed she looked. Was the malaria coming back? Another phase? The doctor said she might have one more cycle before it was over, and the symptoms cleared.

A little gasp escaped her. "Cal?"

He halted halfway to her bed. His heart hammered with joy. "Yes, it's me."

"I-I thought you were dead… I saw them shoot you…I had awful flash-back…"

"I'm okay," he reassured her. "You're coming out of the hold of the malaria." Relieved she was fully conscious and there was no glaze to her eyes this time, sloughed off another layer of worry off his shoulders. Seeing the tears form in her eyes, he moved to her side. "You're here in a Cusco hospital and you're going to be fine." He slipped his hand into Sky's, leaning over and kissing her lightly on the lips. "How are you doing?" As he lifted his head, Cal could see her eyes were clear. She was fully present for the first time. Tears were running down her face and he gave her a gentle look, using his thumbs to brush them away. "You're safe," he said, his voice sounding rough with emotion. "It's all over, Sky. I'm fine and you are on your way out of this malaria episode. What can I do for you, Sweetheart?"

Sky whispered raggedly. "I'm so thirsty, Cal."

"That, I can remedy," he growled, pouring her water and then carefully lifting her upward and holding her against him. "Drink all you want." He sat on the edge of her bed with his hip against her blanketed one. She'd been through so much and then to have the malaria come like a bat out of hell and take her down, leaving her helpless against Alexandrov, tore him apart. She was so much stronger than he'd ever realized. Sky drank nosily, slurping and some of the water slopping out of the corners of her mouth.

Cal retrieved her a second glass and found a straw in a drawer. He smiled down at her and removed the water from the corners of her a mouth first. "This straw will help," he murmured.

Sky was comforted by Cal's nearness. She sucked all the water from the glass, finally sated. Feeling bereft when he eased her back against the bed, he tucked the covers in around her waist, fussed with her uncombed hair, and grazed her cheek with his fingertips.

"Tired?" Cal asked, sitting on the edge of the bed to face her. He moved his hand gently down her exposed left forearm. The blue of the nightgown brought out the stunning color in her weary looking eyes.

"Fatigue is the word you want…still, I feel so much better now." Sky studied Cal's hard face. He was dressed in his usual black T-shirt and jungle cammo cargo pants and boots. He was clean-shaven, his short hair combed and in place. She relished his calloused hand tenderly sliding up and down her forearm in gentle, tender strokes. "I remember everything now," Sky whispered, closing her eyes, feeling tears come. "Julie being shot. And Dylan going down. And you being shot…"

"Look at me, Sky."

She forced her eyes open, holding Cal's somber looking gold-brown eyes. She saw the darkness and grief in them.

"Julie died instantly," he told her in a low voice, entangling his fingers between hers. "She felt no pain, Sky. Dylan is going to live. He received a bullet to the thigh. He's had surgery here in Cusco and has already been flown stateside. They've taken him at the Balboa Naval hospital, in San Diego, and he's doing well in recovery." Grimacing, Cal added, "Julie's body was flown back home to her parents' Virginia farm. Her funeral is today. Dylan can't make it, but her parents are flying out to see him shortly afterward, to visit him at the hospital. He is their son-in-law, and they're good people. They're going to help him all they can."

"T-that's good." She licked her dry lower lip. "I was crazed with fever, Cal. Everything blanked out." Sky made a face. "Malaria is not something you ever want to get. It sucks."

He laughed a little and squeezed her fingers. "The doc said you got it because you probably forgot to take your meds daily. Is that true?"

"Yes…" Sky gave him a helpless look. "Last week… before all this happened, Cal, our lives were in free fall. I just forgot. It was my own fault…"

"No fault, Sweetheart. You're alive and you'll recover. We'll get you through this."

Sky frowned. "Cal, there was this Ukrainian soldier… he helped me… cared for me. I don't even remember his name, but he protected me from Vlad. I know he did…"

"His name is Alex Kazak." And Cal told her the rest of the story about how he helped them escape and that he was in the same hospital as she was in right now. Cal didn't go into detail because he could see Sky rapidly fading. He hoped like hell she didn't have one more virulent cycle of the malaria before it left her alone again.

"I-I'm glad he's alive. From the moment he helped me on the helicopter, I knew he would protect me. It was just a feeling, but it proved to be true. He kept Vlad at bay. I think, but I don't know for sure, he fought Vlad and forced him off me at some point."

Cal saw the pain in Sky's eyes, the grief and sadness for all that had come down around their heads in the last few days. "He did have a fight with him, defending you from Vlad's assault at the hut. He said you reminded him of his little sister."

"He's a real hero, Cal," she said more strongly. "He saved me. He absolutely did." She added, "And so did you. You're going to have to tell me how you managed to find me? And rescue me?"

Cal leaned over and kissed her brow and then her cheek. "In time, Sweet Woman. Right now, you need sleep more than anything else. I've got some calls to make and then I'll stand guard over you. Fair enough?" He thought about telling her that Vlad was dead, but she was so fragile right now, that he didn't want one more emotional shock to halt her recovery. That news would wait until a better time when she was stronger physically and emotionally. He would know when it was appropriate to tell her the rest of the story.

Sky managed a weary smile. "That sounds so good…I love you so much…"

CHAPTER 18

February 3

SKY AWOKE SLOWLY, the room dark. She felt arms around her, a body holding her close. Frowning, fighting her sleepiness, she gradually realized from the soft snore nearby, it was Cal curved around her. Heart opening, Sky lay there on her side, being held by him as he slept. She had no memory of him sleeping with her in her hospital bed. It was a cramped bed at best, slightly larger than a twin. Sky hungrily absorbed his strength and sense of overwhelming protection. She was no longer on an IV in her arm and it felt like freedom to her. She was physically drained in ways she couldn't begin to express in words. And yet she felt buoyant, more hopeful than ever before, as she lay there next to him and inhaled Cal's scent, a mix of male with his pine soap he loved so much. He'd once told her it reminded him of his home in Virginia, the fragrance of the Douglas fir mixed in with maple, oak, elm and beech trees that surrounded his home. Now, she knew why: his hideaway, the place he felt safe and healing to his spirit, was his cedar cabin, hidden away with the meadow and creek below it. He'd shown her several new photos of it surrounded by the thick stands of trees crowning the hill where he'd built it.

"Hey," Cal muttered thickly. "You, okay?" and he eased back, propping himself up on an elbow staring sleepily down into Sky's deeply shadowed face.

"Fine," Sky answered, her voice rusty from not speaking much. "I just woke up on my own. I think, for the first time, I'm symptom-free," and she managed a slight smile. Cal's face was hard, his beard darkening his face, giving him the look of the hunter, he was. She turned onto her back, reached up, feeling new strength returning to her. Sliding her fingers across his cheek, the stubble sending tingles down her fingertips, she whispered, "I love you, Cal…" Sky felt and saw his reaction. He had no game face in place, and she saw his sable and gold eyes narrow upon her, making her feel utterly cosseted by his tall, hard body.

Cal cupped her cheek gently, leaning down whispering against her mouth, "I love you too, Sweetheart…"

Those priceless words flowed into Sky, feeding her heart, and healing her soul. His mouth tender and searching against hers, as if to kiss her hard would injure her in some way. She gave a breathy laugh and pulled away, meeting his burning gaze. "I'm not THAT fragile, Cal."

"Yes," he growled, "you are." And he kissed her gently for a long, long time, reacquainting himself with her womanly taste, the soft pliancy of her lips molding hotly against his own. Cal reluctantly broke the kiss and added with a scowl, "You just don't know it, is all."

Sky languished in his embrace wanting to go nowhere else. "Well, maybe when compared to a SEAL who suffered a terrible sprain, cuts and bruises all over his body, and pushing it beyond any human limit I've ever seen for twenty-five miles, you're right." She gave him a wicked look, her heart soaring with love for this man who ignored his own pain and suffering in service to others. She saw him raise his brows and then give her a wry look. He moved to his back and brought her against him, her head resting on his shoulder, arm curving across his torso. Cal was still dressed, only his combat boots missing from his large sock feet that hung over the end of the hospital bed.

Cal smiled, amusement in his deep voice. "You must be feeling better. You're getting cocky again."

Laughing a little, Sky nodded. "For the first time, I actually feel human." Her stomach growled loudly. She heard Cal chuckle.

"Hungry?"

"I guess I am." Sky sighed. "What time is it?"

Cal looked at his watch. "0300. Middle of the night. Why?"

"I'm craving a hamburger."

Grinning, he murmured, "Best words I've heard since you landed here in the hospital. You're on the mend, Sky."

Sighing, she nodded, content to be held, her body pressed against his. "I'm so glad you're here, Cal. It was nice waking up just now and finding you next to me."

"Shoulda seen the Peruvian nurse the first time she came in here to check on you and saw me in your bed, holding you."

She heard laughter in Cal's voice. "When was this?"

"When they first brought you in off the helicopter. You were going into the fever stage again, fighting the IVs. The doc was going to knock you out with a tranquilizer, and I nixed it." Cal's voice dropped. "Told them if I held you in bed, that you'd settle down. At first, they got all flustered and said it wasn't right for me to lay in your hospital bed with you. That it was against the rules."

Sky managed a short laugh. "They don't know Navy SEALs. You guys break the rules all the time and reinvent them into what you want."

"Well, they found that out. The new shift of nurse coming in the next morning found us asleep in this bed. The nurse about had a hemorrhage. She looked like a deer caught in headlights: stunned into silence," and Cal chuckled. "Good thing she didn't come in a touch me, though," Cal said, getting serious.

"Geeze," Sky said, worried. "Did she leave you alone?"

"Yeah, we traded a few stiff words in Spanish with one another," he drawled. "She got the message. And then I took the medical doctor to task and made it clear I was going to be holding you through those phases and that they weren't going to sedate you. I wouldn't have it. He agreed with me," Cal murmured, pleased with himself.

"You are SUCH a badass, Sinclair."

"Thank you. That's a real compliment."

Sky nuzzled his neck, kissing him several times, feeling him respond. She was nowhere strong enough to make love to him yet, but when she was, he'd better look out. Smiling, Sky closed her eyes. "I'm tired now," she murmured.

"And now, I'm wide awake."

Her lips compressed. "But you love me anyway?" She felt his arm tighten around her shoulders.

"Sweetheart, you are my life. I'll move heaven, hell, and anything else that gets in my way just to be with you and keep you safe."

The words were balm to Sky's exhausted soul. Yesterday evening, Cal had told her Vlad was dead. That Sergeant Mace Killmer, had shot him at the village. He left a lot out because it wasn't necessary to share it. Sky had lived all her young life under his threatening shadow and now, he'd never bother her again. She had laid there and cried with relief, clinging to him. And he'd held her against him, rasping that she was finally free, for the first time in her life. Sky had no idea of how long she cried, but she finally ran out of tears. He patted her cheeks dry with tissue after tissue, cradled her in his arms, and murmured how much he loved her. It was as if an emotional dam had also broken within Cal and he could finally share the vast array of feelings he'd been holding at bay from her. It had startled Sky, but it was something she valued as much as breathing. She wanted to know how Cal felt at any given point, to share his worries, his happiness, his dreams... all of it... with her.

"Maybe this morning," Sky whispered in a hopeful tone, "you could walk over to the local McDonald's when it opens at 0600? Get me two hamburgers? Two huge fries? I'm craving American food." She felt Cal laugh; no sound coming from him, just body movement.

"Want some American coffee to go with your order?" he asked wryly.

"Mmmm, that sounds delicious." Her stomach growled again. This time, Cal chuckled out loud. "What about some of those gooey cinnamon rolls?"

"Yes, that would be great, too."

"They have oats with fruit and nuts on top of it."

"I can't eat that much but thank you."

"Music to my ears," Cal growled. "They open at 0600. I'll bring you back your American breakfast, Ms. Lambert."

Tucking her hand beneath her jaw, she whispered, "Thank you, Cal. You really know how to take care of me..."

"That's because I love the hell out of you. Now go back to sleep, you're starting to slur your words, Sky. What you need is complete rest."

Cal hid his smile as he sat in the chair next to Sky's bed, watching as she attacked the McDonald's breakfast order with gusto. He'd gotten out of bed, pulled on his combat boots, and quietly left her room, leaving her undisturbed and sleeping deeply, a healing sleep. By the time he had returned, she was sitting up in bed, her hair uncombed, but her eyes looking clear, and color slowly returning to her cheeks, waiting anxiously for the food. He'd bought four Egg McMuffins, two boxes of cinnamon rolls, two oatmeal, and two cups of their largest coffee. That was a small breakfast for him.

"This—," Sky muffled between bites, her mouth full, "—is delicious. It tastes SO good, Cal. Thank you..."

"You owe me," he growled, his mouth lifting as he watched her demolish the first Egg McMuffin and quickly open the second one.

"Mmmm," she said between bites and gulps, "I like owing you."

Sky looked hauntingly fragile, but she was more perky this morning, exuding more energy, her eyes dancing with life. Cal was so damned grateful for it, that he felt like crying. Sky's strength, while unseen, was like the Andes mountains: resilient and indomitable. She was bouncing back from trauma he couldn't imagine, and yet, here she was, gulping down food, starved. His smile increased and he shook his head, loving her even more, if that was possible.

Sky was amazing. And she was his. She loved him. Him, of all people! Cal had never thought he had any capacity to fall in love. Or to be loved. He'd felt too shattered by life, unable to give anyone anything. So much had been stolen from him as a child. It had left him hard, taciturn, and blunt, none of which lent to romantic charm. Yet, Sky had stepped into his life and magically changed it by her just being her. Cal knew he'd never get over the fact she loved him, despite himself. He didn't know what she saw in him, but he was so damned thankful for whatever it was. He'd spend the rest of his life loving her with whatever was left of him.

Staring openly at her, Cal felt his heart mushroom with such a fierce love of this woman, it choked him up for a moment and he stopped eating. He watched her considering his challenge, wolfing down the food without apology.

That was another thing he liked about her: Sky was real. She didn't play games. Life had destroyed much of her ability to socialize, he now realized. She'd been ground down to her essence and that's where she lived today. Fine by him because he liked her natural and without airs or playing games. He never found those sorts of people appealing. They all wore masks. Sky wore none. And she was so damned beautiful, it made him want to get down on his knees and weep for joy. Cal knew he was not attractive as males went. Just the opposite. Yet, she loved him. It made him dizzy sometimes, to try and figure out why. What could she possibly see in him? Maybe someday, he'd understand it, but right now he didn't.

"So," Sky said, coming up for air after eating the second McMuffin and swallowing some coffee, "I have to pay a price, Sinclair?" and she gave him a testy look.

He loved her brashness. To look at Sky, one would never think she'd been an aggressive, risk-taking medevac pilot flying into the face of danger and possibly death on every flight. One wouldn't imagine she'd survived her terrible childhood, only to then witness the murder of her two foster parents whom she'd genuinely loved. Anything Sky had loved had been stripped from her. It had built a strength in her he'd never seen in another woman, and maybe that's what drew Cal to her. He sensed his own kind. His childhood left him picking up pieces too, trying to cobble himself back together to get along in society.

He wiped his hands on a paper napkin, then opened the oatmeal in the cup. "Yeah, you gotta pay, Sweetheart."

"What did you have in mind, exactly?" she teased, picking at the hot, delicious cinnamon rolls in the box sitting on her blanketed lap.

Cal struck a thoughtful pose, spooning in the hot oatmeal. "You don't get a choice," he warned.

Chuckling, Sky hooted. "You're SUCH a tough guy when you want to be, Sinclair. Stop threatening me and tell me what I owe you for this amazing, delicious breakfast."

He gave her a hooded look. "IF," he emphasized, "you feel like taking a short distance to a jewelry store that's nearby, I want you to pick out a set of wedding rings for us." He saw her mouth drop open for a moment, then Sky quickly snapped it shut. She was shaken, not expecting this. Cal wondered if it was too soon. He knew Sky hated hospitals. Who didn't? "Look," he soothed, "you don't have to do it. I just thought if you felt up to it, a short walk out in the fresh air and sunshine would do you a world of good. We can do that some other time. It's no big deal."

Tears jammed into Sky's eyes as she sat there regarding him. Cal looked like an anxious little boy in that moment, so wanting to please her, to make her happy. She stopped eating and held his stare. Sky swore she could feel he was silently trying to protect himself from whatever she might say. For a moment, she saw Cal as that gangly innocent seven-year-old boy, without a mother and only an abusive father who showed his love through a leather belt he'd wield against him. Her throat tightened and she looked down at her clasped hands. "No… no, I'd LOVE to do that with you Cal." Sky saw his face soften, saw relief flood his gold-brown eyes that had darkened, as if he were waiting to be hit. Sky would never do that to him. Not ever. She realized this was so important to Cal that he'd exposed himself fully, completely vulnerable to her because he loved her. And this was his way of proposing to her. She loved him so much. So much…

Cal sat up, the oatmeal cup in his hands. "Really? You'd like to do that?" He saw the glistening tears in Sky's eyes, but they never fell. The soft line of her mouth nearly broke him. She looked so utterly happy. Cal had never seen her like this before. That's when he believed her. He put the paper sacks down on the floor, stood up and sat on the edge of her bed, facing her. He gathered Sky's hands into his.

"I didn't exactly say this right," Cal muttered, unhappy with himself. "I want to marry you, Sky. I don't want to wait long, either. What we have," and he held her luminous gaze, "is one for the books." His mouth tightened for a moment as he tried to put his feelings into words. It was hard to do because no one had ever demanded this of him before. As a SEAL, they sure as hell didn't want his emotions anywhere near their kill box. Moving his large, scarred fingers over hers, thinking how long and delicate looking her hands were against his, he cleared his throat, feeling suddenly nervous. Cal looked up at Sky. "I can't think of life without you in it, Sweetheart. I'm not good with words and I'm struggling." Cal broke into a boyish grin. "Hell, I can wade into a firefight with no problem, but telling you I love you, that I want you as my wife, my best friend, my lover for the rest of my sorry-assed life, is tougher than any battlefield."

"Cal," she whispered, lifting her hands from his, framing his face, holding his shaken gaze, "I love you. Yes, I'll marry you. Anytime, anywhere." Sky laughed a little, tears trailing down her cheeks. "For a guy who's well known for his bluntness, you are very diplomatic, your words are beautiful when they come straight from your heart. Do you realize that? I love the man who allows his heart to speak through him. Never stop doing that?"

"You tear me up when you cry, dammit."

Sniffing, Sky leaned forward and whispered, "Tough, crying is good for a person's soul in case you missed that memo. You're such a growly bear when you want to be, Sinclair," and she laid a kiss on him that made him change his mind about her being fragile.

"I like this set," Sky said, pointing down through the glass display case at the Aura Jeweler's store just off Plaza de Armas. Cal had hailed a taxi outside the hospital, not wanting her to walk that much yet. He'd brought a pantsuit of pale blue linen from her closet of their apartment, a soft silk blouse that had a lavender sheen to it, and her favorite pair of gold earrings. She was eager to get rid of the hospital gown and into real clothes, once again. She looked beautiful sitting in the chair at the elegant antique table at the back of the famous jewelry store. He saw Sky pointing to a gold band and a very small solitaire engagement ring. She'd chosen the smallest diamond in the case. The prices were hefty, and he knew what she was doing.

"Maybe," he grunted. He looked at the Peruvian owner, Esteban Morales, dressed in a very expensive dark pinstripe suit, and said, "Bring us any blue diamonds you might have? Do you have any?"

"Of course, we do," Esteban murmured. "A fine choice to match the color of your lady's eyes." He gave them a perfunctory smile and turned, speaking quickly in Spanish to a woman dressed in a white blouse and black skirt waiting in the background. She hurried around the U-shaped displays. In moments, she brought out six blue diamond sets on a gray velvet pad for them to look at.

Cal watched Sky for reaction. He heard her draw in a breath, her eyes widen with surprise as she stared down at the array and choices. Blue diamonds were rare. Cal saw one set that was perfect, nearly matching the color of Sky's eyes. He knew the price was going to be astronomical, but he didn't care. Sky moved her fingers delicately from one set to another, oohing and awing over each one. She reminded Cal of a butterfly alighting gently on each flower, tasting it, testing it, and then moving on to the next. She was enraptured with their faceted beauty.

"Would you wear a blue diamond?" Cal asked, catching her glance.

"Oh, yes. I didn't know they had any! These are so beautiful, Cal!"

No, he thought, *you are. A diamond can't begin to compare to your beauty,* but he kept silent. Again, she did the same thing, pointing to the smallest, least expensive diamond set.

"I like this one."

"But the color," he protested. Cal's fingers were large, but he carefully chose the diamond he had in mind, pulled it out of the velvet pad and laid it in her opened palm. "This is the one. Do you like it?"

Her eyes grew huge. There was the main diamond, probably more than two carats, set in between two smaller once carat diamonds, and then two more half that size, all set in eighteen-carat gold. "But... this is so huge, Cal!"

She turned and lowered her voice. "It has to cost a fortune!"

Cal looked over at the owner. "How much?"

"You, Señor, have very finest of taste," the jeweler said with genuine sincerity. "It almost matches Señorita Lambert's flawless blue eyes." He smiled grandly. "You are a man who wants the best for his lady. It is forty thousand USD."

When Sky heard the price, she nearly fell off the chair: Forty thousand dollars!

"No!" she whispered, giving the jeweler an apologetic glance, and then holding Cal's stare. "That's too much! No one can afford that!" and she chewed on her lower lip, gripping his upper arm as if to shake some sense into him. She saw him give her a patient look. The kind of look a parent would give a petulant child who was acting out.

"Money's no object," Cal told her, serious. "And these diamonds almost match your eyes. That's phenomenal. Go on, just try the set on. See what you think?" and he held out her left hand, sliding on the finely crafted engagement ring.

"This ring, Señorita, is one of a kind, like you," Esteban said, his expression very serious and genuine.

Cal smiled at Sky. "A perfect match. Another reason to buy it."

The jeweler knew he had an advocate in his corner, and all that was left was to convince the unsure señorita who was stunned at the price of it. "Señorita Lambert, surely you cannot turn your husband-to-be down? He knows what is best for you. He holds your heart gently in his hands. Now, surely," Esteban rushed on enthusiastically, "you cannot say no? He is a man and knows what is best for his woman. He must love you very much to give you the finest quality diamond I have ever seen in that particular color. Surely," and he smiled gently, "you must not turn him down. You must accept what he knows is best for you."

Cal damn near smiled. Peruvian males were decades behind American women. No husband in their right mind would think of his wife as something he owned, or that he knew more about something than his wife did. He saw amusement glimmer in Sky's eyes as she moved the stone slowly, the light catching the facets, making it gleam and glitter azure refracted light throughout them. Sky slid Cal a questioning look.

"What are you going to do if I say no?"

"Buy the set anyway. I'll just tuck it away until we get home. Set it out on the kitchen table for you to look at and ponder every day until you decide to start wearing it."

"You wouldn't do that, Sinclair."

Giving her a shrug, Cal met her smile with one of his own. "The color is perfect for you, Sky. By wearing that ring you'll get to see what I get to see every time I look into your eyes." Cal reached out, grazing her bright red cheek, "You might not be able to see it, but I can tell you from where I'm sitting, that color makes me know that you're the only woman in the world who has that incredible shade of blue. And I want to always see your eyes the way they look right now: in love with me."

Her buts, ifs and protests melted away beneath his low, heart spoken admittance. It just totaled Sky, and she gave the diamonds another look, trying to see it from Cal's perspective. She knew her eye color was different. Unique. And he was right: she couldn't see what he saw. The warmth, the love in his eyes, swept away all but one protest. "The cost, Cal," she said, worried.

"That's not a problem, Sky."

She gave him a stunned look. "It's not? As I recall, the military doesn't exactly pay us what we're worth."

She was getting well very quickly. Sky's spunkiness had returned. His lips drew away from his teeth and he leaned back in the chair, and he relished her reactions. "Well," he said, "I'm not discussing finances right now with you, not here at least, but you have to trust me when I tell you I can easily afford that set of rings for you." He held her widening gaze as his words sunk into her. Sky was not marrying a pauper. Cal kept his financial status to himself. Only him and the IRS and Uncle Sam knew his bottom line. He'd invested most of his money every month since age of eighteen, onward to the present. His passion was learning how to use the stock market to his advantage. If he told Sky he was worth over five million dollars, he was afraid she'd faint right off that chair. He watched her worry her lower lip, frowning, looking down at the engagement ring, waffling between her worry and trusting him. She kept touching the blue stones and Cal knew she loved them by the way she caressed them. He was sure because of her situation, she wasn't penniless, but Sky wasn't rich, either. And it was going to feel damn good to let her know tonight, when he made her dinner at their apartment, just how much he was worth. Cal was almost smiling because he knew he'd have to time it carefully or Sky, when she got excited or upset, would lose her appetite. And right now, she desperately needed another twenty pounds on her frame to fill her out to a normal weight for her height.

"Well….," she murmured, giving him a desperate look, "if you're SURE about this, Cal. I mean, forty thousand dollars is a LOT of money…"

"Listen," he growled, sliding his chair closer to hers, capturing her chin and holding her unsure gaze, "no more fence sitting. Yes, or no? If you say no, I'm buying them anyway. You want to make me happy, don't you? I WANT that set for you, Sweetheart. I can afford it, hands down. You just need to get over the sticker shock and we need to move on to the life that is waiting for us…"

With a ragged sigh, Sky said, "You're right." Cal's bluntness was back. And maybe she needed that kind of directness to shake her off the fence she was indeed wobbling upon. "But money… I mean, it takes money to live… you have a mortgage—"

"No," he murmured patiently, "I do NOT have a mortgage on my cabin. My cars are paid off, too, Sky. I have no bills. Does that help you make a final decision?" And then, he saw her hesitate. "I have a nice nest egg in savings." What ELSE would he have to say in front of this jeweler, who was looking more stricken by the second as he moved his gaze from Sky and then back to him, his hands clasped in front of him as if in a silent, fervent prayer, asking God to help her say yes so, he could get his forty thousand US dollars. The man was positively sweating, anxiety written all over his face, wringing his hands.

Cal grinned. "Hey," he teased, "this guy is gonna die of a heart attack if you don't say yes. Is that want you want? The big one to do him in right here and now?" And then, he saw Sky relax, her shoulders come down, the tension dissolve from her face as she smiled shyly over at him.

"No… no more deaths. Okay," and Sky moved her hand over to Cal, "I love this set. Please buy it for me?"

He saw the merriment in her eyes, the happiness shining in them as he pulled out the credit card from his billfold, he kept in a pocket of his cargo pants. Cal grinned at her as the man took it, practically running to the back room, slipping behind the purple velvet curtains where his office was located. "Well? Are you happy with the rings, Ms. Lambert?"

Sky gave him a tender look, hoping all her love was there for Cal to see in her eyes. "Absolutely. I'll never want for anything, ever again," she sighed, admiring the ring on her hand.

"Well," Cal grumped, "I hope you'll want me again."

Laughing softly, Sky reached out, running her hand down his thick bicep. "Oh, that's different. Don't worry, I'm going to keep you very, very busy Sinclair. We have a LOT of time to make up for."

Music to his ears and Cal matched her wicked, heated smile with one that rivaled his own.

CHAPTER 19

February 4

Alex Kazak was hobbling around his room when he had two visitors unexpectedly show up. He straightened, his blackened eyes widening with surprise. The woman he'd saved, Sky Lambert, was dressed as a woman, not as a pilot. She wore a white alpaca wool pantsuit with a cobalt-colored silk blouse that emphasized the incredible color of her eyes. The Peruvian leather sandals made her small feet even prettier; her toenails polished a light blue to match the color of her outfit. She was beautiful! He saw Cal Sinclair enter after her and quietly shut the door. He wore a black t-shirt, cammo pants, and his combat boots. He stood in his long blue robe, his feet bare, the hospital gown of the same color barely reaching his knees. Opening his hands, he nodded in Sky's direction and said, "I never expected to see you again," with emotion in his tone. "You look like another person who has stepped out of a fairy tale book, a very beautiful princess, not a mere human being."

Sky blushed and gave Alex a wobbly smile. "I've just gotten back on my feet after the malaria episode." She approached him, stricken by the beating Cal had warned her about. It made her wince just looking at the Ukrainian's broad face. "I-I'm sorry all this happened to you," Sky said, gesturing toward his face. "You didn't deserve it. You're a hero in my eyes, Alex. You saved my life... thank you..." and she reached out, touching his forearm gently, sliding her long fingers into his scarred, large hand. He was careful how much he squeezed her fingers in return.

Her husky words made him smile a little. It hurt to smile, but her heartfelt thanks touched his badly beaten heart and made him feel good. Alex hobbled over to the bed and carefully sat down. "Thank you, but I am no hero, Sky. Please," and he pointed to the two chairs in the room. "Can you both sit for a while? We can talk?"

Sky saw how lonely Alex was. He had no one here. He was alone in every sense of the word. Cal moved behind Sky and brought up the two chairs near his bed.

"We can stay for a little while," Cal told the man, gesturing for Sky to take a seat. She proudly wore the blue diamond engagement ring on her elegant left hand. She cleaned up amazingly and Cal felt like the luckiest man in the world.

Sky watched the soldier's expression harden into a game face to mask his pain as he slid slowly, with effort, back into his bed. He pulled the bedcovers up to his waist, his huge farm hands clasped in his lap. "How are you doing, Alex?"

"Better," he said. "You look very well considering how sick you were days ago. You know, you have no idea how closely you resemble my sister Kira. She too, loves the color blue." He tipped his head and studied Sky. "Are you sure you were not twins and then taken and separated at birth? Going to different countries to grow up in?"

Sky smiled at his attempt at humor. Now, she had to stop herself from wincing because his features were so distorted and swollen. Still, his hazel eyes gleamed and were clear. "Can you show me her photo? Cal said you showed it to him in that hut."

"Ah," Alex murmured, pleased, as he dug carefully into the pocket of the bathrobe. He rooted around and finally located it. "I carry Kira with me wherever I go," he told her proudly, holding the photo out to her.

Sky took the ragged, frayed photo. It was very old, covered with protective plastic that was aged, some of the color of the photo beneath it, faded. She shook her head. "This is amazing, Alex. Kira really could pass for being my twin sister." She glanced up at Cal, who nodded in agreement. Moving her gaze to Alex, she handed it back to him. "Thank you for letting me see your sister's photo."

Alex carefully posited the photo back into the pocket of his bathrobe. "Now, you can understand when my commander threw you back into the cabin of the helo, I was in shock. Looking at you was like looking at my beloved Kira." His voice lowered, "I'm sure Cal told you the rest of the story about her?"

Nodding, Sky felt her chest tighten with sadness. "Yes… he did. I'm so sorry for her. I-I just can't imagine what it did to Kira. And to you, and your parents. Rape doesn't just affect the woman, it affects her whole family, her children, relatives, and friends. It's a terrible stain that doesn't ever go away." Sky held his sad gaze. "Thank you for saving me from Vlad. I need to tell you the rest of the story about him, because I'm sure you don't know about it," and she began to tell Alex the tale of how Vlad had entered her life in the first place. The Ukrainian listened intently, saying nothing, but occasionally, his game face slipped and she saw the rage in his eyes over what Vlad had done to her as a teenager, and how he'd murdered her foster family. By the time Sky was done, she felt emotionally drained. Wearily, she said, "So now, you understand the why I was so scared of him."

"Thank you for telling me, Sky. I know how hard it is to speak of such terrible things," and Alex touched his chest. "At least Alexandrov is dead now. Removed forever from your life. You are free."

Nodding and feeling deeply for the soldier, Sky uttered, "But your sister… well… that will never go away. And that's the worst part for both of you. She will never be free."

Cal gently placed his hand on her tense shoulders. Sky had wanted to visit the man who had saved her life in so many ways. But he knew she was still recovering from the malaria, and that this tough conversation would drain her. And it had. Sky responded to his light touch, straightening a little and giving him a soft look filled with love.

"You are growing very tired, Sky," Kazak said. "I honor your wanting to see me, but it's very emotionally stressful for you, too, when you need to be resting, also."

"Is that the combat medic in you speaking?" Sky gently teased him. She saw the Ukrainian rally and almost smile. She'd never met Spetsnaz operators until now. And Kazak was so very much like Cal in that regard.

"You can't separate the medic from the rest of me," Alex said, pride in his voice.

Cal sat forward, getting his attention. "I've made a few contacts for you out of Washington, D.C., and elsewhere. There's a woman, an undersecretary at the State Department, Chloe Payson, who is going to set up an appointment to meet with you once they transfer you out of here to Balboa Naval Hospital in San Diego, California. She's got your records and everything else the CIA gave her. She's leaning in your favor, Alex. She's an older woman with a lot of wisdom and she sees through a person and sees who they really are. All you have to do is be honest with her." Cal opened his hands. "She's read the reports from the other American military operators and knows, without a doubt, that you saved both our lives with your choices and actions. Equally important? You are from Ukraine. The State Department and President are working to help the people of that country stand against Russia's authoritarian rule and assault, to remain democratic. Americans love Ukrainians."

"What does this all mean?" Alex asked.

"IF Chloe decides you're the real deal, she's going to set a lot of things in motion for you, Alex. The first thing she'll do is grant Kira a permanent visa to remain in the USA. That way, she'll be a lot safer from the KGB and any Russian Mafia reprisals. Chloe doubts that your name will be linked with Alexandrov's death, and she doesn't feel you and your family will be under threat here in the U.S. So, that's good news."

Alex nodded. "That is. I can't do anything if my sister is not protected."

"Chloe knows that," Cal murmured.

"What then?"

"You'll both be considered Ukrainian immigrants and be placed on the list to enter our country immediately, and then change your citizenship status to become American citizens or, you can choose a dual citizenship with your country and the U.S."

Alex sighed and closed his eyes. He leaned back against his pillow, his mouth pursed. He fought back tears of relief. Not wanting his American friends to see him sob like a child, he tucked his emotions away. Opening his eyes, he said thickly, "Kira and I cannot thank you enough…"

Cal grinned and stood up, offering the man his hand. "Oh, yes you can. You saved Sky. That makes us even."

February 14

THE AMERICAN AIRLINES plane lifted off from the Jorge Chavez International Airport, Lima, Peru at 0800, bound for Washing, D.C. Sky sat in first class with Cal, feeling years of heaviness slowly dissolving off her shoulders. The vibration of the plane soothed her as she thought back through the challenges thrown at her. And now, she was free for the first time in her life. She turned her head and studied Cal's hard, unforgiving profile. He turned toward her, linking his fingers with hers.

"What are you thinking about?" he asked, seeing the sheen of tears in her eyes.

Shrugging noncommittally, she said, "That I loved leaving Cusco on the fifth of February and spending ten days in Los Flores area of Lima. We had such fun. And getting to have dinner and drinks with Mace Killmer and his men, well, that was really special for me. He too, saved our lives in another way." She leaned her head back, slanting a glance toward him. "Now? Today? It's Valentine's Day, and I was reviewing my life. How I'm finally free of Vlad… it's so hard to believe, but I know it's true…"

Cal wanted to haul Sky into his arms. They hadn't made love yet because she was still on the mend. Malaria, as Cal knew, totaled a person for weeks, sometimes months, after a vicious attack. There would be time after they arrived home to love one another. "All Heart's Day… for us. You've fought and won your freedom, Sky. You've earned it, Sweetheart."

Giving Cal a look of apology, Sky quickly wiped the tears from her eyes. "I can hardly wait to get to your cabin. To see who you REALLY are."

Cal gave her a lazy smile. "What you see is what you get. There are no surprises, Sky."

And that was one of the many things she loved about this man, his continuity. Maybe it was because his SEAL training had been permanently stamped into his nature. But there was another part of Cal, the abused little boy, the survivor who had thickened his skin and his resolve and made something better for himself. He'd never surrendered, never became a victim. Instead, he'd devoted himself to a life of service, saving others, and for that, her heart throbbed with pride over what Cal had accomplished. He'd always lived for a higher purpose, never feeling sorry for himself or allowing his father's shortcomings to stop him from being fully who he really was.

Sky looked forward to drawing out Cal's softer, emotional side. It had already begun happening naturally between them. Someday, he would lose that game face, because the man beneath was breathtaking to her. He, too, needed to feel safe and learn to become vulnerable and whole, and to trust once again. Just like she was doing beneath the umbrella of his love for her.

"You know," Cal warned her, "it's going to be cold as hell when we land in Virginia." Sky wore an alpaca wool pantsuit of chocolate color. The cream-colored silk blouse made her look like a fashion model. He'd talked her into wearing sensible shoes because Peruvian sandals in February were not going to make the grade.

"You bought me a gorgeous Alpaca coat," Sky reminded him. It was warm, soft, and beautiful in colors of blue, cream, and gray, reminding her of the mighty slopes of the Andean mountains.

"You're used to tropical heat. This cold is going to take your breath away at times."

Sky could tell he was worried she'd catch flu, or something far worse. Understanding his worry, that he'd almost lost her, she slid her hand over his. "YOU take my breath away. I'll be fine." Would he ever see her as strong and capable? Not fragile? She smiled to herself because no one had ever coddled her, protected her, as Cal did. It was a nice feeling, not suffocating, but to have someone who cared enough to worry and be supportive.

Cal nodded, saying nothing, absorbing the softness of her hand across his. "At least Jack Driscoll will meet us and drive us to the cabin. You'll be warm in the company SUV."

Her love heightened for Cal as he scowled, looking straight ahead at the seat in front of him. "Are you actually trying to figure out all the ways an East Coast winter can kill me?" Sky teased, smiling as he looked up guiltily at her.

"I guess," Cal admitted, drowning in the heat of her smile. Cal wanted to kiss her, but he wasn't one for public displays. He'd wait until they got home to kiss her senseless when no one was watching. "I'm just concerned, Sky, that's all."

"You're acting like an old, broody hen, Sinclair." She patted his hand. "Let's talk of something positive: like our coming marriage. Did you contact Dylan? And if you did, you never told me how he's doing at Balboa Naval Hospital." Sky watched the change in Cal. He immediately moved out of that dark place within himself as he engaged with her.

"Yeah, talked to him yesterday afternoon while you finished packing your clothes. He's getting a lot of company from the teams stationed over at Coronado. It's only about ten miles from where the SEALs train. One of the brothers drops by to see him nearly every day to check up on him, shoot the shit with him, or bring him some fast food, because he hates the hospital food."

Sky laughed. "He's in good spirits, considering everything?" She knew Dylan had to be in deep grieving over the loss of Julie. She wasn't sure she could survive if Cal was suddenly ripped away from her. It made her respect Dylan's inner strength to overcome such a staggering tragedy and heart loss.

"Yes," and Cal hitched a shoulder as the airliner leveled off. The seat belt sign flashed off and the flight attendants were coming through the cabin to hand out breakfast menus and take their drink orders. "He's got hours where he sinks pretty low. Anyone would."

Sky gave Cal an understanding look. "What did Dylan think of us getting married in San Diego? Inviting all your old SEAL teammates to be there for us? And your brother, Chad, and your sister, Tracey, and her husband will be there too?"

"They're all coming," Cal said. "I told him we'd be in town about a week before we get married. He said he'd be walking by then, come hell or high water. They've got Dylan on a brutal physical regime. He said he'd come to our wedding on crutches if you were okay with that."

Laughing softly, Sky nodded. "Of course. I'm just glad he can make it. I think being with other SEALs is helping Dylan so much."

"I do too. We take care of our own, Sky. When a SEAL dies or gets wounded, other SEALs and their families rally around them to care for them for months afterward, helping them through the adjustment phases. They're doing the same for Dylan right now. The SEAL wives bake him up goodies, which really lifts his spirits. We're a family affair, no question."

"And speaking of family," Sky murmured, "wasn't it wonderful that Alex called us yesterday to tell us Kira was already stateside, and that he was leaving the Cusco hospital for San Diego?"

"Yes." Cal drew in a deep breath. "Chloe called me and told me she was recommending Alex for citizenship along with Kira. I'm glad the diplomats and whoever else was involved, are giving them the shot, they deserve."

"I heard you talking to Alex in the other room of our apartment," she murmured. "It sounded like more was going on for him?"

"Yes, I called Jack Driscoll several days earlier after Chloe signed papers for Alex and Kira. He's always looking for overseas operators from different countries because he has business in them. When I told him Alex was from Ukraine, he jumped at it. He is looking for men and women from that country right now, to fill the roster. Once Alex gets out of the hospital in San Diego, Jack has sent him a ticket to fly back to Shield Security in Alexandria, Virginia, and I believe Alex will be employed shortly."

"Will Alex be happy doing that, Cal? Does he want to continue being a security operator?"

"Alex is a team player," Cal murmured, squeezing her hand. "He's great at being just that and in our business? You want people who believe in the team as a whole and support it. Alex needs a team to be fulfilled. I believe if he and Jack get along, that he'll be offered a job. What kind, I don't know, but I'm sure I'll find out about it if it happens."

"Then, he'd have to live in Alexandria, Virginia area?"

"Most likely. All the rest of us who work for Shield do."

"I wonder about his sister, Kira?"

"Oh, that." Cal raised his brows. "She wants to stay in San Diego because she loves the ocean. And Alex thought it was a good decision. He'll always be in touch with her because they are very close to one another. He said that water was always healing for Kira, and that staying there, he felt, would be good for her."

"I hope so," Sky said. "She's been through so much already."

"I'm sure Alex will keep us in the loop if he's hired by Shield. He's a family person."

"So are you, Cal. June sixteenth is the big day, Sinclair," Sky gave him a teasing look. "You have four months to back out of this marriage, big guy."

"Not on your life. You're stuck with me."

"I'm not complaining." Sky's smile widened. "Let's just hope we don't get stuck in the snow trying to get to your fabled cabin hidden on the mountain after we land…"

February 15

THE FEBRUARY SUN was slanting into the west at three p.m. when the American Airlines jet landed at Regan International Airport. They had stayed overnight in Miami, Florida, and taken a morning flight home. The sky was a powder blue, cloudless and it was a balmy twenty degrees Fahrenheit. Sky met Cal's SEAL teammate who owned Shield Security after deplaning. Jack Driscoll shook her hand, welcoming her home. Sky found the man in his mid-thirties to have intense light gray eyes, standing six foot tall, leanly built, but finely honed. He walked with a casualness that belied his SEAL years in the Navy. Sky could spot that easygoing gait anywhere. The man had an oval face, clean-shaven, and was wearing a sheepskin coat over his dark blue fisherman knit sweater and tan corduroy chinos. He too, wore combat boots, like Cal. She stood back, looking at the two men grab one another, pounding each other heartily on the back in welcome. Their camaraderie made her happy for them.

Driscoll had not crushed her fingers when he shook her hand, either. There was an intensity to Jack, but it was well harnessed. No question these two ex-SEALs had that same kind of focus, in her opinion. Cal put his arm around her waist, and they walked more slowly because her stride was shorter than theirs. Sky was happy just to listen to the two men laugh, joke, trade stories and then laugh some more. It lifted her. Cal needed to be with his own kind, his other family, just as Alex Kazak was built the same way. When she'd asked him what kind of work, he was going to do upon returning to Virginia, he said he was thinking of becoming an operations mission planner for those men and women who were sent out into the field for Shield. Sky was relieved to know Cal's days as a security contractor were over. He would no longer be in harm's way. He would be coming home every night—to her.

"D.C.'s weather has been cranky, lately," Jack warned, stepping onto the shuttle that would take them to the main terminal to pick up their luggage. "It was only in the twenties this morning, Cal, and it's still freezing now. Just had another eight inches of snow dumped on us two days ago. Highways are clear, though. I had one of my operators, Lauren Parker, load up your fridge with your favorite foods yesterday. She got a maid service to come in and clean and was always there to ensure security."

"Thanks, brother, I appreciate it," Cal said. He gave Sky a wicked smile. "I even had vegetables, all kinds, added to the grocery list I emailed to Lauren a few days ago."

Sky chuckled. "Good, I won't starve then. Thank you."

Cal felt warmth flow through him. Even though the short afternoon flight hadn't been long, Sky had dozed through most of it. She was tired to her soul, just starting the process of coming out from hiding for nearly all her life, one way or another. It made him feel good to hear that unrestrained laughter bubble up that slender throat of hers. It would take them half an hour to drive to his cabin. He was glad Jack was driving so he could relax, and Sky could sleep if she chose, in the back seat with him. Cal desperately wanted Sky to relax and hoped like hell she would love his home. Would she? What would be her reaction?

Jack dropped them off just as the sun was at its highest for the day. Cal's home was well hidden among a grove of Douglas fir, maple, elm, beech and oak trees on top of a hill. Snow lay everywhere, but the road was graveled and passable, making it easy for them to reach it. Cal thanked his friend and boss, and then turned to Sky. Someone had cleaned off the five cedar steps leading up to a wide, L-shaped porch that wrapped around the two-story cabin.

Sky took in the enormity of Cal's home. He kept his hand beneath her elbow as she climbed the stairs. "I was thinking a small, turn-of-the-century kinda cabin, Sinclair... not this palace!"

"It's my dream come true. And no, it's not a little one-room cabin," he said, grinning. Growing concerned, he said, "We're at two thousand feet here. How are you doing breathing-wise?"

She shrugged. "Just fine," she said, standing on the broad porch, appreciating the massive swing in the corner. Sky gave Cal a sweet smile meant to take away the worry she saw come to his eyes. "Do NOT," she growled playfully, "go into the nattering mother hen mode with me. Okay?"

"Okay, Superwoman." Cal led her to the front door. It was massive. He had carved the door with scene of a dolphin leaping out of the ocean along the San Diego Bay coastline.

"Did you sculpt this?" Sky gasped, lightly touching the door carving.

He felt pride because her eyes were wide with wonder as she gently stroked the smooth, polished carving with her fingertips. "Yes. I decided to honor this bottlenose dolphin who took me out of training for six weeks during some limpet mine training sessions down in the San Diego harbor when I was a SEAL," he said, laughter in his tone. He took out the security pad and punched in a number that opened the door. "That particular dolphin, Max, is a twelve-foot-long Pacific bottlenose male. He weighs eight hundred and twenty pounds. He broke two of my ribs on a swim test I had to pass. Me and my swim buddy had to place fake limpet mines on the hull of a cruiser. We have trained dolphins that are taught to kill anything they see around a military ship. The SEAL trainers turn Max, who already had a nightmare reputation among the teams, loose on us to rattle us and make us fail our test."

"That dolphin broke two of your ribs?" Sky whispered disbelievingly.

"Yeah, the bastard," Cal laughed. "Laid me up for six weeks. I was really pissed. Got the limpet mine on the ship, though, passed my test, and I got back to the Combat Rubber Raiding Craft, or CRRC. Once I got on board, I passed out. I woke up in Balboa Hospital, my ribs taped. My team wasn't laughing, either. They were relieved Max went after me and not the rest of them. Those beasts can swim through the water at twenty miles an hour when they're in attack mode," Cal grumped. "I thought I'd been hit with a Mac truck. Damn near lost consciousness. Max swung around and hit me again, and that's when he broke my ribs. I can laugh about it now, but back then, it wasn't funny at all."

Sky shook her head. "Unbelievable, but it's beautiful carving, Cal. I didn't know you were an artist." The bottlenose was rising up out of the ocean on its tail.

"I'm many things, Sweetheart. Well? Are you ready to step into your new life? Your new home? Or would you like me to carry you over the threshold?" and Cal gave her a teasing look.

Sky pressed her hand against his chest. "I'll walk, Sinclair. You can carry me over the thresh hold after we get married. Okay?"

Nodding, he met her smile and easily pushed open the heavy door. "Welcome home, Sky… to our home…," and Cal stepped aside, gesturing for her to walk into the house he'd built.

Sky felt as if she'd entered another world, a world that was entirely about Nature, and she felt embraced in the warmest of ways. Turning, she looked up in wonder at Cal after he closed the front door. "This… this is…amazing," and she pressed her hand to the base of her throat, staring up at the two-story cathedral-roofed home. It was huge, like Cal. Beautiful, like him. Raw nature, like him. The golden and crimson sheen to the cedar logs, the overhead trusses, the walls rippling, almost alive with their own energy, made Sky catch her breath. She felt Cal stand behind her, settling his large hands on her shoulders.

"Like it?"

Sky leaned against him, her gaze moving constantly around the incredible space. "Like it," she managed, "I love it!" She turned around in his arms and smiled, sliding her hands up across his black t-shirt. "You built this? I just can't believe it. It's so… detailed, stunning and complex…," and she laughed again and shook her head. "Just like you! This house is YOU!" She watched a pleased grin stretch Cal's mouth.

"I knew you'd get it," and he drew her gently into his arms, his mouth descending upon hers, feeling her womanly warmth, her heat, her lushness that he so badly wanted to touch, and then, love her breathless. Cal tasted the chocolate she'd nibbled on earlier, the sweetness of Sky's mouth, and the way she responded willfully in return as he deepened their kiss. That moan of hers drove him crazy as he pushed his hand inside her Alpaca coat, his palms ranging up around her ribcage, gently cupping her small breasts. Cal eased his hands downward and broke the kiss. Sky's eyes were filled with desire, her lips wet and parted, the expression on her face telling him everything.

"Are you feeling up to letting me love you tonight?" he teased, searching her eyes. Cal knew she was tired. But tired never stopped him and he didn't know what her limits were yet, unless she spoke up. He hadn't touched her since coming out of that hellish rescue, only slept with her, and held her safe.

"How about we shower together first? I don't know about you, but I'd like to wash off the hours of jet travel?" He wanted Sky refreshed. Anticipating. The gleam coming to her eyes told him she was sold on his plan.

"I'm in the home of a SEAL. Why wouldn't you want a shower first?" she laughed.

"All right, Sweetheart, hang on," and he swept Sky up into his arms to carry her. Cal heard her give a little gasp of surprise, her arms flying around his shoulders as he settled her comfortably against himself and headed for the curved, massive cedar staircase that would lead up to the master bedroom and bathroom. If Cal had his way, he was going to introduce Sky to his home by making slow, tender love to her. He'd been dreaming of this night for a long time. And now, it was going to come true...

CHAPTER 20

February 16

CAL HEARD SKY walking barefoot across the flagstone floor of the kitchen before he saw her. He turned at the kitchen counter and smiled at her as she stood hesitating at the entrance. The first floor was a series of rooms, each flowing into the other. She stood there wearing his dark blue terrycloth robe. The material hung across her feet, burying her in the folds of thick, soft material. Only her delicate toes peeked out from beneath it. Her hair was deliciously tangled, her lips soft and slightly swollen from their previous night of hungry lovemaking they'd shared. His heart ballooned with a fierce love for her. She looked like a waif, utterly innocent, soft pink color flooding her cheeks.

"Hey," he murmured, wiping off his hands on a nearby towel hanging near the two large kitchen sinks, "you look a little lost." He moved toward her, his boots thunking against the colorful flagstone floor. Cal felt his heart expand as the corners of that lush mouth of hers lifted into a welcoming smile.

"Do you think I look a little overwhelmed in your robe?" Sky asked, picking up a massive fold between her fingers. Her heart took off as she saw the hungry look leap into Cal's eyes as he perused her standing there beneath his amused inspection. He wore a white cowboy shirt, the sleeves carelessly rolled up to just below his elbows. She saw the black t-shirt he wore beneath it. He'd shaven, his hair gleaming from a recent shower. The way he walked toward her reminded Sky of a lion, casual but alert and in charge.

Cal halted, moving his hands across her shoulders and studying his robe hanging all over her. "Looks like we need to do a little shopping in Alexandria today for you," he murmured. "You've got nothing but tropical clothes and Sweetheart, that isn't going to make it here," and his grin widened.

"Just kiss me," Sky breathed, opening her arms, stepping forward. "The clothes aren't going to be on for long, anyway…"

Cal embraced her, his mouth taking her offered one. She tasted sweet beneath his lips, and that throaty sound she made was music to his ears as he kissed her. Easing her back, he said, "Hungry?"

"For you, I am."

Cal grinned and brought her into the kitchen and pulled out one of the black leather stools at the granite island. "Sit here. You need to eat and revive first. Coffee?"

Sky snuggled into the thick, blanket-like robe she wore and made herself at home on the comfy stool, resting her arms on the black granite island. "I'd love some. When did you get up?"

"About an hour ago." He poured her coffee into a mug.

She met his warm gaze as he brought the coffee over, sliding the red cup slowly across to her awaiting hand.

Cal murmured. "I make a mean Denver omelet with old sharp, cheddar cheese. Interested?"

Her stomach growled.

They both laughed.

Sky rubbed her stomach and grumbled, "I guess I am hungry." She saw the sly look he gave her, bringing heat flushing to her cheeks. She honestly had known only one side to Cal, and now she was getting to see the man relaxed in his home. The difference was striking. No longer was the SEAL game face in evidence. She noticed as he set to work at the Wolf stove, a commercial grade appliance only the best chefs in the world used, that even his shoulders appeared relaxed, no longer tense. She sipped the coffee and purred, "This is wonderful coffee, Cal... thank you..."

He whipped up the omelet in a stainless-steel bowl with a whisk. "From Brazil. The best."

Sky sighed. "This home is heaven, Cal. Really, it is."

His heart expanded with silent joy. "So? You think you can live with me here?" and he gave her a glance across his shoulder.

"I know I can. This is like a house set in a land, far, far away kind of setting. When I got up to take my shower, I saw some deer crossing the meadow. It was so fantastic. We're literally sitting here in the arms of Mom Nature."

Cal poured the omelet into an awaiting huge black iron skillet. "I've always found peace here. Time to think. To decompress. It's always been my sanity, my coming back to my center."

Nodding, Sky understood what he was saying. She knew SEALs trained on a continuous two-year cycle. Never a chance for much rest or downtime. "This home is healing for you, Cal." She watched as he busied himself efficiently whipping up the omelet for them. His mouth curved faintly over her comment. She held out her left hand, the blue diamond engagement ring sparkling as she slowly moved it around in the light. Sky would never forget his comment about the color of the ring reminding him of her eyes. Her throat tightened and she slipped her hand around the mug, absorbing the peace in the kitchen, the coming breakfast fragrances, and Cal. "You know," she said softly, "we've come a long way in a very short amount of time."

Cal slid the finished omelet onto a large red ceramic platter. Bringing down two plates from the cupboard, he said, "Funny, I was thinking that same thing earlier this morning." He added two slices of buttered toast to the plates and brought them over to Sky. Sliding one her direction, Cal leaned over, kissing her temple, the strands of her hair damp beneath his lips. "It's been a two-year journey for both of us, so it hasn't really been that short amount of time." Cal poured them more coffee and then sat down next to Sky after giving her flatware and a brick-red colored linen napkin.

"I'm glad you found me."

He gave her a warm look and sat down beside her. "Makes two of us."

Sky's mouth watered as she cut into the colorful omelet. Cal had cut up red and green sweet peppers, onion, and added diced ham and the cheddar cheese to the airy egg concoction. The delectable scents drifted into her nostrils. "Mmmm, this smells so good!"

Shaking his head, Cal muttered, "You're like an excited kid."

Tasting the fare, Sky made a humming sound in the back of her throat. "Who knew you were also a five-star chef, Sinclair?" She looked up at him. "What ELSE do you do?" She saw a ruddy color come to his cheeks, his blush endearing.

Shrugging, "If I need to know how to do something, I teach myself. SEALs are like that. We each bring a set of skills to the team. You never know when someone's particular skill might come in handy out on a patrol," and he grinned. He saw the respect, the admiration in her expression, and her praise felt good. Sky just naturally lifted him, made him feel differently about himself for the first time in his life. It was nice to be looked up to like she was looking at him right now.

"You," Sky said, munching on a piece of her sourdough toast, "are nothing short of amazing. You're talented. You could probably get rich just carving those beautiful scenes in wood and selling them through New York City galleries."

A faint smile curved his mouth. Sky had already scarfed down half the omelet, and it hadn't been a little one. She was attacking the toast now and it wasn't going to survive much longer, either. "Sweetheart," he murmured, catching her gaze, "I make plenty of money in the stock market. I carve because it's satisfying to me. It ramps me down, centers me."

"And you cook like a chef."

"Thank you." The toast was gone. Cal rose and walked over to the counter. "I have some cinnamon rolls. Want one?" and he saw her grin self-consciously.

"I'm eating everything in sight."

"I'm glad," Cal growled, bringing her one of the hand-sized cinnamon rolls being kept warm in the microwave.

Patting her tummy, she laughed a little. "I think I'm eating because I'm no longer under stress." And then she added more softly, giving him a loving look. "And because I'm happy. With you…" Sky watched his face grow tender as he held her gaze. "It's you, Cal. Anything you touch is better off because you did…"

His chest tightened and Cal said nothing as he took the second heated cinnamon roll out of the microwave and set it next to his plate. "I like how you see me. I don't think I deserve it, Sky, but thank you. It makes me feel good about myself."

Turning on the stool, she slid her arms up around his broad shoulders and pulled him down so that she could touch his mouth. "Listen," she whispered fiercely against his lips, "you are the bravest, most incredible man I've ever known. Anything I say to you is the TRUTH, Cal. I've always been honest with you," and she curved her lips against his, feeling him react, hearing a groan rise within him. His arms came around her and he lifted her up and off the stool, onto his thigh and against him. He ravished her, his strong mouth hungry, taking and giving to her. Sky melted against his body, secure in the knowledge he could hold her easily with his male strength. Finally, they separated, each breathing raggedly, staring each other in the eyes, reading what was there.

"Hate to break this to you, Sweetheart," he growled, picking her up and taking her fully into his arms, "but that cinnamon roll is going to wait."

Laughing, Sky threw her arms around his neck. "I'll take you over a cinnamon roll any day."

Giving her a very confident smile as he carried her out of the kitchen, through the large living room, Cal climbed the stairs that would take them to the master bedroom. "Good thing I'm more important than a damn cinnamon roll," he teased her mercilessly, watching the happiness shining in her exquisite blue gaze. Eyes he would drown in every time he looked at her. As he reached the second floor, he absorbed her breathy laughter, the way Sky nuzzled him with her nose and then kissed the column of his neck. Every inch of his skin tingled beneath the soft kisses she rained upon him.

As Cal settled her on the unmade bed, clearing away the blankets, she stretched out languidly, with feline grace, confident in herself as a woman. The sunlight had shifted as it was rising, the columns of light above the bed now striking the other end of the room, the cedar glowing molten gold and crimson beneath the sun's rays. He saw the wicked gleam in Sky's eyes, relishing her boldness, her fearlessness, as he quickly removed his Levi's, pulled off his boots, and dropped the shirt to the floor. After tugging the black t-shirt over his head, standing naked before her, she rose up on her knees and came to the side of the bed, her arms open to him. As she leaned against him, her taut breasts brushing his chest, she strained upward, and he leaned over to meet her parting lips.

"You will ALWAYS be the only man in my life I will EVER love," Sky whispered in a trembling voice. "You saved my life so many times, Cal." Drawing back enough to meet and hold his hooded gaze, she choked and said, "You gave me a reason to live… a reason to hope… it's you, Cal. No one else. Ever…" Sky swallowed against her tightened throat, adding, "And I'm going to spend every day, with every breath I take, showing you just how good a man you are. How much you deserve my love…"

THE BEGINNING…

Don't miss Lindsay McKenna's next Shadow Team series novel, *Collateral Damage*.

Available from Lindsay McKenna and Blue Turtle Publishing and wherever you buy eBooks.

Excerpt from Collateral Damage

C AL SINCLAIR DID not have the heart to interrupt Sky Lambert, the woman he was going to marry in two weeks. He halted near the cedar stairs to their master bedroom on the second floor of his Virginia home he'd built himself over a seven-year period. There, in the alcove where the bay windows looked out over the pristine meadow below, he watched Sky drawing with her pastel chalk set on her easel.

Weeks ago, she'd discovered all his drafting tools and accessories he used to build his two-story cedar home. It sat on a hill surrounded by Douglas fir and oak trees. Cal smiled a little, wrapping his arms across his chest, watching her intently. The morning sunlight was pouring through the cathedral windows that stretched skyward on the eastern side of their bedroom. His body still glowed in memory of them waking up at dawn, Sky's favorite time. She'd been naked against him, sleeping deeply, when he'd aroused from his slumber. He hungrily loved this woman who had stolen his heart and fed his soul like the sunlight drifting silently through the bedroom. They had both lost so much in the past, and Cal felt incredibly grateful as he stood there watching Sky use the pastel colors on the paper attached to the easel as she tried to capture the meadow and stream beyond the bay windows.

His mouth twitched as he remembered looking for Sky and found her rooting around with eager curiosity through every drawer and shelf in the basement. Along one wall, he'd placed all his sketched drawings, some in ink, some in pencil and others in pastel chalks, that he'd imagined his dream home would someday look like. It had been a seven-year vision when he was in the SEALs, and later, two years with Shield Security in Alexandria, Virginia. Any time off was spent building it. Sky had discovered the colorful box of chalk and had been transformed into an excited child, finding sixty of them in a box, touching them as if they were precious jewels. She dragged his easel, the paper and chalks up to her favorite place, the bay windows that overlooked the meadow and stream north of where the house sat.

Cal's heart opened powerfully as he saw Sky working intently, her blond brows drawn down in concentration, trying to capture the meadow where elk and deer crossed it daily at dawn and dusk. Sky had a special connection with the dark green velvet settee that sat facing those windows. After he'd brought her home from Cusco, Peru, from that hellish challenge to get her out of there alive, Sky had settled in with him on Valentine's Day. And over the past months, he'd watched her make his home her home. It was something Cal had wanted desperately for Sky because her childhood had been a nightmare existence. Now she was at peace. He could see it in her oval face, the way her incredible turquoise eyes shined with happiness. Sky WAS happy. Hell, so was he. He loved her. And for whatever reason unknown to him, she loved him just as fiercely in return.

Rousing himself, Cal deliberately made enough noise to catch Sky's attention. He'd been a Navy SEAL and could walk silently with the best of them. Only, it scared the hell out of Sky to be walked up behind and she didn't hear him approaching her. Cal knew it was her past when Vladimir Alexandrov, the other foster child in the Zimmerman family where she lived, had hunted her like the sadistic sexual predator he was. At seventeen, Vlad had trapped Sky in her bedroom and nearly raped her. He'd stalked her for a year previous and it had made her a frightened shadow in the family. Frowning, Cal tucked her terrifying past away. He saw Sky turn, surprise in her expression.

"Cal! I thought you were going into the hardware store?" She halted, pink chalk between her fingers.

"I am," he murmured, allowing his arms to fall to his side as he moved from the stair landing toward her. "Got breakfast going. Interested?" and he grinned as he saw the colorful chalk dust all over her hands, some sprinkled down her bright yellow tee that lovingly outlined her body. A body he never would tire of making love too.

Groaning, Sky looked at her watch. "Oh, crap," she muttered, "I'm sorry, I lost track of time." And then she gave him a childlike grin. "I got carried away," and she pointed to her large chalk drawing on the easel.

Cal wandered over. "Hmmm," he said, lifting his index finger and gently removing a purple smudge on the tip of her nose, "you've really attacked this project," and he held up his finger that now was purple with the chalk dust. He heard Sky's husky laugh, going straight to his lower body. Cal thought about scooping her up into his arms and carrying her over to their king-sized bed, unmade, and taking her slowly, deliciously, once again.

"Well," Sky said wryly, taking the cloth sitting on her easel and wiping off his finger "I get lost in the drawing." Giving him an apologetic look, she quickly wiped off her fingers, the colors smeared across them. "Is breakfast ready?" she asked, setting the chalk in the tray.

"Almost," Cal murmured. Looking across her shoulder, he studied her efforts. "Nice. You've captured the morning shadows across the meadow."

Groaning, Sky said, "You're just saying that Cal." She launched herself against him, curling her arms around his broad, thick shoulders. "Because you say nicest things about my struggling amateur efforts," she whispered against his mouth. "And you have nothing but praise for my poor attempts."

Her whole body went from simmer to boil as his arms swept around her, his mouth opening, curving, and hungrily taking hers. A soft moan of satisfaction caught in her slender throat as she felt his large hands move sinuously from her shoulders, down across her long spine and cup her cheeks, embracing her hard against him. Sky smiled as she broke the kiss, feeling his erection pressing strongly against his Levi's. "I thought you got enough earlier?" she teased. They had left Cusco, Peru months earlier and Sky had found herself nearly insatiable for him, unable to get enough of Cal in every way. She saw the glint in his narrowing gold-brown eyes. She knew that look. The more gold she saw in his eyes, the more turned on, the more he desired her.

Grunting, Cal reluctantly released her. "I will NEVER get enough of you, Sweetheart," and he placed a swift kiss across her wet, smiling lips that he could drown in forever. And that was exactly what was going to happen: he was going to marry Sky in two weeks, on June 16th, in Coronado, the SEAL training center, with San Diego right across the bay from it. She would be his forever.

Sky eased away, slipping her fingers into his large, calloused hand. "I'm hungry, too, but I do need some physical fuel to run on." She gave Cal a wicked, teasing look. "Fuel? You know? For us mere mortals who aren't godlike SEALs, Supermen in disguise? You must have pity upon me," and Sky pulled him along toward the stairs that would lead to the the kitchen and living room below.

Cal preened silently beneath her praise. Yeah, he used to be a SEAL and yeah, they all thought of themselves as impervious to normal human complaints and weakness. He liked that Sky saw him in that way. It made him feel good about himself. "Okay," he offered grudgingly, releasing her hand and allowing her to go down the stairs first, "I'll bow to your need for food."

Available from
Lindsay McKenna

Blue Turtle Publishing

SHADOW TEAM SERIES
Last Stand
Collateral Damage
No Quarter

NON-SERIES BOOKS
Down Range (Reprint)
Dangerous Prey (Reprint)
Love Me Before Dawn (Reprint)
Point of Departure (Reprint)
Touch the Heavens (Reprint)

WOMEN OF GLORY SERIES
No Quarter Given (Reprint)
The Gauntlet (Reprint)
Under Fire (Reprint)

LOVE & GLORY SERIES
A Question of Honor, Book 1 (Reprint)
No Surrender, Book 2 (Reprint)
Return of a Hero, Book 3 (Reprint)
Dawn of Valor, Book 4 (Reprint)

LOVE & DANGER SERIES
Morgan's Son, Book 5 (Reprint)
Morgan's Wife, Book 6 (Reprint)
Morgan's Rescue, Book 7 (Reprint)
Morgan's Marriage, Book 8 (Reprint)

WARRIORS FOR THE LIGHT
Unforgiven, Book 1 (Reprint)
Dark Truth, Book 2 (Reprint)
The Quest, Book 3 (Reprint)
Reunion, Book 4 (Reprint)
The Adversary, Book 5 (Reprint)
Guardian, Book 6 (Reprint)

DELOS

Last Chance, prologue novella to Nowhere to Hide
Nowhere to Hide, Book 1
Tangled Pursuit, Book 2
Forged in Fire, Book 3
Broken Dreams, Book 4
Blind Sided, BN2
Secret Dream, B1B novella, epilogue to Nowhere to Hide
Hold On, Book 5
Hold Me, 5B1, sequel to Hold On
Unbound Pursuit, 2B1 novella, epilogue to Tangled Pursuit
Secrets, 2B2 novella, sequel to Unbound Pursuit, 2B1
Snowflake's Gift, Book 6
Never Enough, 3B1, novella, sequel to Forged in Fire
Dream of Me, 4B1, novella, sequel to Broken Dreams
Trapped, Book 7
Taking a Chance 7B1, novella, sequel to Trapped
The Hidden Heart, 7B2, novella, sequel to Taking A Chance
Boxcar Christmas, Book 8
Sanctuary, Book 9
Dangerous, Book 10
Redemption, 10B1, novella, sequel to Dangerous

Kensington

SILVER CREEK SERIES

Silver Creek Fire
Courage Under Fire

WIND RIVER VALLEY SERIES

Wind River Wrangler
Wind River Rancher
Wind River Cowboy
Christmas with my Cowboy
Wrangler's Challenge
Lone Rider
Wind River Lawman
Kassie's Cowboy
Home to Wind River
Western Weddings: Wind River Wedding
Wind River Protector
Wind River Undercover

Everything Lindsay McKenna

Lindsay's website is dedicated to all my series at lindsaymckenna.com. There are articles on characters, my publishing schedule, and information about each book written by me. You can also learn more about my exclusive newsletter, which covers my upcoming books, publishing schedule, giveaways, exclusive cover peeks and more.